Krystal Harding

A Realm of Flowers and Light

Book Cover by Get Covers

Images from: Vecteezy.com and Canva

1st edition 2024

Paperback ISBN: 979-8-9904093-0-9

Hardback ISBN: 979-8-9904093-1-6

Dedication

Those who have that fire inside that just needs to be let out.
Burn the world baby.

DEAR READERS,

First and foremost, I want to thank you for taking the time to read A Realm of Flowers and Light. It means a lot to me that you wish to continue on with Luna and her mates. However, this book is a lot darker than the previous two. Luna and her mates will experience more terrifying things. Take this as your warning. If you don't want to read triggers, feel free to skip the rest of this page.

Triggers are as follows: family betrayal, on page murder of a parent, on page blood and gore (war), force proximity, attempted murder, MMMFMMM sex, MF sex, bullying, gaslighting, abuse from parent, graphic descriptions of wounds and blood.

If any of these things upset you, I would suggest taking caution when reading. If you need a breakdown of chapters where these themes occur, there will be a list on my website. There is not enough room on this page to list them here. Please keep your mental health in mind when moving forward. Your mental health is important to me.

Without further ado... Enjoy

Krystal Harding

Pronunciation Guide

Characters

Luna Cromwell Embros: Luna Crom-well Em-bros

Damian Ashford: Dam-ian Ash-ford

Bastian Ashford: Bas-t-ian Ash-ford

Valyn Halloran: Val-in Hal-lor-en

Niklaus Adair: Nik-louse Ad-air

Fennik Elrod: Fen-nick El-rod

Elijah Elrod: Eli-jah El-rod

Undas: Un-dahs

Vanalli: Va-na-lee

Erina (Lilliana): E-ree-na

Tanis: Tan-is

Harold: Hair-old

Cassandra Halloran: Cass-an-ra Hal-lor-en

Penelope Ashford: Pen-el-ope Ash-Ford

Scarlet Ashford: Scar-let Ash-ford

Marie Elrod: Ma-re El-rod

Nora Adair: Nor-ah A-dare

Talissa: Ta-lis-sah

River: Riv-er

Claye: Cla-y

Ignis: Ig-nes

Voxis: Vox-es

Lumina: Lu-mean-a

Zekon: Z-con

Illisandra: Ill-e-san-dra

Otius: O-tee-us

Zephir: Ze-fear

Milara: Me-lar-ah

Undine: Un-dine

Jasmine: Jazz-min

Victoria: Vic-tor-e-ah

Alstrom: All-strom

Beatrix: Bee-a-trix

Elenor: Ell-e-nor

Marcloff: Mar-kl-off

Elucia: E-luc-e-ah

Alric: Al-rick

Valmor: Val-more

Aralia: A-ral-eah

Arthur: Ar-ther

Miharu: Me-har-roo

Mina: Me-nah

Celia: Seal-e-ah

Ishtar: Ish-tar

Luther: Lou-th-er

Creatures and Daemons

Ithika: Ith-ick-ca

Lyria: Leer-rhea

Ophelia: O-feel-ia

Ritmer: Rit-mer

Hilmer: Hill-mer

Realms and Cities

Floria: Floor-e-ah

Fildery: Fill-dur-rey

Mirith: Meer-rith

Hildaria: Hill-dar-e-ah

Mirith: Meer-rith

Solaria: Sol-are-ah

Valhime: Val-hime

Daglidell: Dag-li-dell

Endora: end-door-ah

Anchora: Anchor-ah

Celetsia: Cel-es-tea-a

Altaria: All-tear-e-ah

CONTENTS

PROLOGUE

My Dearest Harold,

I am returning to Floria for a little while. With Fennik refusing to have me at the wedding, I need some time to myself to regain my composure before I speak with him again. I want nothing more than to approve of this union, but I know how hard it can be to get the affection one desires from their mate when there are others involved.

Not that you don't love us all equally, sometimes one just needs a little more attention.

Please do not worry about me or follow me. I would like this time alone to clear my head. I will be visiting my brother while I am in Floria. I need to check in on him.

With all my love,
Marie

Of course, she would leave. I shake my head and put the letter in my pocket. I looked around Marie's room, noticing the Versalli suitcase and matching bag was gone. Her scent was stale in the room. She had been gone since before the ceremony even begun was my guess.

"My love?" one of the most beautiful voices sung into the room, bringing my focus to the doorway. Cassandra stood there, her blue and teal floor length dress still shimmering after hours of dancing. Her silver curls bounced around her as she walked toward me. "What's wrong?" she asked, looking around the room.

"You haven't figured it out?" I looked at her, raising an eyebrow. She shrugged her shoulder, and I laughed a little. She wanted to hear it from me, not from her own head.

"Marie has left to go to Floria. Leaving me a letter," I say as I toy with the parchment in my pocket.

"May I?" she asked as she held her hand out for it. I pulled it out, placing it in her soft hands. She closed her eyes and took a deep breath before opening it and reading. "She is such a jealous and possessive bitch." Cassandra snapped as she closed the letter and handed it back to me.

"You're usually a lot calmer than this, my dear Cassandra," I chime, pulling her into my arms and breathing in her summery sun scent. It was soothing to my soul.

"I don't trust her, Harold. Neither does anyone else. You should've seen Erina put her in her place. I think Erina regrets bringing up Tanis and Elijah, but Marie deserved it after what she kept calling Luna." Cassandra took a deep breath again and settled into my chest.

"Why don't you all trust her? I thought we had gotten past this distrust decades ago." I said, pulling Cassandra back to look up at me.

"Her story about Tanis doesn't add up. Harold, if she was mated to him, the refusal would've broken her too. You, being her mate, won't magically make that go away. Also, I don't believe you are her mate. I've had a horrible, uncertain feeling about her since I met her. I've let it go, thinking I was just being irrational, but once Nora, Scarlett and Penelope said they had the same worries," she sighed. "We don't trust her Harold and I have a terrible feeling she is going to hurt you or worse, to try to break apart our bonds. I can't lose you." She cried. I hugged her tightly. Cassandra's feelings and visions are usually not something to sweep under the rug. She was worried about Luna and the boys' first ceremony, and she was right. Something happened.

"I will be cautious. I promise. Let's get back to the others." I place a kiss to her soft pink lips and smile at her. I won't let today be ruined by tears. It's too special. I put my arm around her shoulders and turned her to the door. As the lock on the door clicked shut, I pulled my phone out of my pocket. Cassandra looked up at me. "It's time I called on an old friend of mine from Floria. There's a debt that needs to be repaid."

Part One

Forever Yours

CHAPTER 1
LUNA

"Don't look at me that way," Valdis said to me as he kissed me once more. "You think I rather go to some boring board meeting than stay here in bed with you all day?" He was right. I knew he didn't want to leave me here, but he had to make appearances at these types of things since he is now Infernia's next in line for the throne.

"I get it, I'm just whining," I say as I kiss him back. I hated watching him get ready to leave me. Hell, I hate watching any of them get dressed period. Let alone get dressed to leave me for days at a time. I shoved the blankets down to my thighs and let the early morning air caress my skin. Valdis snapped his head in my direction.

"If you don't cover up, I'm either not going to this meeting and fucking you again for the third time this morning or I'm calling Valyn and Fennik and letting them have their way with you while I sit and watch, then I'll go to the meeting," he smirked at me, and that devilish grin could melt me all over again. I also knew he wasn't kidding. Fennik and Valyn have been having way too much fun with me lately.

"I'm going to go for a run. Niklaus and Damian have decided that I need to keep up with a workout. Things have been a little too calm for everyone's liking," I say as I get up from the bed exposing my naked body to him. I can feel his gaze tracing all the lines of my body as if I was a map and he wanted to memorize it.

"I don't disagree with them. How is Bastian faring in Taiga? Will he be back soon?" Valdis asked and I knew it wasn't because the two of them still had issues. Surprisingly the two of them have gotten along rather splendidly. They all went out to dinner one night and went drinking and the next thing I know they all came back laughing like nothing had happened. I'll take it.

"He should be home today. If he's not, I'm going to Taiga to drag his ass back here." I say stomping my foot on the cold hardwood floor. Valdis just chuckles under his breath while fussing with his tie. I grabbed his T-shirt from yesterday from the chair by the dresser and toss it on before walking over to him.

"Let me help you with that," I smile as I help him fix his tie. He grabs my chin and makes me look up at him. Again, that smile does things to me that has me clenching my thighs together.

"You're such a good helpful girl," he whispers as he kisses me deeply. "Thank you, princess." He breaks the kiss as a knock comes at the door. I growl at the intrusion, but he flicks my nose. "Stop it, unless you want your ass blood red and vibrating." I squeaked and quickly covered my ass.

"Mind if I come in?" a deep voice rumbled through the door and my heart skipped about six beats. I ran to the door and threw it open. Standing there with his black hair pulled back, in a pair of grey sweatpants and a black muscle tank, was my winter prince. He finally was home. I ran into Bastian's arms, not caring that my bare ass was now completely exposed to anyone looking.

"You're home!" I shouted, I wrapped my arms around his waist and took a deep breath, letting his snow and pine scent flood my senses. "I've missed you." I could feel him taking me in.

"I've missed you too. Valdis," he replied as he looked over my head and into the room at Valdis, who was still packing his bag.

"Hey, I'm heading out for a few days. Should I let Damian and Niklaus know you're not going for your morning run?" Valdis smirked. He knew I wanted a way out of the run. Bastian coming home was definitely a good enough reason for me to get out of it now.

"Nah, I'm going to go running with them," Bastian replied, pinching my ass. A yelp squeaked out from between my lips. Chatter filled the hallway, my heart pulled in my chest again as Niklaus and Damian turned the corner in their work out shorts and muscle shirts. Dear gods these men look like they are chiseled out of fucking alabaster. It's no wonder Marie didn't think I was good enough for Fennik.

"Get that thought out of your head, now," Damian growled as he got closer to me. I really need to figure out how to block my thoughts sometimes.

"I'm sorry, I shouldn't be thinking about it, but it's not easy when Marie still hasn't come home. It's been weeks!" I threw my hands up in the air and stalked back into Valdis's room, throwing myself on his bed. The guys didn't follow me inside, instead looking at Valdis. He nodded, letting them enter. The amount of respect that they show each other now is heartwarming.

"Does Fennik know you're worried about his mom?" Damian asked. I just shook my head no. It was the truth; I didn't tell him. Fennik didn't want to hear anything about his mother. He said she chose her side and clearly that side wasn't supporting him. My mother has told me just to let it go, but it's hard. I looked out the window, the sun painted the sky a breathtaking pink and yellow. The stars from the night sky began winking out.

"Okay, time to get you out of your head and up on your feet. I get you're worried, but you don't know Marie. If no one else is worried, then you shouldn't be either. If our father was worried, he would've either gone himself or sent us to go check on her," Niklaus grabbed my hands and pulled me up from the bed. "Let's get some clothes on you before we decide to not go for our run and instead take you here on his bed."

Valdis scoffed, "Not without me you won't." He zipped up his bag and rolled it to the door. I didn't like the feeling I always got when one of them went to leave. It reminds me of when Nikalus left me. Great, abandonment issues at their finest. Niklaus handed me a pair of grey booty shorts out of the dresser. I quickly pulled them up and padded over to Valdis.

"Only a few days. If it has to be longer—" Valdis put his finger to my lips, so I'd pause.

"Princess, if I am going to be gone for more than a few days, I will call you. Or I'll just send Vanessa and Kieran to come get you," He kissed me once more, then looked behind me. "Take care of our girl."

"No worries, I'm home now. Oh, Kieran isn't in Infernia," Bastian winked and the smile across his face was bright. Kieran had made the first move on Hector after our eventful time in Taiga. They've been together since.

"Kieran is going to have to come home to visit soon unless he wants the wrath of Vanessa. She's already made threats to come here and stay if we don't visit often," he chuckled and kissed my cheek once more. "I'll see you soon, my love."

"I'll see you soon, babe." I kissed him once more before he left. The dread threatened to bubble up in my chest. Lucky for me the guys noticed it and I wasn't left alone to think about it. "So where are you all dragging me to this morning?"

"Mistward. We are going to run the mountains," Damian said as he tossed me a bright blue tank top from a bag he had brought in with him.

"Do I need to restock my clothes in your room?" I asked him and he grinned widely at me. He has been removing my workout clothes and sweats for more sexy attire. Tight dresses, lace and fishnets, silks and velvets. He has a fine taste for the luxury items in life. Scarlett says it's because the solar realms are full of high society and is the home of the gods and goddesses.

"We are going out tonight, so you will be getting ready in our room later," he said as he pulled me into a kiss and ran his hands along my sides, stopping right at the waistband of the shorts.

"All right you two, let's get going. Sneakers on," Niklaus was pulling my attention back to the present and it was probably for the best.

"Off to run through Mistward! Yay!" I said with exaggerated excitement. They all laughed. Damn Fennik and Valyn for getting to sleep in.

CHAPTER 2
LUNA

Silver hair caught my attention as we arrived at the gates and my heart tugged strongly. Valyn leaned up against a tree next to the main gate. He looked up as the crunching of rocks under our feet grew louder. He smiled and jogged up to me, gripping my chin and planting a huge kiss on my lips. The taste of sea salt washed over me, and I forgot I was moving. A strong hand grabbed mine and helped me from toppling over into Valyn.

"You really need to be more careful, baby girl," Fennik's voice sung to me, and I spun. His orange hair was a tuft mess on his head but the light in his emerald-green eyes shined so brightly. We were all running together this morning. I looked around at everyone as they all began stretching.

"Here I thought you two would be sleeping in this morning," I poked Valyn in the side. Fennik lead me away from my attempted tickle fight with Valyn to start stretching out.

"We all agreed with Bastian coming home that we should do this together. Valdis wanted to join us, but he has matters to attend to in Infernia. Make sure your shoes are tied tight. I don't need you tripping over your shoelaces," Damian quipped. I fall once and these guys treat me like I am fragile. I was human then!

"So, what's the plan for today? Running then breakfast?" Bastian asked Damian, both sitting almost cross legged with each foot touching the flat bottom of the other. I knew the stretch; they made me do it and it made my inner thighs burn. I hated it, but I knew I had to do it if I didn't want to lock up while running.

"Nox and Virgil need some assistance with a group of Borgs spotted in Tarrium. Valyn, Niklaus and I offered to help them out. I figured with Valdis leaving this morning, your return, and Fennik meeting up with Sirus later, we would give you and Luna some time alone together." Damian said, smiling at me. My heart melted at the way they took care of me. They all knew that I cling to them after a long absence, hence my clinging to Valdis for the last two nights before he left. I did the same thing when Damian came home from Solaria a little over a week ago. This damn bond is making me a psycho stage five clinger and I am not okay with it.

"So, I get our girl all to myself?" Bastian gasped, dramatically placing his hand over his heart. A small giggle escaped from my lips at his theatrics. I missed my playful winter prince. He winked at me, an approval to my reaction and a wicked promise wrapped in one expression. "Seriously though, are you three going to be alright by yourselves?"

"We'll be good. Nox and Virgil will be with us and surprisingly Virgil is really quick and skilled for a human," Valyn replied while stretching out his calves. I watched each of them stretch. It should be illegal to be surrounded by such hot males. I am truly lucky that they are all mine. Niklaus stood up and came up behind me, running the tips of his fingers along my shoulders. A small shudder shook my body, how long has it been since Niklaus, and I have been together?

"Don't worry little one," he whispered into my ear. "You'll be in my bed again soon enough." He kissed my cheek and held his hand out for me to take. I could feel the heat of his gaze as he traced my lips with hunger in his eyes. "Let's get going." The others stood up and looked away. Each trying to respect one another and their stolen moments with me. I patted dirt off my ass and nodded at Niklaus. Time to go running through the damn forest.

I felt like we were running for hours, my legs began burning once we hit the small stream. I wasn't built to run like this. Luckily for me, they didn't seem to notice me stopping at the water and taking a small break. Not that they would give me shit, but I wanted some time alone. I sat down on the edge of the stream and looked up at the now blue sky. The clouds were a nice and fluffy white today, with just a soft breeze to keep me cooled down. It was early spring here in Mistveil and while it's nice, I dread the summer months. I know it's going to get sticky hot.

Rustling in the bushes near me had my head jerking in that direction. I don't have any weapons on me, but fire would always do the trick. Orange fur had my heart calming down quickly. Fennik trotted over to me, laying down beside me, head in my lap. I ran my hands through his fur on the top of his head, petting down his back. He growled softly in approval. "You know where we are don't you?" I asked him. He looked up at me and huffed. "I'll take that as a yes." I laughed as he nudged my hand again.

"To think that last fall, I fed the prince of autumn at my campsite as if he was a common fox. You little trickster," I say as I continue to pet him. He sinks deeper into my lap, and I scratch behind his ears. If you would've told me last year that I would be married and mated to fae princes and a daemon prince, I would've laughed at you and asked what drugs you were on. Sitting here with my autumn prince in his fox form in my lap, I feel complete. I let out a deep breath and looked out across the water. "Hungry?"

His head popped up and cocked to the side, I laughed once more. I didn't have any weapons with me but, I don't think I had anything with me that day either except my bow. I pulled off my shoes and socks, tossing them onto the grass next to me. Fennik moved, sitting up to watch me as I dipped my feet into the cold stream. The waters were filled with different types of fish this time of year, the salmon from up the mountain never came down this far but there were plenty of gullies here. I realized I had nothing to catch them with this time around except my hands. This is going to be fun.

I wade a little into the water and Fennik huffs at me. I look back at him still sitting there on the bank, "You better not laugh at me!" I yelled back at him. I glance down at two gullies swimming between my legs. I focused my breathing and shot my hands into the water and gripped the slightly slimy fish, yanking it out of the water, tossing it toward the bank. It landed with a thump on the ground next to Fennik. He stepped away from it like it was going to jump at him. It was cute to see his reaction to the fish. I grabbed another from the stream and repeated the same thing.

Making my way back over to the bank, I walked out and looked down at the two fish, "Couldn't have just put them out of their misery, could you?" I asked him, shaking my head. I grabbed a few sticks and made a small fire box. There were some potar leaves fresh on the trees, this would make things a little difficult but at least this time I wasn't using a lighter. I grabbed a few leaves and tossed them in the center of the box and snapped my fingers, igniting the leaves.

Fennik dropped two sticks next to my feet. I smiled as I grabbed the sticks and looked at the gullies still flopping around. I have to dispatch them, so they stop suffering. I take one of the sticks, the sharper of the two, and plunge it into the fish head. Not the best way but, it will do for now. I did the same with the other and then pushed the sticks through the fish and began grilling them.

"Should I toss it to you and let you eat it like an animal like before?" I joked, but I think he was seriously going to stay like this. He's been in his fox form more recently. King Harold told me to just let it go and he will return to his true form once he gets out his anger. Apparently, this was a thing he did as a kid to keep himself calm and not taking out his anger on others. I want to go to Floria and drag Marie back by her fucking hair. Self-centered bitch. I turned my attention back to the fish so as not to burn them. I doubt he would care at this point, but I was getting hungry, and the guys were nowhere to be seen. Fennik looked out over the stream at the tree line in the distance. He seemed like he was annoyed by the time he looked back at me.

"Everything okay?" I ask, trying to hear if anything was coming. Nothing. Just the sounds of the forest cresting into the morning. Birds chirping, sticks breaking under the feet of the deer. Nothing out of the ordinary. Maybe that should worry me more than anything. Fennik relaxed and moved closer to me as I finished cooking. "I have no seasoning, so if it tastes bad, don't blame me."

I pulled a gully off for him, placing it on the ground in front of him. I know not to pry. I know he will eventually be okay but, "I'm here for you. You don't have to worry about losing your shit around me. You've seen me go into a rage before and never once judged me. I won't judge you." I kissed the top of his head.

I know. I just don't want my anger to come off the wrong way. I'm not angry at you or the others. I'm pissed at my mother and her bullshit. It's not fair to you.

Just hearing his voice in my head sent a calmness washing over me. "I get it. I'm pissed at her for abandoning you and your father like this. It's not fair." I huffed as I took a bite out of the still scalding hot fish. Bad idea! I spit the fish out on the ground, "FUCK! That hurt! Dumbass move!" I shouted.

"Are you alright?" I didn't hear Valyn come up behind me and my normal sensation when the guys are close didn't alert me to shit. Must've been the damn distraction from the hot fish.

"Yup, I'm just a dumbass that bit into a super-hot fish," I replied, sheepishly grinning up at him.

"So, you cook fire side for Fenn huh?" Valyn teased looking between the two of us. Fennik had already halfway finished his fish. I looked back down at the skewered fish in my hand and sighed. Not my original plan for breakfast.

"This is where I met Fennik. I guess we're just reliving our first date," I said, and I could hear him snort out a laugh in my head. Valyn looked between us and sighed.

"Guess I can't compete with a fox companion for breakfast." Valyn chuckled, sitting down beside me. He looked at the fish skewer in my hands and let out a low whistle. "I'm assuming this was you since Fenn won't get out of his fox form long enough to have a conversation with any of us."

She's good at fishing and hunting. You should see her. Elegant and breathtaking. I bet she would love to try the fish in your realm Valyn. He spoke through our minds like we were sitting here talking aloud.

"Oh really? Then I might have to take you there once the summer festivals come around." Valyn put his arm over my shoulder and pulled me in. "Hey Fenn, are you going to be alright? You've got us all worried. It's different now than it was before. We're all here for you."

Yeah, I know that I just don't want to be a burden or accidentally take my anger out on anyone. I guess it's no different now that you all can hear what's going on in my head. He replied and looked up at me. I'm sorry. I'll switch back in a few minutes. I have to run back and get my clothes. I could hear his laugh, and it made me smile.

"You're fine, I'm not going anywhere right now. Want to try some?" I asked Valyn, holding the skewer up for him. I wasn't truly expecting him to take a bite, but he did and looked at me. "I had no seasonings so don't give me shit." Valyn quickly swallowed and grinned.

"I never said it was bad. I was just shocked that you cooked this. No offense, but I have never seen you cook," he said, and it dawned on me in that moment that I haven't cooked for any of them besides Fennik. We've either had someone at the house making food or we go out to eat. I think I need to change that.

"Maybe I can get Valdis to come home tonight for dinner and I'll make something for us all," I excitedly blurt out. Fennik just chuckled and headed off into the woods.

I'll be right back; the others will probably be here when I return. You don't have to wait up for me if they do. I'll catch up.

"We will stay right here waiting for you," Valyn said, pulling me into his lap as he offered me a bite of the fish which I promptly refused. I burned the shit out of my mouth, and I don't feel like attempting to eat another bite. I shook my head, and he finished it off. Well, I guess I can say that I have fed Valyn now too. I leaned my head back onto his chest and looked up at the sky once more. I let out a sigh and closed my eyes. Valyn ran his fingers through the loose parts of my ponytail. It was probably the most soothing gesture he could do right now.

"Are you good princess?" He whispered into my ear. I know he just wants to help but I know if I say anything mentally between us, everyone could hear it. Just like our talk with Fennik. Everyone heard what Fennik was saying. I need to talk to Sirus about blocking out others while I talk to one.

"I'm frustrated with how Marie is acting. I get it, everyone says to let it go, but it's not fair. Like what is her damn issue with me?" I sighed. I didn't get why she hated me so much.

"It's not you. It's the fact that Fennik didn't mate to someone one on one. How much do you know about Marie? Has your mother told you anything?" He asked, leaving the question open for me to tell him as much or as little as I wanted.

"I don't really know much about her. My mother said there was another before your dad, which seemed to be a big no for everyone. Including your mom. I think she has been the most vocal, aside from Penelope. I wish Marie would just give me the chance to show her I won't put her son on some back burner or treat him wrong." Tears slipped down my cheeks. Having all of my mother-in-laws approve of me was probably the biggest thing I wanted and to know that there is one who despises me for no good reason. It hurts. "Her absolute rejection of me for no reason other than I have more than one mate puts me right back into school when I was rejected by everyone except Kira and Harper because I had natural bright blue hair which is uncommon in human cities. I was an abomination and there were plenty of kids who made it well known. Hence why when you met me, I had blonde covering most of it the best I could. It was Virgil's idea as a way to keep me safe from harsh words or worse. It worked on new kids in town but not the others."

I could feel the tears gliding down my cheeks. Gods, how long has it been since I spoke about the constant bullying and abuse I suffered as a kid. All because I was different. I was unique. And well, now I know, I am a goddess who was never meant to be raised in the mortal world.

"Fuck those people. No one there deserved you. Aside from the twins and Virgil. I may not like how he still looks at you some days, but I can put that aside. As for Marie, she was mated before she met our father. She supposedly broke the mating bond with her first and chose our father. Only thing was, none of our mothers trusted her. If the bond was truly broken, it would've killed her. It would have eaten her alive until one of them died. Knowing a part of your soul is out there alone and rejected won't sit well. Rumor has it her first killed himself after she left him, but that's just a rumor. No way of actually knowing if it is real or not. Marie sure as shit doesn't talk about him. My mom says she's never alone when she goes home for a visit. Our father has been recently talking about going to Floria himself to check in on her. Something he never does. Our realms are our mothers sanctuaries. Unless invited, he doesn't invade their space and private time. Only difference is, no one besides Marie takes that time." Valyn said, running his fingers up and down my spine.

"I got pissed and left when Bastian pulled his shit a few months ago but it was painful. An empty hollow void that I forced myself to ignore. I don't ever think I will be doing that again. No matter how pissed off I am at any of you." I said, opening my eyes to see a beautiful crane landing in the stream in front of us.

"Well, that's good to know," Bastian's deep smoky voice wound its way around me. "I never plan on doing something dumb like that again. I think we all felt the same void without you. So, let's agree that we can be mad, but we will never run away from our problems."

"I can agree to that," I smiled as he reached his hand out to help me up from Valyn's lap.

"I think we all can," replied Damian as he and Niklaus walked up to us. "You do realize you missing out on running now just means we run again later, right?"

"Can I persuade you not to make me run and to do something better?" I asked sheepishly, not wanting to come off weak but also not wanting to play the strong card.

"Maybe something could be arranged baby girl," Niklaus replied, slipping his hand under my chin, forcing me to look up at him.

"I say we can definitely figure something out," Fennik replied as he joined us. I could feel all their eyes drinking me in. I think I may have just fucked up.

CHAPTER 3
LUNA

We made our way back out of Mistward with no issues. I honestly don't think I've been here since the Borg attack last year. Bastian grabbed my hand, intertwining our fingers together. He took care of the Borg that night, he made sure I was safe, and it wouldn't return for me. Still a little pissed that Valdis was the mastermind behind it, even if his intentions were somewhat in the right place.

"Shower then breakfast?" he asked me as we broke the tree line. Most of Mistveil was still slumbering. It was peaceful here.

"That sounds perfect. Joining me?" I asked as he looked out over the small city. A pinch to my ass had me yelping and spinning on the culprit.

"You're mine when we get home little one," Damian was smirking like a cat. His eyes flashed a bright crimson and my heart sped up. I could feel my cheeks heating under his stare.

"He's right. With him, Valyn and Niklaus leaving after breakfast you should spend time with them before they go. I have you all to myself when they leave," Bastian said squeezing my hand then looking over at Fennik. "Well, almost all to myself."

"You'll have her to yourself; I have to go meet with Sirus to check on a few things. But when I get back, she's mine for the night," Fennik winked at me, yup, my cheeks were probably as red as Damians hair at this point.

"You're so cute when you're embarrassed," Bastian said playfully. These men would be the death of me one of these days.

"Where are we going for breakfasts?" I asked desperately trying to change the topic of conversation. Niklaus and Valyn were talking to themselves in the back of the group, so they were no help. Honestly though, they probably would just make me blush ten times harder than I already am.

"I was thinking about The Dewdrop. They have a great selection of breakfast foods and pastries. The chef there used to work at the house. When she said her dream was to start a breakfast and lunch café, we let her go and gave her a nice severance package that was be enough for her to purchase the building, get the equipment and purchase a years' worth of product to get herself started. She's been flourishing ever since," Damian said. I could see the pride as he was explaining the situation with their old chef. A part of me twinged a little with jealousy at the pride for another woman in his eyes. It seemed like such an irrational thing to have. She wasn't competition, especially now that we are bonded and married. I really need to get that part of me under control.

"That was really nice of you guys to do that for her," I forced myself to say, keeping a tight grip on the jealousy I felt so it didn't betray me in my voice.

"We all had agreed, she was like a sister to us. Her husband still works for our father when he needs renovations done or when new buildings need construction. He headed the rebuild of Mirith," Fennik stated from the other side of Bastian and the jealousy I was just feeling deflated like a popped balloon, replaced with guilt. I really need to get shit under control.

"Baby girl, what's going on in that head of yours?" Bastian squeezed my hand to get my attention. I looked up at him with a puzzling look. Why would he ask me that? "Your hand went from burning hot to ice cold within a matter of seconds."

"It did?" I asked, stunned a little that I didn't notice it myself.

"Yes, so out with it," he said with such command that I halted my steps. I looked between him and the others. I didn't want to tell them that I was letting my brain and jealousy get the best of my inner thoughts.

"You can tell us, Luna. We won't judge you," Fennik said. Valyn and Niklaus finally noticed that something was happening and ended their conversation abruptly. I know I could tell them, and they wouldn't judge me, but it didn't make it any easier.

"I got a little jealous," I said looking down at my feet. I didn't want to make eye contact when I was feeling this way. Valyn busted out laughing, breaking me from my self-loathing.

"Kitten, you should know by now not to be embarrassed to tell us if you get jealous. It's taken us how long to not want to kill Virgil every time we're around him?" Valyn stalked up to me and put his finger beneath my chin forcing me to look up at him. His turquoise eyes bright light the seas as he looked down at me. "As long as you don't go killing people for glancing in our direction, it won't be a problem. Can't cover murder up so well." He kissed me and pulled me into a hug. I relaxed into his chest. He was right. They didn't like Virgil for a long time. It took a lot for them to get over him being my first.

"Miranda is the sister we never had. She tried acting like a parent to us when we were younger. Always telling us to knock our dumb shit off. What would our future mate say about our behavior? Things like that. She was right though. Haven't had the chance to tell her she was right, and she won't let us live it down once we do tell her." Niklaus said as he walked up to me.

"Yeah, I'm not looking forward to telling her she was right either." Bastian laughed. "Let's hurry up and get home. The Dewdrop will start to fill up in roughly two hours. I want a good seat."

"I already called and told her to save our booth. She put a reserved marker on it for us. But we should hurry." Damian said as we began walking again. Do I still feel guilty for the jealousy, yes. Will I learn to move on? I have too. They did it for me so I could keep my best friend.

"Oh, Harper is coming over later. She wanted to talk to me about something. The twins have another show coming up soon and I think she wants me to come. I really want to go. I've missed the last few they have had due to other situations," I almost immediately regret the words that come out as Bastian puts his head down. "It's not on you. I didn't handle things well when we fought. Plus, getting trapped in a mirror realm doesn't exactly make it easy either." I chuckled to myself.

"Please don't remind me of that shit. I love your uncle and I get it, but no thank you," Fennik said. We crossed the gate and made our way up to the house. Everyone branched off into little conversations of their own. I enjoyed the lack of questions posed to me. I just want to get in the shower and eat. Harper will be here at some point this afternoon and I am slightly nervous about what she wants to talk about. She's usually never so shy when wanting to talk to me about anything. I wonder if it's about Lilly.

I let my thoughts continue to race through the days activities and what is needed from me. I need to check the kitchen for what to make for dinner. I also need to send Valdis a text about dinner tonight. What is the worst he can say? No, I can't? Eh, I should expect for the rejection. Not because he wouldn't want to. A hand wraps around my wrist breaking my concentration, fire wraps around my wrist instinctually. Shit!

The hand lets go of me faster than it grabbed me. I spun to see the guys all paused in the doorway watching me. It was Damian who caught my attention, his hand a bright red. "I am so sorry!" I say wanting to cry. I didn't mean to hurt him.

"It's okay, I let go fast enough. I didn't mean to startle you, we called your name, but you didn't respond," he hid his hand into his shorts pocket. Tears streamed down my face. I didn't mean to hurt him.

"Stop crying baby girl. It was an accident. You can always make it up to me," he said as he winked at me, tentatively reaching his other hand out for me. I barreled into his chest, sobbing. He stroked my hair and nodded. I could hear footsteps passing by us, a kiss brushed to my shoulders as each of them went to their rooms to get cleaned up. "Come on, let's get you cleaned up."

We made it back to my room without incident. I don't know why I reacted that way. I knew I was safe. I knew I was around my mates. Probably the safest I've been in a long time. So why did my powers react like that. I tried to stay present through my racing thoughts. I didn't want to hurt him again.

"Either you're going to pick out an outfit or I am. If I do it, you're going out in the most obscene lacey thing I can find in that closet of yours," he teased me. I don't know if I was expecting some type of punishment from him for hurting him or not. Maybe if he did, I wouldn't feel as guilty. I didn't answer him, instead stalking into the bathroom and turning on the shower. I needed to clear my head and to be somewhere my fire couldn't hurt him.

I stripped off my clothes and felt his eyes trail the length of my body and the curves they all loved so much. I felt the water before stepping under the pelting rain from the showerhead. Closing my eyes I let the whole situation wash from my mind. I heard his feet step into the water behind me, his hands tentatively brushing against my hips. He stepped closer to me, wrapping his hands around my waist. Placing his forehead on my upper back, he let out a small sigh.

"I'm sorry," he said over the roaring water. I kept my eyes closed, listening to the flow of the water.

"Why are you apologizing? You didn't do anything wrong. I did," I let the feeling of the water flowing down my body consume me, wrapping me up like a blanket of comfort. He held onto me tighter, sinking into me more.

"It was an accident, you're still new to your powers. It's bound to happen to us all a few times. It's okay. No harm done," he replied as he moved his hand from my waist and to my face. He turned me away from the water to look at him. I opened my eyes to see Damian inches from my face. His eyes were like a burning fire I just wanted to dive into. His red hair plastered to the side of his face from the water. I brushed his hair from his face, untangling it from his beard. He grabbed my hand with his and kissed it. The skin on his hand where I burned him didn't show any signs of damage. Thank the gods for that.

I looked at his hand one more time and kissed it. "I know it was an accident, but I never want to hurt you or any of the others," I sobbed out into his hand. He entwined our fingers together and chuckled. I glanced back at his face just in time to see the smirk flash across his lips. His wicked smile sending shivers all over my body.

He grabbed my throat with his free hand and pushed me up against the wall, gently squeezing it. "You need a reminder that there is nothing you can do that would physically cause us harm. Same as us to you. Our bodies and souls are made for one another," he kissed me deeply. His hand loosened around my throat and moved down the center of my chest to my breasts, cupping my left breast in his hand, giving it a firm squeeze.

A moan escaped from my lips at the firm pressure of his calloused hands on my soft skin. He captured my lower lip between his teeth and growled. I felt the heat from him fill my body, desire dripping off him, latching onto my skin. I dragged my nails softly down his back, his eyes flickered with lust. He squeezed my breast harder, moving his fingers to the sensitive pebbled peaks and pinched hard. A yelp freed itself from my mouth, but he was quick to capture the sound in his own.

He pulled his lips just far enough away from mine to speak, "You are forever mine until the day the gods decide we are no longer meant for this world and when that decision is made, you'll be mine in the stars for eternity." His lips crashed hard and heavy into mine. Wetness gathered between my thighs that had nothing to do with the water rushing over us. He wrapped his arms around my waist and tugged me from the wall and closer into him. I went willingly, wrapping my arms around his neck. His erection poked at my thighs, and I giggled.

Oops, not the best thing to do. He broke the kiss and a wicked grin flashed across his lips. "What's so funny baby girl?" he asked, voice as smooth as velvet caressed my skin. I tried to look down at his impressive length to no avail. He pulled his body back just enough for me to get a glimpse of the rock-hard throbbing length that I wanted nothing more than to plunge inside of me.

"Nothing is funny. You just tickled me, that's all," I replied innocently. He didn't fall for it and dipped his fingers between my thighs. A low moan escaped as he dragged his finger through my arousal. His grin didn't falter as he dropped to his knee in the shower, hoisting my leg in the air placing it on his shoulder and devouring me like I was going to be his breakfast. I closed my eyes and let my head fall back, the water soaking my hair. My moans echoed in the small space around us to the point where I couldn't focus on anything else. He huffed a laugh into my pussy which made me look down at him.

"We're not alone baby girl," he said into me as he went right back to devouring my pussy. I didn't understand what he meant; it was just the two of us in here.

"That is a beautiful fucking sight," Valyns voice wrapped around me like a silk scarf. My eyes flung to the opening in the shower, and I watched Valyn take in the sight. He crossed his arms, biting his lower lip, eyes roaming all over my body. Damian bit my clit sending me rolling through an immense amount of pleasure and pain. My head flung back as I rode his face to find my release on his tongue.

"Have I ever told you how fucking amazing you taste?" he asked me, pulling back from between my legs, his beard glossy with my cum all over it. The satisfied smug smile he wore made my legs weaker than they already were. He gently put my leg down and stood up. Somewhere between my watching Valyn and my face riding, Valyn lost his clothes and got in the shower behind me. His hard cock pressed up against my ass and my eyes widened. Damian had palmed his cock and I watched as he stroked it, long and slow. I reached for it, but Valyn grabbed my hand, pulling it behind me to grab his instead.

"You're not touching him, you're going to be a good girl, and do as I say," Valyn whispered in my ear, and I shuddered at the anticipation. It has been a while since these two had been in me at the same time. Damian leaned in and gently kissed my lips, leaving my arousal on my own lips. Valyn reached around and grabbed my breasts, massaging them gently. Damian watched as Valyn caressed me, stroking his cock harder and faster. I didn't want him to waste his release on the shower floor.

"Do you want it?" He asked me, watching my eyes hone in on the glistening of his cock's head. I didn't want anything wasted. I nodded, but I knew what they wanted. I jerked on Valyn's cock, grinding my ass up against it. I want them both to fill me up, my need becoming painful.

"I think she wants both of us," Valyn teased, his breath whispering across my skin. I reached my other hand back and gripped his hips, pulling him into me. His cock pressed firm against my ass, his hands slid to my hips and between my thighs. "I think she is more than ready for us," he said, sliding his fingers into the wetness still pouring down my thighs.

Damian's eyes glistened and I watched his gaze follow Valyn's fingers as he slid them between my ass cheeks, getting my hole nice and wet for him. I've only had Valdis in me like that. Valyn lined the head of his cock up to my entrance and gently pushed in. I winced a little at the pressure of his cock forcing its way into me. He was gentle though and waited until I was comfortable before pulling it out and pushing himself back in. "Fuck! I see why Valdis says we should do this more often. You're so fucking tight." Valyn breathed out.

"My turn," Damian moved up grabbing my legs, he put one leg around his waist and lined his cock up to my dripping wet entrance. He slid in with a little force and it ignited a fire in my blood. Feeling the two of them fill me up was euphoric. Damian grabbed my other leg and wrapped it around him, driving Valyn deeper into me and drilling him up deeper as well. I wrapped my arms around Damian's neck. The feeling of them so deep threatened to shatter me into a million pieces. I was on the brink of exploding from pleasure.

They move in and out of me with the most beautiful rhythm, in and out simultaneously. I bit into Damian's neck hard pulling a out a roar of pleasure as he drove into me deep and hard. Valyn cursed from behind me. "Princess you better be fucking close!" He growled into my skin. My teeth sunk into Damian harder, his fingers bit into my thighs pulling me down hard onto him.

"She's fucking ready!" Damian roared as his released pulsed into my at the same time mine crashed over me. Valyn let out a groan, drilling harder into my ass. The feeling of fullness and love was so intense and so fulfilling.

They both gently removed themselves from me and I whimpered at the emptiness that filled my body where they once were. Valyn grabbed my loofa and soaped it up with my strawberry mint body wash and cleaned me up. Damian washed my hair when Valyn was finished. Both of them cleaned themselves up, not allowing me to do it for them. I whimpered at them removing one of my favorite things to do for them when we showered together, but Damian called out for Niklaus to come get me so they could finish up without making me upset. He didn't hesitate to come get me. Niklaus looked me over and smiled, drying me off with a towel and helping me into the bedroom where Bastian and Fennik sat on the chairs in the corner of the room talking. It was a nice coexistence that I was worried we would never have.

Niklaus picked my outfit out, a crème-colored dress with white corked sandals. I am getting way too spoiled by them washing my hair and my body, picking out my outfits, brushing my hair. I wasn't used to this type of pampering. It was something that most women would want to get used to. Me, I don't. I want to still be able to do some things for myself. But I will never be ungrateful for the time they do it for me. I am lucky. Hell, I am beyond lucky.

"Ready to go to breakfast?" Fennik asked me as Valyn and Damian entered the bedroom fully dressed. My hair was still a little damp, so I just put it up in a pony tail to dry on the way to breakfast.

I looked at everyone and smiled, my heart was so full of love. How could anything go wrong?

CHAPTER 4
LUNA

Never ask what could go wrong! I swear the world has a horrible fucking way of making you feel like you have no control of your life. We entered the Dewdrop about ten minutes ago and everything was fine, perfect honestly. Then I heard Bastian and Damian curse under their breath. I shouldn't have looked in the direction they did. Valyn and Niklaus tried to get me to the table while Fennik stood there with Damian and Bastian as a busty brunette came bouncing up to them. Her olive skin glistened in the morning light, her plump lips painted a playful pink, the black eyeliner winged just right at the corners of her eyes, framed with long dark lashes that were clearly fake.

"Damian! Bastian! What brings you two here? It's been so long!" her voice sounded like nails on a chalkboard, as she screeched at the from across the room. She waved her hand up high so they would notice her. I caught a glimpse of her pulling her shirt down to expose her cleavage more to them as she practically galloped toward them. Valyn cursed and looked down at me. His hand entwined with mine and he gave me a little squeeze.

This woman had the audacity to try and hug my mates. Blatant disregard for the fact that neither of them extended their arms for a hug or anything. They both looked disgusted at her attempt to touch them. Both backing away before she touched them. She began to pout, puffing her bottom lip out and huffing like a petulant child who got their favorite toy taken away.

"That was rude of you both. I've missed you," she attempted to touch Bastian's hand, but he moved it out of her reach. She looked to Damian for some comfort but found none. Both my mates looked down at this woman as if she was the bane of their existence.

"Do not try to touch us. I told you; we don't want anything to do with you," Damian said harshly to the woman. A bell rang in my head. That was Rita. That was the woman the two of them shared their time with before they met me. If I wasn't insecure about my body before, this woman in front of me had me feeling inadequate. Her small hourglass curves, her petite frame. I'm surprised they didn't break the bitch. She tried to touch their hands again, flirting with them despite everyone in the kingdom knowing they were married and mated. I attempted to step forward, but it was Niklaus who stepped in front of me.

"Don't do it. I know what's going through your head, but don't do it," he warned over his shoulder. Fennik glanced back at me and stepped between Bastian, Damian and Rita. I was thankful that he was standing there.

"You don't speak for my Bast. Isn't that right my love?" She batted those fake ass eyelashes at him, and I just wanted to burn them right off her face. This bitch was pushing a line. She tried reaching for Bastian's hand, but he pulled away.

"Don't ever fucking call me that again. You were never my love, nor my brother's love. We both are mated and married. You would do your best to show our mate the respect she deserves. Leave us alone," Bastian said, his eyes staring daggers into her. To her credit she didn't back down, hell no, this bitch doubled down. She fucking laughed. I felt Valyn tense next to me. Niklaus moved closer to me. Both trying to center me before I charred this bitch.

"Your mate is a human whore. Do you really want to share her with that scum prince from Hellis? Let him have the whore and you both can have me instead. At least you know what you get with me," She smiled and grabbed Bastian's crotch. All bets were off. Niklaus and Valyn couldn't grab me fast enough and Fennik's eyes were wide as I passed him.

I gripped her wrist at the vein and pushed my nails into her skin. "If you don't keep your fucking filthy whore hands from my mates, I will remove them for you. As for me being a human whore. I'm not the one chasing after two males who only fucked me when they were high or drunk looking for any hole to stick it in to get their rocks off. And unlike you, I am not a fucking human as you can clearly see. I am a princess and you have just gone and pissed me off." I spat at her as I gripped her wrist tighter. I wanted this bitch to drown.

"You let six men fuck you! You are the epitome of a whore! I don't care if you are some princess. Once you let that daemon cock go in you,

you stained your body for my boys," She spat out, wincing as my grip tightened. This bitch really didn't get it did she. Bastian and Damian rested their hands on my shoulders, but I glared at them both. Each of my mates froze still at the sight of me.

I let out a sinful laugh, "You, again, called my mates your boys. You clearly have no respect and since you have no respect, I'm going to teach you respect," a wicked grin slashed across my face as fire swirled around my arms, the shadows dancing at my feet. But there was something new mixed with this rage. Crystal clear blue water snaked up my arms between the flames like a snake about to strike its prey. She opened her mouth to scream, and I seized the opportunity. I grabbed her throat with my other hand forcing the water to strike down her throat and hold in her airways. She let go of Bastian awhile ago, but I still snapped her wrist with a satisfying crack. I let her drop to the floor, the water still stuck where I put it. She clawed at her throat, trying to scream. I watched the realization spark in her eyes at what I was capable of doing. I smiled and snapped my fingers. Water disappearing as if it never existed.

I stepped up close to her and squatted down to where she could hear me. "If you touch any of my mates, speak ill of any of my mates, talk about me in any way, or even look in our fucking direction, I will kill you. Be it with fire, with water, with your own fucking nightmare. You will die by my fucking hands, and I will smile, enjoying every second." I whispered. Her skin paled, she shook in her place. Devastation settling in at the fact that I would indeed kill her and have a grand time doing it. "Now get the fuck out of here and out of my fucking sight you filthy whore. No one wants you."

I stood up and dusted my dress off and walked back to my mates with a smile on my face, taking my seat in the booth in the corner of the restaurant. They all just looked at me. Shock and something else etched into their faces. I just opened the menu and waited for the trash to see her way out. It didn't take long for her to scramble to her feet and run for the door. Thankfully the place wasn't crowded and the few patrons that were in here seemed to agree with my sentiment of her.

Niklaus was the first to sit at the table with me, Valyn and Bastian sat next followed by Damian and Fennik. I felt all their eyes on me. Sparks needling into my skin as their gaze moved along my body. Niklaus broke the tension with a low whistle.

"Since when, baby girl, could you do that?" he asked, and I was surprised he was the one to ask. Valyn was studying my arms, looking for any sign of the water that was just there.

"No fucking clue, but I will take it. She should be grateful that I was able to summon it though. If not, she would've tasted fire." I replied, still studying the menu. Bastian cleared his throat, bringing my attention to him across the table. "What?"

"Are you okay?" he asked, a mix of worry and fear flashed across his face before he wrestled it into a neutral expression. I wonder if he is actually worried that I would've killed her. Would he have cared for her safety?

"She touched what is mine. Neither of you wanted her to touch you and her lack of respect for the both of you pushed me to a breaking point. She's just lucky I decided that I didn't want murder to be on the list of things I do today," I said flipping over the menu. "What do you recommend here? I kind of want the strawberry pancakes."

The look of disbelief on their faces was enough to have me wondering if I did in fact upset them. I set the menu down and crossed my arms on the table. "If you have something you'd like to get off your chest, by all means; go ahead. If not, I'd like to eat."

It was Valyn who cleared his throat, "Do you feel any different?" He asked me and I wasn't quite sure what he meant by that.

"Like how?" I asked, the adrenaline finally calming down. I took a deep breath, slowly going over what I just did. It slightly scared me that I could go to that level of crazy. It scared me, but it also thrilled me. It was an odd sensation. I looked at them all. They weren't afraid of me. I could sense that. It was more worry and what looked like fear for me. I didn't understand the fear in their eyes or the worry. I mean yeah, I lost my shit a little more than I was expecting. I didn't mean to go full on psycho, but it was so worth it to watch her squirm and knowing that it was up to me if she lived or died there on the floor.

"Your eyes changed," Bastian interjected, stopping Valyn from needing to explain. I gave him a puzzling look. What does he mean that my eyes changed? I didn't feel anything. I mean yeah it was nice finding out I could summon water, that was cool.

"Your eyes turned into a galaxy, my love," Damian whispered. Shock rippled through my body, Sirus's warning during one of our training sessions ringing in my ears.

If you don't control yourself, your power will consume you and turn you into a star in the sky. The true death of a god or goddess. Don't let the darkness consume you.

I need to call my uncle.

CHAPTER 5
HAROLD

My phone rang out from atop the nightstand. Whoever is calling me this damn early better have a good damn reason. Scarlett and Penelope groaned as I moved from between them. I didn't want to leave the warm embrace of my mates. I'm going to strangle whoever is on the other end of this call.

Gently moving around the bed so I don't bump into and wake my preciouses up, I finally grab my phone. Of course, the damn thing goes to voicemail as I reach it. I let out a low growl. I look at the missed call notification, Valyn. That was unusual of him to call me this early. I guess I better put pants on and call him back. I sigh, staring at the two beauties in my bed and grumble as I grab my sweatpants and slide them on. I pulled up the grey fur blanket and covered both of my mates up. I want them to sleep as much as they can. We had a late night.

I put my phone in my pocket and exited the room, Athena was walking down the hallway heading to the stairs with a tray in her hand. Nora is not a morning person by far, so that leaves my only other mate who is home, Cassandra. I walk down the hall, taking in the paintings that I never really took note of until Luna came into my sons' lives. She gushes over them every time she visits. Especially the painting that

Cassandra has outside of her room. It's a slightly larger piece compared to the others in the hall. The golden frame looked tarnished from time in my opinion, but Luna and Cassandra told me I was wrong it was meant to look that way. The ocean scene from the painting was of Fang's Lagoon, Cassandra was telling Luna that it was one she had painted on her last visit to Doria. She said the Lagoon sang to her, she wanted to capture the moment.

Unbeknownst to us, that was where Valyn discovered Luna was fae. I remember her vividly laughing about the incident while Valyn and Bastian sat there clearly not finding humor in the past situation. They both still held themselves responsible for that night, regardless of what Luna or anyone else said to them. Cassandra wasn't happy to hear that this happened, but she knew that sometimes her visions weren't clear and weren't always about her or those she loves. Now, however, she adores Luna, and this was probably just her senses trying to tell her something big would happen there.

I stopped outside Cassandra's room and knocked gently on the oak door. Seashells and waves were etched into the door and framework, I heard the gentle humming on the other side of the door before the knob turned and a stunned Cassandra was standing in the doorway.

"Is everything alright my love? You're never up this early," she asked, taking my hand and allowing me to enter her space. Her room was beautiful, just like her. The cream and different shades of blue that filled the room matched her perfectly. Her bed in this room was sacred to her and I was only allowed in it if she wished. It was one rule I had for all of them. Their rooms were theirs unless they were ill and needed my care or unless they allowed me in or unless I feel they needed comforting from some type of discomfort within the family.

Cassandra led me to the little table that was by the window looking at the North Selpie Sea. She was eating breakfast while taking in the comfort of home. I almost feel bad for bothering her this early. I took my seat, and she waited a moment before taking hers.

"Have you heard from Valyn this morning?" I asked her, taking in her radiant turquoise eyes. My sons take after their mothers in so many ways, but their eyes, they all took after their mothers in that sense.

"No, I haven't. I know he was going running with Luna and the boys this morning, but then Damian, Nikalus and Valyn are heading to Mirith to help with a borg infestation that seems to be creeping into the lands. Nox has been doing well with Virgil, but the boys offered to lend a hand," she replied, her eyes taking in the unspoken words. "Are you looking for him?"

"He called me a little while ago. I meant to call him back immediately, but I noticed Athena with a tray in hand and knew you were awake. I figured I would come see you and also ask if our son had called you so early as well," I stated, I pulled my phone out of my pocket and saw a message that he had sent. "Oh, what's this?"

I need your help. Please call me back.

"Well, that's unusual, he never asks for my help with anything," I say after reading the message aloud for Cassandra. She blinked a few times before taking a deep breath.

"Call him and put him on speaker. Sometimes you don't know how to help in certain situations," she chided me. She wasn't wrong though. I was no good when it came to helping the boys when they were children. I didn't see the need to coddle and cater to their needs or their crying. I didn't care too much about it, but their mothers didn't seem to mind it. Despite my push back about wanting to raise them as warriors and proud leaders. Their mothers all stated they needed to know the softness as well. They were right.

I pressed the call button, Valyn picked up on the first ring. "One second," I could hear him cover the phone to say something to whoever he was with. "I'll be right back in, I promise." There was another long pause and the sound of bells. "Okay, now I can talk."

"Before you speak, your mother is here with me and can hear every word," I cautioned him. Not that he would ever speak ill of his mother, but if it was a topic he didn't want to discuss within her presence I wanted him to know she was listening.

"That's fine. Honestly, mom's input might help too," he sounded worried and slightly rushed and frantic. I didn't like that.

"Okay, let us know what we can do," I announced, letting him know he had our full undivided attention.

"Luna, can control water," his words rushed out like a river rushing down a mountain. Cassandra and I just looked at each other. That wasn't Luna's powers. "Can you control water dad?" His question was a hard one to answer, but I didn't have a chance to say a word before his mother cut in.

"What happened right before she controlled water? Did she use water from a source or make it herself?" My normally calm mate was now frantically asking these questions and it had me worried.

"She created it out of nowhere. She was pissed and went full blown dark side. As hot as it was, her eyes turned into a galaxy, and she is completely calm about this as if nothing happened. She's currently just sitting there eating her pancakes as if she didn't just play with death moments ago," Valyn tried so hard to control the wobble in his voice. He wasn't afraid of her; he was scared for her safety. I know the feeling of worry.

"I can control water, but only if there is a source. If your mother creates a source, I can use the power whenever. Again, I cannot create it from nothing. Have you tried to call King Drake? He might have more insight to her powers." I asked him. Her father might know more than I can offer, but maybe Erina could offer some more insight.

"Niklaus already called him, but he didn't answer. He sent a text saying he was in a meeting. I know a few of us will be there in two hours. We will just talk to him there. Fennik and Bastian will be with Luna while we are gone," Valyn said urgently through the phone. Worry spread across Cassandra's face. I knew she was worried about Luna now.

She needs to come here. Cassandra's voice whispered softly in my head. None of my mates ever felt the need to speak into my mind since the children have all the grown up.

You think you might be able to help her? I whispered back to her. She nodded. Okay then.

"Valyn, bring her here. Or have your brothers bring her here. We might be able to help her understand a few things about where her powers might develop," I spoke firmly into the phone.

"I will attempt to tell Bastian that. He was hoping to have time with her alone since he's been gone for a bit. We still have to tell Valdis what's going on," I could hear him sighing into the phone.

"Tell your brother that I want to see my daughter in law. I know he won't say no," I said assertively. I know it irks my sons that we love to have Luna over. They would rather keep her all locked up in Mistveil Castle then let her come here all the time. I think they think I'll kidnap her and keep her here. They can be strange at times.

"I'll do my best dad," Valyn replied, snapping my attention back to the phone. It's been a long time since any of my boys really called me dad. I know they love me, but I also know that they harbor some loathing toward me as well. I don't blame them.

"If I need to ask Penelope to intervene I will. He will listen to his mother," Cassandra said sweetly. Valyn knew his mother would do just that and Penelope would call Bastian the moment she wakes up and would tell him to get his ass up here with Luna.

"I'll do the best I can. If he fights me on it, I will call you mom. I have to get inside. I love you," Valyn said to his mother. Her smile was so wide and beautiful.

"I love you too son," she replied with the sweetest smile on her face. You could hear the smile in her voice. I knew Valyn would hear it. We hung up the phone and looked at each other. "If she is truly that strong Harold, she is going to need all the help she can get to get through this. But, whose to say she won't develop the powers of all of our boys and Valdis."

I could see the fear in her eyes. Neither of us were afraid of her, no, this fear was bone deep terror that we could lose her if she is truly all powerful. It could kill her.

CHAPTER 6
DAMIAN

I didn't know how to handle that whole situation. Bastian and I were content with telling Rita to fuck off and go on with our day. Everything running through my head right now is telling me that she is going to spiral about this later. She may be calm and acting like nothing has happened, but she almost killed Rita in a rage. I don't want to leave Luna here, but a promise is a promise, and I don't think her brother would let me live it down if I backed out.

I watched her sit there grinning from ear to ear when the pancakes were gently placed in front of her. Her brown eyes had returned to her normal chocolate brown color with the light golden swirl in the irises. She was so beautiful, so loving and so kind. The girl we witnessed with Rita was anything but kind and loving. She was rage and jealousy, but for no reason. I mean, I guess I shouldn't have told her about Rita before, but Rita should've walked away when we told her too. She didn't deserve near death, but she definitely got the message now.

Valyn excused himself from the table a little while ago and I had a feeling I knew who he was calling. Niklaus stepped out first, also making a phone call but he texted me directly telling me he was calling Drake to see if he knew anything about her powers. If anything, maybe

Erina knew something. It was odd not using their titles anymore, but they wouldn't allow us to. I plan on asking Nox later if he knows anything.

"When do you guys leave to head to Mirith?" Luna chimed, dragging my attention back to her from my head. She was still shoving bites of pancakes between her luscious lips. My mind trailed to the most erotic of thoughts of those lips wrapped around my cock. Fuck.

"In a few hours. We don't have a lot we need to take with us so we can spend extra time with you before we go," Niklaus replied when he realized I wasn't replying any time soon. He was also planning on some mischievous shit. I could see his eyes trailing along her lips and lower. She adjusted her hair, pushing it behind her back to expose her collarbones to us. She enjoyed tormenting us.

"Sorry for that. Our dad called and I had to take it," Valyn said, pressing a kiss to her cheek and taking his seat. We all looked at him. So, I was right, he called our dad earlier to get his advice and opinion.

"Is everything alright?" Luna asked, worry striking across her beautiful face. She looked around at all of us trying to make sense of our reactions.

"Oh yeah. He and our mothers wanted to see you today if you have some time. I know you have plans with Harper and Bastian has plans for you as well, but if you could make time to go see them it would be great," Valyn looked apologetically at Bastian knowing the plans he had for Luna later. Bastian just nodded his head, he understood.

"My plans aren't until later this evening. I can take you up there before or after Harper comes over. Do you know when she will be arriving?" Bastian asked Luna. She stopped mid scoop and blinked at him. She was so cute when she was caught off guard. Especially when she's eating. It could be considered weird that I find that attractive, but it was the small cute little quirks that sent my heart fluttering.

"Harper should be over around lunch I think. I'll send her a text closer to ten so that I don't get assaulted for an early morning call," she giggled out. I am wondering if she means literal assault or verbal. I know none of the females liked to be woken up earlier than needed. I remember the sleepover they all had a month ago. I made the mistake of texting her at six in the morning and they all ripped my head off when they saw me four hours later for waking them up early.

"Whenever you hear from her, just let me know. I have to call Bertrum and make sure things are still good back in Taiga," Bastian said as he popped a piece of bacon in his mouth. I could see the defeat in his eyes. We promised him time alone with her. I really hope he was able to get that.

"Want to just go home and fuck all day instead?" She blurted out and the whole damn table lost it. Bastian choked on his bacon, Valyn and Niklaus spit out their drinks through their noses. Fennik's cheeks went bright red, and I half choked on air. She smiled widely at us, a giggle creeping out of her.

"I'm sorry Princess, but since when did you speak such dirty words out in public?" Bastian drawled out, still shocked by her forward approach. "I mean, I am down to fuck you all day long, but I think that would upset quite a few people."

"I don't think you want our moms coming to the house looking for you and them walking in on the two of you," Valyn said, regaining his composure just barely.

"You do realize that Penelope has already caught Bastian and I?" She said popping another piece of pancake in her mouth. Bastian's eyes went wide at what Luna had just confessed.

"What do you mean by already caught us?!" He exclaimed; he was now internally spiraling. I had a feeling one of our mothers would catch us. They always loved to just pop in at random, so it would've been on them. The fact that Penelope hasn't said anything to Bastian though says something.

"Yeah, it was about a week after the wedding when we were trying to figure out a schedule that worked best for us. You were taking me on the couch in the living room. Your mom walked in and abruptly turned around and walked away. I yelled your mom, I thought that gave you a clue," she said, finishing off her pancakes as if she didn't just make Bastian die a little on the inside. "I did call her later that day to apologize, but she just laughed. Saying something about that's what she gets for not calling first."

"I guess that's why they no longer just pop over on a whim," Bastian said rubbing his temples. Luna went back to eating as if nothing had happened and she didn't make a big confession.

Luna looked up from her plate. "I'll ask Harper to come by on a different day," she paused, her eyes swimming around the table, "I can't keep my control over myself with women around you guys. Do I feel bad for practically killing that bitch? No, absolutely not. Should I have handled it better? Yes. I don't want Harper saying something wrong and me snapping on her without a thought. Maybe we can just talk over the phone."

"If you believe that it is best to not have her come around right now, then let her know. We can always schedule a day when you are feeling better," Valyn gave Luna a quick kiss on the cheek. I could tell she was spiraling. The regret, regardless of what she was saying, is taking hold of her. She's too good and kind to be okay with what happened. I looked at Fennik, he was heading to see Sirus later today, maybe he could get us some answers.

I pulled my phone out from under the table and sent him a quick inquiry on what his thoughts were. He took a few minutes to reply just in case Luna was paying more attention to our actions than usual.

I'm going to ask Sirus if he knows anything about gods and goddesses and galaxy eyes. I mean we know she's only part goddess, but maybe there could be a transition or something. He finally replied, putting his phone down on the table to finish his eggs.

I put my phone away and looked around the table. Everyone was on edge but knew better than to show it. We couldn't speak into one another's minds without her hearing us, so that was out of the question. My phone buzzed on the table dragging me back to reality. I looked at it and saw Nox's name on the caller ID.

"I have to take this," I said, excusing myself from the table. No one really acknowledge me leaving except Luna. She was watching my every move like a cat stalking a mouse. It was kind of hot. I left the café and moved to the small seating area out front.

"Hey, what's up?" I said answering the phone trying to sound as normal as I could. Lord knows my brain was not feeling normal by any means.

"What happened with my sister," Nox blurted out, he sounded out of breath like he had either been running or flying.

"What do you mean?" I said, trying to sound calm and collected. I heard a huff from the other end of the phone. He knew better.

"Unless she is sitting right next to you with a knife to your balls, tell me what the fuck just happened to her. Something felt off and our mom is freaking the fuck out," Nox huffed at me. I felt bad talking behind her back, but if it would help the Queen feel safe I had to tell him.

"She went full blown possessive, galaxy eyed, and pulled water out of thin air to drown a former fling of mine and Bastians. Not saying she didn't have it coming, but the water thing was new," I spoke quietly so the two children playing across from the café couldn't hear me.

"Wait, what?! She doesn't have galaxy eyes dude," Nox was in the middle of talking when the phone was snatched away, and Queen Erina spoke into the phone. "Get her here now."

The phone went silent, and a pit of dread formed in my stomach. Erina was never demanding, usually the opposite. Her tone had the hair on my arms sticking up and had me worried. I entered the men's only group chat and sent a text saying we needed to leave and get Luna to Mirith at her mothers demands. I looked back into the café to see Bastian kiss Luna on the head before storming out to me.

"What the fuck! I was supposed to have time alone with her!" He growled as he got in my face. The two children stopped playing to watch us. I slowly pointed to the children so Bastian could control his temper and his language. He pulled back from me but only a step.

"Nox called, he knew something happened to Luna and so did Erina. Apparently it has her freaking out, as Nox put it. She then took the phone from Nox after I told him about her galaxy eyes and demanded that we bring her there now before hanging up on me," I said, waving my hand at the seat next to me. Valyn and Niklaus were the next two out of the café. Fennik and Luna were packing up the massive amount of food she had ordered. "Looks like we're all heading to Mirith. Valyn let dad know what's going on. If our mothers want her there, they might have to go to Mirith to talk to her."

Valyn nodded, not questioning at all what was going on, but Niklaus was like Bastian when it came to her. Hotheaded and thinking with the wrong head half the time. "Why the hell are we taking her to Mirith? I get it her mother is asking for her—"

I cut him off, "It is not a request Niklaus, she told me to bring her there now. There was no, when you get the chance or would you please. You think I want to fuck up her time with Bastian or take her to a land that is becoming infested with Borgs? No!"

Niklaus, to his credit, backed down. I wasn't used to him not pushing the limits. It's weird how we all have grown out of our childish, selfish ways once we met her. Fennik held the door open for Luna who was carrying three bags out of the café. Dear lord, why did she order so much food.

Bastian grabbed two of the bags out of her hand, "I got these for you princess." He teased her. Something she's been allowing us all to do more often.

"Thank you," she said smiling. "What's got us rushing out of here so quick?"

"Your mother wants us to come to Mirith, a bit of an urgent matter that she wouldn't discuss over the phone," I said, trying to convince her that it was something else besides her newly obtained powers.

"Is she alright?!" Luna panicked, but Valyn held her hand, kissing her on the top of her head.

"She's fine, she just wants us all there to talk. I already told my dad where we are going and to let our mothers know you will visit when we return unless they want to come see you there," Valyn said smoothly, I watched her ease a bit at his words and thought to myself how I wish I could calm her as easily as he does.

I'm as calming as the night sea. I heard Valyn speak into my mind and stared at him. I think he is the only one who has figured out how to shield everyone else from talking at once in his head. Lucky fucker.

I rolled my eyes as he turned Luna away and started leading the way home. We had to get to Mirith soon. I just hope that this isn't a mistake. I couldn't live with myself if something happens to Luna.

CHAPTER 7
LUNA

The walk home was quiet, well aside from the buzzing in my chest and head. My head has been hurting since my little episode, I thought food would help. Jokes on me, it didn't. I feel hungrier than I did when I started. The head pounding should have stopped once I ate, any other time I've gotten headaches in the past, food and sleep did the trick. Maybe I just need a nap.

"Is everything okay my love?" Valyn whispered to me as we continued walking hand in hand. I glanced up at him, taking in his turquoise eyes and silver locks, I missed him when we weren't together. He was the one who grounded me the most out of all of them.

"My head just hurts. I think I overdid it with my jealous rage earlier," I admitted not happy to show that I had a weakness when I overextended myself.

"Would you like to stop by the Mor before we get home? I'm sure Maggie would have something to help you," he offered. We were only about a block away from the Mor, but I didn't want Maggie to worry about me or have my mother waiting any longer for me to come visit. My mom can be a little testy if I don't show up when she demands it.

"No thank you, if anything I will just rest when we get to Mirith. I know you guys are still helping my brother and Virgil, but I have to see what the urgency is," I confessed, watching the children file out of their houses with their mothers and fathers, waving at us as we passed them. They were cute, some of the girls were dancing and placing flowers in their hair, some of the boys were rough housing the whole way to their classes.

"Do you want one of your own?" Valyn's question was out of the blue and slightly startled me, I almost tripped over a few stones. I looked at him, mouth agape. When I was a kid I planned on having kids, I wanted them early so I could spend as much time with them before I died. But now, fae don't live for eternity, but they do live for a very long time. Do I want a child right now?

"Maybe one day. But not now, I want to enjoy my life with you all before we bring a child into this world," I said. It was truthful, with war and uncertainties going on right now, I couldn't imagine bringing a child into this. Plus, right now I am way to selfish to share these men with anyone else.

"As long as it's not a complete no," Valyn whispered, kissing the top of my head like he normally does. It's like he's calming my head when he does it. A small grace that he gives me when he places little kisses to the top of my head.

"I promise if I ever change my mind and want one immediately, you will be the first to know," I giggled, a little girl came up to me and offered me a sunbloom, a beautiful type or orange and yellow rose. I took it with a smile and held it close. The girl bounced back to her mother who bowed at us as the little brunette girl smiled and waved.

My mind starts to wander about the future and what I would want from it. Before I knew it we were home. Bastian and Valyn took my bags of food to the kitchen, promising me that we would grab them before we leave for Mirith. I whined a little, but I finally conceded.

Bastian took me to my room and helped me change into jeans and a grey tank top. He was watching me intensely as I changed in front of him. We were promised alone time, and I swear to my grandparents if I don't get that alone time, someone is going to die.

"Are you ready to go?" Bastian asked as he crossed the room pulling me into his arms, his grey eyes a mix of molten silver and granite, bore into me. I could tell he wanted more than to just leave this room.

"Aren't you upset about us losing alone time together?" I whined, pressing my face into his neck.

"Of course I'm upset sweetness," he said, hugging me tighter. "We will have alone time. I promise you. Even if it's not exactly what I had planned. I'm sure I can find something for us in Mirith. There is that lake that you love. We can always go there."

"We can fuck by the lake!" I exclaimed. The lake had some areas around it where we definitely could get some privacy. Bastian pinched my ass. "Oh, come on! Don't act like I am not saying what you're thinking!"

"I'm not saying that, but you need to think about what your mom might want to talk about.," and just like that Bastian had me deflating like a balloon that was popped by a needle.

"Thanks for the reality slap," I droned. He grabbed my chin, forcing me to look up at him. He captured my lower lip between his teeth and growled at me. I forced a kiss between us, one with such passion that threatened to burn the room around us.

"We will get our time. We just need to do adult things first," Bastian entwined his fingers in my own and gently tugged me toward the door. I followed finally submitting to him. The paintings in the hallways had slowly changed over time. I asked Cassandra if I could have the next painting she painted, only if she was willing to part with it. She laughed and promised I could have the next one. That painting of the Selpie sea now hangs in the middle of the hallway a little ways down the hall from my room.

I miss painting myself, maybe I'll ask Cassandra if she's okay with me sitting with her one day and painting. My phone buzzed in my pocket and as I pulled it out, Bastian pulled me tight. I didn't understand what caused him to pull me in, but I would take it.

Please tell me you are on your way. Uncle Sirus just showed up and everyone is in a fucking spiral here. Nox's message didn't make sense. Why was my uncle in Mirith and why the hell was everyone losing their shit?

Yeah, I'll be there shortly. Is everything okay? I didn't like that way this conversation was heading.

No.

The air outside smelled of all the flowers that were blooming in the gardens surrounding the fountain as we crossed into Mirith. My father was standing there waiting for our arrival. Nox and my mother were nowhere to be seen, but Sirus was standing there with my father. A scowl of disapproval littered his face, I'm assuming at what he would call the most appalling scent ever. He wasn't one for the bright florals of spring.

"There's my dear daughter," my father called out to me arms stretched wide awaiting my embrace. I let go of Bastian's hand and moved to give my father a hug. I inhaled his cedar cologne, and I felt grounded for probably the first time today. Not that my mates didn't ground me. Their grounding was different from my mom and my dad. Hell, Nox's scent grounded me to in a weird way. I guess because they are my family. The family I never knew I had and the one I truly belonged to.

"Stop hogging her Drake," Sirus velvety voice cut through my inner peace for a brief moment until he pulled me from my father's arms and gave me a hug. "Holly is here too. She wanted to come visit."

"Oh! I haven't seen her in what feels like ages. How is life in Taiga treating you?" I asked Sirus as he let go of me and took a step back.

"It's cold and grey, but I wouldn't trade it for the world," he looked past me at Bastian and nodded his head. Bastian returned the gesture, some unspoken bond they now have thanks to Sirus staying in Taiga after the wedding.

"What's going on? I know something is off. Nox already said things aren't okay and that everyone is freaking out. Did something happen? Was there another attack?" I rattled off the question after question and slowly watched my father's and Sirus's faces change from smiles and to the look of worry and sorrow.

"Luna, something happened with you today and your mother and I felt it," Sirus said as calmly as he could. My heart began to race, how the hell did they know what happened with me earlier. I turned and looked at my mates, each one of them looking down at the ground, not wanting to look me in the eyes. "Before you get mad at any of them, we knew as it was happening. Your grandparents knew it was going to happen moments before it did. We just don't know exactly what happened."

My heart sunk and I stepped back, how could they feel what was going on with me? I did the best thing I could do in that moment, and I turned away from them all and walked over to the garden wall. I looked out over the city, the busy streets that are full of vendors and workers buzzing about below. The rebuilding is still going on in smaller areas of the city. The library and schools were the first of the main buildings aside from homes that were fixed.

Footsteps on the stone pathway behind me had me tensing. My heart didn't have the gentle pull that happens when my mates are near, but I knew nothing bad would be coming for me here. Not without my mates and family stepping in. A soft hand touched my arm, I looked back to see my mother standing there with a smile on her face, even though it's a forced one.

"It's good to see you sweetheart," my mother gave me a big hug, her body slightly shaking as she holds me. I hug her back but keep it quick. Clearly everyone is on edge with me now that something is happening to me. Great so I uncover new powers, lose my shit and now everyone around me is going to start treating me with kid gloves.

"You requested us to come visit?" I inquired. I now realize that I am the center of everyone losing their shit. I didn't think that everyone would know about my episode, but I guess I was completely wrong about that.

"Your grandparents are on their way. They have been wanting to come visit and after the energy wave that we all felt this morning, they decided that now would be the best opportunity," my mother said, moving her way back down the stone pathway. I guess I had to follow. My mates and my father all had somewhere else to be when we walked back to the fountain. "Your father took them to his office to discuss the borg infestation. Since all of your mates are here, maybe they all can help get this under control before it spreads closer."

"I'm still here. I think it's best that we keep between us," Sirus said, stepping around the fountain and looking at me. "I'm sorry, but we need to know what happened. Every detail."

"Let's get inside first before we discuss this matte. Everyone should be here shortly," my mother, the prim and proper queen that she is made her royal decree. So inside we went, following the endless halls to a large living room. The ruby red curtains were pulled back by thin golden chains to show off the Mitos mountains in the distance. The room was cozy, despite the small fire in the fireplace in the back of the room.

Each chair that lined the small oak table in the center of the room had a smooth, dark magenta fabric accenting the darker wood of the legs. I've been in this room so many times in the past few months, usually getting scolded because I'm not spending enough time here doing royal duties and such, but how the fuck am I supposed to be in two places at once.

I took my normal seat closest to the window, looking out it like I always do. I love my mother and wanted her back in my life, but she is becoming a massive headache.

The large oak doors that we passed through only moments ago opened up with a bit of a thud as the door hit the corner of the built-in bookcase. My grandfather, in all his glory, was a giant man. His auburn hair, cropped tight on the sides, was a little bit of a mess on top, but that was the only thing that was a mess about the god. His olive complexion was beautiful, only marred by three light bands around his right bicep. I wonder what those are from.

His golden eyes landed on me, a grin creeping across his face as he took me in. I hadn't physically seen him since my wedding, but it was the tall beauty behind him that had me still glued to my chair.

My grandmother, Vanalli, was a force in herself. Her silvery white hair was tied back, three hair bands wrapped evenly down her hair kept the strands in place. She was pale compared to Undas. She came up to his shoulders, her body more elegant than mine would ever be. But it was her golden eyes that held me with that unflinching stare.

My mother and uncle were both up and moving within seconds of their parents coming into the room. "Sorry about the bookcase Erina. I didn't realize how hard I opened the door," Undas said as he embraced my mother. She looked like a child in his arms, which must mean I look like a baby when he hugs me. He was practically the size of a mountain.

Vanalli and Sirus were more alike, neither of them were cold, just more blunt than my mother and grandfather. They gave each other a soft smile, but not the bear hugging embrace that my grandfather wrapped my uncle in.

My mother and her mother were going through something. The tension in the air around them was suffocating. I finally managed to get myself up to my feet and crossed the room. I curtsied to my grandparents as I was taught to do by my mother. My grandmother smiled, nodding at me in approval, but my grandfather scoffed, pulling me into a tight embrace that I couldn't help but hug him back just as tightly.

"Let us sit," Vanalli said, practically gliding to the seating area. Undas set me down gently like a toddler, walking with me back over to the chairs. I was surprised when they both took the seat next to me. My mother wasn't pleased at all since Sirus took the other seat.

"It's come to our attention sweet granddaughter of ours, that you have come into new powers," Undas began. Alright, so we are jumping right in head first, no pleasantries.

"Yeah, I created a water snake. Is this something I should be worried about?" I questioned, looking around the room to try and get a read on everyone. I didn't want anyone to worry about me.

"Was Valyn with you?" Vanalli inquired from the other side of Undas. She looked around him to get a better look at me. I nodded.

"Was he using his powers in this situation?" Undas cut in, earning himself an elbow in the side from my grandmother. "Ow! Seriously?"

"I wasn't done," she snapped. The term fighting like an old married couple fit these two like a glove.

"He wasn't using his powers. None of my mates were. I kind of just lost my shit and I just felt this rush of water and the next thing I know I have a beautiful snake wrapping its way around my arm ready to strike the bitch. Not my fault she didn't listen," I shrugged my shoulders. My mother looked at me in pure horror, like I just said I killed someone. "She lived mom, but you can't tell me you wouldn't have tried to kill someone for touching dad."

"What do you mean?" She snapped, "Who was touching who?" Now everyone was staring at me. Great. Time to rage out again.

"Some bitch named Rita. She was a play toy for Bastian and Damian before they mated to me and she wouldn't take no for an answer and kept touching them, calling me a whore, and insisting that they revoke the bond and be with her," I recalled, the rage building again in my chest just looking for a way to get out.

"Take a deep breath Luna," Undas said, placing his huge hand on my knee. "Close your eyes and focus on your breathing."

I scoffed but did what I was told. The air rushing from my lungs in the darkness felt like a hurricane in the forest, rough and hard. I felt a sharp pain in my palms and a wetness flood between my fingers, the smell of iron reaching my nose far to quickly than it normally would've. Great, I dug my nails into my hand and broke skin.

I took another deep breath, trying to calm the still roaring wave of rage. Squeezing my eyes tightly, a faint green light slowly burst into my vision, flowing it's way down to where my hands were placed on my lap. A small gasp came from around the room, but I was too busy focusing on the little greenish white light.

The feeling of wetness faded from my fingers and the sharp pain that was there slowly began to fade to nothing. The light slowly made its way back up my body and settled into my chest, like a cat nuzzling itself against its owner for cuddles.

A calming sense washed over me, replacing the rage and anger from before with a feeling of love and warmth. What an odd little ball of light you are. I thought to myself as I watched it dim itself in my chest, returning me to the darkness of my closed eyes.

"Luna, open your eyes," Sirus's voice trembled as his words rushed out of him like a flowing river. I opened my eyes and looked at everyone. Their eyes locked on me like I had done something wrong.

"Did I do something wrong?" I asked looking at them all.

"Which one of your mates is a healer?" Vanalli asked me. I had to think about that. I wasn't sure if anyone was a healer truthfully.

"Niklaus is from Oakenhall. He inherited the healing ability from Nora," my mother spoke up, well shit, learning something new about my mate without him even being here.

Undas looked at me and then to the rest of the room, "She's going through the changing."

CHAPTER 8
LUNA

What the fuck was the changing?! "Didn't I already do that?" I questioned them all. I thought when I went through my transition from human to full fae that there was nothing left for me but to live happily ever after with my mates for as long as eternity would grant me.

"Luna, you are fae, but not full blooded fae. Your bloodline on your mothers side as you know is that of the gods and goddesses. You are no ordinary being my child. Your change from human to fae was only one in the sense of a magic being lifted from you. It was not the actual changing," Vanalli spoke solemnly staring out the window at the mountains in the distance.

"Our kind usually doesn't leave Valhime. We visit the other realms from time to time, but your mother and uncle are the only two of our kind to live elsewhere. You are now the third. The only difference is that you are mated to the Prince of the solar realms. Valhime is a city inside the solar realm of Solaria," Vanalli continued, even with my mother scoffing.

"Valhime is the City of the Gods. We are our strongest there, it's considered sacred land. I think you should come visit Luna. It might help you to meet others like you. You might be able to gain some semblance of control during your changing while there as well," Undas offered. My mother's brows furrowed, she seemed annoyed at the offer.

"I'd like to visit, but I have some other things I have to handle first," I let out a low sigh.

"If you are talking about Marie, let it go," my mother snapped at me.

"Erina. You will not snap at my granddaughter in front of me. She raised herself for ten years, be it if it's what you wanted or not. She is fully capable of making decisions regarding her relationships," Vanalli scolded my mother right in front of me. I watch my mother turn to look at her mother with a tight-lipped smile.

"I will speak on the matter because unlike you, mother, I know what is going on and Luna should stay out of it," she quipped.

"It's causing issues with Fennik, so no, mother, I will not stay out of it. He is my mate and what's hurting him can be fixed if his mother can stop being so stuck up her own ass and get over herself," I spat out with the same venom she just used at my grandmother. Undas and Sirus sunk back into their seats, leaving us women to basically be at one another's throats with unseen weapons.

"Let's not push Luna anymore. If she can control water, and healing along with the fire and shadow powers she already possesses, who know what else she could possess," Sirus spoke up. I wonder if he meant other elemental powers or if he meant something far more worse.

Both my mother and grandmother seemed to have picked up on what he was implying, sitting back in their chairs. The tension in the air felt as thick as the fog rolling off the Selpie Sea early in the morning. I don't think this conversation is going anywhere near what my mother had planned.

I decided it was time to take my leave. I don't want to snap at my mother or watch the invisible blades my mother and her mother were throwing at each other. I stood up looking dead at my uncle, "We need to talk. Alone."

I headed out onto the patio right outside the room. Sirus followed at a respectable distance, closing the door behind him.

"I assume that you want to tear into me for the gang up in there," he started. I raised my hand, taking a deep breath letting the taste and smell of the garden flood me before speaking.

"You told me before that if I don't control myself, that my power will consume me and turn me into a star in the sky. The true death of a god or goddess and not to let the darkness consume me. Is this what you were talking about?" I let the word tumble from my lips into the space between us. He watched me for a moment, taking in my question before letting out a sigh.

"Luna, you aren't the first goddess to be mated to multiple mates. The last one was Talissa. She, like you, had multiple mates. Each one possessing an elemental power of great magnitude. She was capable of harnessing their powers without them needing to create a source, they ended up being the source. She loved them dearly and what happened was tragic. But war was raging between the deamons and the gods, they sacrificed their lives and power to Talissa so she could defeat the deamons and trap them in Hellis for what was supposed to be for eternity." As Sirus spoke I watched as sadness clouded his eyes.

"Did you know them?" I questioned as he took a pause.

"Yes. Each of them had become my friends during the war. When Talissa's mates made the decision to sacrifice themselves for her, she broke. She took their powers and their souls with it. But without her mates, she had nothing to ground her," tears streamed down his cheeks, I shouldn't have asked him. Before I could tell him to stop, he continued. "Talissa defeated the daemons, but she forced out not only her mates powers and life forces, but hers as well. She didn't want to live without them."

"You think that I could become like her?" I ask, knowing I shouldn't pry but I have to know.

"Possibly. We need to figure out what your source of power is. How was Valyn after you had your explosion of power?" Sirus asked.

I stopped to think for a moment. "He seemed fine. Shocked, obviously, but he didn't seem like he was in pain or anything like that. We can always ask him before he heads off with the guys to take care of the Borgs."

"Get him here. Get Niklaus here too. You just used his healing a few minutes ago. If he felt anything, he would have the better recollection," Sirus stated, turning from me and heading back inside.

I pulled my phone out and sent a quick message to them both. I need you two. That would be enough for them both to come without me needing to explain to much in text.

Is everything alright princess? Your dad has us a little busy. Valyn's voice rung out in my head, with the silence following I can tell no one else can hear him.

Not really. I just need you and Niklaus. Tell my father it's important and you'll be right back. I felt a small caress to my cheek. It was the oddest but most comforting feeling ever.

We are on our way. Niklaus shouted down the mental bond. I could hear Bastian mentally sigh. Looks like our time alone won't actually be happening.

CHAPTER 9
VALYN

Niklaus was several steps behind me as we wound our ways down the luxurious halls of Mirith's castle. Drake and Erina had a flair for the luxury items that Hildaria offered. Reds and golds everywhere you looked. Not that our parents were any different. It seemed like most of the royal families took pleasure in the luxurious things our world has to offer.

Luna's text should've been enough for me to tell Drake that I was needed elsewhere. He was understanding of Luna needing Niklaus and I. I don't know why I hesitated; I shouldn't have.

An icy hand knocked gently on my mental shield; Valdis was panicking but wouldn't let the others know. He was probably the most respectful of not barging into our minds unlike my brothers who all fail miserably at keeping one another out.

I mental open the door to my mind so he can speak just to me. Is she okay?

I honestly don't know. She's exhibiting more power and I'm worried. I spoke back to him. Mentally like this it was more of a feeling, a sense of what the others are thinking or doing. If I was meditating and Valdis was too, we could astral project into one another's heads.

It's something we've been working on to help Luna with our long departures.

Should I come to Mirith? Would I be welcomed? He rattled off the questions so fast that I can tell he's pacing around whatever room he's in.

You know Drake and Erina forgive you for the way everything went down. I had to focus on the hallway before me, so I didn't walk into a wall.

"I take it you're mentally chatting with someone?" Niklaus scoffed behind me as I almost walked into a corner. I stopped and cut him a glare.

"Valdis isn't here, but he can feel Luna's panic. She can't keep everyone out either. He's worried about her," I snap. Niklaus, to his credit, looks like he regrets opening his mouth. They've made up, but the two of them still walk on eggshells around one another when Luna isn't around.

I'm going to head to Mirith then. Kieran and Gabriel are here, and Vanessa is making threats. She's not giving me an option to not come. Valdis's words were soft, but I could tell he was on edge. He needed to see her, so he knew for himself she was safe.

I'll let her know you're coming. I'm about to enter the room she's in. Warning, Bastian is already on edge with his alone time with her being taken from him like it is. We're working with Drake now to make sure they get their time while we're stuck here. I felt him mentally leave my mind as if acknowledging what I said, but knowing there is nothing more to discuss. He will come here and be here for her.

I didn't even have to knock on the door before it flung open and Sirus was staring me dead in the eyes. Something tells me whatever is happening, he knows more than anyone else.

"Glad you could find your way here," Sirus moved out of our way, letting us into the room. Shock flickered across my face, I was not expecting to see Vanalli and Undas here. How the hell do you act in front of the God of fire and wealth and the Goddess of love and peace?

"Valyn my boy, how are you?" Undas's voice boomed through the room like we was speaking through a microphone, pulling me out of my stupor.

"I'm well, sir. How are you?" Stupid fucking question Valyn! He's a fucking god!

His laugh reminded me of my grandfathers, an old man whose seen his share of lifetime experiences, wise and kind. It was warming. "I am doing well. Aside from my granddaughter going through the changing. That's probably the main thing stressing me out at the moment."

"I'm sorry, sir. But did you just say the changing? I thought she already completed the changing?" Niklaus stated, coming out of his own stupor. We've only met these two once before at the wedding. They danced to two songs before politely excusing themselves for the evening. I think a collective breath was shared with everyone in attendance when they left. None of us were raised that the gods walked the realms still so no one knows how to act around them.

"No need for the sir boys, you're family. As for the changing. Luna went through a form of the changing. That was more the magical band-aid being ripped off of her fae body. She was always otherworld-ly; magic is what made her look human. Nothing more," Undas said from the couch. Vanalli smiled at us, waving to the two chairs next to her.

"Please have a seat. There is much we need to discuss," Vanalli ushered us to sit down. I took the seat by the window and saw Luna pacing outside.

"One of us should go out there and talk to her. Let her know we're here," I try to excuse myself, but Vanalli put up here hand.

"Mentally tell her you're here. We know all about the mental con-nection," she replied, smiling at her husband. He winked back at her, so I did as I was told. Luna opened the door a few seconds later, gently grazing her fingers along my arm, then Niklaus's as she took her seat between her uncle and grandfather.

"Valyn, I have a serious question for you, and you as well Niklaus," Undas started off. We both looked at one another, then to him and nodded. "When Luna manifested water earlier Valyn, did you feel weird? Like a part of you was being controlled or did you feel sick in any way?"

I wondered what Undas meant, by a part of me being controlled. "No, I was in shock for sure because I couldn't tell if I should've been worried or turned on." I shrugged. I heard the audible smack of Luna's hand to her forehead. She would regret that.

Vanalli looked over at Niklaus, "Did you happen to feel sick or weird moments ago?" Niklaus just shook his head.

"No, should I have?" he asked. Vanalli looked at Undas and then to Luna. What the hell were we missing.

"How advanced are your healing powers?" Undas asked Niklaus, his brows furrowed a bit. This was a topic he didn't like to talk about.

"Not advanced at all. I can heal minor cuts and wounds, but I can't attach limbs back or do emergency field healing," Niklaus said. To my surprise there was no bitterness to him when he spoke. Not like all the times in the past.

"I wonder," Sirus rubbed his chin and with lightening quick speed, he gouged a slice into Luna's right arm. "Niklaus, heal her." Luna yelped and glared at Sirus, but his command was to Niklaus.

"That's too deep a wound! I can't heal a wound like that! What the fuck?!" Niklaus shouted. He shot over to Luna, trying to heal the wound, but it wasn't working. Nora always told him to practice, yet he never did.

"Stop. Luna, heal it," Sirus grabbed Niklaus and shoved him away from her. Niklaus growled and went to go for Sirus but stopped as a greenish white light enveloped Luna's arm, mending the deep wound. When the light vanished, her arm showed no evidence of the wound to begin with.

"You can heal her, you're just stopping yourself," Sirus said. I watched Erina look at her daughter and then to her brother. Rage building on her face, but I was too busy looking between Luna and

Niklaus. Luna's face looked so calm, but Niklaus had a look in his eyes that I couldn't place.

"Talk to your mother, she can help you harness the power of more than just controlling the earth," Vanalli spoke softly to Niklaus. He broke his stare on Luna to look at Vanalli. "You are strong. You just focused on the physical magic you have, not the emotional magic you wield."

Niklaus gazed back at Luna, something akin to pride and determination flooded his features. Luna looked at me, unsure of what to expect.

"Well, I guess we have to see what else you can control," I teased her. She blushed the cutest rose color. Undas and Vanalli, watched on, waiting to continue the conversation without interrupting the moment.

"I still suggest you come to Valhime soon. Do what you have to do for Fennik but do so quickly. There hasn't been a changing of God proportions done outside of Valhime. I can't say for certain that things won't get worse the longer you wait," Undas announced. The room went silent because we knew what that meant.

If Luna went to Valhime, the only one of her husbands who could go with her was Damian. That wouldn't sit well with any of us I don't think. Maybe we could fight the gods and be let in with her. Maybe we would be judged by our past and found unworthy of being with her during this time.

"Then I guess it's time I head to Floria and get the stuck-up bitch to grow up," Luna announced just as a crash came through the door.

CHAPTER 10
LUNA

The door burst open as a large orange wolf stalked through the doorway coming right for me. I knew it was Fennik, and I could tell he was angry. But was he angry with me or with someone else.

Fennik, please change back. I pleaded with him. *Did I do something wrong?*

No, you didn't do something wrong. A dragon is flying over Mirith. I wanted to check on you and make sure you were safe. We all felt a strong pain sensation then nothing. I needed to see you with my own two eyes. Fennik moved around Sirus who moved to give him a wide berth. He sniffed at my arm and looked up at me.

Go. Niklaus and Valyn will be right behind you. Just be safe. I placed a kiss to the top of his head and watched as Valyn and Niklaus excused themselves from the room, kissing me on the cheek before they left.

"Is everything alright? They normally don't cause such a ruckus when they're here." My mother said, looking at her beautiful door that now has claw marks down the front of it.

"There is a dragon circling above the city. The guys felt Sirus's wonderful pain plan, but then they didn't feel anything once I healed myself. Fennik has been on edge since his mother pulled her shit. He

84

doesn't stay in his human form long now a days because he doesn't want to lash out his anger on anyone. I'll have him fix the door," I said as I stood up and headed for the patio again.

Undas and Sirus followed me outside as we looked for any evidence of an incoming attack. "This sort of thing used to happen all the time back in the day. Sirus, do you remember Ishta?" Undas spoke to his son in fondly, but Sirus just ignored him. I could see him fidgeting at the door entrance.

"Go get her," I grabbed his hands to get his attention. "Bring her back here or to one of the safe rooms. Hell, take my mom and your mom with you. Get them somewhere safe."

Sirus looked at Undas who nodded, then took off through the doors earning a stern shouting from my mother for running in her house.

"You knew what he needed when I didn't. Some father I am," Undas said as he stepped out into the garden. The sun danced across his auburn hair, lighting it up like fire itself. I watched him look up at the sky in search of the dragon that Fennik was talking about.

"I'm sure you are a great father. I just know that panic when danger is around and your mate isn't near you," I said, Undas' head snap back at me. A look of shock rippled across his face. "Oh shit. You didn't know."

"He never said anything about having a mate," Undas said, gazing at the castle like he could see through walls to find his son.

"I only have a feeling. I don't think they've made any official claim or anything like that. I'm sorry, I shouldn't have said anything," I step into the garden and stood next to him. The sun warmed my skin, something I didn't know I needed until now. "I don't want to become a star."

Undas put his arm around my shoulder and pulled me into a hug. "Talissa and her mates were different. Luna, Valyn and Niklaus didn't seem to notice anything. They didn't feel any different. That alone makes you and Talissa very different. Sirus just worries about you. He doesn't want to lose you like he lost her."

"Were they close? I know he said they were friends," I looked up at the sky, not a dragon in sight.

"She was his older sister, your aunt. Vanalli seems to think that Talissa is only sleeping, and that her and her mates will come home to us one day. I want to believe that she is right. I miss my daughter, but it's also why your mother and uncle are so tough on you. They watched their older sister sacrifice herself to save everyone," he paused and looked down at me. "You and your aunt are much more alike than you will ever know. I hope your grandmother is right. I think Talissa will love you."

I don't know enough about my own family. My mother never said she had a sister, Sirus never said anything either. Why would he make me think they were just friends. "I want to go to Valhime. Maybe I can find a way to know for sure if she is only sleeping or if she is truly gone."

"That would be nice," Undas hugged me a little tighter. I couldn't help but wrap my arms around his waist and hug him back.

A dark shadow glided across the garden drawing our attention skyward. A large golden dragon soared high above us, circling the castle. "Ready to fight alongside your grandfather?" Undas asked me as fire circled his arms forming a type of whip in his right hand. He was glowing with a golden swirl of fire.

"You bet," I replied, following suit with shadows and fire wrapping around myself. My grandfather let out a low whistle.

"You are slightly terrifying. I like it," he said as we tracked the path of the dragon. Not knowing if this is friend or foe, I don't want to attack for no reason. I don't see Nox anywhere, but I know he would be in flight if something were to happen.

The golden dragon swooped down toward the front of the castle, so we took off. Running through the garden, trying not to light the place on fire in our wake. Undas was surprisingly quick for someone his age. Hell, I don't even know how old he is. He cut the corner of the house so fast that I couldn't follow. I would be on my ass if I took it as fast as he did.

Three large wolves stalked the front gate, I recognize each one of them. Bastian was flanked by Fennik and Damien, Virgil sword in hand between the wolves. Valyn and Niklaus were in this wolf forms as well guarding the front doors. The silver wolf tracked me from the moment my feet touched the grass on the front lawn. Valyn's turquoise eyes never leaving me.

"Where the hell is my brother?!" I yelled out to Virgil. His hair was longer now, he was also way more muscular than I recall. I guess working with a dragon will do wonders for your physique.

"He's coming. Drake's trying to get through to Alistar but the communication to Infernia has been cut off," Virgil said as I got closer to him.

Valdis, are you safe!? I pushed my thought through to him, focusing on his mind the best I could.

Shit kind of hit the fan here. Are you safe? Valdis replied but I think everyone heard him.

Safe as in she is running into danger with her grandfather. Yes, she's completely safe. Niklaus retorted. I glared over at the beige wolf and bared my teeth.

I am safe. Undas and I are just here to help out if needed. I replied trying to smooth over the panic I felt rising in Valdis's head.

"We've got company!" Undas yelled as the dragon charged for the ground where we stood. I had to break off the conversation with Valdis to focus. I hope he's okay.

"Luna, get inside, we got this," Virgil ordered, but I just snarled at him.

"You don't get to order me around!" I snapped at him. "I am legit covered in fucking fire and all you have is a sword. If anything, you go inside. I have this covered."

Virgil still hasn't fully come to terms with the fact that I indeed didn't need him to protect me anymore. He may be over the fact that we aren't meant to be, but it still doesn't stop him from being overbearing sometimes.

"Stop fighting you two!" Nox growled as he tore out of the front door running for us. "Luna! Ready to go?" I nodded my head and took off running. I could hear the complaints rising from behind me.

Nox started ripping clothes off as his flesh began to transform into shining black scales. As the sunlight danced across the scales a hint of purple could be seen glistening. He stayed low to the ground so I could jump onto his back.

"I swear to our grandparents if you drop me, I will kill you!" I yell, hoping he can hear me over the wind.

Mental talk sis. You know in situations like this it's easier to communicate. He pushed the words into my head. Great another male invading my brain.

Yeah, yeah. What's going on? Valdis said shit hit the fan in Infernia. Did dad get ahold of Alistar? I grab hold of Nox's necklace; one he now wears for me to use a reigns when we ride together.

No, all communications have been shut down. Can you reach Valdis now? Nox was heading straight for the golden dragon which until now was speeding headlong for us.

Yeah, I can try but shouldn't I be more focused on charring this bitch? I asked.

I got them, you just get in touch with Valdis. He may know whose doing this. Just if you can, char the rider while you chat. Nox's laugh echoed in my head.

I focused on Valdis's energy. Valyn was teaching me how to isolate the person I wanted to speak with, but I always failed miserably at it. I could just scream into the void that is our bond, but then everyone would hear it.

I felt a slight tapping at the back of my mind, a soft smoky feeling lingering there. That's him. Valdis, is that you?

Are you hurt? Valdis's voice sung loud and clear in my head as if he was standing next to me,

I'm okay, I'm with Nox and we are heading into a dragon fight, but he wanted me to get ahold of you. Do you have any idea what's going on? I asked, wishing I could see his face.

There's a rumor going around that the King of Limbris sent an army force to Floria, and this is the warning that we are all on notice. Valdis paused as my heart began to race.

We have to get to Marie then. I know she's a bitch and I really don't want her around but if there is a daemon army heading her way we can't just leave her there! I began to panic. Fennik wouldn't want anything happening to his mom, no matter what she did.

Deep breath. We don't know if there is an army going there or not. We got things under control here. Gabrial and Kieran are on their way to Mirith. Me and Vanessa will be following shortly. I love you. His velvety voice caressed me, soothing the oncoming anxiety attack I was having.

I love you too. Just get your ass here. I have to go char a dragon rider. See you soon! I broke off the connection and focused on the glint of a rider's helmet.

Looks like break time is over. Can you get me next to them or should I just scorch them both? I say to Nox through our mental bond. Our bond is so different from the bond that I share with my mates. Nox's voice is foreign to my brain, we've only done this a handful of times and only when he's in his dragon form.

I'll do the best I can, but we're about to have more company. He said back to me. I look to the skies around us, but I don't see anything. My eyes caught sight of a golden eagle soaring through the sky next to us.

Nox took off faster, a loud boom roaring behind us. Whatever magic kept me on his back is strong. I'm grateful for it. I focus on the dragon and rider in front of us. The dragon was large, but not as large as my brother. The golden scales seemed dull, muted almost the closer we got.

The glint of the sun off the rider's helmet told me we were close enough. I took a deep breath extending the small snake of fire from my palm, it launched off so quick bursting into a larger serpent the closer it got to the dragon. The large fire snake wrapped itself tightly around the dragon, burning it's scales as it gripped it. A roar tearing from it's throat was the only indication it gave of pain.

My next focus was the rider, the helm he wore was just like the one Luther had worn during the last attack on Mirith. An icy cold rage worked its way up my arms at the thought of him. I forced the rage out of my body expecting flames or shadows to engulf the rider, but instead what looked like birds made of ice attacked the rider. Each bird that hit, exploded into ice, trapping the rider in place.

My fire serpent strangled the dragons' wings, forcing them from the sky. The sudden whooshing of wind past us as the dragon started to fall directly to the ground had my head snapping.

"We have to catch them!" I yelled. I don't know why I didn't just tell him mentally, but my brain was focusing on those on the ground. The courtyard is going to be ruined again.

Hold on tight, he mentally yelled at me. He arched his body to loop around so we were facing the ground now. The large golden eagle was still with us, flying just as fast as we were.

The golden dragon halted midair, hovering over the courtyard by some unseen force. My fire serpent was still squeezing the dragon as tight as it could. I wasn't letting it go, but I was not the one keeping it from crashing down to the ground.

Nox slowed out descent, aiming us for the clearing right outside of the garden. I jumped off his back landing on the ground before us. I kept my back to him so he could change back into his normal form and conjure up some clothes. I didn't need to see my brother's dick.

"What the hell?" Nox asked as he caught up to me. We watched as the dragon was snarling in the face of Undas. Our grandfather just stood there laughing. "Is he trying to piss off the dragon?"

"I think he's the one holding the dragon," I exhaled a breath that I didn't know I was holding. Undas looked over at Nox and I as we crossed the yard back to where they were standing.

"Good job you two. I think I can take it from here," Undas said with a wicked grin.

"That's great and all, but we need them to be able to talk. Valdis said that there is a rumor of an army from Hellis is Floria. The attack on Infernia and apparently this guy," I wave at the snarling dragon, "are our warnings."

"Did Valdis tell you where in Hellis the army is from?" My father asked as he closed in on us. I didn't even realize he was outside.

"Limbris," I announced. My father paled and looked at Undas. "Do we have to worry?"

"King Reginald isn't a foe that I ever thought I would see again. He was supposed to be locked up, but vermin always have a way of showing up again," Undas scoffed, turning his attention back to the dragon and frozen rider. "Ice?"

"Yeah, I'm assuming that's a power from Bastian," I shrugged. Footsteps came up behind me, my heart tugging at all corners of my being to move to them as they approached.

"Well, it looks like you are mastering our powers faster than we did," Bastian said cooly as he put his arm around my waist. He placed a kiss to my temple, leaving the cold feeling of his lips in their wake.

"I really need to calm the fuck down, I can't keep using your powers like this," I exclaim.

"Can one of you unfreeze his head? And maybe freeze this damn dragon's head instead," Undas said half-jokingly.

I went to remove the ice, but I didn't feel the same way I did when I created the beautiful little ice birds. I was slightly calmer. Instead, Bastian snapped his fingers and the ice from the riders' head shattered before gathering around the dragon's head, freezing it's snarling gaze.

"Don't worry Princess, I got you," he teased, twisting my ponytail between his fingers. The rider took a moment to gather that its head was no longer a giant block of ice, but they couldn't move.

"Release me!" the being hissed. Piercing red eyes glared at us from under the onyx helm it wore. In the sky the helm looked like it shined more than it does right now. "You would do best to do as I say."

"Get fucked," A deep burly voice called out. Shadows erupted across the lawn as Gabrial and Kieran stepped out of a shadow portal and into the courtyard.

"Bite your tongue, bastard prince," the rider snarled at Gabrial who just laughed.

"Ah yes, a bastard prince. Technically though my parents married after my birth so that would remove the bastard part of my title," Gabrial mockingly bowed at the creature. "Unless you are referring to me as a bastard for slaughtering your brethren."

"I will kill you! I will rip your intestines out and feed them to my dragon," the creature snarled, displaying long grotesque yellowish fangs.

"It looks to me like the royalty of Hildaria and Mistveil have you under control," Kieran quipped as he walked over to stand next to me.

"Hello boys, nice to see you again," Undas chimed, blatantly ignoring the snarling rider.

"Hello Undas," Kieran chirped as he stepped up next to me. "Don't worry, Vanessa and Valdis will be here soon."

"Can we just kill the damn thing and be done with it?" Gabrial said, unsheathing the sword at his side. Undas cocked his head to the side as Gabrial dragged the tip of the blade across the golden scales of the dragon. "If we leave it frozen for much longer, it will die."

"Get your filthy blade off my dragon!" The rider snarled, trying to get free of its own icy prison.

Gabrial smirked and turned his attention to the rider, "I can easily jump up there and slice you're head off instead."

"Don't be so brash. We have to keep him for questioning," Valyn sauntered over to me, his exquisite muscles rippling across his chest as he walked. My eyes traced the light tuft of hair from his navel to deep below his waist line. I sighed and looked away. I couldn't be thinking about jumping on his dick right now.

"That will be unnecessary," my heart skipped a beat as the sultry sound of Valdis's voice rang through the courtyard. I watched his cross the yard and step up to his brothers. I looked behind him, my inquiry answered with a nod.

She's inside with your mother and grandmother. She wanted to talk with them first. Valdis sent the image of his sister hugging my mother through our bond, it warmed my heart to know the amount of love they all had for one another.

"You know nothing Prince of Darkness!" The creature snarled and hissed at Valdis as he got closer. I bet if he could run away from him, he would.

"You are a warning are you not?" Valdis questioned, his gaze a burning ember. The creature hissed at him, spewing spit and something black at him. Gabriel went to move his blade to the creature, but Valdis held up his hand. "No need brother."

Valdis ran his hand up the exposed side of the dragon, maneuvering around my flames. I watched panic set into the creatures face, a snarl ripping from it's throat. "STOP!" It yelled at him as if begging. Valdis just looked up and smiled.

"You're dragon is such a beautiful golden color. It's a shame that he isn't just any dragon now is he?" Valdis again questioned, leaving all of us puzzled. His own brothers looked confused at his words. "Do you know that he is trying to declare war on a member of the royal family of Infernia?"

"She is no royal family of Hellis. Not by blood. She will not be seen as such!" he snarled, eyes darting between Valdis and myself.

"His mother," Valid said, shoving his hand hard into the scales of the dragon, "is not of royal blood either. But you and your kin would see her as royalty. My wife is no different."

"Valdis who is the dragon?" Gabrial asked, looking closer at the dragons face as if it would answer his own question.

Valdis's smirk grew into a fiendish grin. One I haven't seen on him in a while. "Gabrial, you don't recognize Prince Emory?" Shock rippled across Gabrial's face. Kieran even took a step back as if he was in the presence of a gorgon.

"Prince Emory is a fucking dragon?!" Gabrial shouted. His eyes now trained to the dragon more. The blade in his hand at the ready to strike.

"Luna, my love, can you please unfreeze the princes head? I want him to hear what I'm about to say," Valdis asked and this task I could easily oblige. Ice turned to water at the snap of my fingers. Bastian let out a low whistle as he watched me work.

"Remind me to help you with that," he said, putting his arm around my shoulders, pulling me into his side. The smell of snow and pine wafted around me, settling a nervous feeling in my stomach that I didn't know was starting.

"Prince Emory, you and your family are in violation of the Hellis peace treaty. Your family signed the treaty under no duress, as you know, the penalty for breaking the treaty is death. Seeing as you are here as a warning that war is on the horizon, your life will make due as payment for your acts of treason. My wife, Luna, is a member of the Royal family and ties the realms together. With her as a princess, soon to be Queen of Hellis, you and yours have declared war on a member of the Infernia Royal family. Fare thee well."

Before the Prince change and speak a word, a loud sloppy plopping sound rung out. Inky blackness pooled under the giant golden dragon. The creature atop the prince screamed out but was no match to Kieran's blade. Both had been dispatched without so much as a fight.

The courtyard was silent, everyone just looking out the body that was once a dragon. I read that a dragon once killed would turn back into their fae self or in this case, daemon self. Prince Emory was a beautiful man, pale skin the color of starlight, voided gold eyes stared up at the sky. I could imagine he wasn't as beautiful of a man in life.

"Well, that was fun, but let's move this little party indoors," Undas said, breaking the tension surrounding us. We always knew war was still around us. We knew that the attack on Mirith was only the beginning. Now they're attacking Floria, and we can't let that happen.

CHAPTER II
VALDIS

Luna followed her grandfather into the house as Gabriel and Valyn helped remove the corpse of the Prince of Limbris from the garden. The creature that was riding with the prince was his bodyguard, a weak little thing he was. Then again, Emory was never on for the battlefield. He would talk a lot of shit, but never got his hands dirty. For a dragon shifter, it's not normal for them not to be in the thick of things.

"Are you okay?" Fennik asked me as we followed Luna and Undas. He has been oddly quiet this whole time.

"I'm not the one whose home is being attacked. How are you holding up?" I return the question, hoping he gives me a real answer.

"I don't know. My mother is in Floria, and I should be running there to make sure she is safe," he stopped talking looking over at Luna.

"But?" I continue, trying to get him to finish his thoughts.

"Luna cares more about my mother's safety right now than I do and I should feel guilty, but I don't," Fennik exhaled. I feel bad for him. I couldn't imagine what I would've done if my mother acted the way his mother did.

"You don't have to feel guilty. Luna is feeling the empathy you can't right not. She isn't as close to your mother as you are. According to my mother, Marie wasn't very kind to or when it came to Luna. My mother had to bite her tongue quite a bit. She wasn't very happy with how your mother spoke about our wife," I recounted my mothers conversation with me about the last time she saw Marie. It didn't go very well.

"I walked in that day and yelled at her. I remember it all too well," Fennik said. I could feel his body radiating from the memories of that meeting.

"You know she is going to want to head to Floria and check on your mom. No discredit to your mother, but Luna has a bigger heart and is kinder. I don't know how she does it, but we could learn a thing from her," I nudged Fennik in the arm. It's odd how we've all fallen into an easy pace around one another. I'll take it though. Not wanting to fight with everyone has been a joy.

Watching Luna was amazing all on it's own. Her hips swaying from side to side as she walks, her long blue hair swishing as she moves, and the way her laugh carries to my ears is like a beautiful symphony. I wonder if she ever notices these little things that I find so adorable.

She peers back over her shoulder and smiles at us. I watch Fennik straighten up as he notices her taking us in. Instinctively I do the same thing. I didn't think I was slouching but be damn if I wasn't.

"You two don't have to stay back there you know," she said over her should to us. We quicken our steps to match her and Undas'. That man is a giant and watching him slow his gait for his granddaughter is endearing. He looks at her with all the love and adoration you would expect from a loving grandfather.

"If Limbris is plotting an attack on the realms, it makes sense that the autumn realm was the first target," Undas continued his conversation with Luna as if we didn't step up beside them.

"The first attack from Hellis forces was on Mirith last fall. I don't know exactly which city it came from, but then we had the smaller attacks in Taiga during the winter. Reapers were killing the guards and patrols around the Hellis gate," Luna cut Undas off and listed off the attacks over the last several months.

"The Reapers are a division of Altaria, they're basically chaotic neutral. If it causes chaos in either realm, they're happy. They don't normally go out of their way to do it though. I wonder if those Reapers we ran into defected to another of the darker realms?" I thought out loud. I don't know why I didn't think of it sooner. Altaria isn't evil in the sense as the last of the cities, but they could be easily swayed.

"That is some food for thought. Maybe we can bring that up to your dad and see what he thinks," Luna was always running things through her head. Sometimes I wanted to pop in just to see what's going on in there and other times, I was afraid to know what I would find.

We stop at a large oak door with a beautiful scene of animal etched into the wood working. The handles, a bone antler, were long and beautifully set in a black iron. The screeching voices on the other side of the doors, however, were not as beautiful as the door. Someone was pissed.

CHAPTER 12
LUNA

Looking up at Undas, I could see the exhaustion on his face. He glanced down at me, giving me a weary smile. We knew the loud screaming voices from inside the room far too well. I rolled my eyes, taking a deep breath before opening the door.

"Can't leave you two alone for more than five minutes before you're at each other's throat can we?" I said, walking into the room and plopping down on the couch next to my grandmother. My mother rolled her eyes, huffing at me.

Fennik and Valdis followed me into the room and stood behind me, both noting the tension in the room. I glanced over at Holly who was sitting curled deep into Sirus's chest. The two of them are the opposite yet the same. Neither like full confrontation nor fighting around them.

Holly looks up from Sirus chest to offer me a small smile. I return it with the same kindness. Holly is a good person, I'm glad she is with my uncle.

"What's the fighting about my love?" My grandfather asked my grandmother as he took up his seat on the other side of her. Vanalli is a strong-willed woman with a fiery temper to match it. No wonder she matched perfectly with Undas. She was the peace for his ever-raging waves, he the calming sea to her erupting volcano, despite being the god of fire himself.

"Your daughter thinks that if we just ignore the problems, they will go away," she snaps. My mother huffed from where she sat, rolling her eyes so far back all we can see if the whites of her eyes at times.

"She is only suggesting that we don't go into this blindly. We don't want another great battle to destroy the lands again," Sirus explained, but my grandmother was having none of it.

"Daemons won't wait to make another attack," Vanalli snaps, then pauses her ranting to look at Valdis. "I'm sorry my boy, but you know I am right."

"You're not wrong. Most of Hellis is happy living in the peace they do. They don't care much for the upper world of Cerulia. But those in the capitals of the lower parts of Hellis aren't as happy with not having dominion over all the realms. They don't like being shackled to Hellis. Each of the lower capitals have towns and smaller cities that would happily wage war again just to be above again," Valdis offered to them, more of an understanding with my grandmother. She meant well, and I can understand her rage. She lost one child to the daemons.

"How many cities would you say could want a war between the realms?" Sirus asked him, cradling Holly closer to him, running his fingers through her blond curls.

"At least three. Limbris for sure, Iterais, and possibly Altaria. Iterais has aligned with Limbris before, they're cities and town boarder each other and Limbris is known for attacking those close if they do not submit and offer to help. Altaria will align with anyone and everyone just for the pure simple enjoyment of chaos. They're neither good nor evil.," Valdis let out a sigh, pinching the bridge of his nose as if he was trying to stave off a headache. "Cerulia will have the alliance of Infernia. Eternius is neutral but will most likely align with Cerulia as well. Minaris and Pretarius will align with Cerulia. They align with my father no matter where he stands."

I count out the amount. Seven cities of Hellis. Eight Realms, and the two main continents. We should have the numbers, but I know we don't. Then it dawns on me, what the Ritmer said back during the first attack on Mirith.

"Limbris is infecting those in the human cities on the continents to possess," I breath out. Everyone just stops and looks at me.

"What did you just say?" Undas asked me, looking all the world worried.

"When Niklaus and I fought the Ritmer during the first attack on Mirith, he was possessing a soldier of the kings army. He said the greying is a deamon infection that allows daemons and other creatures of Hellis to possess those who are effected. I just don't know how they were able to infect Luther," I chewed on my bottom lip, thinking about all the ways they could've gotten him.

"He allowed them too," Niklaus said as he sauntered into the room, making a beeline straight for me. He kissed me on the cheek and took a seat on the arm of the couch. "They used Vikrum to poison his mind.

The seed of doubt is enough that when the offer is made from a Ritmer that they can willingly possess the victim. Vikrum made Luther believe the lies about our father and had him believing you had abandoned him. It was enough to break him."

A sob wrecked out of my mothers throat. Luther and I may be half siblings, but he is my mothers child. I have to keep reminding myself, that while I had him. She didn't have him long enough.

"We will get him back mom. I won't promise it, but I will try my hardest. He's a stubborn ass, but if there is anything left of him inside, I can pull him back," I offered. No promise. I will never make a promise that I can't keep.

Vanalli and Undas look between each other then to their daughter. Vanalli stands, making her way to where my mother was, wrapping her arms tight around her. "I'm sorry. You're going through pain. I should be more understanding."

Well, that wasn't something I was thinking I would see. However, I am glad that they are making up. I look at Undas, catching the silver lining his eyes. They've all been through so much.

"I am going to head to Floria," I announce aloud, I could feel Fennik tense behind me, but I needed to make sure his mom was safe. Even if I wanted to spike the bitch to a wall for harming Fennik.

"Why?" Fennik asked dryly. His fists clenching at his sides. I could feel the anger shoot down our bond. I looked up at him and smiled.

"Your mother. Your father would be shattered if something happened to her. I also want to prove to her that even though she's a bitch that I want to roast, I'm better than that," I smile, letting my hand drift behind the couch to his fist. "You don't have to go with me if you don't want. But we need to know if there is a daemon army in Floria. Could you imagine your people trying to defend themselves against the might of dragons and daemons?"

He took a deep breath and let it go. The anger in our bond simmering down to a dull annoyance. "You're right. It would break our father if something happened to her and despite the fact that I don't want to see her, you are a better person than even I," he grabbed my hand, pressing it to his lips.

"I'll go with you guys," Niklaus offered. Fennik looked from me to his brother. A faint smile graced his lips, the little digs that they used to take at one another have faded to playful jokes and banter.

"I'm coming too. If there is an army in Floria, then the next logical place for them to try to attack in the Summer Realm. Not that the Autumn Realm needs the prince of summer for protection," Valyn said as he entered the room, winking at us. Bastian and Damian followed closely behind along with the others. Our little room was filling up with big bodies, suffocating the space with different scents and testosterone. I looked at Bastian who looked utterly defeated. We were supposed to have time alone together.

The day was drawing closer to an end, my plan to cook dinner for my mates wasn't going to happen tonight. Maybe once we get back from Floria. "We will leave tomorrow. I have a promise that I have to keep for today. I'll have my stuff ready to go first thing in the morning," I announce, slipping from Fennik's light grip. He looked over at Bastian then nodded. If I had to leave Bastian right as he came home, I wanted to spend as much time with him as I could before leaving.

Bastian stepped over to me and pulled me up into his arms. "Please excuse us, we have some plans we must see to before she goes."

With that, we left the room, probably a little less graceful than we wanted and probably before we should. But I'm tired of things getting in the way of my life. I let everyone dictate my life and what was expected of me when I thought I was human.

I am not human. I am a fucking goddess; I will not wait for my life to be over before I can even live it.

CHAPTER 13
BASTIAN

Luna was pulling me through the castle and out the back door heading off through the back courtyard. Nox was still outside talking with Virgil when we burst past them. Nox just shook his head, but Virgil looked pissed off.

I'm still not a hundred percent a fan of his. I still think he wants Luna. He gets too protective and possessive of her, even now that she is married. I know humans don't mate, but damn I wish he would find a mate and leave my wife alone.

I turn my attention back to the blue-haired beauty before me. An electricity sparks between us where our hands touch, a small shock of excitement and thrill that begs to be let out.

"Where are you taking me princess?" I teasingly ask her. I know she said there was a lake close by, but there are actually two that I saw on the map of Hildaria that boarder Mirith. Both are rather large, like they used to be one, but the gods thought it better to split them in half by placing a mountain between them.

"Lake Gilder. The larger of the two lakes. Luther used to come up with a story that the lakes were once real-life lovers who were turned into lakes for forsaking the gods. He would say that the Portos

Mountains were placed between Gilder and Minerva as punishment for loving each other more than loving the gods," she paused her tugging and stopped dead in her tracks. "I don't want to think that it was true, but as a kid I believed him. I thought that if I loved anyone more than the gods that I would be punished. Gunther raised us with a healthy fear of upsetting the gods. I guess Luther was more like him because he continued the healthy fear as we got older."

"My love, you are a goddess. You could never upset the gods," I say, pulling her into my arms. "I mean, you may upset your mother every now and then, but I'm sure that's just normal mother daughter squabbling."

Her laugh is so beautiful, reminding me of a beautiful symphony. I could get drunk off of her laughter alone. She pulled back from me just a little to look up at me. Her bright brown eyes now had gorgeous flecks of gold through out them. I commit this to my memory, her beautiful face peppered with light freckles across her nose, the way her nose wrinkles when my beard tickles her, the little dimples when she truly smiles at me. I drink in every detail of her. I don't plan on being away from her for longer than a week max in the future, but those plans never seem to go how I want them to.

"Do you always go to Lake Gilder?" I ask her as we start walking, hand in hand towards the lakes.

"I've gone to Lake Minerva a few times. It's calm and serene there, plus there are beautiful flowers that bloom along the lake side. Last time I was there was with Lilly and Virgil. Lake Gilder was for our family; it didn't seem right to go there with Virgil," the sadness in her voice had the next question off my lips before I could stop myself.

"Do you wish you never met us?" Instant regret. The smile on her face faltered, but she didn't stop walking.

"No." She sounded so sure of that answer, but I felt like there was more to it.

"Then why do you seem so sad right now?" I ask her, pulling her closer to my side so I could wrap my arm around her.

"Where you all thought you would never have mates, I thought I would've been married to someone else. I had a whole life planned out mentally. Granted, I don't think Virgil would've objected to the life I planned out, but thinking about it, it's not fair," she keeps her pace steady, but I can feel her heart, it aches but I just don't know for what.

"Luna, if you want to explore that option with Virgil, as much as it would drive us insane, we could figure out a way to let you try," I grit my teeth, I've seen my father do it with Nora before Niklaus was born. She was engaged to another man before her bond took hold. Our father wanted to know that she wouldn't regret accepting her bond. Nora took three days before telling our father she couldn't imagine living without him.

He even offered to let her have her fiancé as a lover once they mated and married. Nora refused, but the offer was given. Maybe we could do the same thing for Luna.

It took me a minute, however, to notice that Luna stopped dead in her tracks and was glaring at me. "What?"

"I do not want that. I do not want to explore an option with Virgil. Been there, done that. As much as my heart will always have a place for him, I was ready to let him go. Not my fault Luther stabbed him, and Nox brought him to Mirith and now he just sticks around," she let out the cutest little huff, but my heart was singing with joy that she didn't want to explore a relationship with him.

"Then why do you seem so hurt when you talk about him?" I asked, tugging on her hand to get us moving again. The fields of flowers stretched out on either side of us, encasing us in the smells of spring. Birds chirped happily and even the sky itself seems to smile upon her.

"I was ready to let him go, but I want to stay his friend. It's just hard because how do you take back a few years of romance and go back to being just friends? He still gets protective of me and possessive constantly. Even with you guys right there. He also needs to remember I can light shit on fire now," she snaps her fingers, bringing a little orange and red flame to life, dancing on her finger tips like a little sprite performing to unheard music.

"Don't forget the water trick and ice trick you can do now," I teased her, running my fingers through the end of her pony tail. She pointed at me with the little fire sprite, threatening to let it loose on me. "You won't hurt me." I place a kiss on her cheek, and she just smiles at me.

"Yeah and the healing and shadows. Let's not forget that stuff too," she says as she rolls her eyes. It's a lot to her, hell it was a lot for us when we first developed our powers. The only difference is that we've had them since we were children, she just came into hers.

"We will help you learn to master them all once we figure out how they manifest for you," I offer. She smiles, returning her focus on the path in front of us, looking down at the ground. "Are you making sure you don't trip?"

"No!" She shouts and I can't help but burst out laughing. "Okay, okay! Yes! I don't want to trip and get hurt. You know me, I'll end up in the Mor for six weeks if I trip over a pebble."

"Only you could hurt yourself on a pebble," I tease. "But I'm sure Maggie would love your company."

She waves me off and takes two large steps without looking down. She laughs then takes another, tripping over a twig. I quickly reach out my hand and grab her arm. "Only you." I tease, kissing her on the cheek. I decided enough was enough and pulled her up onto my back. "I'm carrying you the rest of the way my delicate little flower."

She huffs but doesn't fight me. We take in the flowers and the birds dancing around us as they fly in pairs. The sight of Lake Minerva comes into view, and I must saw, it's breathtaking.

Lake Minerva is a rather large lake, curved tight around the edges and like a voluptuous woman. No wonder Luther had told the story about the lakes once being human. Minerva fits the bill. Luna takes a deep breath, letting the air settle into her.

"Don't forget, we're going to Lake Gilder. Unless you rather do it here," she whispered into my neck, her breath sending chills down my body.

"Why wait?" I ask her as she places kisses on my neck, lightly nipping where my neck meets my shoulders. I don't think we are going to make it to Lake Gilder.

CHAPTER 14
LUNA

We indeed did not make it to Lake Gilder. The serenity of Lake Minerva was where we needed to be. My last time here I was laying by the lake with Virgil and Lilly talking amongst themselves. What a different atmosphere today is.

Birds chirping, the wind silently whispering over us as we lay out in the grass. Bastian laid me down gently on the ground, pulling my shirt off of me and tossing it above my head. He kissed every inch of exposed skin that he could land on. I melted into his touch, the hair of his beard tickling my thighs as he kissed up them to my core. A thin fabric was all we had between us that split his lips from my own. My body shuddered at the anticipation, his eyes flickering to molten steel as he looked up at me from between my thighs.

"You are so deserving of this baby girl," Bastian whispered as he pressed a gentle kiss to the fabric now soaked with my arousal. A growl slipped from his throat as he used his teeth to remove my panties, sliding them down my thighs to my feet, his fingers tracing my thighs as he moves. His breath was cool as he placed feather light kisses back up my thighs to exposed center. The sun was warm despite the cool breeze and the winter prince hungry to devour every inch of me. His eyes focused on my pussy as he spread my thighs wider. "Fucking gorgeous." He breathed into me before dropping his mouth over my clit.

Ever so slowly he lapped up every drop from me, nipping my clit to elicit a louder moan from me then quickly licking it to soothe the pain. A vicious cycle of pain and pleasure, one that pulled me closer and closer to release. Arching my hips up from the ground, I expose more of me to him. His hands wrap under and around my legs holding me in place as he devours more and more of me. I begin to tremble as he deliberately circles his tongue slowly around my clit, pulling a moan of utter pleasure from me. "Bastian." His name a whisper on my lips was like unleashing the tether on him, he growled, driving his tongue deep within me dragging me closer and closer to release. A scream of pleasure rippled through me as I came crashing down on his tongue.

He pulled back from me, unraveling his arms and my legs, placing me gently back on the ground. His beard is glistening now with my arousal and normally I would've buried my face in my hands and been embarrassed, but not anymore. I love that he can smell me every time he takes a deep breath. It just makes him want me more. Hell, it makes them all want me more.

"You taste so sweet, princess," he said, collapsing to the ground next to me. He has on too much clothing for my liking. Considering I'm lying here with nothing on my lower half. Still don't know how he managed to get me out of everything so quickly. I frown looking at his shirt. "What's wrong?"

"You have clothes on," I whine. A chuckle escapes from him as he sits up on his elbows and looks at my shirt shaking his head. "I'll take mine off if you take yours off," I tease, pulling at the fabric holding onto me hostage. Another laugh ruptured from him as he pulled his shirt off and tossed it into the field, losing all sight of it in the flowers. I watched his muscle ripple with each movement. He has the body of a god, muscular and tall, larger than life itself. Hell, they all do. I just got very lucky to be with them. I pulled at my shirt, trying to get it off of me with grace, but failed miserably. My hair got caught in my necklace which made it harder to get my shirt off. Note to sell, don't wear necklaces if I know I'm going to get fucked.

Bastian's laugh was contagious, his deep voice is what I imagine silk would feel like if it was a sound. He helped me get my hair free and the shirt removed, tossing it to where his sat. My bra was unclasped within seconds as he kissed me holding my chin in one hand and snapping his fingers on the hooks with the other. He pulled my bra off with the same hand and tossed it, his eyes watched my breasts as they released from the horrible fabric cage.

I was now completely nude, laid fully bare before him. The bulge in his pants, evidence of his need and arousal caught my attention. Again, he was still wearing more clothes than me and I was now frustrated that I was the only one naked. I pushed him back onto his back and got between his legs, undoing the button and zipper on his jeans, pulling them down to his feet. Fucking shoes. I make quick work of them then complete my mission of stripping him down to nothing. His cock bounced out of his boxers once I was able to get them off. I marveled at the sight of precum glistening off the tip of his dick.

The thoughts running through my head were of the naughtiest kind. Licking his cock from balls to tip then just going for a swim, sucking him right to release then running away to see if he can catch me with a raging hard on, or just sucking him off, or even riding him to the morning. All pleasurable ideas, all fun and all sounding like such a good idea.

CHAPTER 15
BASTIAN

She's so cute when she gazes and my dick. Her bright brown eyes widen, showing off the beautiful flecks of gold simmering beneath the iris. I could watch her all day and still find something new about her each and every time. I can see the wheels turning in her head, the ideas simmering within her mind. She's trying to figure out how she wants to attack my dick, and I know better than to help her. As much as I want to wrap my hand in her hair and bring those luscious pink lips to my dick, I'll keep resisting. For now.

She looks up at me and licks her lips. I can't help myself as I reach down to cup her chin to pull her up to me, but she stops me. I cock my head to the side, raising my brow as I watch her. A delightful little grin crept up onto her lips and fuck if I didn't want to just kiss her while burying my dick so deep in her that she would be having my kid regardless of contraceptives. Granted, Maggie does make her a strong ass tea seeing as there's six of us, but I bet I could render it ineffective if she wanted me to.

Before my thoughts could run wild, she made the cutest little gasp before rocking my world. She wrapped her lips around the head of my dick and sucked hard, taking me all the way to the back of her throat.

She held herself down, running the tip of her tongue over my balls as she tried not to gag on my length. Fuck, I tensed as she slowly raised her mouth up my length, making a satisfying popping sound as my tip left her mouth. I couldn't help but growl as she sat there smiling up at me. I know she wouldn't leave me hanging like this. I intentionally make my dick bounce in her face, a wiggle of sorts. She giggles before wrapping her lips around my dick once more. Her tongue twirls around the tip of my dick, making my head fall back against the ground.

Don't grab her hair, don't grab her hair. I can't think straight as she sucks me all the way to the back of her throat. She is fucking perfect. A soft moan vibrates my dick and I'm soaring. She takes my dick deep down her throat, then ever so slowly pops it out. Repeating this over and over, joining her hands in place of her lips. Grazing her nails against my balls rips a moan from me. I fucking love when she has long nails. I can't help myself anymore, I wrap her hair around my hand, guiding her up and down my length. Her moans are so satisfying.

I can feel myself swelling with release, the need to have her drink it all up is intense. Right as I go to guide her back down, she taps on my leg twice, her sign that she needs a second. Without hesitation, I drop my hand from her hair and let her come up for air. Her mascara is running a bit, and she has a little saliva dropping from her lips as she gasps for air. "Too much princess?" I tease, clenching my muscles so my dick bounces for her. The smile on her face was so intoxicating. She looked drunk off of lust, desire sparkling in her eyes.

Without a word, she pushed up from the ground and took off for the lake running as fast as her naked little self could run. I bolt upright to take off after her, but a glint from behind the tree has my attention. I take a small glance and notice, blonde hair behind the tree, eyes following Luna as she runs naked through the field of flowers. How fucking long had Virgil been standing there?! How the fuck did I not notice?

I take a second to decide, go after Luna and thoroughly fuck her while he watches or rip his head off. I decide that ripping his head off wouldn't do me any good, fuck it. Let him watch and see how he should've always fucking treated her. Luna glances over her should just as I take off, she's fast, but she's running slower intentionally so I can catch her. Good, she has no fucking idea what I'm about to do to her.

My little kitten wants to play mouse, then I'll gladly hunt her down and devour her.

It took only a few bounds before I was right on her heels, a little yelp left her lips as she looked back noticing me closing in on her. "You can't get away from me that easily," I called out to her as she picked up her pace a bit. Running naked with a fucking boner is not easy, what the fuck.

"You'll have to try harder, my love," she called back to me, my heart hammering at the words my love. Oh, she is fucked once I get my hands on her. I quicken my pace, reaching my hand out to run through the ends of her hair as she runs. Within a matter of seconds, she was wrapped up in my arms, body pressed against mine as I sunk my teeth into her soft skin, marking her with my victory. The scream of pain and pleasure that danced across her lips had me full erect again, pressed into her ass.

"That wasn't very nice of you," I lick up the blood from the fresh bite on her neck. She shuddered, pressing her ass against my cock as if inviting me to take her right like this.

"I wanted to have a little more fun," she said breathlessly. Her body fit into mine like a glove, her hands reaching behind her to find purchase in my hair. We were closer to the water now and to my surprise the shore wasn't made of rocks or gravel but a beautiful black sand. Perfect. The sightline to the tree Virgil is standing behind is unobstructed, I glance over, watching him try to hide further behind the tree in hopes he hasn't been caught. Jokes on him, he's been caught, and I want him to watch me fuck her.

I gently detangle her hands from my hair and spin her around, so her breasts are pressed firmly against my chest, well right below my chest. She looked up at me with hooded eyes, the scent of her arousal has my head spinning. She is perfection. Putting my hand below her chin, I gently hold her in place as I place a soft kiss to her lips. The only gentleness I plan on showing her before ravaging her and treating her like the goddess she is. I grab her by her waist and pull her up, wrapping her legs around my waist, her pussy slides against my dick pulling a growl from me and a whimper from her.

"I hope you enjoyed your little run," I whisper into her ear as I lay her out on the sand. "Because now it's time for your punishment." Her eyes widen as I press the head of my dick against her slick entrance. I push in gently, once, twice. Her legs began to tremble at the rising anticipation. I couldn't take it any longer, she had me on the verge of release just with her amazing mouth. I slammed my dick deep inside of her, a ripple of pleasure shot through our bond as she screamed out my name. If the guys didn't know what we were up to before, they knew now. Another audience for us, only difference is she can make them feel her pleasure if she chooses too, or unless I fuck her so good she can't control it. I think this is going to be one of those, can't control situations. A smug satisfaction of a smile widens across my face as I watch her eyes roll back the deeper I go.

"Harder!" She screams out, I gladly oblige as she wraps her legs tighter around my waist, pulling my dick in hard and deep. I'm a few pumps away from utter release but I can't do that just yet. Gripping her legs, keeping them wrapped around me, I pull her up with me as I lay back. I pull her down hard on me as she grinds on my dick with each thrust. Her knees spread onto the sand on either side of me as she takes control, sliding up and down feverishly on my dick. I can feel her inner walls tighten around me, her release right on the cusp of spilling over. I move my hands from her waist to her breasts, kneading the soft heavy flesh. She cries out, anticipation at my next move building her closer and closer. I push my upper body up and trap one of her nipples in between my teeth and bite hard. She moans out, driving herself harder onto my dick. She's almost there, and fuck so am I.

I grab both breasts, pushing her nipples together and bite harder on both nipples, licking and sucking them until the harder into little peaks in my mouth. "I'm going to cum!" She screams, grinding harder and faster on my dick. I drop her nipples from my mouth for a quick moment.

"Do it princess, cum all over my cock," I command her before returning to her breasts. As if answering my command, she clenches down on me, riding me through her wave of ecstasy and pleasure as she released all over me. I move me hands fast to her waist and held her down, forcing her to continue grinding on me as I spilled into her, a growl escaped from me as I joined in her ecstasy and please. I fell back on the sand as she collapsed on top of me. Heavy breathing and the smell of sex was all that I could focus on. I placed kisses to the top of her head, running my hand idly through her hair. "Let's get you cleaned up."

She just nods, still shaking in my arms as I gather her up. I take a moment to glance out over the field, not making it obvious that I can see Virgil still standing there, but instead making it look as if I'm trying to find out clothes. Which I partly am. I shrug my shoulders and walk us into Lake Minerva, sending up a silent prayer that we aren't disturbing anyone or any being if the lake truly was a human before. I hold her close as the cool water washes over us, dipping her hair back gently into the water to rinse off the sand and sweat. Her eyes stay closed as I run my fingers through her bright blue locks. She begins humming softly while my hands make their way down her body, between her legs. I can still feel the heat coming off of her through the water. I drop my hands letting her slowly float in the water as I dunked my head under to get the sweat out of my hair and eyes.

Breaking the water to come back to the surface, I watched as Luna swam off to the center of the lake. I couldn't help but follow her, her ass broke the water every so often as she swam, her head dipping below the water as she moved. The water is the more tranquil and serene that I've seen in a very long time. The Hildaria region has some of the most beautiful things, my wife being the most beautiful of all. Watching her pull herself out of the water onto the moss-covered rock in the middle of the lake was a spectacular sight. She was glistening as the sun touched her body, shimmering like a celestial being. One more taste wouldn't kill me.

I swim to where she is laid out, coming up out of the water nestling my face perfectly between her thighs. "Now that is a beautiful sight," I say, pulling myself up just enough to kiss her lower lips. She shivers under my touch, my lips are colder than the others, a side effect of being the Prince of Winter, but she never complains. I watch as her skin pimples and take the moment to take her in. The little freckles all over her body, the few scars that mar her perfect skin. I lower my mouth to her entrance, making eye contact with her the entire time as she looks all the world ravenous. Her lip kicks up in a grin, her eyebrows raising with her lip. I take that as a challenge and clamp my teeth on her sensitive clit, her hands go straight into my hair as I devour her, right here in the open for all to see. I hope Virgil is taking notes for whatever female he takes to bed in the future.

Greedily I drink her up, every drop until her legs starts shaking around my head and I know I've won. I have one of her legs up over my shoulder as the other lays off the rock into the water, I run my free hand up her leg, toying with her clit with my fingers pulling her release. "Bastian I—"

I plunge my fingers into her, dragging her to a full release all over my hand. She looked down at me with a satisfied grin on her face, sex haze fogging her mind as she rests her head back. I pull my fingers from her and look over at the tree, Virgil is no longer hiding behind it. He's blatantly watching now. I lift my hand still covered in her juices and lick them, savoring every drop, then I wave at him with a smile on my face. Virgil quickly turns and practically runs away. Thank the gods she didn't see him; I gently pull her off the rock and back into the water with me to clean her up for real this time.

"Did he finally stop watching?"

CHAPTER 16
VIRGIL

I should've walked away. I should have just gone to Lake Gilder instead, but no I just had to go to Lake Minerva to try to clear my head. I just happened to come across them in the flower field and I fucking froze. I forgot how beautiful Luna was completely naked. Granted most of our times together were quick and we never really had an official let me take you to bed moment, but how the fuck would I ever be able to compete with fucking in the middle of a flower field and upon a rock in a fucking lake?!

Rubbing my finger against the bridge of my nose, I wander aimlessly down the dirt path towards Lake Gilder. Nox had told me that it was the stronger of the two lakes, it had the heart of a heartbroken man and that I should go there to think some things through. While I have gotten closer to the princes and tried to make nice with them, it's hard. I wasn't ready to let go of Luna. When Kira and Harper came to Mirith with Lilly, they gave me a note Luna had written before Luther had stabbed me. She didn't know what I was going through. It wasn't her fault. When I saw her for the first time in Mirith with the guys I just wanted to protect her. I wanted to show her that I was the man she needed me to be. Sadly, I didn't know that she had let me go.

I can't blame her though. I didn't start acting upon my feelings until it was too late. I wish I had the chance to do things differently, like going back in time to be with her properly. Gunther gave me his blessing, but apparently, he wasn't the one I needed to ask. King Drake and King Harold are completely different from the men we are told to fear in Celvenia. Always being told they rule with an iron fist and that we as humans are expendable. I've learned firsthand that it's not the case. King Drake offered me a place in his royal guard after the attack and I took it. I was allowed to go home to see if my family wanted to come live with me in Mirith, but I was shunned the moment I told my family. Abandoning my post was what I was accused of. Fuck it. The Celvenia royal army was a joke, not even led by the actual King of Mistveil. Once upon a time they were, but now they were just a shell of the mighty warriors.

My mind lingered back to that field and the fucking lake. Luna running naked through the field of flowers, fitting in so beautifully with her surroundings running her hands over the tall grass and the multicolored petals as she ran. Bastian, however, was a stark standout in the field. A warrior on the hunt; his prey being Luna. I wanted to put him down as he chased her, running after her like she some wounded animal. A jealous rage built up in my chest and I had to take a deep breath. That is one of her husbands and her mate. I have to come to terms that she is not mine anymore, and not just because she doesn't want to be mine. She found her other halves and I really should be happy for her. Part of me is, but a big part of me misses her.

The way they all treat her is so much better than I ever did. I didn't mean to watch those intimate moments between her and Bastian. I just couldn't help but watch. He was pleasuring her in ways I never did. He was devouring her, bringing her to the point where she was screaming his name. Something I was never able to make her do. I was selfish with her, always worrying about myself, then again, we were always rushing because we were trying to hide what we were doing. I thought it was out of love, but really, it was out of a desire to shield her from Luther that I never made it public. In reality I was just afraid to commit to her.

Tears streamed down my face as I made my way closer to Lake Gilder. I fucked up a good thing, and now she's being loved and doted on by men who deserve her more than I ever did.

CHAPTER 17
LUNA

Bastian and I spent the next few hours swimming naked in Lake Minerva and laying out in the flowers half naked. My clothes were more destroyed than we originally thought so I was now wearing Bastians T-shirt and my underwear. He had his pants half slung up around his hips, my bra hooked to the side belt loop like a damn trophy. I was happily content with living out the rest of my day like this, but I know we have to go back to reality. I chewed on my bottom lip, thinking of how I was going to handle this Marie situation. Her and I don't get along, but I don't want anything happening to her if there really is an army from Limbris readying to take Floria.

"What's got your mind running princess?" Bastian asked me as he ran his fingers through my hair. We had been watching the clouds as the danced across the sky, I lost track of how long we've been alone. It was much needed time, but it wasn't enough time. I curled up into his arms and nuzzled myself into his chest, breathing in the scent of him.

"We have to go to Floria. The sooner the better. I just don't want to leave you yet," I sigh into his chest as he rubs my back. I want to just forget about the war, forget about the drama. I want to curl into a ball of limbs with my husbands and enjoy each of them.

"You think I want you to leave me? I'm tempted to go with you to Floria myself and drag Marie back to Mistveil by any means necessary," Bastian kisses the top of my head, treating me with such gentleness that is so contrary to how to looks. My fearsome looking prince is a damn teddy bear, and I love it. Rolling back onto my back I look up at the sky once more. Stars begin to twinkle into the violet sky, the sun setting in the distance.

"We should probably head back. I have a feeling if my mom and grandmother have it their way, a search party will be looking for us soon," I sigh, sitting up, bringing my knees to my chest. "As much as I want you and Damien and Valdis with me. I know that you all are best needed here, I'm just selfish."

Bastian sat up next to me, wrapping his arm around my shoulder, pulling me against him. "Princess, if you are selfish than so am I. I would rather run away with you, taking you all over Cerulia to see the realms and more than have any of us go into war. I want nothing more than to fuck you in every majestic place around the world, and after this war is over, I will do just that." He placed a kiss to my temple and stood up, offering me his hand.

I grabbed it as he hauled me up to my feet. He grabbed my shoes and tied them together at the laces, tossing them over his shoulder before entwining our fingers together. "Can we agree on doing this again when I get back?" I tease glancing back at the lake with a smile.

"As many times as you would like," he replied, kissing my cheek over and over again.

We did the best we could when it came to sneaking into my bedroom at my parents' house. My lack of pants and clothes that I left with was an explanation I didn't feel like answering right now. Bastian, despite his size, is quite light on his feet. He got us into my room with no detection. Well at least by my relative, my mates were all sprawled out on my bed and the couch in the room. None of them were sleeping though. Fennik and Niklaus sat on the couch, flipping through the random novels that I kept on the shelves here. Valyn laid across my bed like he was trying to tune out the chatter around the room, while Damian and Valdis talked strategy at the end of the bed. Their heads all snapped up when we walked into the room. A smile flashed upon their faces as we crossed the room.

"Had some fun?" Valyn winked at me as he grabbed my hand, pulling me onto the bed. "Where did your clothes go?" He took in Bastian's shirt that barely covered my ass. I just pointed at Bastian, who shrugged while he plopped down on the chair next to Niklaus.

"You missed dinner. Are you hungry?" Valdis asked, moving from the bed. I hadn't even realized how long we had been gone or how long it had taken to get back. We were too busy talking about the stars and future plans.

"Honestly, I just want to get some sleep. It's been a long day and tomorrow is going to be a test on my patience," I say throwing myself back onto the pillows and curling up still wearing Bastian's shirt. "By the way, you're not getting this back tonight." I hug the shirt closer to my chest. Bastian chuckles, flicking my bra still attached to his belt loop.

"You can keep it as long as you want princess, that just means I keep your bra until I get it back," he blows me a kiss and smiles. I let it go, I honestly don't care that he has my bra. I curl up into Valyn, feeling the large bed ebb and flow as my mates all join in. This bed was custom made for us for when we visit. My father thought it was best instead of trying to keep them in their own rooms.

The scents of my mate's waft over me, creating the most beautiful, serene atmosphere for me to sleep. My eye lids feel so heavy as I slowly drift off to sleep. Tomorrow will be a nightmare but tonight will be a dream.

CHAPTER 18
LUNA

Floria was beautiful. The smell of bonfires and apples swirled in the air as we stepped through the portal. Leaves the colors of fire decorated the trees all around us, dancing in the wind. The sound of morning birds chirping in the distance was a pleasant one. If the army from Limbris was here, I doubt we would be hearing such beautiful music. It seemed so peaceful, but why did I have this nagging feeling that something is terribly wrong. Niklaus stepped out of the portal before me, taking in the sights of his home. He fit in here, the orange of his hair dancing in the wind, his emerald, green eyes sparkling in the morning sunlight reminding me of the lush green fields from Mirith. Valyn and Nikalus stepped out behind me, all three keeping me in the center of them just in case we walked into a war zone.

"Does something feel off to you guys?" I asked them as we made our way through the courtyard. The castle in front of us was modest honestly. It was on the smaller side compared to Castle Mistveil or even my parent's home. The white stone exterior is pristine, the orange and red accents on the tower roofs blend in so beautifully to the morning sunrise. It's gorgeous here.

"I don't feel anything except annoyance. Everything seems fine, can we go home now?" Fennik's clearly annoyed that we're here. He's called his mother selfish on many occasions and maybe we should've done this without him. It's not like Nox didn't offer to come instead so things were less awkward for Fennik. Instead, he had decided that if I was going to his realm that he needed to be with me. I looked out at the orchards, filled with apples off all colors. The pumpkin patches in the distance already had large pumpkins on them, with smaller ones all around. I wonder if they celebrate the Day of Souls here.

"We have to at least see your mom, dude. As much as I'd love to go home and deal with other matters," Niklaus wrapped his arm around my shoulder, pulling me into him. "If we don't get eyes on her, Dad will just come here himself and if that happens, we are all going to have to come back." Niklaus placed a kiss to the top of my head as Valyn entwined his fingers in mine.

"We will make it quick Fen. We all don't want to force you to do something you don't want to do. If anything, I can go in and check on her alone so you three can stay outside," Valyn offered. Fennik took a moment to chew on that. I didn't like the idea of Valyn doing this alone. It's not why we came here together.

"I'll go in. She already doesn't like me, and I can explain that I was sent on behalf of King Harold to check on his mate, and hopefully return with her, while everyone else is preparing for another attack. She can easily dismiss me.," I plan out how I would handle it if she refused to come back to Mistveil with us. Fennik's eyes met mine and I could see the resolve there.

"I'm not letting you guys do this alone. She's my mother and I just need to suck it up and deal with it. I can't avoid her forever," Fennik resigns, turning back towards the house and sighing. "Let's just get this over with. If she doesn't want to come with us, we can tell dad, and he can order her back."

We follow Fennik through the courtyard and up to the large red doors that lead inside. He doesn't bother to knock, but I guess he doesn't have to, this place is his house after all. The doors creak open revealing a beautiful main room. A large staircase accents the left wall, leaves carved into the oak handrailing with such exquisite detail, each vein of the leaf is detailed out to show the life of the leaves. A lush green carpet covered the stairs like grass covers the dirt. The entire castle had a cozy feeling to it, but something oozed of sludge and darkness in the shadows. I could feel it. A deep hatred manifesting in the corners of the room. Clearly I was the only one concerned because no one else seemed to notice it.

Valyn and Niklaus let me go for a quick moment to check on Fennik who was just standing in the center of the room taking in the space. A table sat in the entrance way that had fresh apples in a bowl with two pumpkins sitting on it as well. Some acorns and walnuts were mixed into the bowl of apples making the whole thing look festive. A freshness that the rest of the house didn't seem to have. Like Marie was planning on staying here for longer than she let on. I pulled out my phone, glancing at the picture on the screen of me and all my mates, the day we got married. The smiles on each of our faces, the light in our eyes. I want this back.

I have a really bad feeling about being here. Something feels off.

I send the text to my uncle before slipping the phone back into my pocket. If no one else feels it, then maybe I'm feeling something weird, but maybe I'm not. At least if I tell Sirus that something feels off, he will know what to do if shit hits the fan. A buzz has me pulling my phone back out.

What has you feeling off? How large is the army? Do you see any dragons? I could hear his voice as I read off his questions.

That's the thing, there's nothing here. No army, no dragons, not even a beast or daemon in sight. But I have this weird feeling of dread and a feeling of ooze in the shadows. Somethings not right.

I push out the message and put the phone back in my pocket. The last thing I want is to have my uncle worrying about me, but something is wrong. I haven't seen a single staff member either, which seems very odd if Marie is staying here. That woman never lifts a finger on her own.

I step up to my mates as a musical laughter fills the room. The hair on my arms slowly start to stick up, a chill running down my spine. I recognize that laugh. Marie was having a blast here, or at least that's what it sounded like. I glanced at Fennik, watching the rage build back in his eyes. I walked up behind him, wrapping my arms around his waist and pressing a kiss to his shoulder. "We can do this. We just have to tell her what is going on and leave it with whatever she wants to do."

He nods, turning around in my arms. I look at him and smile, we can go this. We can get this all done and over with. Niklaus and Valyn leaned up against the far wall letting us have a moment to ourselves. He wrapped his arms around my waist and pulled me closer, pressing his lips against mine. I could taste the cinnamon on his lips before they even parted. "We do this together, then we leave. She chooses to stay, then it's on her." He broke the kiss for just a moment so I could nod, then pulled me in for a more passionate kiss. I could hear the small chuckles from across the room, but they weren't laughing at us, they were laughing because they knew the feeling.

"Can we hurry up a little bit? Sorry Fen but your realm is always a little chillier than I prefer," Valyn said, coming up behind us. Fennik growled just a bit at the disruption and being forced to deal with him mother soon than later. He slowly lets me out of his arms as the room takes a collective breath. None of us wanted to do this, but I gave everyone no choice. So here goes nothing.

CHAPTER 19
FENNIK

My mother's laughter set my blood on fire. How could she be here just living it up while the rest of us have been dealing with political bullshit and war. No, this is a damn vacation for her. She is just throwing a tantrum because dad didn't fucking take her side on forcing me to reject Luna's bond. She was selfish and she wanted me to be like her, even when my dad loved her so unconditionally, regardless of having other mates. Luna is the same with us all, not favoring one over the other. I think we all worried that she would favor one more than the other, but she worked out a whole ass schedule around royal duties that we all have had, vacations she wants to go on with each of us as a group and individual times she wants to spend with us. I have never felt more love than I do when I am with her. Hell, our dad only has time for five mates, yet Luna has six.

"When we get home, can we all just go somewhere together?" I ask before stepping up to the large door leading into the living area. The smell of cinnamon and apples too overpowering for even my liking, it almost seems forced.

"I would love that," Luna chimes in as she grabs my hand in hers, giving it a little squeeze. Her way of reminding me that she is here with me and that I am not alone. The scent of pineapples and citrus from behind me let me know my brothers are right here with me as well. I can do this as long as they are here with me. We can do this together.

"Let's get this over with then," I reply, pushing open the door to the large room. The fireplace against the far wall is fully lit up with a roaring fire that's keeping the room nice and warm. Blankets laid out across the couches in the room, one even on the chair that our dad always sits in when we visit. Today however, another takes a seat in that chair, a twin to my mother. Long, straight red hair flows over his shoulders like lava covering the earth, his eyes a match to my own, a bright green flicker to look over at me. He smiles but does nothing more. I haven't seen my uncle in a few years, but he still looks the same. He was much nicer than my mother, I always wondered how they happened to be siblings.

My mother notices the look on my uncle's face and turns around on the couch. The affectionate smile and laughter stop as she takes in me and my mate, her eyes flickering to my brothers behind me. A deep sigh drags out from between her ruby lips, the look of disgust dragging across her face. My uncle shook his head and stood up, crossing the room to me. "It's been too long nephew. Who is this stunning beauty and why am I just now meeting her?" My uncle asks, taking Luna's hand in his and pressing a kiss to the back of it as he bows to her. I could hear my mother's eyes rolling from here, the scoff and added punction.

"This is my mate and wife, Luna. I would've come sooner, but I didn't realize you were feeling up for company," I offer him a smile. "Ah, let me not be rude. You know my brother's Valyn and Niklaus. Luna, this is my uncle Malicah. He is my mother's twin." Luna smiles sweetly at him, bowing her head in a sign of respect.

"It's a pleasure to meet you sir," Luna says so sweetly. She is the most endearing person I've ever met. I think my uncle would love her. Despite my mother and her bullshit.

"The pleasure is all mine. Your mother was saying you finally mated and that you mated in a large group as well. I'm glad you have mates to look after you Fen," he released Luna's hand a messed with my hair before pulling me into a hug. My uncle smelled of apples and something bitter, a smell that I wasn't familiar with.

"Malicah, don't overdo it. Today is just one of your good days brother," my mother chimed, and I could see the look on his face drop as he glanced back over his shoulder to the couch. This was very unusual for him to look at my mother with anything but adoration. Something between them must be strained, maybe she has been bossing him about his life. No mate, no children. Not even a marriage of convenience to sire an heir to continue their family line. She was very upset about that and always took the time to tell him that, every visit. I always wondered why he admired her as much as he did.

"I'm fine Marie. You figured you'd be a little happier that your son has shown up to see you," he retorted before giving me an apologetic look. I know my uncle means well, but he doesn't realize what drama has been going on between us. My mother looks over her shoulder, shrugging before returning to her tea. I go to open my mouth, but it is Luna who is quicker to respond.

"Pardon the intrusion, there was an attack on Mirith. Nothing compared to the first attack, this was just a dragon and a rider, but the implication was that an army is headed for Floria. We came here to warn the people, and hopefully return you to Mistveil with King Harold for safety. He has been worried about you and upon hearing the news of a possible army coming this way, the King himself wanted to come. We, however, offered instead so he could prepare the troops with my father," Luna spoke so eloquently and so formal. From what I understood from Lilly when we spoke about Luna's childhood, she never backed down from Gunther but was always a loyal daughter. Lilly said she learned how to take scrutiny and harsh words from the children making fun of her and bullying her for being different in school and from Luther and Gunther constantly telling her she was always doing something wrong. No wonder she handles judgement so well.

"If my husband wanted me home, he would've come for me himself, regardless of what some ill-bred princess claims," my mother scoffed, taking a sip of her tea. Niklaus took a step forward to say something, but Luna raised her hand and smiled, releasing my other hand, she took a few steps to put herself in my mothers line of sight.

"Again, your husband wished to come, but your son decided it was best to come get you instead. You would think that would mean a little something more to you, seeing as you have a straining relationship because of your lack of respect. Let it be known, I don't care if you respect me or not. You are my husbands mother and with that said, I will show you respect. Even if it hasn't been earned. I was raised better than that," Luna smiled widely at my mother and I swore my uncle about choked on his own spit.

"How dare you speak to me like that in my own home," my mother set her teacup on the table, her anger simmering all around her. I could feel the energy in the room change and immediately stalked to where Luna was standing. She just held up her hand, stopping me dead in my tracks. My mother could control some forms of electricity, lightening, currents in the air around us. She could create storms from nothing. So could I, but I learned to control my emotions a little better than her.

Be careful, she controls electricity. Valyn spoke into all our minds, like we all needed a reminder.

She needs to be careful what she says to me or about any of you. I love you Fen, but I don't have an ounce of respect for her. Luna spoke calmly into my mind. I don't know if that terrified me more than if she would be angry.

"I could kill you right now and you wouldn't even feel it." My mother's threat was charged with the current in the air. The pressure in the room got heavier as a storm began to brew outside.

"And? You don't know what I am capable of. You never took the chance to get to know me. One thing you might actually regret," Luna was cocky, but she wasn't wrong. My mother knew nothing about her. Powers, goddess status, fighting abilities, even her childhood. She knew nothing. A cool breeze busted open the window on the far side of the room, smothering the fire. Luna looked at the fireplace and snapped her fingers. A large roaring fire replaced the one that was just snuffed out. I could see the look on my mothers face of anger, but my uncle just looked on in wonder at what Luna had just done. A loud crack sounded outside of the house, lightening striking a tree right outside of the room. My mother trying to show her powers as well. A pissing contest of sorts. I thought only us men did that shit.

"You can play with fire, so what?" My mother laughed, looking back over at me with a sadistic smile on her face. One of a crazed woman who was in love with a man she couldn't have so she murders the man's love just to get his affection. "Fennik, do you still choose her over me?"

The look of shock rippled across my uncle's face. "You tried to make him choose you over his mate?! Marie, you have no right to do that! Would you make me choose you over a mate if I ever had one? Are we not allowed to be happy?!" Now it was my turn to be shocked. My uncle never would speak to my mother like this in the past. I am surprised he is being so bold with her now.

"My son deserves to be mated to one person, not have to share his mate with not only all of his brothers but a disgusting daemon prince of Hellis! You would have a mate by now if you weren't so sick and dying. Be grateful I come and take care of you the way I do. You should both love me over anyone else. I am the one who has not only raised my son, but I take care of you my dear sweet brother. Learn to be grateful," she snaps at us. Luna starts laughing and the whole room goes cold, the once roaring fire has been smothered out by ice as it creeps along the floor to where she is standing.

"Keep speaking ill of my mates and you won't have a tongue left in your fucking mouth," Luna spat, her usual chocolate brown eyes now completely voided into nothing but stars. My mother would be wise to stop talking, but she's not wise.

She never was.

CHAPTER 20
NIKLAUS

We all knew what could happen when Luna looked like this. We all witnessed it the other morning in the cafe. Valyn and I glance at each other, stepping around Fennik as he watches his mother and our wife. Valyn was probably the fastest of the two of us, he could make it to Luna faster than me for sure. As much as I rather let Luna destroy Marie, she would regret it, not being able to look at Fen or our father again. Marie doesn't deserve an ounce of kindness from Luna, yet Luna keeps giving it to her.

"Fennik, would you really let your wife hurt your mother?" Marie asks him, the look on her face is deranged and twisted. Fennik looks at his mother then to his uncle. Malicah's face was a mix of anger and sympathy. He was looking at Luna with sorrow in his eyes, then to Fennik with the same sad expression. "Fennik, tell your wife to learn her place. If she can't submit to you, then you must make her."

A snap ripped through our bond; whatever tether Luna had on herself had just broke. Shadows formed around the room, darkening the morning light that was coming in through the windows. Malicah stepped closer to the wall, giving me a wider berth to get to Luna. Luna shined like the sun in the darkness, an ethereal glow surrounding her, she was pissed, but a laugh from her was the next thing we heard. A beautiful, yet terrifying laugh.

"You put your son in such horrible positions, as a mother you should be ashamed of yourself for treating your son the way you have. You gave birth to him, he didn't ask you to raise him, that is your job as a parent. You had the aid of not only Harold but of my other mother in laws. They would've helped you, so don't pin that blame of you doing it alone on him. As for your brother," Luna paused, looking over a Malicah, who to his credit, looked her right back in the eyes. "If he is sick and you are holding your help over his head, you're more disgusting than the creatures trying to attack us. My sister was sick and dying and I stayed by her side, doing everything I could to save her from the greying. She is better now, thanks to Maggie, but I would never hold that over her head! She didn't ask to be sick and nor did you brother! No one asks to be sick!"

A ray of light shot out around the room from Luna, like a light beam shooting through a crystal, fracturing the light. Marie just laughed. "You think I wanted to be a mother?" she choked out. Looking back at Fennik she smiled, "He's not even Harold's son! The only child I wanted was my first born with my true mate! They were robbed from me the moment I met Harold. Before I completed the mating bond with Harold, I slept with my love once more because I knew the moment I took that bonding oath, it would kill him and with him my first born would die. You'll see, someone from your past who you loved so much will be taken from you, and you'll lose every ounce of love you have for my son."

Valyn was already at Luna's side when the words crashed into me. Fennik isn't my brother? No. That's not right. I remember when Marie was pregnant with him. I remember growing up side by side with him. She has to be lying. Malicah yelled something from the wall, but I couldn't make it out. Valyn had grabbed Luna, spinning her to look at him, trying to get her to calm down before she did something she would regret. Fennik stood there in utter shock as Marie smiled widely at him.

"You'll see my son. She can't love you the way I can," she said, charging for Luna. A glint of light coming out of her side. I moved, but not fast enough. The room started to spin as a shattering pain tore through me bringing me to my knees. Fennik was on the ground seconds later, followed by a howling Valyn. Marie stood above Luna, blood dripping from the dagger that she held in her hand. She knelt down over her body, wiping the blood on Luna's shirt, smiling the whole time. Malicah was at Fennik's side trying to get him up off the floor.

Valyn shoved Marie away from Luna, staggering her back from where she was leaning over Luna. I couldn't move, I felt like a part of me was just ripped from my chest.

Luna. Luna, can you hear me?! I try to scream down the bond, but my words echo into the darkness that once held her light. I can't hear my brother's either. It's too quiet in my mind.

Marie laughs, turning to Fennik and Malicah. "I told you Fennik, you should've chosen me over her. You deserve to find someone who loves you and only you. It's a shame you had to see that. But now we can be a family again," she laughed. A tall figure stepped into the doorway, the light behind him blocking out most of his features. "Tanis my love, I need your help."

The man stepped into the room with ease. Without Luna, the darkness and ice that once filled this room vanished. Tanis, the mate that supposedly was ripped from her. The one who she let go of to be with my father, he was still fucking alive. The closer he got the more I could make out, bright emerald, green eyes, short slicked back black hair, tan and covered in light scars. He was a warrior no doubt. Fennik's voice broke through me taking inventory of this man.

"You... You killed her!" He roared. He spoke the words my brain didn't want to think of. Luna, my wife, my mate, my life. She was taken from me by this woman who didn't deserve to live.

"She did you a favor boy. You would be wise to stop talking and respect your mother," Tanis's words to Fennik were that of a displeased father. Not someone who had just met. Tanis was not Fennik's father though. There was no fucking way.

"Fuck off Tanis. She did it just to get her son to love her. It won't work Marie. You lied to everyone when you said Tanis and Elijah died. You lied when you said his death was because he lost his mate. You just burdened your son with the lie you've told everyone," Malicah spat at them. Tanis, ignoring the vitriol being spat at him, wrapped his arm around Marie's waist and pulled her close to him.

"What of it? I have my mate and now both of my son's home with me. Malicah, you're only alive because I allow it. You might want to watch your tongue," Marie spoke as if Valyn and I weren't in the room. "Tanis, can you remove the filth from the room please. I need to speak with Fennik alone."

"Of course, my Queen," Tanis kissed her before releasing her and turning his attention to Luna and Valyn. Valyn looked at me, he was going to get Luna out of here at all costs, even if it meant his own life. I nodded, slowly pushing myself up from the ground. I'll take this fucker down with us if I have to.

Fennik and Malicah must've sensed what we were about to do. Fennik was on his feet a moment later, Malicah bracing himself on the ground behind him. Valyn summoned water from the melted ice on the floor, wrapping Tanis in a tidal wave to drown.

Marie spun around screaming, "LET HIM GO!"

I charged at Tanis, sliding through the water to get to Valyn and Luna. The portal to Mirith was closer than the one to Mistveil. "Get her to Mirith. Her mother will be able to help her better than we can!" I shout, shoving Valyn and Luna toward the door. "I've got Fennik!"

Valyn nodded, pulling Luna closer to his chest and running for the portal. He would get her home safe. They could figure out how to save her. She can't be dead. I turned in time to see Fennik charging at his mother. A squelching sound ripped through the air; blood splattering all over Fennik's face.

Marie let out a scream that turned into a gurgle as she choked on her own blood. Tanis let out a roar, trying to clutch his chest as the water fell to the ground. Valyn was no longer in the autumn realm and Fennik had just killed his mother.

We need to leave, and we need to leave now. I run to Fennik, grab him by his arm and heave him toward the back door, gripping Malic-ah's arm dragging him along with us. "We are going back to Mistveil. Just stay with me!"

CHAPTER 21
DAMIAN

Bastian was the first one on the ground gripping his chest, Valdis was next. I was only seconds behind them, a rip tearing through me so fast and so hard that I felt like I was going to die. A scream ripped from my throat as Nox and Virgil stood there in a panic watching us all drop. Gabrial and Kieran came running into the room with Undas and Drake hot on their heels.

"What happened?" Drake yelled as he burst into the room, looking at Nox and Virgil for an answer but neither of them could answer. They didn't know.

"They just went down one by one, gripping their chests," Nox stuttered out, leaning over Bastian trying to help him up from the ground but he wasn't moving. The hole in my chest was getting wider. I couldn't feel any of them in my head. A hollowness filled me, the silence too loud.

Vanalli and Vanessa came into the room shortly after with Erina, Holly and Sirus. Vanalli took one look at Undas and began to cry. Everyone just stopped what they were doing and looked at her. A tear struck down Sirus's face as he looked at his mother and held her. Undas was shaking. What did they know?! Erina was the last one to drop to her knees screaming. A heartbreaking sound tore through the room. No one understood what was going on.

I reached out mentally to Luna, but there was nothing. No sound, just an empty wind down the bond as if the bridge between her and us had collapsed. Valdis fought the pain and got to his knees before collapsing forward onto his hands. His breathing labored. "What is going on?" He tried to demand, but his words were nothing but air.

Bastian and I were still clutching our chests. The pain was so intense I couldn't move. "Why can't I hear Luna?" I asked, the air rushing from my lungs had me feeling like I was about to pass out.

The doors to the room flung open once more and our father and mothers were rushing into the room. Our mothers wrapping themselves around Erina. My father looking like rage and fury in a firestorm. "Where the fuck are they Drake?" My father demanded.

"They went to Floria to get Marie back home for you," Drake spat. The rage between them was palpable. I've never seen them rage at one another. They were like brothers almost.

"Where the fuck is Valyn and Luna?!" Harold shouted. My blood ran cold, why was he asking where they were. Drake just told him.

"They went to Floria with Fennik and Niklaus!" They were in each others faces now. Nox and Virgil took a stance behind Drake. Undas cleared his throat.

"Niklaus? Fennik? Where is my granddaughter and your brother?" Undas asked, my gaze shot to the door, horrified by what I saw. Fennik was covered in blood, and Niklaus was barely able to stand upright.

"Valyn was supposed to bring Luna here. Is he not here?" Niklaus said with a panic to his voice, falling forward only to be caught by Sirus.

"They're not here," Nox said, looking around the room. "What do you mean he was supposed to bring her here. What the fuck happened to my sister!?"

"Marie killed her," Fennik's voice was broken. He took a step into the room, collapsing to the floor. An arm shot out grabbing his shirt and hauling him up into his arms.

"Malicah!" my father yelled, "What are you doing here? You're supposed to be in Floria."

"My sister just imploded Fennik's life. And your other sons' lives. Niklaus didn't leave me there to suffer Tanis's wrath." Malicah said as he carried Fennik into the room placing him on the couch. "Marie's dead by the way."

"If she was dead Harold would know," Penelope began, but stopped and looked at Bastian and I. "Oh no. No. No. No!"

"You were right Cassandra. I guess she fooled me," my father said, placing his hand on Penelope, gathering her in his arms. All of our mothers began sobbing. Not for the loss of Marie, no. Reality just hit me like a ton of bricks.

"NO! You have to be wrong! Luna can't be dead!" I roared, fighting through the pain to get to Niklaus. Bastian's head snapped to me. The pain in our chests, the hollowness. The death of a mate is basically a literal death to those left living.

A throat cleared in the doorway, my head turning to see Valyn leaning against the doorframe, exhaustion spread across his face. "She's with Bethany. We need help." Valyn collapsed onto the floor, but our father was quick to catch him before he smacked his face into the hardwood. Nora moved faster than I'd seen her move in a very long time, she was up and out of the room in the blink of an eye. I meant to follow her, but I just blacked out as I tried to move.

Commotion around the room had me trying to sit up, but I couldn't move. My eyes opened to people moving about a brightly lit room, chatter coming from everywhere. People sounded angry, some sounded sad, and others sounded worried. A flash of black hair caught my eye, Bethany was moving about quickly. Checking in on several different beds all at once. We were at Listhrum. We had all passed out so badly that we needed medical attention. Fucking great.

"Prince Damian, please do not move. We had to restrain you and your brothers to keep you all safe. You guys were thrashing about, and it made it unsafe for us to try to administer any care," another of the younger priestesses spoke to me as if she was terrified of me.

"I'm sorry if we caused you all any issues. That was not the intent," I offered my apology. I felt bad for causing them any trouble. The young girl nodded her head and stepped up to the side of the bed to undo my restraints.

"High Priestess Maggie from the Mor is here overseeing you and your brothers care. She is currently seeing to Princess Luna with Queen Nora," she said as she unstrapped the last of the restraints. I sat up on the bed, taking in the room. The beds, the sitting couches, the chairs all filled in with bodies of our loved ones. Undas is the only one who didn't take a seat, he was pacing the room. I looked at each bed, Luna wasn't in a single one of them.

"Where are they?" I asked the young girl, but it was my brother who answered.

"She's in the main room, Maggie has forbidden us to go inside," Bastian said, sitting up on his own bed, staring a hole through the door as if he could see all the way through it to her. The aching hole in my chest wasn't feeling any better. I want to hug her; I wanted to wrap my arms around her and kiss her and for her to tell me everything is alright. She needs to be alright. I need her back.

"You all might not want to hear this, but she can't stay here. If Maggie and Nora can't bring her back here there are only two options. Oakenhall and Solaria. Oakenhall, you all can join. Solaria, none of you can come, well none except Damian," Vanalli said to us once we all were sitting up in our beds. I didn't even notice my other brothers were sitting in the room as well. I want to lash out at them for letting something happen to her, but Valyn looked like he was about to break, I couldn't do that to him.

"How would we know if they can bring her back?" Niklaus asked. The room fell silent. If they can't bring her back, I don't know what's going to happen to us if that happens. It can't happen. I won't let it happen.

"Not bringing her back isn't an option. Skip Oakenhall, take her to Valhime. I know that's what you mean Undas. She would have a better chance of being brought back in the city of the Gods," I say, looking straight at Undas as he stops in the center of the room.

"I don't want to forgo trying Oakenhall. They have some of the best healers there," Drake said and I understood why. If she goes to Valhime, he can't visit her.

"The healers are great in Oakenhall, but they are best for healing the living. Luna is no longer among the living, and we all know it. I don't want to acknowledge it, but only the death of a mate could render us incapable of moving and incapacitating us," I reply. "I want my wife back." I can feel the tears streaming down my face. I just want my wife.

Undas nodded, placing a hand on Drake's shoulder. "They have a right to make the choice, they are her husbands and mates. I know she is your daughter, but they have her best interest at heart."

"I know, I just feel like that should be a last resort. I don't want to send her to Valhime, you know Erina won't be happy about it," Drake said, head in hands. He was breaking just as much as we were. He just got her back.

"My sister wants her child back at any cost. Mom had Maggie give Erina a sedative. She is going to be down for a while. Holly and Vanessa said they will stay with Erina to make sure she is safe and doesn't do anything stupid. But we need to do something now. I adore your wife Harold, but her and Maggie can't bring her back," Sirus spoke as bluntly as possible. He wants her back just as much as the rest of us.

"Then let's go." I say, gently moving myself from the bed. I felt like I was walking on a ship. "The guys can come with us and stay at my place in Solaria. Everyone will be close enough to Valhime with them not being able to venture into the city itself. Sound like a good plan?"

The resounding yeses and nods gave me hope. We all want our wife back. I looked over at Fennik who hadn't moved from his bed. "Fen, what's wrong?" I ask him, moving closer to his bed. His uncle said he killed his mother; I couldn't imagine how that must have him feeling mentally.

"She said I wasn't his son," he said the words like an echo of himself. What the hell was he talking about. "She said she had a son before me and that she didn't want to be a mother to me."

Our father stood up, crossing the room to sit on the end of Fenniks bed. "You are my son. Your mother was going back to visit Floria often before we married. I swore she was my mate. Cassandra however did not. Instead of listening to her, I foolishly believed that your mother was my mate. Maggie however told me that she wanted to run a test when she found out that Marie was pregnant with you. Cassandra had told her that the others and her worried that something wasn't right. She ran the test as a blood test, claiming it would tell us what your powers would be before you were born. It confirmed that you were my child."

Fennik looked up at our father, tears swelling in his eyes, "So I'm still your son and their brother?"

"Yes, Fennik. You have always been my son. Your mother did have a child with Tanis a few years before you. His name is Elijah. I don't know much about him, but your uncle does. He hasn't really been sick. He's been taking a toxin that while it won't kill him, it will make him deathly ill. He feared that she was hiding something and that it was something that could hurt us all, so he called me and said if I ever needed his help, he was there. The toxin he's been taking for the last few years was to help him get your mother to Floria so he could see Elijah. He said Tanis was still alive, but I wasn't sure until tonight when Niklaus told me what happened. Are you alright?" Our father dumped all that information on Fennik and it was a lot to take in. I can't imagine him being alright.

"I thought you would be mad at me. I'm so sorry. I didn't mean to kill her, I just lost it when I saw what she did to Luna," Fennik sobbed out. My heart ached for my brother. I can't imagine what he went through. Our father hugged him tightly and looked back at us all.

"It's not your fault, I'm not mad at you. I love you. Boys, Fennik will stay here with me. I want to have him stay close with us while we get things fixed up around here," he said. We decided this was going to be the best option for Fennik. He needed the time and we needed to get going, we couldn't wait any longer.

"Boys, we have to get going. I'll get Luna from Maggie and Nora. Be ready to go when I get back," Undas said leaving us all in the room. We each gave Fennik a hug and moved out of the small, cramped room. Each of us had to get our things and get back to Mistveil quick. There was no portal to Solaria from anywhere in Hildaria. We have to get back home and fast. I don't want to think about how much time Luna has left before we can't bring her back.

CHAPTER 22
VALDIS

We paced around the main hall of Mistveil waiting for Undas to bring Luna through the portal from Mirith home. The aching pain in my chest was more and more unbearable as the night went on. Kieran called our parents to tell them what had happened, I wasn't expecting them to come to Mirith. My mother had always said that Erina and she were friends, it wasn't until tonight that I truly believed her. I had seen them all be nice with one another during the wedding and some political meetings here and there, but tonight was different. My mother embraced Erina and my father hugged Drake. I watched my mother sit with the other mothers consoling Erina and Vanalli. Harold, Drake and my father all sat there, drink in hands. The look of despair across their faces every time they looked our way.

We came here to Mistveil to get things ready to head to Solaria. A place I never once thought I would be invited to. War with Limbris would have to wait. If they do indeed take Floria while we are dealing with this, it just means that we will have to kill everyone in sight. I look over at Valyn who has been sitting on his suitcase for the past ten minutes, his eyes far away, sadness radiating from him. I cross the hall and take a seat next to him.

"You don't look alright. Do you want to stay here or go back to Mirith?" I ask him. I know that however long it takes, it's going to be painful and grueling. He watched it all happen in front of him, Niklaus too.

"She was in my arms Valdis. I couldn't stop Marie from hurting her. It all happened so fast," Valyn let the words spill from him like a confession he needed to get out.

"It's not your fault. You couldn't have predicted what she was going to do to her," I tried to comfort him. This was Luna's forte not mine. "What all happened? How did Marie get close enough to get to her?"

"Luna went full blown ethereal on her. Shadows blocking out all the natural sunlight, the only light we had was Luna. She was lit up like the fucking sun. But Niklaus and I saw her eyes shift to a galaxy like the other morning in the cafe. We knew that Luna was about to lose her shit. Niklaus and I both knew that if Luna hurt Marie, she wouldn't forgive herself. Fennik was in shock thanks to his mother and her absolute betrayal, he couldn't help. I managed to get to Luna first, I distracted her. I turned her away from Marie and that's when she struck. It's my fault she's gone Valdis. I couldn't save her," Valyn put his head in his hands, sobbing. Bastian walked over to us, dropping to his knees in front of his brother.

"This is not your fault. This is not anyone's fault but that of Marie's. They can help Luna in Valhime. Vanalli and Undas believe it, so I will keep my faith in the gods. I want Luna back, just as much as you do. Valyn, Luna wouldn't blame you. You know that. Do not blame yourself," he rested his hand on Valyn's knee. I should've known that they would be able to help each other. I may not be an outsider anymore, but I am not their brother.

"I love her Bastian. I feel like I let her down when she needed me most," Valyn looked up at his brother, whispering only enough for us to hear him. He glanced at me and placed a hand on my shoulder. "Thank you, brother."

"Undas will be here momentarily. We have to get ready to go," Damian expressed as he walked into the room. Before any of us could say anything, Undas walked into the room, carrying Luna in a black blanket. She looked so peaceful; her flesh paler than usual, the bright luster of her blue hair was dull and faded. I didn't want this image of her in my mind. I want her warmth and her laughter to be at the forefront of my mind, not this. I don't want to lose her. I love her so much.

"Let's get going. Vanalli will meet us there," Undas said somberly. I can't imagine what is going through his mind. The love for his granddaughter was strong. They had become like best friends since the wedding. I stood up, grabbing my suitcase. I packed some clothes for Luna for when they bring her back. I'm sure the others did as well. At least she'll have options. I wait for Bastian and Valyn, Niklaus was already pacing downstairs. He had followed Damian when he went to prep his home in Solaria for visitors. According to Bastian, they had family living close by that were eager to meet Luna after having to miss the wedding. Damian had to prepare them for what had happened.

Damian led us down a spiraling staircase, sconces lighting up in frosted glass enclosures as we walked down the steps. The staircase was carpeted with a plush black carpet that was soft under foot. As our feet hit the stone floor at the bottom, there were five doors ahead of us, each a beautiful different type of wood with an engravement of each realm, except the last one. It just had an M engraved in the center. That must be his room here. He reached for the door with a stunning sun engraved in the center, the blonde oak of the door a compliment to the realm beyond.

As Damian pushed open the door for Solaria, my breath was stolen as the stunning city sprawled out beyond. It was gorgeous, tall spires of gold danced in the sunlight from the ground up. The city was sparkling gold as the sun shined brightly on the white and gold buildings. A tall clock tower with a golden bell sat in what looked to be the center of the city. "Welcome to Solaria. I should warn you, today is a day for the dead. We celebrate those we lost, and those who are still fighting their battles. My aunt Allura reminded me of this when I came here to give them the heads up of the situation with Luna. Getting to Valhime through the secondary portal will be the best option, Undas."

Undas just nodded and stepped through the door, bending slightly at the waist to make it through. He's been silent since the news of Luna's death. Sirus wanted to come with us, but someone needed to be around Fennik and the rest of her family. They needed the strength. Hell, we all did.

One by one we all crossed over; I went through last to make sure Valyn went through first. He was a little better now that we talked to him and let him get out his feelings, but I am still very worried about him. Undas followed Damian to another door on the opposite side of the courtyard, the door was painted gold with a constellation I didn't recognize etched into the door. "That's the door to Valhime. The constellation on the door is Pitreo. The guiding light home, or at least that's what we are told. Supposedly, it is one of the gods we lost during the first war," Bastian leaned in, whispering to me.

"Are all the constellations named after gods?" I asked as we moved further into the courtyard. It's intriguing that every portal leads into a courtyard in the family's homes. Out are somewhat similar, I guess. Each doorway to another city is directly tied to another Royal family's home. Luckily, we need to extend and invite to the others to allow them to us our doors.

"That's the belief. Every time a god or goddess falls, their souls become a constellation. I'm hoping we don't see another one in the sky tonight," Bastian whispered the last part. I don't want to see a new one either. My heart wouldn't be able to take it. Undas didn't wait for any of us to catch up before walking through the door to Valhime. I don't blame him though. His wife was already home and waiting for him. Damian turned around to see us just standing there watching.

"Allura is inside. She has set up rooms for everyone. Please make yourselves at home. Once I get everything situated here, I will be joining Undas and Vanalli in Valhime," he announced, stepping past us heading for the house.

"Wait, why can you go, and we can't?" I blurted out, I wanted to be by her side when she woke up.

"The gods have allowed the royal family of the solar and lunar realms access to the city for political purposes and in some instances, religious purposes. How do you think the world got word of the religious texts and how the temples were made in the likeness of the gods? They instructed everything to be created the way it was. Solaria is home to the most religious and loyal citizens to the gods. No offense to Undas and Vanalli or to Luna and her family, but that's why I don't come here very often. I am not a fan of the overly religious folk here," Damian explained as we entered his home.

There was so much white and gold that Damian looked out of place. His dark red hair and beard were stark against the marble white flooring and the white walls. It looked like we were inside a temple. I'm not fully happy with how bright it is here. I don't think any of us like the brightness, Bastian is scowling at the room, Valyn hasn't stopped looking at the floor and Niklaus has had his nose turned up since the moment we walked in.

We stopped in front of a large grand staircase, plush gold carpet flowing down the stairs with silver trim. Things this bright usually are eviler than the darkest of places I've ever been to. A tall, curvy woman appeared at the top of the stairs. short golden hair accentuated her face, but it was her stark blue eyes that had me concerned at who she might be. She wore a floor length white gown that hugged her hips and breasts, gold arm cuffs accentuated his biceps. The look on her face was reserved, almost calculating. Clearly, she was older than Niklaus, but looking at the others, they didn't seem to back down from that look.

"Allura," Bastian said by way of greeting. "This is Valdis, he is part of our mating group. Don't be a bitch to him, he's not like the others." Ah, so that explains the look she's giving me. She either is old enough to remember the first war or was a part of the second one. Both happened before my time. She, however, look too young to have been in either. Maybe she read about them or knew someone who told her stories. Either way, I was not a part of either of those wars. That blood is not on my hands.

"I will make my decision on him once I speak to him alone. He will not be permitted to walk the streets of our sacred city, we don't need panic," she scoffed at me. I wanted to say something, but I was raised with manner, my mother would be appalled if I was rude or disrespectful to an elder. I bowed to her.

"I completely understand, I wouldn't want to cause anyone alarm or panic," I say, forcing my words to not sound harsh. I should've expected this once Damian gave the backstory of the realm. But I am not like the daemons who attacked here all those millennia ago. I straighten and look to the rest of the group, Bastian and Damian kept their gazes laser focus on Allura, Niklaus was staring at me wide eyed I guess in disbelief that I was being so kind to her blatant rudeness, but it was Valyn who stepped up next to me and put his hand on my shoulder. A silent but very public display of loyalty, one I didn't know I needed.

He looked over at Damian, "I think if Allura wants to execute a daemon inquisition, we might better be suited to wait elsewhere," Valyn said to Damian. I was expecting some type of retort about us leaving and being elsewhere, but none came.

"I think that's a grand idea. Please tell Melody that I appreciate her setting up rooms, but we won't be staying where one of our brothers will be kept inside like a prisoner. Do be mindful though Allura, I will let my mother know of Valdis's treatment. I don't think she will take kindly to it," he spoke as if he was giving a deep warning that I didn't notice.

Allura laughed, "If your mother wants to have words, by all means, tell her to come seek me out. Penelope too. I am not afraid of my sisters." She turned from us, "By the way, I sent Meldoy away the moment you called on her. She isn't here." Damian let out a growl, but Bastian held onto his shoulder.

"She's not worth it. I already sent a message to our moms. Let them handle the salty bitch. Melody probably went to Noctum. Let's just go there. I know it's slightly further away from Valhime, but I can get them there. You go to Undas and tell him what's going on," Bastian had a clearer head today than the rest of us. Maybe it's because he had Luna last, he was with her alone for the longest time. Either that or he was just more determined than we knew.

"I can handle the accusations and being blamed for what former daemons did. I can handle whatever she throws my way. We don't have to leave," I say, trying to convince them not to put themselves out on my account.

"Absolutely not. Also, could you imagine when Luna comes back to us her finding out that our aunt treated you like trash how that would end for Allura. I don't think we'd have an aunt left," Damian chuckled.

"I'm not against that. I'm also not against telling her about Allura's poor treatment of Valdis just so she can make her bite her words," Bastian shrugged. Everyone chuckled. Talking about Luna is probably the only thing keeping us from cracking. Damian leads way to four doors similar to those in Mistveil.

"These doors will take you to the other realms. Feel free to come and go as you please. Just a warning, there is a door in the dusk realm that will take you to the twilight realm, it's an inescapable prison that if you get stuck in there, it will take me some time to get you out," Damian's warning sent a chill down my spine. Okay, no going through random doors in the dusk realm, got it. "I'm going to head to Valhime now. I'll message you guys once I know more. Be safe."

Without Luna, these goodbyes seem harder on us. "Be safe, Damian. We will see you soon." I say as I follow the others through the door, "and thank you." With that, the door closed, leaving us to find out way through Noctum. We looked up at the night sky and a sob ripped through me. No.

"There, next to the Northern Star, is that a?" Niklaus questioned, but we already knew. A new constellation formed next to the Northern Star. Our Luna was now apart of the stars.

Part Two

Only Stardust

CHAPTER 23
LUNA

Darkness swallowed me up, stars twinkling all around me, an unknown voice calling my name in the distance. I felt like I was floating, soaring through the midnight sky with nothing to bother me, no pain, no sorrow, no agony. Just me, endlessly existing in the stars. That voice calls out to me once more, trying to drag me back to the world of light and darkness. I don't want to feel that pain anymore, I don't want to return to the world below. There's nothing expected of me here. No fighting, no war, no sorrow.

"There is also very little love for you here, Luna," a female voice tenderly speaks to me, as if answering my complaints aloud.

"That's not true Talissa, stop being mean," another female voice chides the first. I hear giggling and others lowly speaking around me. The stars are so noisy, I wasn't expecting that. "Of course, the stars are noisy, it's not like we are just balls of gas that are lit up by the moon silly. Open your eyes."

Huh? My eyes are open, at least that's what I thought. I tried to remember how to function, my eyes felt heavy, my limbs like lead. Ugh, so I guess I was just dreaming of a more beautiful peaceful existence. I finally crack my eyes open and look up, the blinding light from my surroundings has me squinting to see the two clearly female figures standing over me. "Come on, let's get you up," the first female voice says again, what did the other one call her? Talissa? Why did that name sound so damn familiar?

"Where am I?" I ask, my voice sounding so foreign to me. A light lithe undertone has my voice coming out more ethereal, a higher octave than before. I look down at my body, still pale like a porcelain doll, but with a shimmer of glitter covering me. "And why am I covered in glitter?"

A giggle escapes the other woman's lips, "that's not glitter, it's stardust. You're in Illeria, the home of the gods and goddesses who have passed on from Cerulia." She was sweet, a kind smile graced her lips. "We're here to great you and welcome you to your afterlife. We know all about you Luna, and everything you went through while you were alive."

"Lumina, give her a moment. She needs to adjust before you start bombarding her with information," Talissa said, her voice sounding so much like my mother and my grandmother. Her skin was like mine, porcelain, a light. Her long, wavy silver hair had hints of opal coloring shining through as she moved about. She had freckles like me, except hers looks more like stars of purple and blues, but her eyes, a beautiful lavender reminded me of Vanalli.

"I know you," I whisper, causing her to whip her head back to me. "You're Talissa, my aunt." Talissa looked at Lumina, a shocked expression crossing their faces.

"You shouldn't know about me. Well, at least you shouldn't be able to remember what was told to you about me," Talissa replied, her eyes reflecting a warning of sorts as she looked at Lumina, immediately putting herself between the two of us. "You're going to have to come with us, Illeria keeps families together. Hence why we came to get you, but we are usually the ones who have to remind you of your life. You shouldn't be able to remember anything."

Talissa reaches down to grab my hand and help me up. I take a few staggering steps forward, watching as they move with such grace and elegance. I must look like a newly born deer trying to walk for the first time. They slow their pace for me as we make our way into a city that looked like stardust and moonlight all combined. I guess that makes sense since the only time you can see the gods is during the night.

"There are others here, your great grandparents, a great aunt, a great uncle and then myself and my mates. You will get to meet those that have passed long before you, I feel like we should probably have you meet your great grandparents first. You remind me of my sister. Is she well?" Talissa asked me as we crossed through a large black archway made of obsidian. The city is beautiful, everything looked like it was modern. The homes were cottage style, lush greenery and flowers decorated yards and front porches. The walkways were paved with pavers that looked like onyx, but I could be wrong. But everyone seemed happy. There wasn't any arguing that I could hear, no rumors of the impending war, nothing bad seemed to be going on here.

"You said I have other family here, are they also constellations?" I ask as I catch up to Talissa and Lumina. "I was told that every constellation is a god or goddess."

Lumina laughed, her green eyes reminded me of Fennik's, but her long, wavy golden hair reminded me of Niklaus. A pain shot through my chest as the memory of my death flashed before my eyes. I stopped walking and dropped to my knees in the middle of the walking path. "Talissa!" Lumina cried, dropping to her knees beside me. "What's wrong Luna?"

"My chest, it hurts," I gasp out. Talissa moves to the other side of me, helping me back to my feet.

"It will hurt, you might have just confirmed my theory about you not belonging here. We need to hurry," Talissa threw my arm over her shoulder, she carried most of my weight as I felt like I was on fire. "Your mates are still alive right?" I nod, I can't speak through this pain. "They are feeling the same thing. It's the bond refusing to let you go. Mine was the same way, so was my mates. We need to get you to Illisandra and Otius. They're my mother's parents, they also were one of the first families in Illeria. They should have some answers for you."

We enter a rather large castle like home, made of stone and obsidian, the front door was a beautiful cherry oak with an engravement of the moon phases on it. Talissa pushed open the door and entered, Lumina on her heels. My pain subsided a few minutes ago so I was able to walk the rest of the way. Talissa warned me it could come and go in waves. The inside of the castle was just as magnificent as the outside. Plush deep purple rugs lined the floors, all a dark hardwood. The fireplace in the room was roaring to life with a fire of blue flames. A couch and two chairs were occupied when we entered the room. One male looked over the back of the couch with a wide smile on his face. He was handsome, olive skin pulled tight on extreme muscles, blue eyes the color of the seas, with raven black hair cropped tight on the sides. I just wasn't expecting him to be towering over me when he stood. He rivaled even my grandfather in size.

"Talissa, Lumina! You're back!" He rushed over to Talissa, wrapping her up in his arms and planting kisses all over her face. Her smile was infectious, her laugh the sound of a beautiful symphony that I could picture Kira and Harper dancing too. Another wave of sadness ruptured through me, but I could hold myself together for this one.

"Who is this?" The man set Talissa down gently, still keeping his arm around Talissa. I straightened up and held my hand out.

"My name is Princess Luna Embros, daughter of Drake and Erina Embros, granddaughter of Undas and Vanalli. It's a pleasure to meet you," I put on my best official voice, but listing it all off stung. I took a moment and added, "at least that was my title." I looked down at the floor, trying to hold back tears.

The man took my hand and shook his gingerly, "It's a pleasure to meet you princess. The names River, I am one of Talissa's mates. And seeing as you named her sister as your mother, that means I'm technically your uncle." He laughed and let go of Talissa for the first time since meeting him. "That fiery redhead over there is Ignis, the stunning blue-haired goddess over there is Voxis, and the grumpy looking shorty over there is Claye. We are all mates to your aunt. Welcome to the family."

His smile was broad, I looked at each of the gods that he named and smiled, then to the goddess Voxis, she was watching me with intense eyes. "What are your powers?" she asked bluntly as she stood up, moving between myself and Talissa.

"That's so rude of you," Lumina said to Voxis, but I understood. Even though I was family, I was an outsider to them, a risk she needed to assess.

"It's okay, let's see, mainly I can control fire and shadows, but before my untimely demise I was learning to control water, ice and snow, and some healing. There was a belief that I might've been able to control the same things that my husbands could. I guess I won't know now," the sadness threatened to collapse me again. Talissa pushed past Voxis and River and grabbed my hands.

"It's okay, if I'm right, you don't belong here. You might be able to go back to them," she smiled at me, she was much softer now than she was when I first met her. "Let's get you upstairs, Otius is most likely in his office and if he's in there Illisandra will be with him. They should have some answers for you."

"Wait, you said you can control the elements. Is that with the help of your mates or can you produce elements without them?" Ignis asked from the chair he was sitting in, looking around at everyone, I noticed a tension in the room that I didn't sense previously.

"I can produce it without them. They aren't my source. We were going to be exploring that after I got home from Floria. Clearly that isn't going to happen," I say, balling my hands into fists. I swear if Marie hurt anyone else, I will find a way to haunt her ass.

"Why didn't you return home?" Voxis asked, her cool voice slowly warming as she took in my reaction.

"My mother-in-law stabbed me. I should say monster-in-law, the woman hated me from the moment she found out that I was mated to her son. She was happy when I mated to three of my mates but when her son's bond kicked in, I was the monster stealing her son away from the life she wanted for him," I said, anger still seeping through me.

"Talissa, how does she remember things? Isn't she new here?" Claye asks from across the room. I guess Claye and Ignis didn't see me as a threat like Voxis did. "It took us a very long time and help from your grandparents to remember everything."

"I don't know," Talissa admitted. She looked at me with sorrow in her eyes. "I'm sorry your mother-in-law treated you so badly and hurt you. That's not okay." She threw her arms around me and squeezed me.

"Luna," Lumina said my name with a curiousness to it. "You asked if all gods and goddesses became constellations. Why did you ask that?" I straighten, and step back from Talissa, looking over at Lumina.

"You all are the Northen Star. The holy union in the sky. I was told that each constellation is that of a fallen god or goddess and that you all were blessed to be together in the stars forever. I thought that was a thing. Granted Undas believes you all are just resting, regaining your strength and selves to return to Cerulia." As I spoke, I watch shadows darken each of their eyes. Maybe we were wrong. Maybe the constellations had nothing to do with a fallen all mighty.

"When did this Northen Star appear?" River asked, pulling Talissa in tight to his side, shielding her from the rest of the room.

"I don't know. The way it seemed to me was that it appeared shortly after you all," I stopped myself from saying the word. I didn't think it was right to, especially with them right in front of me. Attainable, in physical forms.

"After we died." Voxis bluntly continued my sentence for me. I nod, but I feel incredibly stupid for even asking. "Are you sure your grandparents will know what to do with her Talissa?"

"I hope so. My niece doesn't deserve to be here. I can feel it. I know Otius doesn't believe in my feelings, but maybe this time he will," she said, her face still buried in River's chest. I knew that feeling all too well. Being so overwhelmed by my surroundings that only the comfort of my mates can calm me. I miss them all so much.

"Maybe we should talk to Milara and Zephir first. They may be able to help when it comes to talking to Otius," Ignis offers, standing looking back at the stairs. "I've only met them a few times, but they are more likely to try and help then turn you away for your feelings." Talissa looks at him with fondness in her eyes, nodding.

"Is it wrong that I have no idea who you're talking about?" I ask, feeling out of place right now.

"My father and mother haven't talked to you about their families?" Talissa seemed shocked by this revelation. Lumina made it seem like they knew all about me. Maybe that was a lie to make me feel safe.

"What all do you know about me?" I asked rather bluntly. Talissa glanced over at Lumina, she was smiling from ear to ear as if I had just asked her to give out a research report on some type of far-off planet.

"I know that you are a very powerful goddess, coming into her powers newly so not much is known on exactly what you're capable of. I also know that you were forcibly abandoned by your mom when you were younger. You grew up to fast, taking care of a sibling who is not blood, a half sibling who treated you so poorly and a false father who could've told you the truth whenever he wanted. You have several mates like your aunt here, each a descendant from our bloodlines, well all but one. I also know that you've only recently gone through the changing where most of our kind go through it much younger. That's wrong actually, you didn't go through the true changing. You only went through a magical changing of sorts. You are going through the true change now," Lumina listed off my life up until Floria as if it was written in stone.

"Wait! She hasn't gone through the changing yet?!" River exclaims, looking at me with a wide smile. Lumina jumped slightly at his outburst. Talissa looked up at River with a questioning look in her eyes. "She hasn't gone through the changing, yet she's here. How is that possible?"

As if realizing something that they missed, Lumina gasped loudly. Everyone huddled around us now, I was used to big groups, but this was different; not a single mate was mine. What I wouldn't give to be with Bastian back at Lake Minerva just one more time, or in Oakenhall with Niklaus in my room. Or in Bastian's backyard with Fennik and Valdis again. I miss Valyn, I miss Damian. I miss feeling safe and just curling up in their arms as if nothing is wrong.

"She's not dead," Lumina breathed out. The whole room stopped breathing. What did she just say?

"How is that?" Voxis questioned, looking at me like I was wrong. Like something was wrong with me. Maybe there is something wrong with me. Maybe I have always been defective. Can't even die right.

"She is going through the changing now, don't you remember when you went through it?" She glances around at everyone, each giving her a look like she was crazy. "We become invincible during the change. That's why it happens when we are children. She had a magical suppression on her, she wasn't able to go through it when she was a child. Also, what was used to stab you?"

Lumina turns her gaze to me and I just shrug, "I don't know. I kind of wasn't myself when it happened, I was legit stabbed in the back. Valyn was trying to calm me down, so I didn't obliterate my mother-in-law. Still wish he would've just let me live with the guilt."

"There is only a certain blade found in the Ruins of Decay on the Isle of Souls. The only people who are cleared to enter the ruins however are the royal families of the solar and lunar realms. No one else can go in there without triggering a set of traps and being stuck inside for at minimum a year. Alric and Elucia had a very sick twisted mind when it came to keeping people out of the temples that originally sat there before becoming ruins." Lumina explained to everyone. "If that blade wasn't retrieved, there is no way you should be here. Talissa is right."

"Undas believes you all don't belong here either. He talked about you becoming stars just to basically recharge," I went on to explain everything Undas had told me. Tears streamed down Talissa's face by the time I was done and I felt horrible.

"My father is such a kind and gentle man despite looking like he is a wild bear half the time. I miss him," Talissa spoke softly, I wasn't sure if she was talkin to me or to the rest of the room. "Luna, I don't think he is right though. We have been here for so long that if his theory was correct, wouldn't we be alive again?"

"What if something's stopping you from going back? I mean, you can physically touch me and according to you and Lumina, I shouldn't be here. Maybe you just haven't found your path back yet," I blurt out, clearly thinking out loud. "What if that's why I'm here?"

"I would ask Otius, he was one of the first gods here. An original one might say," Voxis spoke, her tone softening as she spoke to me. "Ignis could be right though. Milara and Zephir might have more answers. They were also one of the first families here too."

"Wanna go meet your great-grandparents?" Talissa asks me as she removes herself from River's arms. Voxis pulls her over to her, wrapping her arms around her, placing a few soft kisses to her head.

"What do I have to lose?"

CHAPTER 24
TALISSA

Seeing Luna in the flesh is completely different from seeing her in Lumina's crystals. Her blue hair reminding me of Voxis, her pale skin a mirror image to mine, her brown and golden eyes a mix of Claye's and Ignis's. From watching her through the crystals, her personality is a sparking match to River's, carefree and loving. She displays Lumina's determination as well. She is just as fierce to protect her mates like me, and she has put herself in danger to save them so many times. To know that she hasn't even gone through the changing yet, she's ran into danger as a human, as a fae. She is unbelievable.

"Solima has taken a liking to Luna," River said as he entered into our room. Solima was a cute little doglike creature, translucent most of the times, but black and white when it forced itself to be physical. "You should've seen her face, she immediately dropped to her knees and started giving it all the loves and pets. She reminds me of you."

"I see all of us in her. I don't know how though; she is Erina's child. And I see my little sister in her so much," I think long and hard. I haven't seen Erina in so long. Does she even remember me. What about Sirus? We were so close, he needed the protection from himself, and I haven't been there for him like I should've been.

"Your nose is crinkling sweetheart. What is going on in that beautiful mind of yours?" River collapsed on the bed next to me, running his fingers through my hair. Voxis and Ignis said they were going to get us set up for the morning to go see Milara and Zephir. I wish I would've taken their offer to come live with them when I first came here, I feel like they would've treated me a little better. Nothing against Illisandra and Otius, but they are so strict. It's no wonder my mother was such a rebellious woman.

"I'm thinking about my siblings. About Sirus and if he has ever found love or his mate. About Erina going through hell being forced out of Luna's life. Hell, I have a half nephew who is apparently a little shit, and then there's my other nephew who is intensely protective of my niece. I left them, I chose to go into battle alone that night River. If I would've just listened to my father, we all would still be walking the lands of Cerulia, not existing here." I sigh, ever since she got here something felt off. I always felt like something was wrong here. Like none of us belonged, the gods and goddesses can die, but normally never killed unless it was with a sacred blade like Lumina said. Daemons couldn't kill us, yet here are. "What if Luna is right and we aren't supposed to be here?"

"We gave you our powers to defeat the Daemons. You exhausted all power you carried with you and that's how we are here. Talissa, if she is right, then we are stopping ourselves from returning to Cerulia. Zephir said something along the lines that we shouldn't be here long. He made it seem like this was just a temporary existence we were blessed with. At least that's how I looked at it, that we had one last time together before moving on to our true end," River placed kisses on my shoulders up to my neck. "As for your sister and brother, why don't you just ask Luna how they are? She has been with them; she may be able to set your heart and mind at ease."

"That if we can go back. Would we still remember our time from here, will we remember each other? I don't want to risk losing you all again. I can't do that," tears stream down my face. River catches each tear, wiping them away and flicking them into the air, turning them into little water creatures before they vanish. He was trying to make me smile.

"Lissa, if we are going to ask the question, it's something we want. You miss your family, we all have our elders here, which is nice, but we each miss our families. A chance to see them all again would be lovely," River whispers into my skin, as his fingers slowly run up and down my back mindlessly. "Also, if we go back, we can start that family we always said we wanted."

Shivers ran down my spine as his words settled low between my thighs. We always said we wanted a baby. We just never said who would start first. Voxis and Lumina were against having babies, but I think they might soften up to the idea if we can actually go back home and have one. I always wanted one. It was my dream to be a mom. I was looking forward to it, but when the war got worse, I gave up the idea of having one. I didn't want to raise a child in a warzone.

"If we go back, there is another war going on. The only difference is my niece is in my place. She has mates who would gladly sacrifice themselves for her, she clearly would sacrifice herself for them," before I could finish my sentence River had my lips trapped with his. He pulled me on top of him, thrusting his hands in my hair as he held me in this kiss of passion.

"She has something we didn't have," he whispers on my lips. "She has a prince of Hellis as her mate. You and I both know that he could be the changing point for her in this war." River kissed me once more, biting at my lower lip. "All we can do is be there for her, the way her mother and your brother were there for us."

I pressed myself against River's body steadying my breathing, "You're right," I breath. "She might have a better chance of coming out of this alive, if we can get her back that is."

River ran his hands down my back, holding me tightly to him. I took a deep breath, breathing in the salty sea on him. He hasn't been in the seas in so long that his scent is slowly starting to fade. Everyone is, we are starting to smell like here. I don't know how I feel about our scents mixing with this place. I always felt out of place here, like I didn't belong. Maybe she is right; maybe we aren't meant to be here. I press my lips to Rivers, one day at a time. We always took things one day at a time. This will be no different.

River knew what I needed, his hands gliding down my skin. We didn't need to have sex to get our fill of each other. Granted, sex is fun. But tonight our minds aren't on that, it's on the future. One we all thought was out of reach. "If we do make it back to Cerulia and Luna is right, I want to start our family immediately."

River chuckled and kissed me on the nose, "Sweetheart, the moment our feet touch Cerulia soil, you will get everything you want." He pulled me close, letting me snuggle into his chest until I was slowly falling into a deep slumber. Tomorrow would start the beginning of a future for us, hopefully.

CHAPTER 25
LUNA

I wasn't expecting to sleep like I did. The night and day here merge into one, you can't tell what's nighttime and what's daytime as easily as you can on Cerulia. I mean they probably have their way of figuring it out, but I'm hoping not to be here long enough to find out. Lumina and Claye have been buzzing about this morning, getting things together to go see my great-grandparents. Talissa seemed shocked that I didn't know who they were, but I guess part of me just didn't realize that I could have great-grandparents that I would ever meet. I also never thought to ask Undas or Vanalli about their parents. I wonder if they have siblings.

"Do you need help?" I ask Lumina as she puts together meals for us while we travel. I wasn't sure how far we had to go, but the way they were acting, it must be slightly far. Lumina placed sandwiches and water skins in a basket, adding fresh fruits and some cut up vegetables to the mix too.

"I think we have everything ready to go. Oh, Undas hasn't told you about his parents, has he?" Lumina's question was innocent, but I felt bad because I could've asked him when I had the chance. It's not all on him. I shook my head instead of letting the guilt eat at me. "That's slightly odd, but not as much as Talissa is making it seem. Undas and his parents had a beautiful relationship, but they passed away before Talissa was born. Undas was devastated, he took care of his sister the moment he was old enough to so his parents didn't have to. Gods who lived as long as they did just pass from extreme old age. I'm not sure exactly how old they were, but I know Undas used to say that they were alive when Cerulia was born." Lumina answered one of my questions without me even having to ask.

"Is Undas' sister here?" I ask, curiosity eating at me. Lumina just shook her head. Well, I guess that was a good thing, hopefully he still had her.

"You can meet her if you ever make it to Valhime. She lives on the outskirts of the city in Fireheart Manor with your grandparents. She is the legit meaning of intensity. I got to know her before the war. She would love you," Lumina quipped as she finished loading the basket. I chewed on my bottom lip thinking about everything I didn't know about. I know Undas and Vanalli wanted me to come visit them in Valhime, and I was planning on it when things calmed down between Fennik and Marie. Would I even be able to go there now?

"You are just like your mother," Talissa remarked as her and River walked into the room. Claye pulled Talissa into his arms, planting a big kiss on her cheek. Her words confused me, I didn't think I was anything like my mom. Well aside from my eyes.

"How so?" I ask, taking a seat at the table where Lumina was pushing me, putting fruits and cheese in front of me. I poked around the plate, eyes the glass of water Lumina had placed in front of me. It had an opalescent hue to it, why? I must've made a face because they started laughing at me. Looking up at them all, I noticed the smiles on everyone's faces. I had no idea Ignis, Voxis or River had entered the room, but they all looked so happy.

"It's not poisoned if that's what you're worried about," Claye's booming voice echoed through the small room. Grabbing a glass off of the counter he filled it from the same pitcher that Lumina had filled mine with. The same hue danced and swirled around in his glass, he put it to his lips and down the hatch it went. "We don't know why the water is like that here, but it hasn't done any damage to us." He chuckles.

"How do you know it hasn't done damage?" I ask, but Talissa took a seat in the chair across from me and smiled. She was taking in my features, the way I held myself. Not expecting a royal princess to be sitting across from her. Thank the gods for that because I forgot all of my formal training.

"To answer your first question, you look like your mother and act like her too. At least the Erina I remember. I don't know what she's like right now, but she questioned everything when she was younger. A sweet, innocent child. She used to chew on her lip too when she was deep in thought," Talissa laughed. "As for the water, we can't tell if it is causing issues or not. But we've been drinking it since we got here, and nothing has happened. If you don't want to drink it, that's fine.

There's a juicer thing in the cabinet if you would rather make yourself some juice before we leave."

"Thank you, I appreciate it. I just don't trust things that shine when they're not supposed to," I said. Lumina pulled the juicer out, placing it on the counter for me. I did what I would always do for Lilly when she was sick and made fresh orange juice, but enough for everyone not just me. I poured it out into glasses and placed them on the counter. "I used to make fresh juice for my sister when she was sick. It's not going to be super sweet, but it's all natural."

River was the first person to grab a glass off of the table and take a sip. His eyes widened and he chugged the whole thing down before looking at the others. "Why haven't we ever used that thing?"

"Because it's a pain in the ass," Ignis retorted, grabbing a glass and sniffing it before taking a sip. His eyes flashed a bright gold with flecks of green sparkling throughout. They weren't that bright the other day. It made me take a look at Rivers eyes; they were a much brighter blue with teal specks peppered throughout them. That definitely wasn't there yesterday.

One by one they each grabbed a glass of juice and drank it. One by one, their eyes all sparkled with flecks of other colors throughout. What the hell could that be from? "Let's get going. The trips not that long, but it's still early, less people to run into," Voxis announced, her shoulder length blue hair braided back. She looked like such an elegant warrior, slender and lean, tall, stoic even. She smiled at me, a nodded her head. I didn't understand whatever she was trying to get through to me, but something was different this morning.

"Ready whenever you guys are," I said, drinking my juice down and rinsing the glass. The water here just looked like I couldn't trust it and I wasn't going to trust it.

They all broke off to talk around the island in the middle of the kitchen. The room was made of stone and wood, with an assortment of herbs and flowers drying out on rope that was hanging along the far side wall. The kitchen was cozy and looked utterly like nature was spilling into the room. Lumina separated from the group, grabbing a pot from the counter and filling it with water. I watched as she placed the pot on the stove, lighting the burner below it.

"Lumina is always trying to find answers to things. We never questioned anything here. You now have us questioning a few things. Lumina, Claye and Voxis are going to be staying behind. So, you're stuck with me, Ignis and Talissa. Hope you're cool with that," River explained, I jumped a little, not noticing that he had parted off from the group.

"What do you mean, I have you questioning things?" I ask, curiously raising my brow as I stare up at the giant of a man. He cracks a wide smile at me and I feel slightly uneasy, not like he's about to hurt me, but more like I asked the right question.

"Let's save that for the walk over to your grandparents," River said, nudging my arm before excusing himself to be back by Talissa's side.

He reminded me so much of Valyn. His body language around Talissa reminds me of how carefree Valyn was with me. I wonder if he's okay.

"Let's get going. I have a feeling they're already expecting us," Talissa announced, kissing each of her mates as she made her way through the kitchen. I grabbed the basket Lumina packed for us off of the counter. Lumina looked at me, giving me the sweetest of smiles, before turning back to some random concoction she was making on the stove. Talissa moved quickly through the house, Ignis and River flanking her like they have probably done every day since they mated. I watched as I took her in. The way she moved with fluid grace, her hair swishing around her waist as she walked, the way she laughed and danced around River as he playfully teased her. My attention turned to Ignis; his eyes locked onto every movement she made. He kept close enough to subtly stroke her fingers as she gently reached out to him, while still talking to River. Ignis seemed just happy to enjoy the subtleness of her touches, and just being in her presence.

We headed outside, the sky still dark with stars and galaxies dancing above us. It was weird to think that we are in a physical place even though we have died. I don't feel any different, aside from some poking and prodding I feel around my wound. I couldn't see it; I couldn't inspect it to make sure it was there. I bet it would leave a gnarly scar if I was alive. All of my mates would love the scar as if it was a part of me since they day they met me. My heart ached thinking about them. Worry about how they are feeling, how they are handling my death. Valyn most of all, I was in his arms.

The bond in my chest is still yearns for them, beckoning me to go to them. I don't think it realizes that I can't. River slowed his pace and walked next to me, grabbing the basket from my hands, "I got his. Should've grabbed it sooner." I watched as Ignis and Talissa fell into their own loving pace, holding each other's hands as we walked the stone path out of the small town.

"Thank you," I whispered, averting my gaze to the ground in front of me. My bond lit up a bright teal light in my chest. I closed my eyes, picturing my loving summer prince. His silver hair and bright teal eyes flash in my mind, the look of sadness and despair written across his face. *I miss you so much*. I think to the image of Valyn, his eyes snap up to look dead at me.

Luna?! Is that you?!

CHAPTER 26
VALYN

I heard her! I know I fucking heard her. I kick back from the table, the wooden chair crashing to the stone floor behind me. The quiet chattering of voices around me stills as they all look at me. Bastian comes up beside me, placing his hand on my shoulder.

"What is it?" he whispers just so I can hear him. Tears streak down my cheeks, disappearing into my beard. I turn my head to look at him once more. My eyes pained from crying, meet with his own red, puffy eyes.

"I heard her," I whisper. No one was breathing at this point. Every set of eyes that could see me, kept watch as I pushed back from the table, pacing. "I fucking heard her voice and don't tell me it's just what I want to hear." I glare at Niklaus who has been drowning himself in bourbon since we got to Noctum.

"What do you mean you heard her?" He looked at me with a puzzling gaze. Bastian was standing still, frozen to the spot. It was bad enough that we saw a new constellation next to the Northern Star when we entered Noctum, but we all refused to believe she was gone.

"She said I miss you so much. I fucking saw her; I saw stars around her and a tall figure with her. I don't know who that figure was or where she could be, but my bond has been screaming at me to find her," I say dropping half assed back into the chair.

"A tall figure?" Valdis questioned me as he sat at the table across from me. "Out of all of us you had the closer mental bond with her. You were teaching me how to mentally be with her from Hellis. Focus Valyn, if anyone can reach her in the afterlife, it's you."

A glass shattered against the wall behind us. The bourbon glass that was in Niklaus's hand was now shattered all over the floor, amber liquid splashed on the wall. "You're talking as if she is dead." Niklaus bit out the words, clutching his hands into fists. "They will fix everything in Valhime. She will be okay. Maybe this is a sign she's not dead."

That thought never occurred to me. What if they already brought her back in Valhime but something went wrong? I close my eyes and try to follow the faint blue flame back to her. A small little ember explodes as I close my eyes tighter and focus on her energy. The wildfire in her soul, those chocolate brown eyes with flecks of gold throughout, her free spirit, everything that makes her who she is. The little ember so close to my heart dances happily, it's probably the most comforting thing I have had since I lost her.

Suddenly, I see her again. The tall figure beside her is a giant of a man, hair as dark as the night sky, eyes a brilliant sapphire, his skin looked like he was out in the sun for hours a day. I feel something akin to comfort that he is with her. I don't know who he is, or why I wouldn't feel jealous, but I don't. I can see through her eyes, the world around her looks like it's hanging in the stars, and maybe it is. The man is making her laugh, and others. Luna is surrounded by two others as well. A woman who looks almost identical to her, and another man with fiery red hair and golden eyes. They were all smiling.

I miss you so much my love. I am so sorry I failed you. I love you. I hope you can hear me wherever you are. I push my words to her, hoping she can hear me. Maybe that she can feel me trying to hold her.

Valyn if this is really you and not my heart just being an asshole, you didn't fail me. If anything, I failed you all. I love you so much. Her words dance around my mind, pulling me to her. I can make out her body, the porcelain skin now dusted with glitter, her eyes don't look the same though. The once golden flecked brown eyes are now the color of the galaxy, blues, purples, and greens, the brown still hiding behind the new hues fighting for control. Her dark blue hair had an opalescent hue to it as she moved, her little freckles shine light stars across her cheeks and nose. She's the same woman I fell in love with, the same woman I married and mated with, but she was also someone completely new to me now.

It's me, I'm here. Where are you? We miss you so much. Are you safe at least? Each question had me antsy. I just want her home. I want her in my arms. I pause for a second trying to find the teether to my brothers and Valdis. They need to know she is safe. I only feel one, a teether straight to Damian. *Luna, I'm going to try something.*

Okay. I don't know how long I have until we get to my grandparents' house, but I know we are trying to get answers. I don't know what all you can see or hear, but I'm with my aunt and two of her mates. Valyn, they remind me so much of us. River reminds me of you, funny, cleaver and can make a room laugh with little effort. Tell Undas, I found her. Please. She misses him and can't tell him herself. She fed me so much information that my head was spinning a bit.

Is River the man next to you? I ask her, she looked up at him and I can see the bright smile he has as he looks at the other two who are with them.

Yeah, I think he realizes that I am not okay mentally. Physically I feel fine. The biggest parts of me aren't with me, so I don't have the same amount of contentment as they have. But I wish you could meet them. You would love them, Valyn. I could feel the sadness in her, the void of emptiness. Even with this little dancing ember, she still feels so far away from me.

Lu-Luna?! Damian followed my teether to her. Thank the gods, because I didn't know if I was dreaming right now or not. *How am I seeing you right now? What is going on? Are you okay? I miss you!*

I am safe, well as safe as I can be. Talissa and her mates think that I shouldn't be here. That I wasn't meant to die. We're trying to get answers now. I miss you too Damian! Her voice cracks a little as she speaks his name and my heart breaks even more. I can't imagine what Damian is going through.

Why does that name sound familiar? I ask her, the name strikes a chord with me, but I can't think of why.

She's the warrior who took on the daemon army in the first war and claimed victory by banishing them to the deepest levels of Hellis.

200

Her mates sacrificed themselves to her so she could use their powers to strengthen her in battle. It's sad she expended it all and they became the Northern Star. My mother had told me of the great sacrifice of Talissa and her mates. I didn't realize that she was related to you Luna. Damian explained to me, I guess that was his way of making sure Luna didn't have to just dump a lot of information on me at once.

They don't know they are the Northern Star, Damian. They never heard of gods and goddesses being turned into stars upon death. They just assumed we all come here when we die or the eternal resting place. Like I said, still trying to work out details. How in all the realms are we talking right now? Luna explains, that gives a whole new meaning to what we were told. I thought it was a given that they all become one with the universe when they die. Are we missing a bigger piece of the puzzle?

I don't know. Damian says. We all felt the chasm of our hearts rip open when she passed. The bond going eerily quiet, but in the most painful of ways imaginable.

My guilt and grief most likely. I couldn't, no, I wouldn't come to terms that you were gone. Seeing as I can see you and all of your spectacular changes, you're not gone. I can almost feel you. I say, wondering how much longer we have to talk with her before this connection is severed again.

Who is that man ahead of you? Damian asked, Luna looked over at the man who was holding onto her aunt tightly.

201

That's Ignis. He is one of my aunt's mates. Kind of standoffish but, I like him. He's as protective of her as you are of me. Wait until you meet Claye, Voxis and Lumina. They are all really nice. Voxis is kind of blunt, but I finally saw her smile this morning. Lumina is a sweetheart! Kind, fun-loving, caring. Claye and I haven't had too much interaction yet, but I think you'd like them all. She burst out with excitement as she lists off the rest of the mates we can't see. The ones who aren't on their journey with them. I could see the expression of happiness grace her face and it made me so happy to hear the smile in her voice again.

I feel a strange connection to him. Like looking in a mirror. Where is he from? Damian is just as curious of Ignis as I am of River. A feeling of connection between us. It's an odd feeling since I never met the man.

I don't know. I can ask. Luna broke away from our conversation to check in with the group she is with. They all stopped walking, eyes widely taking in whatever Luna is saying to them. Talissa moves in front of Luna, placing a hand on her cheek, a smile gracing her face. She looks just like Luna, so much so that it makes me miss her more. Ignis and River move into view, broad smiles on both of their faces. Ignis is saying something to her, with River commenting after, then they stop. *He says he's from Solaria, he was born and raised there. River wanted me to tell you Valyn, that he is from Doria.*

I'm confused, I'm sure the names of the world were different when they roamed the earth. How would they know the names now? I hate questioning her or her new friends, well I mean family. But how could they know much of the changes from Cerulia when they've been gone for millennia?

Lumina is brilliant with magic. She has the ability to help them see Cerulia. They learn things about the world we're in. That's why Talissa doesn't think I belong here. The way they are talking is that I was in the process of changing into a full-fledged goddess, that would make me invincible to where only one weapon could kill me. And seeing as they know the twins who guard the ruins, they know the weapons are still sealed and safe. So, something is wrong. Unless Marie made it to the Ruins of Decay on the Isle of Souls. But according to Lumina, Alric and Elucia are twisted. So, unless a royal from the Solar and Lunar Realms entered and took the blade, I shouldn't be here. Luna drops the bomb like it's something we should know about. Or at least, should've known about.

I'll talk to my mother. I highly doubt anyone from our family would've given Marie the blade. Damian assures her, and I do not doubt that the moment this connection is lost that he will be on the phone with his mother within seconds.

Okay, we are close to Milara and Zephir's house. I don't want to lose my connection with you both. I don't know how I can talk to you or sense you, but I am so glad I am able to. She half sobs down the bond. I wish she was in my arms right now, curled up in bed with me reading one of her books with that cute little smile that she wears when she gets to the naughty parts.

I am too. I say, placing a kiss to her lips. I knew the others didn't figure out how to be able to physically touch through our bond, the only one who even tried was Valdis. A thought then dawned on me. *Wait, do you think that we can talk to her because we could be descendants of the mates she's close to?*

Like a light went off in her head, her eyes widened as she looked at us or at least our bond. *Lumina said I am mated to a descendant of their bloodlines. They haven't had children, but maybe you're in the bloodline of a sibling. Well, she said all but one. I'm assuming Valdis is the one who isn't a descendant. If that's the case, when I get back near the others, I want to try to connect with everyone. I just don't know how to tell Valdis that I love him.*

I got you covered my love. Damian spoke so softly as though he needed a moment to recover the fact that she's not lost to us. *Can you ask them why we felt hollow when you died, but now there is a small little ember sparking again?*

Luna stepped away again, talking to the others. Talissa was talking this time, a soft smile on her face. Again, she placed a hand on Luna's cheek, and I noticed the tears there. Luna was crying because she thought she had lost us forever. Talissa cared about Luna, I could see it. By the time she stopped talking I noticed Ignis and River move closer to Talissa, both gently touching her in some way for comfort. Something I wish I could do for Luna right now.

Talissa believes it's because I am going through the changing. That I am not truly dead, but that my body is just in a coma-like state. She said it can happen when you are injured during the start of the changing. Apparently Ignis's baby sister was injured as her changing was occurring and they thought she had died. It was Lumina that told them she was just in a deep, deep sleep. That might be what's wrong with me. She whispered that last part, as if trying to only speak to herself.

I'm in Solaria now, Undas took your body to Valhime. I can enter since I am part of the royal family of the solar and lunar realms. I can get this information to him and Vanalli. Sweetness, I love you with all my heart. I will see you soon, if what they think is true. I don't want to leave, but I need to tell them you're not gone. Damian said, a tear flickering through the bond between them. I should look away and give them some privacy, but I'm afraid if I do, I will lose her all over again.

Did a new constellation appear after I died? She asked the simple question that I knew Damian didn't even know the answer to.

Yes, right next to the Northern Star. I say, tears forming in my eyes.

Who knows, maybe we don't turn to constellations when we die, we just become the stars to be reborn once we're healed up enough. Her words sounded full of resolve. She is trying to see the brighter side of things.

I know you have to go, but can I ask one more thing? I ask her before we have to let the connection slip away from us. She nods and smiles. *Who is Milara and Zephir?*

Oh! Yeah, they are my grandparents. At least Undas's parents. Tell my grandfather I want to know about his sister when I return, oh and my grandmother that she's not out of hot water with me either. I'll be meeting her parents soon too. Luna smirked, her eyes wide and sparkling. I really hope she is right. I hope she returns to us, and soon. *I love you both with all of my being. Please tell the others that I love them and miss them so much. I wish I could tell them myself, but I haven't had any luck getting my bond to go their way.*

We got it Luna, I promise you. I love you so much princess. I'll see you soon. I try to wrap myself around her and hope I can feel her warmth and she can feel mine. I press a gentle kiss to the top of her head before the little ember decided to dance its way back into my heart. I blink several times, clearing my eyes from what seemed like a fog. Bastian and Valdis were hovering above me, while Niklaus slumped in the chair across from me.

Before I could say a word, Damian was calling my phone. I answered and put it on speaker so everyone could hear. "That was really her right Val?"

"Yeah, that was her. She' still alive," I replied, Bastian and Valdis slumped down into opposite chairs staring at the phone. "Go tell Undas what she said, I'll fill in everyone here."

"Already on my way there now," Damian said, then hung up. The room was silent, so I took this moment to just let it all out. Every detail she gave us, the information we gathered about possible connections to her aunts mates and what she wants to do later. Valdis looked depressed, but his eyes sparkled.

"I may not be a descendant to a mate of her aunt, but if the bond is strong enough maybe I can join through one of you," he paused and looked at us. "That is if you're okay with that."

"I think Luna would kill us if we told you no," Bastian teased. I looked at Niklaus who was busy staring a hole into my phone.

"I'll call our father, he should be able to tell Fennik and the others. Or maybe you should Valyn. You were the lucky one after all," Niklaus was slurring his words, stumbling out of the chair before falling face first into the couch.

"He's drinking more than he did before he met Luna. I really hope she's right and we can talk to her. It won't just do us good," Bastian said and I nodded. I just hope her visit to her grandparents can help her.

CHAPTER 27
DAMIAN

"**I** saw her! We talked to her! She isn't dead!" I yelled into my phone, as I ran to the doorway leading directly into Valhime. Nox was the first person I called. I don't know why I didn't call my father or even her father, no Nox was my first call. He picked up on the first ring and has been quietly listening to me lose my mind. I explained to him everything she had to us. The possibility that she is just in a deep sleep and not dead was the biggest news ever. Nox let out a sigh and I stopped my ranting.

"Are you sure you actually saw her and it wasn't a dream? I want my sister back as much as you do, I just don't want to tell our parents there's hope if by chance it wasn't real. Be honest with me, do you think that it was her or just your grief letting you see and hear her?" Nox's questioning didn't piss me off as much as it would've hours ago. I get it, false hope is probably one of the most dangerous things you can give someone.

"I'm heading to Valhime now to talk to Undas and Vanalli. Maybe they can shed some light on what Luna had said. Nox, can I ask you something?" I paused, never really thinking anything of Nox's powers until now.

"Sure, what is it?" He paused his and I can hear someone talking in the background. I think it's Virgil and a part of me rages. I know everyone else has slowly accepted him, but I don't know if I ever will be able to.

"You're a god as well. Did you go through the changing?" I asked hesitantly. I wasn't as close to Nox as Valyn and Fennik happen to be. I've been so busy with things in my own realms that I haven't been able to attend the dinners and parties that Erina sets up. I always feel bad for having to miss them, but Valyn usually takes Luna. He's also more sociable compared to me.

"Yes, I was a child at the time though. Why do you ask?" Nox asked, his curiosity peeking through the phone.

"Some of the information that Luna said was that most gods and goddesses go through the changing as children which makes them invincible. Were you ever invincible during that time? Like could anything hurt you?" I could tell by the hum from the other end of the phone that something had just occurred to him.

"Actually, yes, I practically was. Nothing could injure me, and trust me, I tried testing everything from jumping off roofs to stepping into arrow fire. What's going through your brain Damian?" I'm sure Nox's brain was already following the path that I was on, he just needed confirmation.

"Luna said that your aunts mate Lumina thinks that she isn't dead. She thinks that because Luna was going through the changing that she should've been invincible. She explained that this happened with

Ignis's sister. She was injured right as the changing began and she stayed in a coma-like state until the changing completed. They think it's the same things with Luna. They also said something about a weapon that could kill a god, but that it is guarded heavily by a set of twin gods. The only fae allowed to enter are of the royal family to the lunar and solar realms. Meaning my mother's family. She's my next call once I'm done talking to Undas," I say, my hand now on the doorknob that will lead me into Valhime.

"Your mom is still here. I can ask her so you can focus on what you need to. Damian," Nox paused, taking a deep steadying breath, "bring my sister home to us."

"I already plan on it," I reply, pushing open the door into the city of the gods.

The city of the gods was the most ethereal looking place I had ever been too. The city sprawled out with silver, gold and white everywhere. Tall buildings reaching for the sky with large windows looked so cold. It reminded me of the human city of Themal, they are advanced for a human culture, but they seem so clinical that no one seemed happy. I could make out a temple in the center of the city, a silvery blue light swirling around the building. I could feel the tiny ember next to my heart dance as I gazed upon the temple a little longer. Alright, that's where I'm heading to then.

I make my way down the white brick streets; the coldness of this place makes me wonder why anyone would choose to live here. I pass a few buildings that look like housing, a few people loitering around inside the doors. Some of the places looked like shops of finery, with jewelry and clothes littering racks inside of them. Luna would hate it here. She needs to the grass under her feet, the wind in her hair, the water between her fingers. Her laugh rung out in my head, startling me. I searched our bond, but the little ember was curled up around my heart as if trying to keep is warm.

I wish that I could hold her tightly. I miss her so much. I don't understand how she could still be alive, not with the way the bond in my chest went hollow, but I'll take it. I hasten my steps, going as fast as I can without looking like I am a man, making my way to the temple. The blue flame still burning strong around it.

There were a few little children playing around the yard of the temple when I approached. Two twins stopped playing as I stepped closer to the steps. "You can't go in there. Undas said something very bad had happened and told us to keep out." The little pink haired girl spoke softly to me.

"Aralia, don't talk to strangers!" her twin chastised her, making her fiddle with her little fingers. He was the same height as her, his pink hair cropped shorter to his head compared to her long pink locks.

"My name is Prince Damian, I come from Solaria to speak with Undas about the girl who he brought here with him," I spoke softly to both of them. I didn't want to frighten them; the little boy wasn't wrong by assuming that I was a stranger.

"My names Aralia, this my brother Arthur. It's a pleasure to meet you, your highness," the young girl bowed to me, an odd thing seeing as she was essentially a young goddess. Her brother followed suit, bowing begrudgingly to me. I folded my arms, one in front of my stomach and one behind my back, bowing deeply back at the both of them. Both of them seemed a little shocked by my display.

"It's a pleasure to meet you both as well. Can I ask you why you're playing out here alone?" I asked them both, curious as to why two children were playing on a temple lawn. Both of them looked at each other snickering.

"Our mother is inside. She is one of the healing goddesses, Miharu. She's one of the best there is!" Aralia chanted excitedly. Arthur however, rolled his eyes looking at the flame around the temple.

"That's not normal, is it?" I question, he stares up at it, shaking his head. "I'm pretty sure I know what it's from." Both children look up at me and the innocence in their lavender eyes is stark. They don't know about the horrors of the outside world. Why would they? I take a deep breath before continuing. "My wife was injured badly. Although I am fae, she is a goddess. Those blue flames are as blue as her hair and as wild as her heart. I'm hoping that it's a good sign."

"Is she Undas's granddaughter?" Aralia asked, looking up at the flames herself, her eyes sparkling with stardust. I nod at her with a simple hum of a response. "Then it's a good sign." The little pink-haired goddess looked away from the temple and smiled at me. An odd sense of relief rushed through me in that moment. Aralia and Arthur stepped back over to their ball and started playing again.

Arthur glanced over at me, "Go ahead on in. If that is your wife, you're going to want to be in there." I wave to the children, a warmth blossoming in my chest. Is that what mine and Luna's child could look like? I made my way up the steps of the temple, my feet sounding off on the alabaster steps. The large mahogany doors leading into the temple were open, exposing the marble flooring to the sun. I took notice that everything inside glistened with a shimmer of gold as I entered the building. Acolytes dashed off into alcoves and rooms as I walked down the halls, following the pull of that little ember in my chest.

I stopped in front of a large door, the wood a dark cherry, but it was a symbol on the door that had my heart thumping heavily in my chest. I reached my hand out, fingers grazing the engraving of the moon phase across the door, but it was the ravens etched into the full moon that had me pausing. The door suddenly pulled away from my hand and staring at me with wide eyes was Undas.

"Is everything okay?" He asked me as I dropped my hand to my side again. "I talked to Luna. The connection isn't great, but I have a message for you from Talissa."

CHAPTER 28
LUNA

The trek over to my great grandparents' home wasn't as far as I thought it would be. Or at least it didn't seem like it was that far, for all I know it took us hours to get here. Time seemed so different here, so did distance. I looked back half expecting to see the town we left this morning in the distance, but I saw nothing but fields of endless nightblooms and stargazers.

I talked with Talissa about how I think my bond woke up again being close to her mates, since my own could be descendants from their bloodlines. Talissa seemed to think that I could be right or at least on the right path. When I explained my thought process about wanting to try it around the others when I got back, River was all on board, Ignis shockingly was too. I guess because I seemed less depressed after speaking with Valyn and Damian.

My heart soared thinking about them, the smile on their faces, the happiness in their voices, the love I could feel even being so far away from them. It was the best feeling ever. As we walked up the stone path, I noticed flowers of all sorts in a small garden near what I would assume was a wild oak tree. I saw fireblooms, sapphireblooms, nightblooms, stargazers, fire lily's, snow snappers and so many other flowers that reminded me of home.

As we approached the house I took in the small stone cottage, the thatched roof and stick made windows. It looked so humble and small compared to the other houses from the town. Talissa stepped up, tapping me on the shoulder. "Don't let the outside fool you. They choose to live here because it's far away from your other great grandparents. At one time they got along, but something happened. I'm not sure what that was, but Milara would rather pluck Otius's eyes out then live close to him."

"Or be in the same room as him. Zephir has done well at keeping Milara as far away from Otius as possible. I slightly feel bad for the man," River said, wrapping his arms around Talissa's waist. I look over at the garden once more before the oak door open to reveal a beautiful slender woman, with the most brilliant bright smile I have only seen one other place.

"Talissa darling! Zephir! Our granddaughter is here!" The woman shouted into the house before coming out and wrapping her arms around Talissa pulling her into a deep hug. River and Ignis stood back letting the woman have her moment. She pulled back from Talissa, reaching for River and Ignis, gripping them both tightly into a group hug.

"It's good to see you as well Milara," River said, hugging the woman, Milara, back. A rough chuckle came from the doorway and my jaw almost dropped. This man was almost a spitting image of Undas. His hair, a brilliant orange, reminded me of the fruit itself. It was on the longer side which seemed to be a thing for the older gods. He stepped out onto the lawn and held his arms open, Talissa gave him a large hug before looking at me.

"Zephir, Milara, meet your great-great granddaughter, Luna. She is Erina's daughter," Talissa said, stepping away from Zephir. Milara finally let go of River and Ignis, turning her attention to me. Zephir stepped next to his wife, both looking me up and down. I began chewing on my bottom lip like a nervous child about to be scolded.

"There it is!" Milara exclaimed loudly. She walked ever so gracefully over to me, sashaying the whole way. Nora would love to have her as a model in one of her shows. Long legs, slender with lean muscles, a gait that would put others to shame, her long curly blonde hair bounced ever so perfectly around her hips, but as she got closer, I noticed her eyes. They would tear the soul out of any man who dare gaze at her longer than a moment, the color of the darkest pits, mixed with the brightest night. They were obsidian with flecks of stars. Taken aback by her beauty, I didn't notice how close she had gotten to me.

"There what is?" I asked, blinking my eyes a few times to refocus back on her. She placed a hand on each of my shoulders, taking me in. She felt so warm despite looking like her touch would be freezing. Elegant beauty frozen in time. I wouldn't ever expect this woman to be the mother of my grandfather. Maybe his sister, but definitely not his mother. Zephir walked up behind his wife, placing a gentle loving hand on her lower back. Her smile widened, but her hands didn't move.

"You remind her of our granddaughter. Erina was a curious little child, always exploring the world around her, but also chewed endlessly on her lower lip when she was thinking or concentrating on something," Zephir replied when Milara didn't. His voice was deep, a beautiful rich smokey tenor I should've expected. I took him in, his long orange hair draped over his right shoulder was braided tight to the left side of his head, silver beads adorning a few of the strands. At this closeness I could make out his golden eyes, the flecks of sapphire in them that looked like blue gullies swimming in the rivers right as the sun was setting perfectly.

"You would know more about her than I do. I didn't have much time with her when I was growing up. We just recently reconnected," I said, looking up at the stars above us. I took a deep breath. "I'm sorry, I miss my mother, just her and I have been butting heads lately and I am just hearing her voice in my head telling me she was right."

"That sounds like Erina. Even as she got older, she never let anyone forget that she was right. One thing that I told her would cause her problems in her future relationships. She's strong willed, you have to understand she means well," Milara finally spoke, dropping her hands from my face and pulling her arms closer to her chest as if trying to warm up from the cold. Zephir watched his wife's movement, putting his arm around her shoulders, pulling her in tight to him. "I'm not cold my love. At least not in that sense. Luna honey, while I am so happy to meet you, why are you here?"

Her question gave me pause. How do I answer this? Hi, yeah, I'm here because my dumbass wanted to save a heartless bitch and instead took a dagger to the back. How would that make me look? "I got stabbed," I said, hoping that she wouldn't ask me how or why it had happened.

"I already know that sweetie, I mean why are you here? Like why are you in Urfalo? Why are you here on our front porch?" Milara smiled sweetly like her question was obvious but that she is humoring me. Talissa stepped up next to me, her hand resting on my shoulder.

"We were hoping you could tell us. I had a feeling she wasn't supposed to be here. She said a few things as well that have me curious, and you're always more receptive to my thoughts and feelings. I was hoping you might have some answers for us. If you don't mind," Talissa requested. Milara and Zephir exchanged a concerned glance between each other before Zephir turned, heading back to the house.

"Let's go inside. Luna you can explain things once we get inside," Milara said, looping her arms in mine and Talissa's, ushering us along the stone path up to the house. So, she's where Undas gets it from.

The outside of their home was fucking deceptive! The inside was huge, it looked like I stepped through portal and into an enchanted forest in the middle of Oakenhall or Floria. Plants and flowers were blossoming in pots and ivy climbed the walls and wrapped around the ceiling. The kitchen was made of wood, with granite counter tops, the table was clearly handmade out of a large tree. The pots and pans were a beautiful copper color that also looked handmade, with exquisite craftsmanship. I honestly was very envious of the way their house looked. Cottage core mixed with minor little modern touches throughout.

Milara led us to the table where I traced every groove and grain with my fingers to stop myself for exploring the flowers and plants. The room felt so alive, like everything was breathing and living out its most wonderful life. Ignis watched my movements, leaning down to inspect the groove my finger was currently following. He placed his hand over a spot about three inches away from where my finger was. I looked up at him, he smiled down at me. "There's a loose splinter of wood right here. It would hurt badly if it went up your fingernail," he spoke softly, his voice barely a whisper to me.

"Thank you," I whispered back, moving onto another groove. Talissa and River stood over the island in the middle of the room, chatting idly with Milara, each one with the brightest smile on their faces. Zephir, however, sat with Ignis and I. He was also watching me toy with the grain and grooves, a smile played on his lips as his eyes followed my every movement. I don't know why I was fixating on the grains of wood, but it was calming some anxiety that I was having over how Milara knew I was stabbed without me having to tell her anything. What the hell is her power?

As if sensing my train of thought, Milara walked back over to the table with five copper cups on a tray, placing it on the table before taking her seat next to her husband. I watched the way his hand immediately found hers and how quick they fell into each other's embrace. I see a lot of my grandfather in his parents. Milara fixated her midnight eyes on me, smiling the warmest smile before beginning. "You have been having quite the difficulty going through your changing. Overload of power bursts, quick rage and possessiveness, and ethereal possession. It's all okay though. You weren't able to go through the changing earlier in your life like you should have due to the magical suppression Erina placed on you to stop you from killing your childhood playmates and to keep your identity a secret. I'm not thrilled with that if I am being honest with you. I understand why she did it, but I'm not pleased. Going through the changing into your adult years can actually be worse than if you did it as a child. The worst most children do is light a house on fire or resurrect their dead pet or the occasional turning their sibling into a creature of sorts when they are being picked on," Milara gave a pointed look at Talissa as she spoke. Talissa just lowered her gaze to the table.

"As an adult, you've developed so much more than in your adolescence. For you, this is particularly dangerous because you are mated. Your protection bond goes deeper than just protecting yourself as a child would. Hence your rage at that woman in the cafe," Milara paused as I raised an eyebrow at her. "I am the Goddess of Sight. Past, Present and Future. One simple touch and I can see all of your life. I'm sorry for the invasion of privacy, but I needed to know why you were here. I didn't see you coming." She looked ashamed, a layer of guilt pooled in my stomach.

"It's okay. I'm kind of used to it at this point. I'm sure you already know that when you have a mate, your thoughts are semi no longer yours. My mate Valyn has been doing really well at teaching me how to block unwanted thoughts from escaping or the others from invading my head by accident. I do have a question though, since you are so wise," I say. She lets out a low giggle, but nods for me to continue. "When Talissa and her mates passed on Cerulia, the Northern Star came to life in the sky. The little connection I had with my mates, they said when they first saw the night sky after I died, a new constellation appeared next to the Northern Star. They believe it's me. But when I brought that up to Talissa and the others, they hadn't heard of that before. Is that normal?"

Zephir's brows furrowed, "No Luna, it's not. Gods and Goddesses do not become stars or constellations. Who told you this?"

"Undas seemed to believe it. Because the Northern Star only appeared after they passed," I looked at Talissa, River and Ignis. My heart pounding so loud in my chest that I could hear it in my ears.

"Deep breaths Luna," Milara spoke softly as she reached her free hand out to soothingly stroke my arm. "You're having an anxiety attack. If you don't calm down, you could end up burning the house down and then I'll make you rebuild it by hand." She laughed a little but continued to stroke my arm. Zephir took this time to speak.

"Technically, Gods and Goddesses cannot die. They go dormant for as long as a few millennia to recharge their powers. Slairra is a resting place for our kind to do just that. Some of us choose to stay to keep an eye on others who come here and to guide them back. You aren't dead and neither is Talissa or her mates." Zephir's words hit me like a ton of bricks, but it wasn't me I was worried about. My eyes shot to Talissa as the copper cup in her hands dropped, clattering loudly on the table. River and Ignis looked between each other, then to Talissa. Zephir continued, "You should've already been strong enough to go back sweetheart. Why do you think we wanted you to come out here to Urfalo with us? Otius plays a big part in why you aren't strong enough yet. I wish you would've listened to us sooner."

I looked between everyone, then a thought struck me. "It's the water," I said, just barely above a whisper. I knew something was off with it the moment I looked at it. It's another reason I hadn't touched the tea that was offered to me here. I didn't see the water that was used to make it. Zephir looked at me, then to Milara.

"What do you know?" Milara asked me, she let go of Zephir's hand to grab both of mine, "Please tell me you haven't drank any of it."

"She refused it this morning, forgoing it for freshly made juice," Ignis replied for me. Milara looked utterly relieved by his words. "You warned us before moving out here to not trust the hand that so openly feeds. What didn't you tell us then? What happened between you and Illisandra and Otius?"

"We didn't leave on our own if you remember correctly Ignis. I tried so hard to get you all to leave with us as we were being ushered out of Slairra like the banished. We could've left and returned to Cerulia any time we wanted. We stayed for you all. I tried to warn you about drinking the water. Do you not recall me making you drinks from fruits and nuts and berries? I never once used the water there when I visited. Always a bottle or two that I brought in with us. Luna, what made you think the water was the problem?" Milara turned her attention back to me as my head began to spin.

"I didn't like the way it looked. The weird shine inside the water didn't feel right. I made everyone juice this morning and I noticed a change in their eyes. Everyone's eyes got brighter," I replied. I pushed my fingers to the bridge of my nose, trying to stop a headache from forming. I could feel the dull throbbing starting behind my eyes. We ate the sandwiches on the way here, and all the fruit, but that had to have been hours ago at this point. River got up from the table and grabbed a starfruit from the bowl on the counter.

"Eat this. You're not used to how time works here and how frequently that you eat," he said, taking his seat next to Talissa again. Something switched in the room, the air that was once warm began to smell of a fresh rainstorm, thunder rumbling in the distance. Could is storm here?

"Luna, I need to you eat that now," it was Talissa, who spoke sternly to me. It reminded me of my mother a little, her voice full of concern. I quickly took a bite of the yellow fruit, juice poured into my mouth like I had just bitten into a handful of the juiciest of grapes. I take a moment and close my eyes, the throbbing behind my eyes has turned to a dull throbbing in my jaw. Quickly finishing the fruit, I look at the cup of tea sitting on the table.

"Drink it. The water from Slairra doesn't flow here, it's clean," Zephir said but Milara already had a glass of water in her hand showing me proof that the water wasn't tainted. I grabbed the tea, gulping it down quickly. "Milara, make her a cup of honey root tea for her. That should soothe the aching. Luna, I need you to listen to me the best you can. You are about to experience one of the worst pains you can imagine during the changing. Your canines have yet to come in, they are going to force their way into your mouth through your gums. It's going to be bloody and painful, but the honey root should help soothe the pain."

I look over at the rest of the table, Talissa is barely keeping it together with Ignis running his fingers through her hair, but River kept an eye on me, his hand placed gently on Talissa's. He knew I had to go through this without my mates, I don't think that is sitting well with him. Suddenly a sharp jolt of pain ripped through my jaw, drawing all eyes to me. Talissa immediately put her hand on my lower back, I had no idea where the others were. Talissa's hand was grounding, I tried to focus on where her hand connected with my back to distract myself from the rupturing pain.

"Why don't I remember going through this much pain when my canines came in?" Talissa asked Zephir, her hand rubbing small circles along my back to help soothe the pain in her own away. The sharp pain slowed down slightly when Milara returned to the table, placing the honey root tea in front of me.

"Drink up darling, it won't take away the pain, but it will help," Milara said, placing her hand on my arm. "I know it's not much comfort, but you have us here to help you through this." She assured me and as much as I want to laugh at the thought of unknown family helping through this personal level of Hellis I am living in, it means the world to me that they are here with me.

I grab the hot tea and sip gingerly from the cup as the throbbing continues to dull. Milara was right, this stuff tastes good and I don't feel the sharp, stabbing pain in my mouth. The throbbing is still there, along with a pressure building up, but I'll take it. "Thank you," I manage to utter out before another wave of pain ripples through the bones in my upper jaw. I do my best to grit and bare it but fuck if it doesn't hurt.

"You were the same way Talissa. So was your sister. Sirus, however, took the pain in silence. He was such an old souled little child, always wearing the worry of the world on his face. I miss my old soul grandson," Milara reminisced about the past, but it was Ignis who brought the conversation back to the main point. Despite my pain and agony, we came here for answers.

"I hate to break up the memory lane, but what is keeping us here Milara? If we can go home, and I'm sure I don't speak for myself alone, but I miss my family, how can we make that happen?" Zephir and Milara gazed into each other's eyes. I watched as a silent conversation passed between them. Concern, worry and fear all played out in their expression. Even in my disorientated state, I know somethings wrong.

"Stop drinking the water, leave Slairra and come here. Otius has been poisoning the water supply in the city with crushed nightbloom and belladonna. It's not fatally poisonous to gods and goddesses, only to humans. He is using it to keep everyone there weak so they can stay and in his eyes be safe. Not having to go through the resurrection and returning to Cerulia just to get put through pain and heartache over again," Zephir dolefully spoke to the table, watching his words sink into everyone around him.

"Why would he do that?! Why would Illisandra sit by and let it happen?!" Talissa howled, the sorrow in her voice twisting my heart tightly. They were being poisoned by the ones who said they loved her so much.

"Because you are here. They watched you and your mates sacrifice yourselves to save Cerulia. They don't want you to suffer any more than you already have. Clearly, we didn't agree hence our public banishing, but we didn't care. We just wanted you all out with us. Sadly, you refused to leave. If you want to go back to Cerulia with Luna when she is finished the changing, you need to come here. We want to go back to you know," Milara spoke gently to us. Talissa looked at her mates, tears streaming down her face. Something clicked in my head at that moment.

"Wait, I can go home once I finish the changing?" I studder, the question hanging in the air. I look to Talissa, River and Ignis, "Will you guys come with me?"

They looked at each other, then to Milara and Zephir. River smirks, "I hope you have room for us here Zephir. We're a rowdy bunch."

CHAPTER 29

LUNA

The pain of canines coming in through pre-existing teeth was probably the most painful thing that I could've experienced. At least an hour or two has had to have passed since we all decided we were going to move into Zephir and Milara's house until my changing was complete. Ignis and River left shortly after to go retrieve the others from Otius's house, they were going to tell them to pack for a few days and explain the whole situation on the way over here.

Milara made a large kettles worth of honey root tea for me while Zephir walked outside with Talissa. She was upset, feeling utterly betrayed. I couldn't blame her. That was a big secret and let's face it, I know what that can do to people. I've seen it with my own two eyes and watched as I almost lost who I was in the process. Milara watched me intently, her chin resting on her fist, elbow on the table. "Can I ask you about what brought you here? I know the detail of how it happened but what caused that woman to go berserk on you? I mean aside from the fact that you were in goddess rage mode."

"She is the mother of one of my mates, Fennik. They had a falling out when she found out that he was mated to me instead of someone else. She didn't want him to have to share me with his brothers or a daemon prince. She demanded we revoke our mating bond, and he find someone else. Someone better than me. I had held onto that since our wedding day when she made the demands and Fennik banished her from attending the wedding," I paused as Talissa and Zephir came back into the house and took their places on the couches. Milara and I joined them instead of sitting at the table any longer. My ass was starting to fall asleep in the wooden chairs anyways. "Mirith was attacked right before my untimely changing, there was a warning of a dragon army from Limbris coming to attack Floria. My mother had told me to stay out of it and let Fennik or his father go and check on Marie. All I wanted to do was make things right between Fennik and his mother."

"She sounds like a peach. She also reminds me of Claye's mother. She didn't accept me until Claye threatened to leave the family in the hands of his uncle and never return if she didn't accept that I was his mate. She probably hates me even more now," Talissa sighed as she lifted a pillow off the couch. tossing it into her lap and hugging it tightly.

"Well at least she didn't throw some horrible news at your mate right as she put a blade in you," I said, shrugging my shoulders. "His mother is a sick twisted person. When I get back, I can't guarantee that I won't gut that bitch for stabbing me and hurting Fennik."

"Why are all the women in my life violent little creatures?" Zephir sighed as he pushed loose strands of Milara's blonde hair out of her face. "I guess it could be worse. You all could be submissive, and I would have to step in, putting men in their places."

"Do you forget how your son raised me?" Talissa laughed, tossing another pillow at Zephir as though they were siblings. Zephir laughed and sent the pillow flying right back at her. Roaring laughs filled the room as Milara shook her head, letting out a soft laugh of her own.

"Tell us about your mates. Lumina can only see so much with her crystals, and I am curious how you all mesh well with a daemon prince," Talissa said, putting her chin on her fists. Zephir snuggled up to Milara, pulling her into his arms so they could relax while I spoke.

"Fennik is the prince of the autumn realm, he is super kind and sweet and gentle. I almost shot him with a bow and arrow when we first met. I was hunting with my half-brother Luther for food. I ended up making it up to him by catching fish and offering him some. I didn't know that he was more than a damn fox at the time, but he looked after me from that moment forward," I paused, thinking about the first time I laid eyes on my beautiful orange-haired prince. I really hope he is okay. I hope Damian or Valyn told him I'm okay.

"Then there is Damian. He is the prince of the solar and lunar realms, currently he is with Undas in Valhime with my body. Apparently, he is filling Undas in on everything we spoke about on the way here. He is the one who saved me from a borg killing me on my way to Mistveil when I was still a fake human," that brought a laugh from all in attendance, but it was true. Technically I wasn't a real human. I was dressed up in a human meat suite for years of my life.

"Bastian is the prince of winter. Think giant, overprotective alpha male. I love him dearly, we had an issue a few months ago when I was kidnapped by Valdis for a night, but we are good now," I smiled widely. The look of shock crossed Talissa's face at the mention of being kidnapped.

"You were kidnapped?!" Milara exclaimed, hand now pressed against her chest. Alright, so Undas gets his overdramatic theatrics from his mom. I'm really glad I am getting this time with them though. Even if they say they are coming back to Cerulia with us, this is time I might not get when we return.

"Yeah, Valdis, Prince of Infernia. Niklaus, the prince of spring, made a bargain with Valdis. He offered his future mate as payment for his brothers to accept him. Of course, all of my mates didn't believe that they would ever have a mate, so he didn't think anything of it. However, Valdis knew that I would be not only Niklaus's mate but all of their mates, his including. It caused a rift in my bonded group, but honestly it was necessary. We banded together to help Sirus with his previous lover and then kind of just came to terms that this is what was needed." Thinking about the bullshit we went through, although it was worth it in the end, I don't ever want to go through that again.

"Lastly, there is my summer prince, Valyn. He is the biggest care-taker. I mean they all have that caretaker energy, but his is the biggest. Think of how River is with you. Amplify that. Valyn is the one who makes sure I drink my water, I'm not too cold or too hot. He's also the one who holds the most guilt over what happened to me. I told him it's not his fault, but I'm going to have to convince him when I get back. He as the one who realized I was fae, when the suppression was on me. Fae wine got me super drunk, and I lit two mermaids on fire underwater. Oops," I laughed, shrugging my shoulders. I should feel bad about that, but those bitches tried to kill me.

I miss them all so much. I want to be in each of their arms for years with no pauses between. Talissa cleared her throat, dragging me from my daydream of them. "When you return, you will be stronger than any of them. Will you fight in the war that's going on now?"

"They will not step foot onto a battlefield without me as long as there is air in my lungs. I will defend them with my last breath and then some. They are my world, my eternity, my life. I cannot and will not go on without them. So yes, I will fight in the war, and I will bring those assholes down. I don't care what it takes," I said without an ounce of hesitation.

The door opened up, revealing five figures as they each entered the small space one by one. "Good to hear, because we've decided to join you. If we have the chance to go back and finish the fight that we were in all those years ago, we want in." Voxis said as they surrounded us. "Just know that Talissa likes to be in charge on the battlefield and will try to fight you for command."

Talissa jumped up from the couch, throwing her arms around Voxis and kissing her deeply, "To the ends of the world I will fight by your sides. This time you guys aren't leaving me."

Suddenly, I felt a burst of energy flood through me, the hollow emptiness of my bond igniting like wildfire in my chest. A sudden ripple of images flooded my brain. The pain my mates went through when I died, the shattering of their hearts when they thought they lost me. Fennik becoming an empty shell, Niklaus drinking himself stupid, Bastian unsure of what to do, Damian rushing to a temple in the middle of a spotless white and gold city, Valdis pacing around a room, and Valyn making calls after calls, filling everyone in on what is happening.

I take a deep breath, catching myself as tears streamed down my face. I could hear their voices, see their faces, feel them throughout me. I look at everyone in the room with me, forcing myself to stay grounded. Lumina peeked over Claye's shoulder and smiled. Milara placed her hand on my shoulder. "Try it darling, we all can feel the vibrations coming off of you."

I smile widely, letting the tears flow. I close my eyes and take one last deep breath.

I'm coming home soon boys. Be ready for me.

CHAPTER 30
FENNIK

Malicah has been sitting with me since my brother had left for Solaria. All I want to do is sleep, the emptiness I feel in my chest is deafening. She's gone. They're both gone. How could my father not be ripped apart the loss of my mother or angry with me for taking her life? Nox has been checking in on me almost hourly, seeing if I'm feeling any better, if I need anything or if I want company aside from my uncle. I know he cares and that I should talk to him, but I can't bring myself to face him and his parents after my mother killed their child. Erina was in here last night talking with Malicah.

"You need to get out of this bed Fennik," Malicah began his normal pestering again. He wanted me out of bed all day yesterday and today. He doesn't understand the void that I have right now. I lost my wife, my mate, the soul that was made to match my own. How can I move on? "Alright, you leave me no choice." He grumbled before leaving the room, slamming the door behind him as he stalked out.

I knew who he was going to get, it was kind of obvious. My father hasn't come to see me since we all parted ways the other night. Malicah swears up and down that my father doesn't hate me, that he is just busy with getting things ready for a strike from Tanis. He believes that with my mother's death, Tanis will retaliate and what better way to do so than align with our enemy.

A soft knock came at my door, again I ignored it. Everyone knew I was in here; I just don't want to talk to anyone right now. I hear the doorknob turn and let out a sigh. I try to focus on the Mitos Mountains in the distance. The bright colors of spring dusting the leaves and trees, the songbirds singing songs in the distance, the smell of fresh baked bread and sweets wafting through the open window that broke my heart. Vanilla and citrus danced around me, pulling at my heart, which perks up at the scent. A small little ember peeks out from behind my heart, like it's trying to find her.

"Fennik, you have to come out of this room," Erina's voice lingered over me, the sound full of authority. I should listen to her; this is her home after all. I let out a long sigh and sit up, facing not just her, but also my father-in-law and brother-in-law. Erina and Drake took a seat in the chairs in the room, Nox standing propped up against the wall. I dropped my gaze to the sheets around me. I've been in her room since they all left. I didn't want to uncurl myself from her sheets. "I know it's hard, but she wouldn't want you sitting in here moping about. She would want you out there protecting your realm."

"Son, I get that your heart is broken. I think out of everyone here, we understand the most, but Erina is right. Our daughter wouldn't want you suffering or holding that guilt on your shoulders. I don't think any of us expect you to come out and dance around with a smile on your face. The loss of our daughter is hard on us all, you and the others a little more so. But they're doing what they have to. They're going to call us when they know more. I could really use your help, you know Floria best. Malicah has been a decent help, but it's not his realm, it's yours," Drake's comforting measures were kind. I would expect rage from them, hell I expected rage from everyone once they learned my mother killed Luna. Why wouldn't they hate me, it was my mother, and I couldn't stop her.

Nox kicked off the wall and sat on the foot of the bed, staring a hole right into me. "Stop feeling sorry for yourself and guilty. You didn't put the blade in your mothers' hand, and you didn't kill my sister. You killed your mother. Would I expect that not to hurt you? No. I expect it to hurt like hell and the guilt is going to try to cripple you. Do I expect you to act as if you didn't just go through the most traumatic experience ever? No. But sitting in her bed, feeling sorry for yourself as if you're the only one going through it is pathetic. You want to make it up to us? To yourself? Get the fuck up and do something about it. My sister wanted to save Floria. Do what she can't. Get up and do it."

"Nox, you be nice!" Erina shrieked at him, but he was right. What good am I doing sitting here in this bed? I look at Nox, he nods at me, and I throw the sheets back, moving up from the bed.

"You're right. She went to Floria to save my mother, and she was going to help us fight an army of daemons to protect my people. The least I can do is pull my shit together to do it myself," I say to Nox, a smile gracing his face. "Whatever you need from me, I'm here."

Drake stood up from his chair, clasping me on the shoulders before pulling me into a hug. "Thank you. Let's get the bastards invading your land."

I nod, feeling a soft gentle hand on my back, "If you need to talk to someone, my door is open for you. Do not hesitate to come to me." Erina pulled me from Drakes arms and gave me a hug. I know my brother's mothers would be there for me too, I just have to have the courage to talk to them.

"I'm not going to hug you, but—" Nox was cut off by his phone ringing. "Excuse me." He excused himself from the room and I could hear Virgil's voice outside of the room. Part of me thinks he hates me too. Even though Luna is our wife, our mate, she was his first. I can't imagine the pain and heartbreak he is going through.

"Has anyone told Lilly, Kira and Harper what happened?" I asked Erina. She looked up at Drake who just shook his head. I walked to the door, pulling it open to see Virgil pressed up against the wall across from the room. He looked up at me, and I could see the red puffiness of his eyes. He's been crying. I guess I can imagine how he is feeling. "Have you talked to the Nightfall sisters or Lilly?"

"Yeah, they know. Why do you ask?" Virgil asked as if I didn't have a right to ask him. I can't blame him; he didn't know how close I was with the sisters. Kira and Harper were at the castle pretty often visiting with Luna. The girls all had a luncheon a few weeks ago along with their book club.

"I just want to make sure they know and that they are being looked after. I know it's hard on us, I can only imagine how hard it is for them. How is Lilly?" I ask, my voice soft and gentle. I expect Virgil to get in my face, yell at me, shove me, something. His calm demeanor was unsettling.

"Lilly hasn't been handling it well. Her and Harper have been staying in the guest room since the night you all brought her here. You would know that if you came out of the room at all," Virgil sniped. There it was the subtle dig I was expecting. Virgil pushed off the wall as Erina and Drake entered the hallway. Nox was still talking on the other end of the hallway, pacing back and forth.

For a moment, I could hear Luna's voice calling my name. I shook my head a few times, I must just be hallucinating. Erina put her hand on my shoulder, "Are you alright Fennik?" I heard her words but couldn't bring myself to answer her. My name echoing in my skull in her sultry voice had me pinned. I stumbled back into the wall, my chest feeling like it was on fire. Drake said something to Virgil that had him bolting down the hallway towards the main floor. Erina was next to me, trying to keep me stable. The little ember that was hugging my heart earlier was dancing around my heart now. I closed my eyes, focusing on the little thing, watching it pull at the bond. The bond went taught in the little embers' hands, and I could feel a sense of warmth and love flood me.

There you are my love, Luna's voice rang out loudly in my mind. I had to be so desperate for me to play this type of trick on myself. *You're not desperate or going out of your mind.*

If I'm not going insane, then how can I hear you? I asked down the bond, wishing I could see her, even hold her one last time.

Because I'm not dead. She whispered down the bond to me. The little flame danced about at the thought that she is still with us. *If you don't believe me, ask Valyn or Damian. I spoke to both of them already. I just needed a little boost to get to you.* I heard footsteps rushing toward me, I could feel Erina holding me steady against the wall. Drake's voice was coming through my ears, but he was inaudible. I couldn't make out his words. *Listen to me, Fennik. I love you and I miss you so much. Hopefully I will be strong enough soon to come home. You better be there when I do.*

I promise. I am so sorry I couldn't save you Luna. I'm so— she cuts me off, showing me the world around her. *Where are you?*

Urfalo. It's part of Celestia, the healing world of the gods. There's a lot of stuff going on that I will fill you in on later. I'm going to try to reach everyone, there's a theory I'm working on, and I think I might be right. Suddenly a flash of a tall, blue haired woman with tan skin burst into view. Something felt familiar about her, like a calling I couldn't put my finger on. *That's Voxis, I think you could learn a lot from her.* The next thing Luna showed me was a stunning pale beauty, with Lavendar eyes and silver hair. *Tell my mom if you see her that Talissa says hi, and she'll see them soon. I have to go for now, but I promise I will get back in touch with you soon. Hopefully physically touching you sooner rather than later. I love you.*

I love you too. I hope to see you soon. I'll tell your mom as soon as we're done. I vow to her, I hear her giggle once more, then the bond goes slack again. The little ember hugging onto my heart nice and tight. She's coming home soon. She's still alive. I open my eyes and take in the hallway, no one tried to move me thank the gods. My father and brothers' mothers were all in the hallway along with Sirus and Holly.

"She's not dead," I said, falling to my ass as I watch as Nox walks up to us, a grin on his face. "Erina, Luna wanted me to tell you, Talissa says hi, and she will see you soon." Erina and Sirus look at me with wide eyes.

"What did you just say?" Sirus asked, glancing between me and Erina. He took a step closer to his sister, putting his hand on her arm for comfort.

"He said Talissa said hi. Scarlett, I have a question for you from your son. He said he spoke to Luna through a bond connection and that she is still alive, just going through the changing. Theory is that she is in a coma like Ignis's little sister," he paused gauging his mother's reaction to the name before continuing. "Basically, she was in the process of starting the changing, but she was injured at just the right time that the invincibility that should have been protecting her wasn't fully formed. At least that's what Lumina told her. She apparently has this theory that the only blade that can kill a god or goddess is locked inside the ruins of decay. Could that be true?"

Scarlet steadied herself, looking between Erina and Drake. "It's true. The only weapon that can kill an immortal being is held in the ruins of decay, but Nox please understand that no one can get in there. While the royals of the Solar and Lunar realms are allowed access, it's not to be taken. It's too dangerous to enter the ruins. The gods who guard the place are ruthless and can be unforgiving tricksters. Alric and Elucia aren't to be meddled with," Scarlet said, pausing for a moment. "There is no way Marie would've made it in and out alive. I know that for a fact. The tricksters don't play nicely with those not from God bloodlines or from the royal family. Harold can't even step foot in the ruins, and he is my mate."

"She's right though. There is a weapon out there that can kill her," I said, looking at Erina and Sirus, then to Nox. If it can kill Luna, it can kill them too. "Why is there a weapon that can kill a god? Why hasn't it been destroyed?"

"We will figure it out. While it's nice to know that a normal blade can't kill us, it's unsettling to know that there is a blade out there specifically to kill gods and goddesses," Sirus said, offering his hand to help me up off my ass. "Let's take a trip to the Isle of Souls. I know Elucia and Alric, tricksters they are, but they are some of the most fearsome gods and goddesses I know. They won't just let anyone on the isle or in the ruins."

I take his hand and pull myself up. "Let's go then." I smile at him. This will either be the death of me or the start of something new. I just hope I can keep my promise to Luna.

CHAPTER 31
LUNA

"How do we go about getting ourselves ready to return to Cerulia. Is it going to hurt?" I ask Milara, she just laughs at my curiosity. "What? This is new to me. How am I supposed to know what it's going to feel like." Everyone was sitting around the living room cuddled up and cozy. I was able to talk to Fennik for a little while with Voxis being close by me. I guess our theory was right on that, each of Talissa's mates share a bloodline with my own. Well almost all of mine, there is no counterpart in her bond that would share a bloodline with Valdis. My heart pulls hard at the still slackened bond in my chest where he belongs. I can't talk to him, but through the others I can probably see him.

The chatter in the room starts up again, my questions still hanging in the air. I wonder if they even know the answers themselves. Something else pops into my mind, this one more pressing than anything. "Wait," I pipe up. The chatter stops again, and all eyes are on me, "I just recently expired sort of, my body is still fresh with just an extremely faint heartbeat from what I'm guessing. But, if you all go back, what would your bodies be like?"

For the first time since we started talking about going back, the smiles slipped from their faces. Zephir cleared his throat, "Just as yours. Despite being asleep for a very long time, their bodies went into a sort of stasis state. Basically, their bodies went on ice. Frozen in time just the way they were the day they left them. If everything was done properly, which I'm sure it was if my son had any say in the matter, they were all put together in our family temple in Valhime."

A wave of relief washed over me and the rest of the room; Undas would've made sure that was the case. He loved his daughter; I can only imagine what he would've done to bring her back. What he is possibly doing not to lose me. Hopefully Damian got to him and told him that we all will be back to him sooner rather than later. "That's a relief to hear," Talissa said, nuzzling back into Claye's arms. They curled up into each other the moment he pulled her into his arms. They all have a way with her that is so effortless, it reminds me of how I am around my husbands.

"When can we go back? How long do you think it will be, I mean," Ignis asked the question we all were thinking. I took a sip from my teacup, trying not to make a weird slurping sound with how hot it was. No such luck. A giggle escaped Lumina at the sound, she quickly covered her mouth to hide the smile. Talissa just laughed. It was an easy feeling being around them, much easier than being around my mother recently. Even though we fight, I miss her. I hope she's okay, I hope someone told her that I'm not dead. The dread of my mother thinking that she just got me back to lose me all over again is too much to think about.

"We have to get the poison out of your systems. Luna, you haven't drunk the water, right?" Milara asks, placing her mug on the table in front of us. I shake head. "Good, then you are just here long enough to regain your strength and complete the changing. It shouldn't be long for you. As for the rest of you, whenever the poison is out of your system, you'll be strong enough to go home. It's just having the will to return home."

"You two haven't been drinking the water, why haven't you gone back yet?" Lumina asks, toying with a strand of Talissa's hair, twirling it around her fingers. The light from the chandelier twinkling in her hair reminded me of the stars in the midnight sky in Taiga.

"We haven't returned by choice. When you're as old as we are, you can have more control how long you stay. Our powers also need a little more time to recuperate. Granted, we hit that mark a few centuries ago, we didn't want to leave you here alone with Otius. Illisandra wants to go home to her children, but Otius rather keep everyone here safe under his protection. He thinks that the longer you stay here, the more likely everyone is to come together here, and no one would have to be used as a weapon," Zephir replied.

I watched the revelation sink in, the longer Talissa and her mates were here, the longer Milara and Zephir were away from their children. Children you can clearly tell they absolutely love and adore. Lumina seemed satisfied with the answer that Zephir gave as she curled up into Talissa's arms, Claye still holding Talissa tight. River and Ignis excused themselves outside and Voxis moved to the window to watch. I finished my cup of tea and took it to the kitchen. Everyone here had someone to comfort them. Granted they're my family, but they don't know me, and I don't know them.

I excused myself outside, keeping an eye on where River and Ignis were so they didn't think I was spying on them or something and headed to the garden. All the flowers that are growing in Milara's garden match the same ones that we grow back home. Lilly used to garden when she was younger. Not as much since she got since, and not much after. I think when I get back, after I get situated that I will help her start up a new garden. I think she would like that.

"They're beautiful aren't they?" a deep smoky voice pulled me from my train of thought. I turned to see River standing a few feet away from me. "Milara and Talissa created this garden centuries ago. They missed their garden back home. I wish they would've told us sooner that we could've gone home by now." River clenched his hands into a fist before dropping them to his side.

"I don't know Otius or Illisandra. Hell, until I woke up here, I had no idea I had great grandparents. They seem to love you all, be it in some fucked up way like Milara and Zephir said, Otius wants to protect you guys. I could imagine my own grandfather doing something similar if it meant I was kept from danger and harm. Undas is probably trying to figure out how to put me in a bubble for when I return," I laughed at the thought of him putting me in some sort of bubble.

"Either way, it seems like everyone has agreed that you all have suffered enough and Otius just wants to keep you all from suffering anymore. Milara and Zephir want you all to be happy but they want to give you the choice. What Otius did was wrong by not giving you the choice. But at least he was looking out for you."

I stare at the sapphire blooms, dredging up memories of Celvenia, the paths from the gates into Mistward forest, the way the shined so brightly. I was always told that one day I would shine like one of them, bright under the moonlight. I never understood it, frankly I still don't. I have so much going on in my head right now that I don't know how to tell anyone that my body is feeling weird. At least the body that I'm currently in. I feel off kilter like I the world is spinning yet not all at once. Ignis stepped up beside me before I knew it, "You're right, they want the best for us, but no one talked to us. Our families aren't here. Talissa misses her parents, her siblings. We all do. I guess that's where my anger is coming into play." Ignis said, plucking a dead vine off of the lattice. "I miss my sister, my father and my mother. We all left a family when we sacrificed our powers to Talissa back then."

"We would do it again in a heartbeat if it meant saving everyone we love. So don't take this as us complaining. We just have our missing pieces too," River clarified as he leaned up against the tree. A horrible neighing sounded off in the distance pulling River from the tree, and next to me in a few steps. "Luna, get inside. NOW!" He yelled and I listened to him as a large black horse came galloping down the pathway toward the house.

As I got to the door Voxis and Zephir were already pulling it open, ushering me inside and stepping outside, Claye following closely. The door slammed shut behind me, rattling the little trinkets and bottles on the shelves. Lumina held Talissa close to her chest, stroking her hair in a comforting motion. Milara was griping in the kitchen, moving pots onto the stove and mixing something that smelled of sweet apples and something absolutely rotten. "What the hell is that smell?" I complain, staring out the window as the lonely horse comes into view. Only it isn't lonely at all. Two white horses followed the gorgeous black mare that was being ridden by a wall of a man. The white horses pulled a dark wooden carriage behind it.

"That is Otius and Illisandra. They must've realized that we opened our mouths when everyone left all at once. I guess I shouldn't be surprised really. Otius won't let you all leave without him trying to defend his decision. This stuff is going to be disgusting to drink, but it will speed up the process of getting the poison out of your systems and getting your guys back home," Milara said, quickly mixing the vile concoction on the stove. I looked back at Talissa and Lumina, Lumina wrinkled her nose, but the tear that ran down Talissa's cheek told me everything I needed to know. We were leaving the others here and going home, forcefully.

CHAPTER 32
TALISSA

I knew what Milara wanted me to do. Lumina knew it too. I just couldn't bring myself to leave them behind. Claye, Ignis, Voxis. Any minute River is going to come rushing through those doors and we will all take the horrible smelling tea that Milara made us and hope to the heavens it's enough to get the poison out of our system and help boost Luna's changing so we can get her home safe.

Milara and Zephir were right. The moment that Otius realized we were gone, he would come for us. I wasn't expecting it to be so soon. I wasn't expecting him to come looking for us like we were prisoners who just escaped, yet here they are. Horse drawn carriage big enough for us all to fit.

"Talissa, if you are feeling some sort of way, now's the time to say something," Milara spoke sweetly over the kitchen counter despite just cursing Otius's name. Luna was watching everything out the small window next to the door. She looked in awe at Tirnag, the large black war horse that Otius rides. Granted, he's only an image of the great war horse. The real Tirnag is back on Cerulia, either roaming the lands or waiting patiently for its master's return.

"I'm not having second thoughts; however, I am having slight doubts. What if it isn't strong enough to finish Luna's changing? What if she is stuck here and we go back without her?" I say, watching as my niece turned to me, her gaze locking on with mine. She hasn't been here long compared to our time, but she has been here long enough that her changing is almost done.

Her blue hair has gotten brighter, with steaks of silver slowly dancing with the blue. The golden flecks that danced in her brown eyes have slowly morphed into the midnight sky. The gold and brown still resided there, but the galaxy in her eyes was prominent. Maybe it was just because she was here, or maybe it's just because I can see what people are fully capable of. Her freckles have turned like mine, a stunning pearlescent glitter across the bridge of her nose.

Will we even look like this when we return home? So many questions and not enough time to get the answers we seek. I should've asked more questions when I had the chance instead of curling up with my mates in blissful ignorance. This isn't second thoughts; this is pure anxiety taking hold. What if it doesn't work?

"She's almost done with the changing. Her outward appearance should be a clear indicator of that. Luna, how are you feeling? Can you call on any of your powers?" Milara asked as she danced around the little kitchen pulling vials and bottles out of the cabinets and placing them on the counter next to the stove. One by one she filled each with the rancid smelling concoction, the red liquid shimmered like the stars themselves were put inside the bottles and vials. She capped all seven of the vials and bottles before walking over and handing a bottle to Luna, a vial to Lumina and a vial to me. "Zephir and I will make sure they all get home to you. Luna, drink that whole bottle now and tell me how you feel."

Luna nodded her head. She inspected the bottle before popping the cap on. Milara could've just left ours uncapped. She placed the bottle under her nose and took a nice big sniff before slugging it down like she was at some party. Her nose crinkled and she made a loud gagging sound, but she got it down. "That is the most disgusting thing I have ever tasted." She reached for the teacup that was discarded on the counter, but Milara tapped her hand.

"You can't drink anything else. That has to work its way through your system. I know it's gross, but it is our only chance of getting you out of here before Otius sees you," Milara warned. A panic set in my chest that I didn't like. Why didn't they want Otius seeing her?

"Down the hatch!" Lumina announced as she popped the cap on the vial and shot down the shimmering liquid. Her browns furrowed, lips pursing but she was able to get it all down. She looked at me with the biggest smile on her face. I looked down at the vial in my hand, uncapping it slowly. I glanced up at the door, River needs to hurry the fuck up. I slam the vial down my throat trying not to let it sit on my tongue for long. It smelled like rotten fruit and horribly made shine. I guess I should be lucky it wasn't the latter.

Milara handed Lumina another vial, "For River. He's going to need to drink it fast once he comes through those doors." Nodding, Lumina

250

took the vial, holding it tight to her chest. It's odd, you think Claye the God of the Earth would be my rock, but it wasn't. River was my rock; he flowed just like the water he commanded but in times where I doubted myself or my abilities, he was there for me.

"Am I supposed to feel like I have ants crawling all over me?" Luna asked, looking back out the window. "River is heading back to the house. He looks pissed off." She stumbled from the window, catching herself on the couch. The door busted open as River walked in, indeed pissed off. He took one look at Luna as she tried to take a step toward him. Luckily for her that he walked in when he did, he quickly shut the door behind him and grabbed her before she face planted the floor.

"What the hell is wrong with her?" River questioned, looking over at Lumina as she began to sway.

"Here you have to take this so we can go," Lumina stumbled across the room, handing him the vial before falling next to Luna. Both were on the ground within seconds of each other, that means I'm not far behind. Milara moved fast, she gripped River's jaw forcing the liquid down his throat before he could protest, then whispered something in his ear. He looked back at her and nodded.

"Sweetheart, I love you with all my heart. Tell your father to expect company soon, we will be coming home, and your mates will be with us. When you wake up find Luna. She's going to need your help; you are the goddess of destruction and renewal. She is the goddess of all. Help her find her way," Milara said as she pulled me into a hug. My vision began to blur, my head spinning and throbbing. Everything was bright and loud. The lights in the room emanated a loud buzzing sound that had me on edge. River placed Luna next to Lumina as he reached out for me.

"Let's go home," he said as the world went black around me.

The calmness and weightlessness of the universe felt like floating in the ocean at night. I remember this feeling from long ago. The war had ended, the daemons back in Hellis where they belonged, but I was bleeding out, powers seeping through the ground around me as I lay there alone and what I thought was dying up until recently. Each of my mates had found a way to sacrifice their power to me to make me as strong as I could be before the battle. Each one left me to walk the battlefield alone, everyone but him. He walked with me all those years ago.

He was one of them, but also one of us. He was another connection in the world that I had. Another lover, another partner. He just couldn't be loved by others so easily for what he was or who he was. As I walked onto that battlefield that morning, he begged me not to go, pleaded with me to stay with him. He didn't want to lose me; he didn't want me to suffer. He couldn't go out there with me without complications, I knew that. Yet he walked with me as far as I would let him. I didn't want to die and leave him alone, but we knew what would happen. At least we thought we did.

He never made it to Celestia. I made him leave me on that field so long ago. I hope he doesn't think that I hate him. I hope he is still the kind loving King that I once loved so many years ago. I hope his brother hasn't corrupted him after my death.

Zekon, I am coming home. I just hope you can forgive me for leaving you, my mate, my husband, my free spirit.

Part Three

Resurrection

CHAPTER 33
NIKLAUS

My head was spinning from all the alcohol I'd consumed since Luna's death. Everyone handled their grief differently, Valyn imagined hearing her out of desperation. He blames himself and part of me blames him too. If he would've just let her fry Marie, Luna would be here, Fennik wouldn't be a clusterfuck right now and we wouldn't be so fucking lonely.

Then there is that nagging voice in the back of my head that this is my fault. I should've been faster. I should've gotten to Marie before she got to Luna. I should've sensed the fucking danger! I grip my fist tighter on the neck of the almost completely empty bottle of bourbon. I head it cracking, feeling the glass about to shatter in my hands. I throw the bottle as hard as I can at the wall.

Luna should be here! If they can't save her, then I will find any way possible to be with her again. I can't live a life without her. I refuse to.

A knock at the door pulled me from my train of thought. "What?!" I snap at whoever is on the other side of the mahogany wooden door. The door opened and it was the wings I saw first before Valdis fully entered the room. I noticed recently that the more anxious he is, the more he can't control those damn things from coming out or at least being fucking visible. "What the fuck do you want?"

"To check on you. We heard another bottle being shattered. It was either I come up here and talk to you or Bastian comes up here and beats the ever-living shit out of you for getting drunk and not taking anyone else's feelings into account. Your choice. I can easily go get him," Valdis's smoky voice was like a bucket of cold water splashed on me. Bastian was pissed, and he was willing to break his promise to Luna because I had them on edge. Again.

"I don't need the icy asshole breaking his promise to Luna. She may be gone, but he wouldn't forgive himself. Go tell him I'll calm the fuck down. Not like there's any more alcohol in the house anyways," I say before throwing myself down on the bed. The room was spinning, and I didn't trust the air coming up my chest to be just a burp. "You might want to go unless you're not bothered by vomit."

I felt the acid burning up my throat and quickly grabbed the rubbish bin that was next to the bed. I wasn't making it to the bathroom, and I wasn't about to try. I didn't want to leave a mess for whoever cleaned this place up. Expelling my stomach contents into a random rubbish bin was not what I had on my plans of things to do anymore. I had practically quit drinking and partying after mating with Luna and marrying her. I mean, we drank together on occasion, usually for the fun effects that fae wine still gave her. I heard the door finally click closed once I stopped heaving. Placing the bin on the floor, I rolled onto my back and stared up at the ceiling. It was painted like the night sky, constellations and stars littered the ceiling to the top of the walls. Everything else was decorated in blacks and silvers and purples.

I closed my eyes, letting the image of Luna flood my mind. The last images I have of her and I alone flood into my vision, her atop of me in a black lace thong with a matching lacey black bra that was practically see-through. Her blue hair was curled and half up in a cute little bun, her cheeks flush from the ride she was taking. It's like I could hear her breathy little moans each time she dropped herself deep on my cock. I knew she wasn't in this room with me, I knew I couldn't reach out and grab her breasts or grab her plump fucking ass. But gods I wanted too.

I tried to get my mind to focus on another time with her, one that wouldn't have my cock rock fucking hard. It did work. Instead, I was stuck in our first time together. The ivy vines spreading her wide for me as I plunge myself in her. Her screams of pleasure, her nails raking down my back, her body arching into mine. Fuck it. If I am going to be stuck in Luna sex loop, I may as well take care of my problem. I listened to the sounds of my heart, the memories I have of her and I, sifting through all of them to find that one where I can focus on her and nothing more.

Each memory I shifted through brought me back to our last time together. She had her nails sharpened to points for me. I loved when she could draw blood from me with her nails, she didn't have canines like us, but they would come eventually, and I can't wait until they came in. She already had a powerful marking bite. I could just imagine what it would really be like once she could mark me properly. I lingered on her features as I freed my cock from my pants, letting it release free. I swear I could still smell her scent all over me even though it's been a few weeks since I last had her all to myself.

I focused more on her body and how she moved, rocking her hips every time she got me fully inside of her. The looks of pure satisfaction as her pussy walls clenched my dick. The little smirk she would give every time she dragged a moan out of me. I missed her. I palmed my cock, focusing on the imagery of her riding me, stroking myself long and slow before picking up the rhythm she always rode me with. Long and slow, torturously then faster and harder, her nails biting into the skin around my neck as she got closer to her climax. I knew I was doomed once we got close, she'd ride my dick to the very tip and slowly slide my head in and out of her before coming down hard and fast so the tip of my dick was so deep in her that she knew I could break her. She would clench her pussy around my dick as I came hard, spilling my seed deep inside of her, milking every last fucking drop from me.

I kept pace with my memory, stroke for stroke, breath for breath. I was close to releasing when a small ember sparked in my chest, forcing me to release as her scent washed over me. Vanilla and citrus filled my nostrils. Her giggle filling my head.

Glad to see just the thought of me can make you cum just as hard as the real thing. Her voice rang out so clear in my head. Fucking bourbon playing tricks on my mind. I opened my eyes and grabbed a tissue from the nightstand. I wasn't about to leave this mess for someone else to clean up. *Niklaus Adair! I know you are not blaming this on fucking alcohol!*

She sounded so mad. *How else can I keep you close without breaking down like everyone else?! I rather have drunk delusions of you riding my dick then have the harsh reality that you're gone!* I tossed the tissue into the rubbish bin and tied the bag up. I'll take that out later. I move from the bed toward the bathroom to clean up and hopefully sober up just a bit.

You are hopeless Niklaus. I am not dead. Has Valyn, Damian or Fennik not said a word to you about me?! Luna's voice was a lullaby and a nightmare all at once. I missed her so much, but I can't let myself fall for the delusion that she's coming back to me. Stupid fucking me had to drink all the alcohol, fuck. *Niklaus, I swear to the heavens when I get back to you, I am slapping you straight across the face.*

The ember flickered in my chest, tugging at my bond that was now- when they fuck did it come back to life?! I closed my eyes and followed the bond to Luna, anger simmering in her brown eyes. Something was different about her. Hell, a lot of things were different about her. Silver highlights her once fully blue hair, her dark brown eyes once flecked with specks of gold now swim with the colors of the night sky. But it was her freckles that now illuminated under the moonlight. *Where the fuck are you?!* I growl.

I'm coming home Niklaus. Be there when I wake up. Please. She pleaded with me and ever fiber in my being buzzed. I want to blame the alcohol; I want to say this is all just a fever dream. But the pull in my chest is tight, the hollowness slowly fading.

I can't. We're in Noctum and you are in Valhime. Only Damian can enter Valhime. I can promise you this, the moment you wake up and I can sense you, I will be ripping at the door to Valhime until I can have you in my arms. I vow to her. A vow I intend to keep. *Do the others know?*

Damian, Valyn and Fennik I was able to get ahold of. I haven't been able to reach Bastian yet. And I can't reach Valdis until I'm closer to home. But I promise I'm almost there. I can feel it.

Then I will get them ready to go back to Solaria. I'll do everything to be there for you! The rage on her face was replaced with the brightest of smiles. *There's my wife. I love you, Luna. Hurry home.*

I'm coming back as fast as I can. Just know that I want all of that. She smiled and gestured to my cock that was still dangling out of my pants.

Well, that's embarrassing. I said, and she let out that cute little giggle that always makes me hard as fuck because it's almost always followed by her dropping to her knees.

Get to Solaria. If Milara was right, I should be back and fully changed soon. She blew me a kiss and I caught it.

I'll see you soon my love. I blew a kiss back before the vision of her faded and the little ember tucked itself into my heart. She was coming home.

CHAPTER 34
FENNIK

I don't know how the hell Luna rides on Nox's back without getting nauseous or falling off. I've legit almost fallen off over the North Selpie Sea twice now. Nox had told me we can't talk like him and Luna can when he's in his dragon form, but I understood. My brothers and I couldn't speak to one another when we weren't in our usual forms either. I envy my wife, the way the two of them fight side by side is incredible, but the way she manages not to fall off is more incredible.

We had been flying for at least two days, stopping every so often to let Nox rest and to relieve ourselves. We tried to eat quick little meals as we went, but we just wanted to get there as fast as we could. We were losing daylight quick, but Nox swore during our last stop that we would make it to the Isle of Souls before nightfall. He wasn't wrong. I expected to see more wraiths and spirits walking the land, but I guess that's just my inner child trying to recreate a scary Hollow's Eve story.

Nox swoops in low to the ground, fog covers the grass and dirt, weaving through trees that look like they have long since died. Everything was grey, black and gloomy. He found a spot to finally land close to a large stone building. It was decaying, grey bricks lay scattered around the structure as if it had just crumbled off what I can only imagine was once a tower. Nox shifted back, his black scales folding into his body as he cracked her knuckles and back.

"We need to find a better way back. No offense to you, but Luna is lighter," he laughed, surveying the area. He walked up to the crumbling tower, placing his hand on the stone before looking at the tree line in the distance. "Ever feel like you're being watched?"

I glanced at the tree line, watching as a small blue flame danced in the trees. "Is that a will-o-wisp?" I whisper, Nox shakes his head, placing a finger to his lips to keep me quiet. The blue flame flickered, taking the form of a small child, a boy from the looks of the short hair. A pink flame bounded behind the little boy as he ran, laughing and dancing around the trees. Nox looked at me then back to the small boy, playing with the pink flame. The boy stopped and looked at the pink flame, then smiled.

A burst of bright light came from the woods, smoke and flames engulfed the trees surrounding the boy. I went to move, but Nox grabbed my arm tight, dragging me behind the decaying tower. "I don't think they're kids."

"Kids?! There is only one!" I exclaim as Nox shoves his hand over my mouth, pulling me onto the ground and forcing me to look into the flames. What I saw had my jaw drop. There were two figures in the middle of the flames, both small and childlike, but both laughing like this is just a game to them.

"Alric, that wasn't nice!" The pink flame was no longer a flame at all. In place was a young girl, stomping her feet and thrashing her arms. The little boy just laughed; the flames immediately went out. I watched as the girl threw a rock at the boy with a wave of her hand. I looked between Nox and the children in front of me. Both immortal beings, both the ones we came here to meet. I'm now fucking terrified.

The two were arguing with one another like their little game was ruined. I mean, I guess it was by a huge fire explosion. "There is no way in Hellis that they are the gods we were told about," I studder out. Nox just keeps his finger over his lips. Watching them intently as they transform back into little embers and take off into the woods. Once they're far enough from our line of sight, he turns to me.

"We were told they were siblings right?" Nox's question had me confused. I think that's what was said. I shrugged my shoulders, "They don't smell like family. At least not the blood type of family."

"You think they're mates?" I tried to think of everything that was said about the god and goddess who protect the ruins. "Didn't someone call them twins?"

"Tricksters. They're lower-level gods but are very dangerous. If they are truly the ones we came to find, they could cause us some issues and not ones of the easily fixed without one of us, if not both of us on fire," Nox huffed, helping me up from the ground. "Wisteria isn't far from here to the east. I just have a feeling going there would be a bad idea."

"Why is that?" I ask, looking over at the massive hole in the forest where trees once stood. Dead and decaying, but still standing. I glanced around the ground, taking in the shape of the stone littering the dirt, the lines of stones still protruding from the ground, the outline of a room. I looked further back, more stones, wood splinters lay around the ground like the world was trying to reclaim the ruins of a home. "Nox, I think something used to be here. Like a house or something."

Nox was quiet. I didn't even hear his breathing. A chill coasted down my spine as a little female giggle, trilled through the air. "Alric! We have visitors!" Fucking hell.

CHAPTER 35
LUNA

An endless feeling of being alone, stars and darkness covering me from head to toe. A voice in my head called out to me, but it wasn't a voice I recognized. Or was it? Should I know who this is?

You've been in different since you started this life. Pure, joy, bliss. A child that the universe blessed with vast great power. You just needed to unlock it. The well of power in your chest will flow through you freely once you return to Cerulia and truly mate with your bonds. Just know you've never been alone; I've been here this whole time.

The voice sounded distorted, but loving. I wasn't afraid of it. I wasn't afraid of losing myself to whatever it was. I laid there floating in the universe, content with my calming surroundings. The voice hummed in my head filling the time that still needed to pass. I wonder if I could talk to it.

Yes. I've been with you for your life and the eternity that your powers were looking for you, patiently waiting for you to be born. I may not have all the answers, but I should have enough.

Interesting. I thought, thinking of how much more powerful I could be. *Can I stop this war without sacrificing anyone I love?*

That's a harder question to answer. You are powerful, like you have an endless well of power you can pull from. Your aunt had the same type of power for destruction and resurrection, but she never fully mated to her mates. Just accepting them and marrying them does not work for gods like it does for the fae. We are stronger than them, but unlike her your mates are fae. However, they come from the same god bloodline as her mates. I'm sure you could sense the connection. I know I could.

You speak as though you are a separate person from me, are you?

Kind of, but not really. I am the inner beast that you have locked down deep inside of you. I peeked out every now and then when you had enough rage to wake the dead though. Nice job with Rita. Hopefully she learns to stay away from the brothers now.

A giggle slipped from me. I don't know why I thought it was funny, but it was. *They didn't find it funny though. I think I scared them. Do you think they fear me?*

Absolutely not. They just didn't know what to expect from you. Piss poor decision on your family not to fully tell you what to expect, but I don't think they knew what to expect either. Truthfully, they will always worry about you, never fear you. I should warn you what to expect when you wake. The voice went from playful to serious so fast.

I opened my eyes, taking the shadow twin sitting beside me. My eyes, my hair, my body, just full of shadows, stars and moonlight. *When you wake up, hopefully all of your mates are close. You're going to need them, the urge to claim them is going to be strong. Once you claim them fully, not only will your powers be fully unlocked, but so will theirs.*

267

Sadly, thinking about it, you probably won't remember a single thing I am saying to you right now. But, once you are at your full potential, you and I can talk better. I will guide you through everything you need to bring the daemon king down.

That won't affect Valdis, will it? I questioned. *If I won't remember anything else from this conversation, I at least need that comfort. And will they want that kind of claiming?*

Marcloff is a douche that no one likes. The few kings that align with him due so out of fear of being attacked and destroyed. Most daemons just want a peaceful life, can they be insane and out of control at times? Yes and no. Most of the cities around Limbris are tainted by daemons who crave violence and depravity. Others just want to live their lives without the fear of war and destruction. So, Valdis will not be hurt. He is not family to Marcloff. But Luna, you must be completely ready to destroy him without doubt in your heart. If you doubt yourself, I fear he will use that against you and hurt you in the worst way imaginable. The voice comforted me. I've witnessed the daemons and fae that resided in Infernia. They seemed just like us, just with some extra features.

Will you tell me who you are? I asked, the final thing I needed to know before returning home.

Not now, but soon. Just know that I will protect you in times where you can't protect yourself.

And just like that I drifted off into a wonderful dream, filled with love and compassion and those I miss dearly. Soon I will see them all again, soon I will be reunited and whole.

CHAPTER 36
TALISSA

Darkness swallowed me up, the musty smell of wetness and stone echoed into my senses. I ached, every muscle in my body hurt like I had moved in centuries. Well, I guess that was a good sign then, because my body hasn't moved in a millennium. I shouldn't be surprised that I can't move. I pressed my hands firmly above me, feeling the cool stone against my palms. A rush of adrenaline flooded me as the top flew off, shattering against a far wall. River peeked inside with a grin.

"Well hello to you too beautiful," he said, reaching in to pull me out of this coffin. I looked around the room, three coffins laid closed still. Fresh flowers laid out on each one. Claye, Voxis and Ignis still lay slumbering until their return, which I hope happens sooner rather than later. River set me down atop a stone bench that was sitting on the far side of the room. Someone came here and kept this place clean, placed fresh flowers on our graves and looked after us.

"It smells like your aunt and mother have been here," Lumina said as she straightened her skirt and blouse. Her luscious blonde curls laid limp; her skin so much paler than it was when we were in Slairra. I guess there were some pros to staying there, but we can always make ourselves healthier once we are out of here.

Shattering glass echoed down the hallway of the temple, a scream tearing from the voice of someone had us sprinting down the halls to where the voice came from. If my body wasn't already screaming at me for moving in that coffin, it sure as shit hated me now. I knew if I was hurting that Lumina and River would be hurting just as bad. No one complained as our feet slammed on marble. We turned a corner to see Celia standing in the center of glass, water and flowers, Milara was sitting up in her own coffin looking like death warmed over. Well, I guess we all kind of looked like that.

"Celia my dear, could you be a dear and help your mother out of here. It's quite uncomfortable." Milara was stretching the best she could, but her coffin was just as small as ours. I nudged River in the ribs, *you help her.* Luckily here our bond was stronger, especially without the toxin in our bodies. River placed his hand on Celia's shoulder, scooping her up out of the center of the mess and placing her next to Lumina before helping my grandmother out of her coffin. "Ah, thank you River darling."

"Of course, glad to be of service," River cracked a wide grin at her, carrying her past the mess and placing her on the stone bench in her room.

"Mom?!" Celia's voice finally caught up with her brain as she took in her mother, sitting there within arm's reach instead of sleeping inside a stone coffin. Celia took three steps before pausing and spinning around to look at us. "Talissa, River, Lumina? You're alive?!"

"Yes, yes, we will get to that shortly. The others will be along shortly. Your father had to have some words with Otius before his departure. I'm almost positive that snake will be returning as well," Milara ranted as she stood up, smoothing out the wrinkles in her white floor length gown. "Any who, let's get inside and get washed up. You three can make use of the guest house, unless it's being used." She looked at Celia with a questioning look.

"It's not in use. I can make up the beds and get fresh towels and clothes. I'm sure my brother has something still laying around that will fit you, River. Lumina, Talissa, I should have stuff that will fit you both," Celia nodded like a subservient woman, obeying orders. This was not the aunt that I remembered. I smiled at her before pulling her into a hug.

"You don't have to do much for us. I've missed you Aunt Celia," I whispered as she wrapped her arms around my waist hugging me tight. "If I have to kill someone for hurting you, I will. Just say the word and they will die."

Celia startled but recovered quickly. She grinned at me, "I've been here dealing with the living. They're probably way worse than the dead. Shit, that was probably insensitive I—" I put my hand up.

"You're not insensitive, knock it off. I promise we didn't know that we could return home once we recovered our powers. But there was also an outside force that was kind of a bitch keeping us where we were.

Let's get inside before Milara starts the toe tapping. I shouldn't have to remind you how impatient she can be," we laughed, locking arms and waltzing to the doors.

"Shit I have to clean—" Celia paused, looking back at where the vase broke then stopped speaking. River and Lumina had cleaned up the mess quickly while we were talking, and I couldn't be more grateful for having the most understanding and kindest mates out there. "Thank you." She said, glancing back at River and Lumina. Both wore faint smiles; we all were sore and tired.

Celia ushered Milara into Firehearth Manor after directing us to the guest house that I had stayed in numerous times when I was younger. Sirus and Erina would call it our camping trip because only us kids wanted to be out here by ourselves. Mother and father were always inside dealing with the politics and social schmoozing that came with their titles. I never wanted any of the fancy politics and parties, that was all Erina.

The cottage was big enough for me, all of my mate and then some. Luna and her brood could come here if they wanted too. The place looked like it hadn't been used in a very long time. Thinking about it, it probably hasn't seen life inside it since before I died, unless Celia was bringing people here. Maybe that was the look my grandmother gave her.

River stripped his clothes off the moment the door closed. I watched as my muscled man stretched out his muscles. I can only imagine the atrophy they have suffered with him just lying there for so long. Lumina followed suit, losing the blouse and skirt by the door. I'd be glad never seeing these clothes again I thought as I kicked the shreds of leggings and blouse that I wore into the pile. Lumina watched me as I moved across the room to the stairs, I needed a shower desperately. Aside from the stench of decay that rippled off of me, I still had daemon blood under my fingernails and in my hair. You would think I would've been cleaned off properly before being laid to rest, but I guess Luna was right and my father refused to believe I was gone. He wouldn't have let anyone undress or bathe me other than my mates.

River followed me up the stairs, stopping at the hall closet to grab two towels and a washcloth. I skipped all of that and went straight into the bathroom, turning on the hot water letting it steam up the room. River tossed the towels on the sink counter before pulling me close against his skin. His lips finding mine quickly, one hand pressed above me on the wall, the other caressing my cheek as he kissed me slow and deep. A growl rippled from his throat to his lips, vibrating my lips. I wrap my arms around his waist trying to pull him closer to me, but he stops me. "I had you the night before we left, I can wait a little longer," he whispered onto my lips as Lumina walked into the bathroom, her eyes wholly focused on me and my body.

I missed her bare breasts pressed up against mine, her soft ass in my hands, her clit between my teeth. Hell, I missed her devouring me like I was an endless dessert buffet. She sauntered into the room, pushing River aside and claiming my lips between hers. The taste of lemon tarts and vanilla mixed with cinnamon swirled in my mouth. Gods, we have been together since our death, but this takes the cake having our real bodies, feeling and tasting who we are. It's a bliss I didn't realize I missed so desperately. I pushed my hands through her hair, embracing her kiss, pressing her breasts and against mine. The feel of her nipples peaking as the touch my skin sent a chill through me, her lips not moving from mine. Not even the growls of satisfaction from River pulled our attention from one another.

I knew what he wanted, any other time I would gladly cave and let him join us, but right now, I am hers. Lumina ran her hands down my sides, her fingers gently brushing the underside of my breasts sent shivers down my spine. I was desperate to have her touch me, I arched my hips as her fingers ran idle circles haphazardly on my hips. A whimper escaped from my lips, pulling her bright emerald eyes to look me in mine. "Use your words silly."

"Fuck me," I whispered, Lumina slid her hand between my thighs her fingers sliding through my wetness. She let out a purr of satisfaction that had me melting in her hands. Lucky for me her nails weren't crazy long, as she plunged two fingers inside of me eliciting a loud moan from me. Her fingers were like fucking magic, pressing all the right spots as she pulled me closer and closer to release.

She kissed me once more before separating herself from me and dropping to her knees, fingers still pulling me towards the best climax I've had. She pressed her mouth over the sensative bundle at the top of my entrance, sucking and biting hard on my clit. I was right there about to cum all over her fingers and tongue and she fucking knew it. I chanced a glance over at River who was stroking his cock in the most delicious way. Lumina caught my gaze and pulled her mouth away. "Get over here and fuck her, just know she's coming on my tongue, regardless if your dicks in her or not." She closed her mouth over my clit once more and had me moaning so loudly I felt bad if my aunt came in to drop off clothes any time soon.

River moved Lumina back just a bit so he could get behind me and slide his dick into me. the full feeling of him had me reeling. I was ready to cum all over him and her without a second thought. Lumina bit my clit hard as River plunged in and out of me hard and deep. His cock stretched me, filling me completely, leaving me a puddle for Lumina. These two always loved to tag team me. My first two mates, the two who had me the longest to themselves. They knew how to work me between them. It was torturous and I loved every second of it.

"Come for me baby girl," River whispered in my ear as he sunk his canines into my shoulder, Lumina sinking hers into my clit. The rush of pain ad bliss sent me over the top as I came so hard on his dick and her tongue. River thrusted deep in me once more, holding me down tightly on his cock as he released deep inside of me. He slid himself out leaving me all to Lumina, but I stopped her for a moment, turning around to face River. I gripped him by the throat pulling his neck down to my level and sunk my canines into him hard. He was hard again in an instant, my free hand gripped his cock, sliding up and down fast and hard as I kept my canines deep into his neck drinking him up. I felt the moment he was about to cum. I unattached from his neck dropping down to my knees, sucking his cock so deep down my throat that he fisted my hair into a ponytail and face fucked me until he came.

I turned my attention to Lumina who was watching intently, her fingers playing in her pussy, her clit all swollen. I lifted her up onto the sink and dropped to my knees, moving her hands to her side on the counter. Quickly lapping up the sweetest of nectar that she was delivering. Her breathy moans were all I needed to hear as I plunged two fingers into her with my thumb rubbing her clit. Her eyes rolled back in her head, her moans getting louder and louder. I felt her inner walls begin to tighten and went for it. I pushed my fingers in and out of her rapidly as I bit her clit hard, canines in her like hers were in mine. She screamed so loudly with pleasure as she came on my tongue. It had been a while since I was able to pleasure her so thoroughly. I missed her screaming my name.

"I think we should shower before your aunt comes in and yells at us for using all the hot water," River said, helping Lumina down from the counter. He moved us both into the shower after checking the temperature.

"Can we do that again?" I asked, they both looked at me and smiled widely.

"Gladly!" The exclaimed in unison. Round two it is I guess.

CHAPTER 37
Nox

Her flames weren't as hot as I was expecting. It was like she didn't want to hurt me, just scare me. It didn't work though. I wasn't afraid of her, I was more afraid of her psycho mate, Alric. "What brings you to our wonderful little isle?" He asked, circling Fennik. I was surprised he didn't try to fight the kid. Kudos to him for that. Fennik looked at me, then to the girl beside me. Her dark magenta hair was in wave that hung to her hips, her eyes the color of an opal moonstone. She was a cute kid, but she was anything but that.

"You want an answer, and I want to speak to the real you. Not the image of innocence the two of you portray," Fennik said, some grit in voice. Not going to lie, but I wasn't expecting him to call them out like that. Fennik always seemed the soft spoken one, but since losing Luna he's been anything but. His orange hair that was usually gelled back or tossed to the side was wild, his green eyes not as bright as I had seen them in the past. He was lost without her, and lost people do stupid shit.

"You think you have the right to speak to me like that?" Alric said, glaring at Fennik. The girl beside me let out the cutest little giggle, genuinely acting like the child she was trying to portray. "Elucia, stop laughing. It's not funny."

"Oh, but it is my love. They can see through the deception we have used countless of times with others who have come here. What the harm in letting them see the real us before they die?" Elucia was just as fucking psycho. Holy shit. She looked up at me and smiled, snapping her fingers. Pink flames licked up her body starting at her toes, elongating her legs and arms, baring large breasts and a great looking ass. Her hair was still hanging in curls around her hips, her lips plump and full were beautiful. But it was the sultry look on her eyes that had my heart hammering out of my chest. The innocent dress she was wearing transformed into a long black lace dress with a high thigh slit and a tight black velvet choker adorned her neck, lace gloves hugging her arms, "Like what you see?"

"Of course he does. No one could resist your beauty my love," Alric huffed before blue flames engulfed him. His body grew, muscles coiling around his arms and legs, his opal eyes the same as hers, seemed to glow within his fire. His dark blue hair laid back as if it was held back by water or gel. The tight black pants coupled with a white t-shirt and black sneakers seemed so off compared to the light brown khakis and white button up he wore just moments ago. Gone were the innocent looking children, they were now full-grown ass powerful gods, and we just pissed them off by landing on their land.

"What brings you to the Isle of Souls if not to die?" Elucia's voice was like a lulling melody, inviting like a siren. How the fuck did this woman go from innocent child to deadly siren with the turn of flames.

"I am Prince Nox Embros of Mirith. My sister is Princess Luna Embros, Princess of both the Hildaria and Mistveil regions and a Princess of Hellis. She was stabbed by a blade that put her into a stasis like coma. We were told there is only one blade that can kill a Goddess or a God and that it is here. The thought is she was stabbed with it before her full changing into full goddesshood. Unlike me, she had a magical suppression on her since birth, she didn't go through the changing until just now. We need to know if the blade is still here," I try to say without insulting them. Elucia's eyes flick to Alric's, a silent conversation between the two of them.

"He is?" She tilts her head to where Fennik stands, Alric right behind him as if ready to strike at a moment's notice.

"Prince Fennik Elrod of the Autumn Realm. He is one of my sister's mates. We mean no harm or disrespect. We just want to make sure the weapon is still here," I reply, hoping that they can sense the urgency in my tone.

"And why should we believe you?" Alric said from behind Fennik. Suddenly, shadows engulfed the area, leaving only the four of us with little to no light aside from the glow of the pink flame.

"Because that is my nephew," a deep voice echoed in the darkness. Sirus finally fucking got here. He didn't want to ride with us claiming he would get motion sickness, but I have a feeling he just wanted to make a grand fucking entrance. I love him, but I never understood him. Alric spun around looking for the source of the voice not knowing that Sirus is right behind me. A hand gentle pressed my shoulder, alerting me to his proximity so I don't accidentally shift and maim him.

I watch as Fennik closes his eyes, something is going through his head, and I am hoping it's Luna. I'm hoping I will see a smirk cross his face telling me she is home and alive again. "Who the fuck is there!" Alric screeched into the darkness. A laugh slipped from my lips before I could catch it. "You think this is fucking funny! Who did you bring?!"

"Alric, wait," Elucia put up a hand stopping his advance on me, a flame dagger in hand. "You wouldn't be able to kill him. Sirus, is that you?" Like a bucket of water was doused on Alric, the flame dagger vanished. His eyes widened with what I thought was fear, but this was something deeper.

"Of course, it would be you to recognize me Elucia. It's good to see you again," Sirus released the darkness around us revealing himself a breath away from her face. "Need I remind you the last time you threatened someone in my family what happened?"

"No, you don't," Elucia snapped her fingers and the pink flame that held me in place vanished. I took a step to be by my uncle's side, waiting for Fennik to come up beside me. It wasn't long before Fennik was standing beside me, staring down Alric who was now standing with his arm resting on Elucia's lower back.

"So, his sister is your niece. Explains why these two are dumb enough to bother us," Alric spat in our direction like we were beneath him. Sirus smirked, the shadows still dancing around Alric's feet grabbed his ankles tight.

"You remember my sister Talissa correct? The one who you refused to help all those years ago," Sirus said to Elucia who looked down at the ground, guilt all over her face. "She is the Goddess of Destruction AND Renewal. My niece, however, is the Goddess of All. Life, Death, and everything in between. She is the cataclysm that could rip this world apart and remake it into the image she wants when she comes to full power. Talissa is returning with Luna. Do you think you want to piss either of them off. I highly doubt Talissa has forgiven you. I know I haven't."

"We should've helped. But what other choice did we have? We had people to protect to you know!" Elucia was a mix of emotions, rage, sadness, guilt. It was all over her face and I honestly started to feel bad for her.

"I know. But you didn't lose your loved ones. I did," Sirus snapped back was so cold. I'd seen him be harsh, I've heard him be cruel. But I've never seen him be like this to someone.

"You said Talissa is coming back. How is that possible?" Alric asked, pulling Elucia tighter to his side.

"Something is going on in the afterlife. Apparently, we can only die by the weapons you guard here. Talissa and her mates just sacrificed their powers and went into a stasis. Hence why we are here. We need to make sure the weapon is still here," Sirus said. "Look, I will forgive you if you prove to me that you are worthy of it."

"How the hell do we do that?" Alric said, putting Elucia behind him, probably the first defensive thing I've seen him do since meeting him.

"By proving to me that the blade is still where the fuck it should be," Sirus snapped, the shadows tightening around Alric's leg caused visible pain. I put my hand on his shoulder to stop him. If we wanted their help, we needed to not be dicks about it. Sirus looked over his shoulder at me, then back over to Alric who was now wincing pain. "You're lucky my nephew is here and doesn't want to see harm come to you."

Sirus released his shadow grip on Alric, turning and stalking off to the crumbling tower. He leaned up against it and waved his hand for me to continue. "Look, I don't know what happened between you both and my family. Honestly, I don't care. I just want to know that the weapon that can kill us all is safely tucked away from those who would wish to kill a god."

The two looked at each other than past me to Sirus. "We owe your family a debt. One we can never fully repay, but if this is a path to forgiveness, then we will show you. The only problem is, once we lay traps, they have to be set off to get to the armory. We can't just deactivate them." Elucia smiled. Her opal eyes twinkled against her pale skin. Great so we have to play a game with tricksters to get what we came here for.

"No tricks Elucia. The first sign of bullshit and I will rip you to fucking shreds," Sirus threatened as he pushed off the tower and stalked back to where we were. Fennik to his credit has kept his mouth shut and stayed close. I guess self-preservation is more important to him then commenting. Fennik stepped to the side allowing Sirus a wide berth to pass, shadows licked at the ground as he moved. Elucia and Alric turned, leading us to the ruins of decay.

I don't know what I was expecting, but it sure as shit wasn't a fucking labyrinth! A fucking huge ass stone maze with ivy crawling all over the dark mold encrusted rocks. Elucia and Alric stood at the entrance, waiting for us to follow them inside.

"Are we really going in there?" Fennik asked, looking at Sirus for an answer that I'm sure he really didn't want to know. He knew we had to go inside, but maybe he was hoping Sirus had a different plan.

"We have no choice. It would be a little better if we had Niklaus here. He could follow the ivy on stones to the center of the labyrinth," Sirus sighed, pinching the bridge of his nose. "Seeing as he isn't here and it's just us, we have to go in ourselves and do things the old fashion way. My shadows can help detect most of the traps, Fennik what can you do besides act nervous. You've read every book in Floria and Fildrey, correct?"

Fennik nodded as she pulled a notebook from his bag. It was tan, leather bound with a blue gemstone in the center and an odd assortment of designs on the front. He undid the clasp and flicked through some pages. He stopped on a page that had a picture of the two gods on it. He did his research on Alric and Elucia before we got here. "According to my research, they are tricksters, but they are honest. There is a misconception that they are siblings, but that's not true. They are mates. Elucia has a fondness for children, they lost one in the battle between the daemon king of Limbris. Their son went off to help Talissa against their wishes when they refused to offer aid. Their stance on keeping him safe failed because their son had more of a conscious then they did. Valmor was his name. He died in battle trying to protect Talissa from a daemon attack," Fennik listed off the biggest reason they owe my family a debt, my aunt sacrificed herself to save the world, but in return for their selfishness, they lost a child.

"Sirus, did you know about their son?" I asked him, but he just shook his head. "Then you owe them forgiveness regardless of them showing us the weapons." It dawned on me in that moment, the reality of it all. "Their son came back."

Sirus and Fennik both looked utterly shocked at my revelation. Turning on my heels I ran to Alric and Elucia. "When did Valmor come back to you?!" I shouted. That is the true debt they are paying.

My aunt didn't return to this plain of existence like their son. Alric and Elucia looked at me with pity in their eyes.

"About a year later. He told us everything, about how Talissa and her mates sacrificed themselves and how he took a blade for her since her mates had died. That was the moment we knew that the weapons we hide here weren't tampered with or replicated. If King Marcloff had replicated our weaponry, our son wouldn't have come home to us. A year is a long time, but he came back at full potential. I think he came back stronger. Valmor, however, decided to align himself with King Zekon. Talissa's only mate that couldn't sacrifice himself."

"Zekon wasn't her mate, he was her informant. Your son has his facts wrong," Sirus spat as he walked up to us, Fennik on his heels. "If Zekon was her mate, she would've told us, and he wouldn't be able to run a kingdom."

"Talissa and Zekon were married. Just like her and her other mates, the difference was that Zekon couldn't give up his lineage or else he would be of no use to her. His own brother has sided with your family. Zekon is playing a role, and a very dangerous one. He walked onto that battlefield with your sister Sirus. He just couldn't fight by her side," Alric stepped between us and his mate. She put her hand on his shoulder, moving past him to step in front of Sirus.

"My son adored your sister, so much so that he went against our orders to be with her on the front lines. We lost our son that day, we are so sorry that your sister hasn't come back to you until now. I truly hope you are right about that. I can only imagine how long she's been incomplete. We will go in with you and try to disengage some of the traps, but you're going to need to help. Whenever you're ready," Elucia stepped into the labyrinth, followed by Alric. Fennik followed suite much to my surprise.

Sirus hesitated, "If they are right, then there is a big missing piece that we didn't know. That also makes the prophecy Valdis talked about much more real."

"In what way?" I asked as I started for the entrance. Sirus finally moved his feet, and we followed them. The entrance was cold, the smell of mold was strong, but not as strong as the sweet smell coming from inside the labyrinth.

"He said Luna was his mate, he envisioned her. His uncle Zekon had a gift from the goddess that was his mother, it was future sight. Zekon could tell you where someone was going to pop out of a good three minutes before the enemy attacked. It was worth it to have him around. But Valdis would make another descendant of Talissa's mates. Luna is following my sisters mating line, that means that there is a chance she can suffer the same fate as Talissa if the war continues on the same pathway as before." Sirus took a deep breath before moving past me further into the labyrinth.

If he was right, that means my sister can suffer like Talissa, possibly even die and take forever to return to us just like my aunt. My brain started wandering until a snap resonated through the stone halls. A bright light flashed, then squelching flesh and blood hitting the floor was all I could hear.

CHAPTER 38
BASTIAN

I've been staring at the same black spec on the ceiling for at least an hour now, or so it feels. Valyn's outburst about Luna had me hopeful, but I didn't trust Niklaus to call Drake. He was too fucking drunk to walk straight let alone have a serious conversation. I made the call on my way to the room that was set up for me when I got here. We hadn't seen Melody yet, and something tells me her mother will make sure that we don't. Fucking bitch.

The call with Drake went as well as I thought it would. He said he would tell Erina and the others. My father took the phone to make sure we all were good, sadly I had to tell him Niklaus wasn't doing well at all. We need to get Luna back before his liver is beyond repair. Not like he couldn't just get it repaired but still that's beside the point. Nora threatened to come get him and throw him in rehab until father told her that wasn't the wisest of ideas at the current moment. The drinking may not be the best thing for him but it's keeping him present and stopping him from doing something even dumber. Nore grumbled but conceded. We hung up about forty minutes ago and now I'm just laying here waiting.

Endless things ran through my mind, the biggest of which is how I plan on protecting her once she is back in my arms. I refuse to let anything else happen to her. I hope that Fennik and the others are making headway with the gods. Hopefully the weapon is still where it should be, and we don't have to go on a treasure hunt.

A shadow creeps over the ceiling, descending down the wall towards the floor, the smell of vanilla swirled around me, her giggle echoing off the walls. I closed my eyes and focused on our bond. A small little ember peeked out around my heart, tugging on the bond until it went taut. She was close. I guess I was lucky to finally get a visit from my beautiful wife.

Hello darling. I drawl as she comes into view. Her beautiful face lit up like a star in the darkness. She has changed slightly, her dark blue hair now highlighted with silver was breathtaking. The chocolate brown eyes that I lost myself in now had the galaxy swimming in them beneath the brown. She's stunning, I can't open my mouth to say a single word as I take in her new features. Her smile is what melts me. She was floating, her hair splayed out around her as she swam her way through what I can only imagine is the night sky.

She glanced over at me, her smile beaming widely at me. *It's really you?* She questioned as if the sight of me was a trick her mind was playing on her. I smiled back at her, realizing that I was now floating with her in the vast emptiness of the world. I made my way to her, even if this was just a dream of me wanting her around, I would take it gladly. Reaching out, I cup her cheek in my hand and fuck if she didn't feel so real to me.

I wasn't expecting her to float into my arms, nuzzling herself into my chest. I couldn't help myself; I pushed my face into her hair and took a deep breath in. Vanilla and citrus flooded my senses leaving me disorientated. *I can't believe it worked!* She chimed all happy and content. I just squeezed her tightly too afraid to let go. I didn't want to let go of her and her just vanish from my sight.

Tell me you are almost home. I need you. I whisper into her hair as she hugs me tightly. I swear I can feel her body pressed against mine, her heart beating strong. I press a long kiss to her head.

I am and you are proof! I could only talk to the others when I was close to my aunts' mates since somehow you all are descended from the same blood line. I was going to try to reach all of you at once when I was around everyone, but things kind of went sideways and we had to rush our departure. I was worried I wasn't ready to come home, but now I know I am. Bastian I miss you so much. I need to know you will be there when I wake up. She looked up at me, her eyes bright.

Of course. We are in Daglidell, but it's a stone through from Solaria through the portal. I can get us all back to Solaria once I'm ready to let go of this bliss. I pressed light kisses to her cheeks, then her nose as she giggles from my beard tickling her. It felt as though she had never left me.

Good, I don't want to leave your arms. I want to stay here where nothing bad is happening, but I know that's not right. It's selfish of me for wanting that. Once the war is over, can we all just go away somewhere and hide for a century or so? She asked, pouting out her lower lip. She's so cute.

I'm down for that. I kissed her once more before letting out a deep sigh. *We have to break this now, don't we?* She nodded and I understood. Soon she will be back in my arms for real. I let out another deep sigh, pulling him chin up to look at me. *Promise me that you will come back to me in one piece.*

I promise. She kissed me, a fire igniting between us as we entangled one last time in universal bliss before fading away into darkness.

She's coming home.

CHAPTER 39
VALDIS

First Valyn, then Niklaus, now Bastian. Bulls in a China shop as my mother would say. They were recklessly running around gathering their things, demanding I be ready to go as soon as they're ready. I never unpacked though. I never wanted to. Unpacking seemed like this was going to drag out long, much longer than I wanted. I had called Vanessa to ask her how things were going in Mistveil. According to her, our parents had decided to make an appearance. They loved and adored Luna. My father has finally forgiven me foe the kidnapping fiasco, so that was a plus.

Vanessa has been pacing around going crazy, apparently so have my brothers. My family adored her, Gabrial has finally come around her and trusting her which for him has been the hardest thing for him to do. Either way I am lucky that my family is being supportive right now. I know my father is probably talking business about how to handle the army that's making its way to Floria as deal with this, but we have to have a plan.

"Are you ready to go? You've been sitting here like nothing has happened," Niklaus snapped as he set his bags by the door. Valyn and Bastian hurried themselves down the hall, they weren't nearly as snappy with me as Niklaus was.

"His bag is already over here Nik. Give him a break," Bastian chimed, setting his bag next to mine, giving me an apologetic look. Valyn pushed past Niklaus and toward the pile of bags by the door.

"You would think hearing that we talked to our mate and that she is coming back to us would make him not drag his ass and he would be up ready to go like the rest of us," Niklaus spat. The alcohol still lingered on his breath. It didn't matter though; I was up in his face slamming him against the wall. Bastian took a step toward us but stopped, putting his arm out to stop Valyn from intervening.

"You got to see her! You got to hold her! YOU GOT TO HEAR HER! What did I get?! Not a gods damned thing! I'm not lucky to be a descendant of her aunts mating group! I miss her just as fucking much as you if not fucking more since I didn't get my fucking fix!" I snarl watching as every word hit like a blow to the gut. "You have the reassurance she is okay! So do they! I don't! So, before your drunk self wants to tell me I don't want her back or I'm not in a rush. I am, I just didn't get the adrenaline rush you all did."

I let go of him, letting his body fall to the floor. His mouth was open, but no words left his lips. I didn't expect them too. I didn't expect an apology from him, hell I don't expect an apology from any of them. I just happened to be the unlucky mate. I plop down on the chair I was occupying before Niklaus's bullshit started. Valyn took the seat across from me and gave me the pure look of sadness. Great I should've kept my fucking mouth shut.

"I'm sorry. I should've thought about that when she reached out to me. I didn't think about anyone really myself," Valyn spoke softly, he was always probably the most genuine of the brothers. Fennik a close second. I looked to Bastian who was always blunt as fuck with me, the apologetic looks in his eyes was almost too much to bear. They were all in their own heads and didn't think of me, which is completely fine. They owe me nothing, especially with her not around at the current moment.

"You're allowed to be selfish. You were able to see her, hear her, and hold her. Something I wish I could do, but I just have to wait patiently for her to return to me. So sorry if I'm not outward bursting with emotion, I'm mentally preparing myself to see her for myself. See the changes you have all described to me. I'm ready to go when you guys are," I got up, grabbed my bag and headed for the door. No one spoke a word; they just followed me out the door.

Back to Solaria, and now back to waiting. At least this time we know she's coming back.

CHAPTER 40
FENNIK

What in the actual fuck! The light finally dissipated to reveal the most disgusting of creatures I could ever imagine. The creature had skin as red as the blood that now poured across the grey stone floor, mangled sharp teeth that protruded from its mouth in all different directions, two horns on either side of its head, and a foul sickly-sweet smell that was a pungent assault on my nose. I looked around to make sure everyone was safe, luckily the only blood on the ground was that of the creature.

"What the fuck is that?" Nox said with disgust, as he covered his nose with his arm. Sirus looked down on the creature before turning to stare at Alric. He was wiping off a silver dagger on his pants, red blood dripping from his hand.

"A Riven. They're a type of goblin that seem to love the dead of the land. Usually, they don't come in here often, but every once and awhile one gets in and sets off a trap or six," he spoke so casually of this thing infiltrating their land. "Don't worry they never get far."

"They are foul smelling," Elucia said as she covered her nose with her hand and moved further into the labyrinth just leaving the thing there to rot. "Don't worry, it won't be there by the time we return."

She turned right at the corner, each of us stepping over the creature to follow her. She led us down a long corridor with doors and turns on either side. She walked down to the second to last door on the left and entered it. Normally I wouldn't trust a well-known trickster, but we know her secret now. A guilt that clearly eats at her more than her husband.

"How much longer?" Sirus impatiently asked. Elucia just kept walking, ignoring the question all together as she took deliberate steps over certain stones. I put my arms out stopping Nox and Sirus from stepping the wrong way.

"Follow my exact steps. They said they would lead us, they never said they would tell us their secrets," I pointed at where Alric was following the same exact path that Elucia walked. I copied their movements, step for step, making sure not to miss a single stone. I really hope this doesn't haunt me. I finally reach the door where Elucia and Alric stopped to watch. A smile crested her lips as she watched Nox follow my steps, one by one until he was beside me.

Sirus, however, didn't trust the process and took a step on the wrong stone first, setting off a javelin that shot straight across the room barely missing Sirus's chest. Elucia and Alric let out a collective sigh, pushing past Nox and me. "You're stubborn. If you follow the rest of the steps properly, you won't have to dodge things." Alric called out to him, but Sirus being head headed, took another wrong step. Another javelin shot from the opposite wall, narrowly missing our God of death. Sirus let out a low curse before stepping, finally, on a correct stone. I went to open my mouth, but Alric put his hand up. "He has to help himself at this point. You already told him what to do and he didn't listen. He never does."

Nox watched on as Sirus followed the remaining correct stones to reach us. "Was that so fucking hard?" he snapped at his uncle who was bent over, hands on his knees as he tried to catch his breath. It didn't stop Nox from reading him the riot act as we continued our way to the armory. Nox was still snapping at Sirus and bickering when we reached a large room. Elucia lifted her hand, pausing our advances.

"The armory isn't much further. I know it hasn't felt like forever, but it's been over an hour. If you step wrong in this room, the labyrinth will twist and send you back to the beginning. Changing the entire labyrinth on just you. You won't be able to follow the same path to get back to this room. So don't be fucking stubborn or else we cannot help you," Elucia said, pointing her glare at Sirus. I could feel the heat from her stare when I stood next to him.

"Fine. I'll follow orders," Sirus conceded. I wasn't sure how much I believed him, but I wasn't about to be lost from the only two who could help us. Alric started first. Three steps forward, two to the right, four forward, five to the left, two forward then to safety. I watched Elucia follow the exact same path, I glanced at Nox before nodding and taking the first steps onto the floor. He followed me closely a step or so behind me. Sirus, watched as we made our way across the floor. His eyes focusing on where we stepped. As we crossed into safety,

Sirus called out, "Three forward, two right, four forward, five left, two forward. Right Fenn?"

"Yeah!" I shouted back to him. He took each step quick, stopping at the last stone of each order. I couldn't tell if he was trying to decide if he wanted to step off of the path and move forward onto another stone or not. If he could race through this labyrinth alone, would he look for the weapon or something else? He continued until he was right beside us. He smirked at Elucia and I didn't understand the taunt. She was being helpful. Why was he being a dick?

"It's right this way," Alric said, ushering Elucia through the door to the left of the hallway. I watched Sirus hesitate before following them. I understand that he doesn't trust them, but I don't have a reason not to trust them. I will follow my heart until they give me a reason not to trust them. Nox was behind me watching the whole thing go down.

"Do you have a feeling we are being led into a trap?" Nox whispered to me as we followed them down another hallway, the stones becoming less moldy and more pristine. The grey granite turned into a white and grey marble, the stone floor changing into a beautiful hardwood finish with plush ruby red carpeting. The sconces along the walls became more elegant the further in we went. I still didn't get a bad feeling.

"No, I think we are going into their home. I think the remnants of the home we landed in, was their home at one point. Something bad happened and they're taking refuge here. I don't think they want to hurt us, but who the hell knows. I could be wrong and just want to trust someone," I replied, shrugging my shoulders. Nox gripped my shoulder hand, stopping me from taking another step.

"It may not be us they're trying to trap," he gave a pointed glance at Sirus who was following but taking in his surroundings as if an attack was imminent. "He doesn't trust them at all. He has reasons not to. You and I have no reason not to trust them."

"Then we keep Sirus close to us until we get out of here. Maybe not let the God of death piss off two tricksters who could kill him with the weapons they guard," I complain. Sirus is a grown ass god who distrusts almost everyone he meets, has caused us our own problems before and has risked not just his life but Luna and Valdis's as well. Great so now we are babysitters.

We both seemingly agreed to watch him closely, but I wasn't about to let Elucia and Alric out of my sight. The two of them were talking quietly amongst themselves as they walked. The labyrinth had officially turned into a beautiful home, I realized I wasn't off when I said it was their home. Alric had opened a door to the right of the hallway and stepped inside, Elucia paused outside waiting for us. Sirus paused before the door as we got to them.

"Where are they?!" Alric yelled. "They were here this morning! No one has been here since you all landed!" Elucia looked worried and rushed into the room Sirus hot on her heels. We followed her into the room, noticing the bare shelf that had a blade holder on it. "Otius's Hand is missing!"

CHAPTER 41
Nox

Worry spun a web in my head, the sounds of yelling and arguing mingled with the thought that the blade is gone. I pulled my phone out of my pocket and called Undas. The phone rang twice before his gruff voice answered. "What is it, Nox?"

"The weapon's name is Otius's Hand. Did you know about this?" I tried to keep my voice steady; I tried to let the rage I was feeling not explode on him. I could hear a deep sigh through the phone. A soft female voice spoke in the background.

"Hand me the phone," I could hear the voice much clearer now. "What is the problem my dear boy?" Vanalli's voice was soft and usually soothing. I could hear her tapping her nails on whatever surface she had available.

"The weapon that can kill the gods is called Otius's Hand. Did you know the blade was named after your father? Did he create the damn thing?" I snarled. I was raised with respect, but I was beyond fucking pissed. I heard more voices in the background, male and female. "Has my sister woken up yet?"

"Your sister's vitals are coming back slowly. To answer your other question, my father forged an array of weapons not to kill the Gods but to kill a daemon king. We only know that there is something in the metal that can harm us. What that is? We don't know, but it can kill a daemon king. That we know for sure. Why are you so upset about this? All weapons that were made are all locked up in the ruins of decay with Alric and Elucia. Aren't you there?" Vanalli's words danced around my brain. It took me a moment to process the information I had just been given.

"Otius's Hand is missing," I said flatly. The room around me went silent, all eyes on me. "I adore you, but your father just put all our lives at risk. I don't care why he made the blade; it should've been destroyed. Now we have to worry about who has it."

"Elucia and Alric have traps set inside the ruins. There is no way that someone got in without setting off the traps. Are you with them?" Vanalli's voice was high pitched, and face paced.

"Yeah, they're here currently fighting with your son. Want to talk to one of them?" I ask, clenching my fist tight around the phone. Don't break the phone dumbass.

"Please put Elucia on," Vanalli spoke with a sternness to her that I wasn't used to hearing.

"Elucia, my grandmother wishes to speak with you," I grunted, holding out the phone for her to take. Elucia gingerly took the phone from my hands, her pale complexion a bit green now. She looked sick, so did Alric.

"Good evening Vanalli," she spoke softly into the phone, and I wish I could hear what my grandmother was saying. Elucia looked terrified, her eyes wide as she watched everyone in the room. Alric and Sirus had stopped arguing long enough to see the fear flash across Elucia's face. Fennik looked like he was about to be sick his own self. I guess he realizes the implications of what this means for everyone he's standing with in this room. Someone stole a god killing weapon from under the noses of the tricksters. Whoever stole it knew the way.

I glanced at Alric thinking long and hard about the question I was about to ask him. "Is there anyone who knows the labyrinth as well as you both? Valmor?" Alric took a moment before answering.

"If Valmor came home and didn't say anything to his mother, he knows the wrath she would inflict upon him, even from afar. The only other visitor we have gotten aside from you lot was Allura from Solaria a few weeks ago. She was inquiring that the blade was still safely tucked away from the world. She said something about waves being made thanks to a new power player and she worried that someone would come for the blade. Elucia and I showed her that she had nothing to worry about and that we protect our own. We sent her own her way, despite her being very rude to us about our lack of hospitality," Alric rolled his eyes, but I locked eyes with Fennik.

"Allura is Scarlett and Penelope's sister. She wasn't lucky enough to mate with my father, and she was pissed about it from what I've been told. you don't think that she would steal the blade and help my mother, do you?!" Fennik's panic was a rush of emotions. Allura had a reason to help Marie. Jealousy. One of the worst traits to ever consume humans and fae alike. Not that Gods were immune, absolutely not, Luna was a prime example of that.

"We need to get back to Mirith. If the blade isn't here, then we need to figure out where it is," announcing the next move aloud seemed so cliche like they really needed me to tell them what we should do. "If Allura has the blade, or even gave it to Marie, we need to warn my parents." Fennik was too busy texting on the phone to pay much attention to what I was saying. Elucia tapped me on the shoulder and handed me back my phone.

"We are being summoned to Valhime to speak with Vanalli and Undas. There is nothing to protect here. At least not at the moment. Vanalli heard what you said about Allura, she is currently holed up in Solaria. I was told to tell you both that Prince Damian is in Valhime with them and Princess Luna. Sirus, your mother has asked that I pass along a message. She wants you in Valhime with us, your sister is also being summoned as we speak." Elucia moved to Alric's side, he wasted no time pulling her into his embrace. Suddenly I found myself pitying her. She looked shaken up by whatever else my grandmother had said to her.

"Fine, we all head to Solaria, I'll tell the others to meet us there," I clicked my phone on, but Fennik was already ahead of me.

"Sorry, I already told everyone to meet us there now. I figured adding you a group chat would eliminate the back and forth and different messages," Fennik said with a smile on his face.

"We can get you out of here safely and we can travel together as long as you're not opposed to teleportation. It's a specialty of Alric's," Elucia said with a smile to her lover.

"We could've just transported here from the beginning?" Sirus griped from behind us.

"Not exactly, I can't do it inside the labyrinth. It's a measure we took to make sure no one could use me to get to the blade. Clever don't you think?" Alric flashed a grin at us. Probably the first time I didn't see him with the scowl he's had since we showed up. "We're going to have to retrace our steps, but the traps that were set to get in here should be lifted since we passed and made it safely inside."

"Then let's get going. No disrespect, but if my mother summoned us, we best not make her wait," Sirus headed for the door to the room and waited for everyone else to catch up with him. Elucia and Alric took point with Fennik and I flanking Sirus. I guess we will have to make one hell of a team if we have to fight someone with a blessed blade.

Why can't my life every be easy around these guys?

CHAPTER 42
LUNA

Everything was so bright. The lights dancing in little circles, the bright yellows, blues, purples and pinks inside the white bulbs. I could hear the electricity buzzing through them as if someone was amplifying the noise just to be annoying. I could smell everything. The smell of smoke filled my nostrils, but didn't alarm me, instead it sent a thrill through my body unlike ever before. I tried to focus my gaze on the room around me, the people standing over me, hovering and shoving one another. I didn't care who stood there, I needed my prince of darkness. The man who matched the inner beast within me that raged to be set free and alone together. A throaty growl came from the side of me, a delicious sound that sent shivers down my spine to the pool between my thighs.

I heard someone sound like they were clearing their throat, trying to drag the feral beast's attention to the others in the room, but I could not give two fucks less at who was in the room, only that they needed to fucking leave. A hand pressed itself against my forehead. It was soft, delicate and smelled of elderberries and puffin flowers. Maggie. The high priestess who had saved my life on countless fucking occasions and never once begged me to stop. Never once commanded I be a lady and act like the princess that was demanded of me. No, she understood my need not to be protected but to be the protector. "She doesn't have a fever, but her senses are going to be extremely heightened. I would be very cautious with how you interact with her from this moment forward." She was warning the room. Smart woman. Then again, she was always smart. I adored that about her, that and the fact that she never once questioned me or the things that I did. She may have been stern a few times because I made her worry, but I can appreciate that.

"Will she remember everyone?" A deeper, gruff voice spoke up. I recognized it immediately. Undas. My grandfather. Talissa's father. The one who I gained my flames from. He wants nothing but the best for me. Don't kill him, I told my beast as she cracked an eye open to take in the large fiery god at the end of the bed. He won't hurt us.

"She will. She may already but give her time and get her mates here now. Her mating bond is waking up with full power and will need them all to bring her back down. Figure out a way to give them a pass into Valhime like you did me. She cannot be let out of her until she has bonded with each of them as a full-fledged goddess." Maggie told the room. My beast purred in my chest, giving a silent approval of her words. She wasn't wrong. I want to pounce on the only mate that is within arm's reach right now, but that might embarrass him.

"Leave us then. I can match her bond until the others arrive," he growled, his beast tearing at his insides to get to me. His bond as hungry for me as mine is for him. Not a physical beast, no. Something more powerful, more raw, more intense. He will be worshipping me the moment that door closes, even if I have to ride his face until he can't breathe or taps the fuck out. He's mine.

I heard the door the loud shuffling of shoes on carpet, grumbles and slight complaints about being ushered from the room and a simple whisper saying hush. Good, they're leaving, soon it will be just him and I. Then all bets are off. I heard a softer male's voice speak to my mate, "Remember she's more powerful than before. Be careful with her for your safety, but don't back down." I recognized my uncle's voice, the death god warning the mate to the universe about safety. I wouldn't dare hurt him, a part of me wanted to snarl at him for insinuating I would hurt what is mine, but the rational side of me understands. This is just as new to them as it is to me.

The door opened once more as he left someone entered behind him. The scent of apples and fire wafted into the room, alerting my beast to another who belongs to me. A growl slipped from his lips as he took me in, laying here with nothing but a sheet to cover me. A very bright sheet that touched too much of my skin for my liking, it was scratching my skin like nails. My first mate knew it, could feel it. Thankfully, he ripped the sheet off and tossed it across the room. A feral growl echoed in the room as he spread my legs wide.

"Look at this beautiful pussy, already dripping for me," he growled as he lowered his head between my legs, taking in a deep breath of my scent. "I think that needs to be handled." He gripped my thighs so tight, dragging his nails softly down my thighs, eliciting a growl from me. I hadn't been in my own body for a little while, but I had full control of my limbs and actions. Propping myself up on my elbows, I cocked a grin at him before grabbing his beard and pulling him up the length of my body, biting his lower lip to drag him into a kiss.

His hands roamed my body, squeezing my hips, digging his nails in as he passionately kissed me back, devouring every inch of our kiss. His smokey taste lingered on my tongue, a new taste mingled in with the familiar smoke though. Rain, salty rain. It hit me then when I broke out kiss that he had tears streaming down his face. Light reflecting off those beautiful crimson eyes, mapped out different hues of reds and black in his iris, something I never noticed before this. Kissing away his tears, I moved him from a top of me to lay on his back. My eyes fixate on my mate at the door, his bright orange hair an absolute mess, but his beast is gnawing at the bit to get me. He is just as hungry for me as this one. I straddle my smokey beast, digging my nails deep into his chest, red lines appear, some with droplets of blood peeking through the marks. Lowering myself down his body, I lick up the blood, sweet and sticky, but delicious.

His cock twitches between my legs, I can feel him aching for me through his jeans. The beast in me roars in me to be released to fully claim this one for myself in a way I haven't before, but I wanted to play. I glanced at the other one standing at the door watching, the outline of his cock pressing hard against his own jeans. A playful smile graced my lips as I got off of my mate and sauntered over to the other. My smokey mate watched me as I walked across and thrusted my hand down my autumn mate's pants, gripping his cock firmly in my hand. I loved it, his cock was so hot and hard. I pulled him by his cock over to the bed that my other mate was sprawled out on, "Undo them. Now." I commanded. Without hesitation, both males removed their pants for me. The one standing let his fall to the floor, the one laying down kicked his off the side of the bed, waiting patiently for my next move.

The bed was big enough for a plethora of people, all of my mates will fit lovely on this bed together once we are all united. I dropped my autumn mates' cock, sliding onto the bed until I was straddled over my smokey mates face. "I hope you don't like to breathe," I whisper as I lower my pussy over his mouth. His tongue immediately began lapping up the sweet nectar that I offered him. The other one watched as I sat upon my mates' face. "On the bed. Now."

Without question he was on the bed in seconds, his cock bouncing with the movements. I gripped his hair roughly, pulling him into a kiss. The taste of apples and cinnamon coated the inside of my mouth, dancing with the taste of smoke. It was a delicious mix of flavors that made me gush more. My mate didn't tap out to my surprise, his beast was craving me. I grinded hard on his face, the sensitive bundle of nerves at my entrance toying with his mustache as I brought myself closer and closer to releasing myself on his tongue. My autumn mate gripped my hair, breaking our kiss.

"I'm sorry. I'm so sorry," he whispered onto my lips. I watched as his jade and emerald eyes looked over me for the first time like this, realizing I didn't care about the past. I just want the future, and I want it now. He pulled me back into a passionate kiss, one hand in my hair the other pinching my nipple hard. "Come on his face, then take my cock however you please." He growled into my ear.

The door flew open, pulling my beast further to the forefront of my mind. *Claim them. Claim them now!* I let the urge take hold and as I rode my smokey mates face until I came so hard on his tongue, I plunged my canines into my autumn mates' neck, pulling deeply from him. His beast roared forward, sinking its own canines into me. Our blood mixing, our power and bond tightening and strengthening. We completed out bonding the proper way. His make on me, my mark on him. Satisfied by this, my beast slowly released him, letting him fall back into the chair against the wall. Cock still throbbing hard between his legs. I slid off my smokey mates face, his beard glistening with my juices, a grin plastered on his face as he sat up on his elbows. "My turn," he whispered as he gripped my waist, tossing me on my back as he plunged his cock deep in me.

He grinned up at my other mates in the doorway. "Close the fucking door and lose your clothes before she makes you lose them," he barked out as he kept a hard, fast rhythm while he fucked me so thoroughly my beast was tame and satiated. For now. He covered me with his full body as he pulled me closer and closer to another release, only this time, my canines would be sinking into him. "Are you ready princess?" He whispered into my ear sending chills down my spine.

"I was born ready prince," I whispered back as I sunk my teeth deep into his neck, his blood tasted like the most exquisite bourbon money could buy. A sharp pain in my neck turned to pure bliss as he plunged deep in me with not just his teeth. He pulled me deep as we drank from one another. He pulled back to look down at me as my blood dripped from his lips to mine and kissed me once more as he wrapped my legs around his arms and plunged deep and hard into me. I came undone as I felt him fill me up. He twitched for a few moments before unsheathing himself from me.

Wings covered me in an instant, shadows danced around us as my daemon mate covered me with his body. "I've missed you, my love. I have a feeling if we keeping doing this one by one, you're going to be too sore for the others. What do you say about three of us at once?" His velvety smooth voice sent a heat through me that I couldn't focus on. The beast inside me was writhing and pulling at the idea of taking three of them at once.

"I have two hands to you know. That would cover everyone," I teased. Something inside me snapped tight as an invasion in my mind had my mouth watering. My summer mate filled my vision, naked, hard and fisting his cock, greedily waiting his turn. I need them all. My smokey mate, was well satiated in the chair, but the others needed release. "All. Now!" I let out the command and at my will they all moved.

"If it's okay, I am going to sit this one out and catch my breath," my lunar mate called to me. I growled but conceded. I could have more of him later. My snow mate brushed his fingers through my hair, violet eyes wide as he took me in. I was still laid out on the bed as he bounced his cock in my face. I could easily pop it into my mouth like a fucking lollipop. Precum glistened on the tip, I needed to taste him. I reached out to grab him, but my daemon mate stopped me.

"Not yet, princess. We need to adjust you first and as much as I want to plow that beautiful pussy of yours, I think Valyn would rip me apart if I don't let him go first," my daemon mate helped me up as my summer mate laid out on the bed. His cock was so beautiful, thick and hard and glorious. I couldn't help myself as the beast took over, pouncing on him like he was my prey.

"Go ahead and be greedy princess. Take all of me," his said as I slide myself on his length, he was so big, I felt myself stretch and tighten around him. I settled down finally as hands gripped me ass. I took a deep breath as my daemon mate, spread my ass cheeks and slowly inched his way inside of me. The feeling of fullness was intense, the beast in my chest pulsated and writhed gleefully at the feeling. My snow mate finally lined his cock back up to my lips, greedily I sucked him right in between my lips to a cursed moan. It was perfect. My autumn mate and spring mate filled my hands and started moving. I knew I couldn't mark them all like this, or maybe I could.

My body was on fire, filled by my mates as they fucked me and used me to their satisfaction. The daemon one grabbed my hair, pulling my head back, forcing my winter mates' cock from my mouth, the friction inside me from my daemon and my summer mate was dragging me closer and close to release myself. "Be a good girl and cum on his dick while you claim me," his velvety voice caressed the skin on my neck, and I willingly came all over my summer mate as they both thrusted deep into me. "Good girl." He leaned down and kissed my neck, exposing his own to me. I opened my mouth and claimed him rough and hard. His blood pouring into my mouth was a bit tart with a floral taste that I wasn't expecting, but before I could react, he was sinking his canines into the flesh at my collarbone.

I felt my summer mate start to twitch beneath me, his beast ready to claim me. But he didn't say anything. He waited until the daemon was done. The autumn one was next his movements in my palm, vigorous and needy, He grabbed my head, pushing me down toward his cock. I knew what he needed and so did the beast writhing inside of me to taste him again. I popped the tip of his cock into my mouth, flicking my tongue against the bottom of his head as he came all over my tongue. I growled, staggering back from us all looking for purchase on a wall or couch. The daemon was already watching us, satisfied by his seed leaking from me.

The spring mate was next, he was gentler with me. More than my beast wanted him to be, and I thought he would put his cock in my mouth but instead he kissed me, guiding my head to my winter mates' cock instead. They both took time guiding me up and down his length, slow then fast. My winter mate growled as he tilted my head just right to shove his cock to the back of my throat, shooting his load straight down. He dropped to his knees before me, gripped my chin and kissed me, breaking so my beast could take what it was craving. His blood. Another claim, another mark that would stay with us for eternity. I sunk my teeth into his skin, letting the warm blood trickle down my throat.

Two more. Two more to satiate the beast inside of me. I turned my head to watch my spring mate line his cock up with my ass before he plunged himself into me, my summer mate growling at the friction pressing against him through me. Sweat dripped from me onto my mate, but his turquoise eyes just shown bright, bits of gold flecked through as I got so close. The spring prince gripped my waist and plunged himself deep. "Luna!" he yelled as his beast took over and sunk its teeth into my shoulder. A wave of bliss and passion washed over me as he filled and claimed me. I reached for his wrist and clamped down tight with my canines, piercing the flesh right below his wrist.

My summer mate edged himself so long, but he did it to himself. His smile widened as the spring one moved away from us. Everyone in the room exhausted and panting. Everyone but him. He gripped my waist hard and forced me down on his cock, stretching me and filling me in one thrust. Lust filled me as I rode him like my life depended on it, his smile only widened as I lost control. "Take me baby girl. Do your worst." He winked at me and all bets were off. I dug my nails into his shoulders as I grinded him into me deeper and harder. I want him to fill me up, I want to not be able to walk when he is done with me. *As you wish.* I heard his voice in my head as his arm wrapped around me, moving me to my back while he rose up above me tossing my legs on his shoulders as he drove his cock so deep in me, I let out a scream. My nails digging into his forearms, drawing blood from him.

He smiled down at me once more. Claim me baby girl. Take everything you need. Just come for me first. His voice sung in my mind like a beautiful song written just for me and I gladly obeyed. He moved my legs to his hips and lowered his body over me, exposing his neck to me. Inching my lips to his neck, I liked the salty skin before sinking my canines deep into him, he returned the favor. We drank deeply from one another as we rolled into a crashing wave of release.

We laid there on the bed for so long, our bodies mingling, his blood dripping down my lips. Time seemed to slow as my beast let its hold on me go. Names slowly started coming back to me. My beast didn't care about their names, just that they belonged to us and that everyone needed to know that I would slaughter anyone who tries to take them or hurt them.

"You're a murderous little creature aren't you, my love?" Valdis said aloud, dragging my thoughts from rage to bliss. He got up from his seat, still naked as the day he was born, and crossed the room. "Don't ever leave us like that again."

"Nothing on this planet will take me from any of you ever again if I have any say about it," I pushed myself up on my elbows and kissed him.

"Not to drag the moment down, but what happened when you died Luna?" Damian asked as he joined us on the bed, Bastian crossed the room and got me a glass of water before joining. Niklaus and Fennik seemed content to sit on the couch close to the bed. So many deliciously naked bodies surrounded me. I could go again. A smile tipped my lips skyward. Oh fuck!

"Shit! Where are we?!" I asked forcing myself up from the bed. They all gave me a puzzled look, like I was about to break. "My aunt and her ma—"

The door opened, despite protests outside of the room a tall man entered the room, a grin from ear to ear on his face. "Well damn, I thought we were the only ones who came back horny as fuck." River said, eyes twinkling. My mates all went to get in his face until Lumina poked her head out from behind him with a wide grin on her face. "Your aunts outside, she said we shouldn't bother you but," he walked into the room with Lumina and took a seat. "We couldn't help but wonder how you handled the change."

"Don't let him fool you, he wanted to see if you had any better positioning ideas," Lumina chimed in taking her seat next to him. "But truly, all jokes aside, we wanted to make sure you were okay and that you made it back safely."

I didn't think, I just jumped up from the bed and ran to them, pulling them into a hugging embrace. "Thank you both. I am so glad you're back safe! Is there any word on Ignis? Voxis? What about Claye?"

"They're coming," Talissa's voice rang from the doorway as she closed it behind her. "Milara followed behind us. Zephir should be here soon. Luna honey, I love that you are so free with your body, but would you mind?" Her question trailed off and then it hit me. I was hugging her mates butt ass naked.

"Shit! I am so sorry!" I jumped up and grabbed a sheet from the bed, tossing it around me. Everyone laughed including my aunt. "I wasn't thinking. I didn't mean to offend you."

"Offend her?! Please! This is the same woman who wanted to prove to Voxis that she would be jealous if another person not in our group looked at her naked, so she stripped in the middle of the street and began dancing. Don't let her fool you, you take after her in many ways," River laughed. Each of my mates quickly got dressed, pulling out bags with clothes for me from the side of the room.

"We each brought you clothes that we had in our rooms. You have options," Bastian smirked, kissing me deeply.

"Well, that's a plus, but you might want to hurry. Milara is here and she is kicking up threats of violence. Apparently, the almighty god killing blade is missing and we have to go find it," Talissa said as she sat on River's lap. She caressed Lumina's cheek, placing a soft kiss to her lips.

"Wait, so you all returned from the dead," Niklaus started, "and you all came back horny?" His head tilted to the side as he watched my aunt make out with Lumina. Not going to lie I can't imagine what it's like for them.

"Apparently it's a side effect on our physical bodies. We wake up with a craving. It's supposed to go away but no one told us how fast, or how much we'd have to fuck to satiate it," River said, running circles on Talissa's back. Lumina broke the kiss, gasping for air, a giggle bubbled up from Talissa as if she was a child again.

"Sorry about that, you just taste so good," Talissa said, a smile playing on her lips. "My little lemon tart." She moved a strand of blonde curls from Lumina's face, Lumina swatting at Talissa's hand to stop.

"That's it, embarrass me more!" Lumina was flushed and blushing. It was cute. I wonder if I would've been the same had I mated to a female. I looked at my mates, a warmth filling me. I'm mated to exactly who I need to be with.

"I am going in regardless of how they are all dressed or not!" Milara's voice rang through the door. Well, honeymoon's over.

CHAPTER 43
UNDAS

My sister had called me to warn me about our mother randomly waking up and the craziness that has been happening in Firehearth manor over the last several hours. What she failed to mention was that my beloved Talissa had returned as well. Not only has my granddaughter woken up, but my daughter is back. I don't know how to feel about all of this, the time I lost with her, the regret I have from that day. I can't take back things that I said back then, I can only hope that she forgives me.

Considering I got a hug before she went in to talk to Luna, that is a positive sign, but my mother had to come in and ruin it with her barging in and yelling to gain entrance to Luna's room. Honestly, I was just as shocked as Vanalli when Luna opened the doors so my mother wouldn't destroy them to get in. My mother and Luna embraced before shutting the door in our faces, mainly my mother keeping us out.

"What do you think they're talking about in there?" Vanalli asked me quietly as Sirus and Nox sat in the corner by the fireplace. We called Erina to let her know Luna had woken up, but she told us she couldn't leave something bad had happened in Floria and they were on their way there with Harold. We need to get there to help them, but not knowing how strong Luna is, we have to keep her close. She needs to recover.

"Your father's death blade and the fact that it's missing," I replied. Otius and I never really saw eye to eye after how he treated Vanalli for staying with me instead of returning home. Didn't matter that we were mates to him, just that he needed to keep his daughter in a gilded cage, and I refused to let her be kept like that. She is a wildfire, despite how she carries herself now.

"I don't understand how they lost the fucking blade. It wasn't that hard to stay put and set traps to stop people from getting close. But also, how did they not know someone got in and stole the blade?" She was twisting her hair around her fingers above her chest. Anything she was nervous or stressed that was what comforted her, our daughter all do the same and now so does my granddaughter.

"When do you want to go talk to them?" I knew Elucia and Alric had come with Sirus and the others, but we haven't had the chance to speak to them since Luna woke up. I put my arm around Vanalli and pulled her close to me, pressing a kiss on the top of her head.

"I think while they are all busy, we should probably go talk to them. I don't want Elucia to think I requested her here just to have her waiting," Vanalli kissed me before standing, running her hands over her dress to smooth out any wrinkles. My queen always wanting to look one hundred percent at all times.

"Then let's do it. Sirus," I said, pulling his attention from Nox. "Would you let your sister and niece know that we will meet up with them for dinner when they're done with your grandmother."

"Yeah, are we worried that she's here without Zephir?" Sirus was close with his grandfather, at least my father. It's not surprising to me that he is the one he's worried about. As much as I worry about my father, I know if my mother is here and isn't causing a fuss about him, then I shouldn't worry. Now if she was in hysterics, all bets would be off.

"No, just keep an ear out on them please. I don't know what they are plotting or how bad things are about to get for all of us," I said, entwining my fingers in my wife's fingers as we began out walk to the main hall. Nox bowed every time we walked by him, and I still can't for the life of me get him to stop. I know he is military, and I know they breed that kind of respect into the soldiers, but that is my grandson. I need him to relax more around us.

Vanalli held my hand the entire way down the marbled hallways. Our footsteps echoed off the walls, making me so uncomfortable. I love our home in Firehearth, simple, cozy and inviting. Not like the places here in Valhime, cold and clinical. It's annoying that we have here to take care of meetings and things here. I'd rather do it somewhere not so damn cold!

"You're frowning my love," Vanalli spoke softly as we moved through the halls to the main office where Elucia and Alric were waiting for us. We wanted to address the matter immediately, but our

321

granddaughter waking up took precedence. They understood and said they would wait for us to return.

"I hate it here. I know we had to come here to save Luna, but can we please go home after this? Like let's take her and everyone else and go to Firehearth. There's room enough for everyone," I tried to plead my case with my wife, but she was raised here. She was used to the coldness Valhime. It wasn't until she lived with me in Firehearth that she realized the world was such a warm place to be. She flourished there, we flourished there.

"I'd be more than happy to return home. I have a sinking feeling that if your mother and father have returned, my parents won't be far behind. I'd prefer not to be here when they return," she said, worry and concern were like a mask on her face. She was very always worried her parents would return.

"Shall we call your brother and sister?" I asked slightly hesitant. She was close with her sister, but her brother saw things a little different when she decided to stay with me. It didn't matter that we were mates, she betrayed them in his eyes. Even though he was the one who forced her to take that agreement all those many moons ago.

"I'll call them and alert them. Ithalu might want to get Mina out of here quickly before they return," she spoke softly as we came up to the office door. She turned to look at me. "If my brother and sister decide to run from them, will you allow them rooms at Firehearth?"

I cupped her chin in my free hand, tilting her head up before placing a gentle kiss to her lips, "Your brother and I may have our issues, but I would never refuse them safety my love."

With that she kissed me once more before turning back to the door and letting the mask of disappointment slip back on as if it never left. She was really good at making sure that if she wanted us to feel bad about something, we would. I took a deep breath myself before settling back into my own mask of rage. These two are so fucked. I open the door, letting her go in first, watching as both tricksters raise from the seats in acknowledgment.

"Please be seated," Vanalli demanded disgusting the demand as pleasantries. I swear I need to learn how she does it. She took her seat behind the desk as I took my place behind her. "I'm sure you already understand where I stand and the amount of disappointment I feel. You two were tasked with a simple task of guarding a blade that could kill us all. Yet, my son and grandson go to make sure that it's still where it should be resting and what do they find? Two gods disguising themselves as children to torment the locals, setting fire to a forest for fun, playing games instead of actually guarding the weapons that you were entrusted with. And please spare me the excuse of your traps being foolproof. Clearly, that is not true or else we wouldn't be sitting her trying to figure out how to find the blade."

"I wish that I had an answer as to who got past our labyrinth. You can ask your grandson, we led them through, but we didn't tell them how to get through. Your granddaughters mate figured out what we were doing. Sirus distrusted us from the beginning, but that is to be expected. We understand how you feel towards us for not helping your daughter. For that, I am deeply sorry," Elucia said, a picture of calmness. She was truly sorry for refusing to aid Talissa, at least her son wasn't as weak as they were. I just wish they would've told us what happened. The truth that he came home to them a year later.

"When were you going to tell us about Valmor?" Well, I guess she was going to bring it up sooner or later. Vanalli folder her hands on the desk looking between the two as they gazed at each other. Vanalli was pissed when she found out about Valmor. "Let me be clear, I was grief stricken when our children were taken from us. My anger and disappointment did not stop me from checking in on you once I found out that Valmor left behind your backs and join my daughter and the cause. When news reached us of his death, I was distraught, my heart aching and breaking for you both. Yet, neither of you check in on us once since Talissa passed. I thought it odd, but now knowing that one year later Valmor returned to you, and you failed to tell us. It would've given us hope, it would've given my other children hope that their sister would one day come back to them."

"We didn't want to give you false hope and no offense, you were our last thoughts," Alric said before Elucia could speak. "Valmor also left us shortly after returning to us. His own anger with us for staying neutral outweighed his love for us. He aligned with Zekon, and we haven't seen or spoken to him since. It was like losing him all over again. So sorry we didn't think of your feelings as our world crumbled around us."

Vanalli looked like she had been slapped across the face. "Zekon died in the war. Do not treat us as idiots. My daughter lost all of her mates that day," Vanalli raged, my kind, sweet, loving wife was white hot. A silent flame flickering to life. Fuck, I need to stop her before she does something she will regret.

"If that is true, you must know a way to contact Valmor. I would love to speak with him myself," I interject, as I watch the look of shock and confusion break through Vanalli's mask. *If they are right my love, then we need to know why Zekon didn't come back to us.*

I hope he didn't think we would hate him, she responded, her hands now shaking on the table in front of her. She looked up at Elucia who had tears in her eyes, the heartbreak of a mother who lost her child not once, but twice. She grabbed a tissue from the side of the desk and handed it to Elucia. "I'm sorry, but we thought Zekon died that day. If you know otherwise, we really do need to talk to him."

"Why don't you talk to the daemon princes? Isn't your granddaughter also mated to King Alistar's son?" Alric spat, disrespectful little shit. "Our son won't return our calls or speak with us, and you want us to try to help you talk to him. No. I'll take responsibility for the blade going missing, but I won't help you torture my wife." Elucia laid her hand on Alric's arm. *I understand that need to protect your mate, especially after something tragic happens.*

"It's okay, maybe us helping them this time will show him that we have grown. We can't sit idle anymore Alric, as much as I would love to," Elucia said, pulling out her phone and flicking through the contacts. "This is the last number I had for him. I think he wanted to open communication decades ago, but I think he waged a war internally as to forgive us or not. It was a call then a quick hang up when I said hello. But again, that was decades ago."

"Thank you. If we happen to talk to him, I will tell them how you are helping us. We might need to call on aid from the others as well as you both. Cerulia is under attack again by King Marcloff. We cannot let him win," Vanalli spoke sternly, locking eyes with Elucia who nodded her head.

A soft knock came at the door, "Come in."

The door pushed open and standing in the doorway was Kieran and Vanessa. "We might be able to help you."

Alric and Elucia looked at each other than to the door, but Vanalli looked at Vanessa. "Come in darlings."

CHAPTER 44
LUNA

I am so glad that I am quick at getting dressed, Milara wasn't waiting for me to be decent. I'm just grateful she didn't interrupt my fun time when I woke up. I'm going to be sore for a fucking week, but it was so worth it. Valyn pulled me into his arms and help me as Milara came into the room with a bright smile on her face. I can just imagine how insane I look, hair is probably a complete mess, any make up that I possibly still had on was probably smeared, and I know I am sporting some nice rosy cheeks. I should be embarrassed, but I'm not.

"It's so wonderful to see you on this side of the earth my dear," Milara said as she crossed the room, pulling me into a bear hug. "Zephir and the others should be along shortly. We, however, have business to discuss." She finally released me and took up residence in the abandoned chair by my aunt. I just sat on the bed, nestled in Valyn's lap, content to stay here for a while longer.

"You're not even back for more than a few hours and already you are plotting," Talissa said, shaking her head. River had her pulled close to his chest, slightly protective. I guess he was nervous of what Milara was about to say. Valyn squeezed me tighter in the same type of protectiveness. Everyone else was laid out on the massive bed, Valdis the closest to me.

"I'm not plotting. There was a war already raging before we stepped foot back onto Cerulia soil. I know we all want a few moments of bliss and contentment before we start up the mess of figuring out how to get out of this mess unscathed," Milara spoke softly to us all. "I know you don't want to hear this; I didn't want to hear it either. Otius's blade was stolen. Otius and Illisandra are going to return as well. I, for one, don't want to be here when they return. I might just kill him again with my own bare hands or at least try. Anyways, there are a lot of people out there waiting on you to emerge from this room Luna. I suggest you get that done and over with. Expect the gawking at your new appearance, but more so expect the suspicion. You are more powerful than your aunt. Sorry Talissa darling."

Talissa just shrugged her shoulders as she reached her hand out to Lumina who gladly took it with a smile. "What is needed of us?"

"I'm so glad you asked. Once the others return, which Celia is aware of and waiting for, I need you all to go searching for Otius's blade. We can't have a god killing blade out in the world. That is just stupid. I hate that your grandfather even had that thing made. I know you might want to go elsewhere," Milara said, eyeing up Valdis who was running idle circle on my thigh. "But we can cross that bridge in private."

"My bond is already reawakened; he knows I'm alive. I just need to get out of Valhime so I can be with him," Talissa replied, Lumina and River both smiling at her. "Once the others awaken, we will head out.

Is there any idea of where the blade might be or who might've stolen it?"

"Only royals from the solar and lunar realms are allowed in without question. I didn't go in and nor did my mother," Damian announced from the pillows. "Apologies for interjecting."

"You're fine dear. I appreciate you offering the information," Milara smiled at Damian, but I watched Talissa take him in. She probably saw the same thing I saw when I looked at Ignis. They have similarities, and a lot of them. But her attention to Valdis had me wondering if she hated him because he's a daemon.

"Can I ask something?" I looked at Talissa, her attention shot from Valdis to me. "Why do you keep staring at my mate like that?" Milara sighed loudly, standing up from the chair.

"Get ready to leave, we are leaving for Firehearth manor shortly. I'm sure the others would love to see you before taking off. Talissa, think before you speak," with that ominous warning, Milara excused herself from the room, slightly slamming the door behind her.

"What the hell was that about?" Bastian asked, as he moved from the bed. Everyone relaxed more the moment the door closed. Like a small collective breath was released. Were we all holding our breath or was it just a mental thing?

"I'm sorry that I kept staring, it was rude of me," Talissa apologized to Valdis, then turned her attention to me. "Milara has her hesitation with daemons, and not to sound disrespectful, but she has good reasons." River scoffed behind Talissa, earning a glare. "While yes, things between the gods, fae and daemons have been anything but good or cohesive. There have been daemons that didn't want the first war to take place at all. Those who wanted to live peacefully with our sides and just exist. I have another mate. His name is Zekon. He couldn't do for me what the others did. He had to play a role on both sides of the war, but he was the only one who walked onto that battlefield with me that day. Well at least halfway onto the field. He couldn't be seen by his uncles. His brother was helping the fae come up with a plan of action to keep the fatalities to a minimum. They made it work, but there were casualties on both sides. By the time the war ended, and King Marcloff was locked away in Limbris, my power had begun to fade. Zekon got to me right before I succumb to the darkness. He promised to keep the rebellion alive in Hellis until we could be united again."

Valdis was silent, standing far too still for my liking. "You're... You're my uncle's mate," Valdis whispered out. "Zekon never talked about what happened and he refused to let anyone know who his mate was. Everyone knew he was mated, but no one knew to who. Women threw themselves at him, men did too. He never once mentioned why he never took up any offers. Gabrial used to say he was infertile, and his mate left him for someone else. I remember our father beating him within an inch of his life. Our mother had to step in and stop him."

"I thought you looked like him. Alistar was always very protective of Zekon, him and I had quite a few words and exchanged a few blow ourselves back in the day before he accepted me," Talissa said. She smiled at him. "Well Luna, that explains why he was the only one you couldn't contact through the bond."

"I don't understand. Legend says all of your mates sacrificed themselves to give you the power to defeat King Marcloff, but he wasn't defeated and not all of your mates sacrificed themselves. Is the legend a lie?" Valyn asked, watching River smile at Talissa. I wasn't expecting him to be the one to answer.

"We did sacrifice ourselves. Or so we thought at least. We gave Talissa all of our power and strength so she could kill Marcloff. We were told by the fates that it was what had to be done. However, when Talissa showed up in Slairra, we knew something went wrong. She was supposed to live along with Zekon and have the family she deserved to have. The one we all wanted together," River started, a distance in his eyes. "After all the time we spent in Slairra, we figured out that it was supposed to be all of us. Zekon included. If Zekon would've given up his power to her though, our plan wouldn't have worked. It would've put Alistar in Zekon's place to stage the coupe and draw Marcloff out into the open. Zekon never would've allowed Alistar to take that risk, especially not after he had just found Lisbeth."

"Not to mention, Talissa being mated to Zekon wasn't public knowledge. They kept it a secret from almost everyone. It was the only way to keep Marcloff from killing Zekon to weaken Talissa. Then again, we didn't know about the not being able to die thing," Lumina added.

"But daemons can die," Valdis retorted. Talissa watched him, sadness flickering in her eyes.

"Zekon and your father aren't full daemons though," Talissa said, I watched the moment hit Valdis like a sack of bricks being thrown at his chest.

"What do you mean?" Niklaus added as he gathered up things from around the room to tidy up. I watched him touch a little ivy plant in the corner of the room to bring it back to life. Most of the plants in this room looked dead if I am being honest.

"Your grandmother is a goddess; your grandfather is a daemon. Not sure where he is, but I've met your grandmother. She is a sweetheart, but that makes your father and uncle, therefore you and your siblings Nephilim. Halflings with strong powers. Why do you think your family is prone to helping the fae and humans?" Talissa dropped the bombshell that had me wondering what the hell she was talking about. What the hell is a Nephilim?

I'll tell you later. Right now, we need to go see your parents, they need to know you're alive and they aren't answering their phones. Valyn whispered down the bond. "Excuse me, I hate to do this since we just got Luna back and you have just returned, but we need to find your sister." Valyn turned his phone over, scanning the screen as a flood of texts come through. "Sadly, we need to go now."

"What's wrong with my sister?" Talissa said, standing up and walking over to the bed. "If something has happened, I should know. She doesn't know I'm home."

"Unsure, Nox is saying their parents aren't answering phone calls or texts and I can't reach our father either," Valyn said glancing over at Damian who had his phone to his ear. From the expression on his face something was wrong.

"We will go find my parent's. Mind keeping Milara busy while we escape?" I asked as I took inventory of all the clothes my mates brought me. A slip wasn't going to help me if I needed to fight. I noticed a pair of deep blue jeans and a black T-shirt sitting on Bastian's bag. Niklaus has a pair of my fuzzy grey socks on his bag, but it was the sigh of relief when I saw my boots sitting with Valdis's things. I looked at Valyn's things and to my surprise he had my black leather jacket in his belongings. I smiled as I grabbed my things and headed to the bathroom.

"I'll do what I can, but something tells me you are going to need my help with whatever is going on," Talissa interjected from the room as I changed quickly. I pulled my hair up into a high ponytail before running my hands down my body. I felt something in my jacket pocket and reached in to retrieve it. The necklace that held their rings was wrapped up in a silk handkerchief. I unclasped the silver chain and put it around my neck. My mates were always tehre for me. Always a part of me, no matter how far we are from each other. I walked back into the room; a cocky little grin graced my lips.

"Any news on where they were headed?" I ask as I sit on the bed to lace up my boots. Valdis dropped to his knee in front of me, not allowing me to do it myself. He worshipped me and I adored him for it.

333

They all did in their own ways. I am the luckiest girl alive. Valdis looked up at me and I saw it for the first time, a silver swirl laid stark in his dark violet eyes. I leaned in to give him a kiss, but the door busted open forcing my inner beast to take over and shot a powerful shield around those in the room. It was visible, a faint shimmer separating us from my brother. "Nox! You can't just barge in here! What if I would've hurt you?!"

He laughed and poked the shield, the shimmers rippling at his touch. "Well, I'm not dangerous so you can drop it any time now." I took a deep breath and released the high alertness that built up in my stomach.

"Impressive," Lumina marveled at the shield as it vanished. "Next time we get the chance, I need to examine that more, if you're okay with that."

"Sounds fine to me." I beamed.

"Luna, I am glad you're back and I hate to rush you, but I can't get ahold of mom and dad. Something is wrong, King Harold isn't answering his phone either. According to Cassandra, they left for Floria. Something bad is happening there," Nox noted Fennik in the corner as his head snapped up at the mention of his home.

"Then that's where we will go," I declared, no one seemed to object so that was a plus. Talissa watched as everyone moved together out of the room.

"You and I have much to discuss when this is over," she whispered to me as we locked arms and headed out the of the room.

"Agreed," I said, giving her a quick hug before following my mates down the long hallway, leaving her and her mates to distract our grandmother alone. I will see her again soon. I know it.

CHAPTER 45
VANALLI

Vanessa had such confidence when entering the room, commanding all eyes on her. I can only imagine how she will do as advisor to Hellis for Luna, she's been looking forward to her new role for a while now. It should've happened by now, but my daughter never liked Luna going to Hellis.

"How can you help with our dilemma?" Undas asked her, brows raised a little at the intrusion. I glanced up at him just shaking my head. I guess he forgot who Zekon's brother was.

"Zekon is our uncle. He has been secluded a bit and doesn't leave Minaris much these days. Most of the people in his rule are considered chaotic neutrals, but they tend to lean more towards the doing what's right and good. Most of them just want to live in peace, and thankfully our uncle has done good at keeping the spawn from Limbris and Iterais at bay. I've met Valmor a few times during my visits to Minaris, really nice guy, he happens to be my uncle's advisor," she spoke of Hellis politics like a true professional. She knows firsthand the hate people in Hellis must endure thanks to Marcloff's rule in Limbris and the first war.

"You can talk to our son?" Elucia questioned her. Vanessa just nodded, giving Elucia a moment to ask the questions she needs to know. "Is he doing alright? Does he have a mate yet? Does he still hate us?"

I watched as Vanessa pondered which questions to answer and how to answer them. She's a smart girl; she knows better than to give Elucia all the answers she is searching for. "I don't have answers for you on the latter of your questions, but he is safe and happy. He enjoys his role as head advisor and has on more than one occasion told me that I should treat my position as advisor with the utmost respect and honor. It's a role of trust. I look up to him."

Smart girl. Vanessa looked at me and winked. She was standing outside the door this whole time, listening in on the conversation and coming in just in time to give hope, but not enough answers to where they won't help us. Elucia seems to want to do right by us, Alric however seems content with the answer.

"What do you want from us?" Alric blurted out; his intention clear. He will assist, but there will be a cost. For tricksters like him, there is always a price to pay, and I know just what it is.

"I make no promise that your son will speak with you or want to see you, if that is the condition of your assistance," I proclaim. "If you want to assist, do it because you want to make right. Not to see what you can gain from it."

"My Queen, what can we do to help you?" Elucia finally acknowledged my title. I wasn't expecting that, clearly my husband wasn't either. I'll take it with a smile though. Alric looks at his wife utterly befuddled by her acknowledgement that he looks down at the ground. It doesn't surprise me that he isn't opening his mouth. Elucia had made up her mind. There was no changing it.

"Did anyone visit the ruins recently?" I asked, trying to keep myself calm. I already knew the answer though, this was a test to see if they would tell me the truth or not. Vanessa took her place next to Kieran who was here more for moral support than anything else.

"Allura. She visited the ruins not long before your Sirus and your grandson showed up. What she was looking for, we don't know. As far as I know, she did not enter the ruins," Alric stated. At least they didn't lie about her visit. Then again, if they did it would be pretty stupid since I was on the phone with Elucia when Alric told the boys about it.

"What happened after she left?" Undas chimed in. I wish he would sit down or at least tell me when he is about to speak. I don't need to be jumping from him being silent for so long then interjecting and startling me.

"She left on a ship. We left for Wisteria shortly after her departure. We needed to pick up food from the local market there. In case you haven't noticed, not much grows around the ruins," Alric replied, albeit a little snarky. Elucia picked up on the disrespect as well and kicked his leg discreetly.

"How far away was the ship when you left? Is there anywhere the ship could've hidden to get out of sight fast?" I ask, it's been far too long since I've been to the Isle of Souls. I guess that is my own fault. I should've been keeping an eye on the blade just as much as they were.

"There is a cove off the coast that they could've possibly hid in, but we weren't gone long enough for them to have come back and made it through the labyrinth that fast," Elucia replied, crossing her arms in front of her. I could see the wheels in her head turning. "I didn't recognize the ship she came on. It didn't bare the Solaria Royal crest. It was more like a commoner's ship. Black sails and a dark mahogany hull. I can't recall if there was a name on the ship or not. I don't know why I didn't think of it sooner. You don't think she could've stolen the blade, do you? I don't know Allura like that."

"I only know that she is the sister of Scarlet and Penelope. Nothing more. But why would anyone from the solar realms want to steal Otius's Blade?" Undas replied for me. I couldn't think straight. Allura was a loyal servant of the gods. Why would she steal a blade that could kill us?

A knock at the door drew me from thought, I looked up at Kieran who headed to the door. "Should I see who it is?" He asked, the perfect image of a Prince. I nodded, allowing him to answer the door. As the door drew open revealing the small, veiled priestess in the doorway, my heart sunk.

"Pardon the intrusion my lady, but Princess Luna and her mates have left the sanctuary. Princess Talissa is still here with Lady Milara, whom is not very pleased at the disappearing act of the young princess. I thought you should know." The priestess was small in stature, a minor goddess who studied under the teachings of Lumina's people. They vowed to never show their faces, instead taking up the white and gold veils with the Cross of Lumina on the front. I wonder if Lumina has noticed her symbol from the past adorning the walls and priestesses here.

"Did they say where they were going?" I asked the young woman, a gentle smile on my face as to assure her that the intrusion isn't an issue.

"I overheard them saying they were looking for Queen Erina, King Drake and King Harold. There has been no contact since they reached Floria. The Princess and the Prince seemed very worried," she replied, hands folded in front of her, head bowed to the floor.

"Was my son with them?" I ask, trying to mask the worry. I don't want to seem alarmed or panicked in front of our guests. The young goddess shook her head.

"No, my lady. He remained behind with his sister as they await the arrival of Lord Zephir. I just wanted to inform you; Princess Luna is not one hundred percent healed. She may be awake, but her powers have not fully taken root yet. I tried to tell them that before they rushed out the door, but there was no stopping them. I worry for her safety," I could hear the worry in her voice. Luna is a strong goddess, but how powerful she really is, no one knows.

"I will call her or at least try to. Thank you. You are free to go," I dismissed the young woman, clearly sensing her urgency to leave after delivering her news. I am grateful that the priestesses hold us in high regards. Who knows if we were anyone else how they would have handled the situation.

I look to Undas, "I guess we know what has to happen next." Elucia and Alric stood up from their chairs, bowing at the waist. Vanessa and Kieran taking up flank behind them.

"We are at your disposal. We might not be as powerful as your family, but we offer what we have," Elucia broke the bow to stare me in the eye. "I am sorry I didn't tell you sooner about our son. I am also sorry it took so long for your daughter to return. Let me make things right, please."

I nodded, turning my attention to Vanessa, "I hope you're ready for a fight."

She cracked her knuckles together, grinning widely at me. "I've been ready."

CHAPTER 46
LUNA

Getting out of Valhime was much easier than I expected. Not sure why I was thinking that there would be security stopping us from leaving or anything like that, but who knows how this place works. I clearly don't. Damian led us all the way back to Solaria, the place looked just as cold as Valhime. I guess it makes sense though since it's modeled after the city of the Gods. I just prefer the liveliness of the other realms. Hell, Taiga is the land of winter and doesn't even feel this cold.

"We can take the portal back to Mistveil and resupply before heading to Floria. Unless you rather go straight there," Damian said as we crossed the courtyard to the main house.

"The sooner we get to Floria, the better. But stopping at the armory in Mistveil sounds like a good idea," I replied, glancing back over my shoulder at my brother. I could see the worry on his face, and the sleepless nights that he's been dealing with. It made me look around at all of them, dark circles formed under their eyes, their movements not as on par as I remembered. Then again, when was the last time they all had a good night's rest? "Why don't we rest in Mistveil, regroup and come up with a plan. You all look like death warmed over and like you haven't slept in months."

Valyn laughed, throwing his arm around my shoulder, "My love, do you think we slept at all while you were away?" Guilt formed a pit in my stomach, it's my fault they were all worried. If I could've just controlled my anger and my powers, I could've had a calmer head dealing with Marie. I still haven't even gotten a chance to talk to Fennik. I have no idea what happened after I got stabbed. I can't imagine things went over well with a drink and food.

"I'm sorry," I whispered. Everyone halted, including my brother. Valyn put his fingers beneath my chin, I refused to let him guide my sight up to his. A tear slipped down my cheek, "I should've had better control over everything. I'm so sorry that I caused you all pain." I let the tears flow, no matter what they say, it is my fault that they suffered. It is my fault they didn't sleep and were worried.

I didn't expect to be removed from Valyn's hold. I didn't expect the flash of orange to cloud my blurry vision. "Princess, you had no control what happened. No matter how out of control you were of your powers, your love is intense. It was used against you. My mother knew what she was doing when she incited your rage. She had a smile on her face after she took you from us, and I did what I had to do." Fennik's voice was like a soft blanket wrapping itself around me and holding me tight. I wrapped my arms around him tightly, my tears soaking into his shirt. His hand idly caressed my head as he just let me sob into him. No one tried to move me or stop me. No one dared.

"Come on now, we can't have you looking like you've been crying when we get back to our families, that won't go over well."

I can't help but giggle at that last bit. I pull back from his chest to see his smiling face. "Okay, but can we at least rest and come up with a plan. You know Floria best. We're going to need to find a way in that isn't the most conventional way. I can fly in with Nox and we can scout out the situation in Floria once he gets some sleep."

"I don't need sleep," Nox interjected. I shot him a warning glance as he put his hands up in surrender, "Fine. We rest for the night in Mistveil, then you and I head to Floria at first light. The others can join once we see how things look around the castle. If they can use the portal over me making trips, that would work best."

"I can meet you there by sea," Valyn said. Before anyone could respond footsteps sounded from the halls inside the castle. Something didn't feel right about the presence that was heading our way. I didn't like it. A tall woman appeared in the doorway, pulling a groan out of Damian and Bastian. I took in the woman, the beauty and the darkness twisting around her. I leaned into Fennik.

"Who is that?" I whispered as Damian went to move toward her. I grabbed his arm, stopping him from heading to her. "Damian, we need to leave. Now!"

"She's my aunt Luna. Allura, we were just about to leave," he called out to her, but she didn't respond. An eerie silence took over the courtyard. Damian looked back at me then to his aunt. He noticed something was off too, he put himself between her and I looking over at his brothers and Valdis. "Get her out of here!" he shouted.

I couldn't say anything as Valdis grabbed me and flew me to the portal door to Mistveil. He got me through as the others followed, all except Damian. The door slammed shut as Bastian made his way through it. "NO!!" I screamed running back for the door. Niklaus and Bastian grabbed me, holding me back.

"You can't go back there!" Niklaus yelled trying to force me into submission in his arms. Bastian put himself in my line of sight, forcing me to stop.

"Damian's got this. He will have help shortly, I promise. Our cousins are there, and they won't let anything happen to him. Focus on your bond with him, he will be fine. We just need to hurry the fuck up and get to Floria and get to your parents and our father," Bastian's words calmed me as I sent my ember down the bond to Damian.

I swear to the gods above that if you die, I will burn the worlds until you're returned to me. I threaten. His laugh comes down the bond letting me know he heard me, and he knows I will keep that threat.

I will be fine. I will join you in Floria the moment I am done with this. I love you. He assured me. Not like I would let him live it down if he wasn't safe. I pull my phone out of my pocket and send a text to my uncle telling him to get his ass to Solaria to help Damian. I wasn't about to have someone I know could help him so close and not do anything. Sirus didn't hesitate to reply.

On the way, with plenty of backup.

Good, hopefully he means Talissa, River and Lumina are offering to help him. "Okay, help is on the way for him. Nox, you have about three hours to rest. Valyn, if you are coming with us, then rest up now while you can," I barked out the commands as I stalk through the halls of Mistveil heading for the armory. They all followed me as I pushed open the heavy wooden door. I wasn't going to Floria for talks, if my parents are being held captive. I will slaughter all those who stand between us.

"I can fly with you, I may have smaller wings, but I can get in and out with less suspicion in the area. Golden eagles aren't unheard of around the area," Niklaus said, perching himself on the windowsill. I looked over at him as I pulled a crossbow from its place on the wall.

"Honestly, only 2 of your mates don't have wings. I can join you as well, maybe even play decoy if I need—" I cut Valdis off before he could even utter another word.

"You are not playing fucking bait!" I snarled at him. I wasn't about to lose him because he wanted to do something stupid. They all decided to sit back and not bother stopping me from pulling more weapons from the walls. "Anyone going with us, get your asses in a fucking bed and sleep. Three hours. No longer." I shove bolts and arrows into a bag and toss it by the door, laying the crossbow across the bag before grabbing two daggers and a sword from their resting spots. I placed everything on the bag of supplies before leaving them all in the armory. Three hours is all I gave them, so that's all I can give myself. I stalk the halls to my room. I haven't been in this room alone in what feels like an eternity, and I alright with that until now. I need to be alone. I need to go over the few maps I have of Floria from when I was studying the realms.

I close the door behind me, locking it so no one will enter without my permission. I tried to call my mom's phone once I sat down. It just rang and rang until the voicemail picked up. "You've reached Erina, leave a message after the beep." A sighed, ending the call. I tried my dad's phone too, same thing. I didn't like that they weren't answering me. I pulled out a large rolled up map and spread it across my bed. Floria was in the far southeast of the realm. If we left from Port Ilsa, we could get there by ship within two days. If Nox and I flew from here to Floria, it would take anywhere from three to five days with us having to stop frequently.

I grabbed another map, spreading it out along the bed. This one was a quick sketch I had drawn up one day of where all the realms were located, towns and cities, rivers, lakes, mountains and oceans, even all the ruin locations were mapped out perfectly. I outlined where all the portals between the realms were. We could always travel to Fildrey through a portal then make our way to Floria by land. It may take two or three days that way. I scanned over the map once more, my finger stopping on the Temple of Waters right outside of Port Ilsa. There was a portal there that could get them to the port city within minutes. Maybe we will be able to borrow a ship from the port and sail across. This way we can all go together.

The idea of splitting up didn't sit well with me at all. Leaving Bastian and Fennik behind was wrong. It was Fennik's people who needed to be saved and how else better to save them then to have their Prince right there with us. Throwing myself back on my pillows I let out the deepest sigh of frustration. Why is this happening? This war seems so pointless. Why can't the daemons come to the surface? If they don't want to cause harm, and they just want to be seen as people too, then why the hell not let them?!

Come to Cerulia, just follow our rules as you would want us to follow the rules of your homeland. It doesn't seem like it should be hard, but yet, here we are. Fear is the root of all evil truly. The fear of the unknown and the fear of what's to come. It can be caging to those who are afraid of change, but without it we can't evolve and grow into better beings. Maybe the world should just be washed away and made anew.

That's a thought.

CHAPTER 47
DRAKE

The smell of mold and rot filled the air. The stone beneath me bit hard into my feet, the metal clamped around my ankles bit even harder. I swear when I get out of here, I will rip that bastard apart. His laugh when he ambushed us as our feet made landfall still plays on repeat in my head.

"What a nice little surprise," Tanis had laughed when we made our way through the portal. I don't think any of us expected him to be staying at the castle. Harold was calmer than I would've imagined seeing Tanis, but then again, he knew the truth when no one else did.

I looked about the cell, a bowl of water was pushed under the door with what looked like moldy bread and rotting fruit. Not surprising that they wouldn't actually give us anything edible. I hope Erina is alright. Whatever spell they have on the cells has blocked all attempts I've made at contacting her through our bond. I can still feel it though, so that is a great sign. Then again, Tanis wouldn't want us. He would make do with Harold and just leave Erina and I to rot in these cells until we starve to death.

There was no actual bed in here, just some hay thrown into the corner in a pile. Not even enough for a horse to lay on comfortably.

I've had to take to relieving myself in the corner of the cell furthest from where I knew I would be sleeping. Guards did rotations every so often, but it gave me something to mark the time. Sixty ticks for a minute, thirty-six thousand for an hour. Every eighteen hundredth tick, they change the guard. If my math is correct and my observation skills aren't lacking, we've been here for at least four days. I wonder if anyone has noticed that we've gone radio silent. I wonder if Luna has woken up yet.

My thoughts wandered around in circles. Fear for my wife's life, fear for my daughter's life, worry that my son will do something reckless. If something happens to me or Erina, Nox and Luna will take over as leaders of the Hildaria region. Nox will give up that title so fast, Luna won't know what to do. Thankfully she has mates who have all been raised to rule their own lands. I shake my head, washing away the image of my children being forced to take over something they neither want nor are ready to have. We will make it out of here alive. We will return to our children. We will all go home safe.

Yelling came from outside of my cell. A deep burly voice followed by a lighter voice were barking orders, screams of agony and pain filled the halls. What the hell was going on out there? "Your majesty, if you are awake move away from the door!" The deep burly voice called in before I heard chanting from the softer voice. I ran to the back of the cell, my foot cutting open on a rock, toppled me down to the ground right as the door exploded into little splinters into the room.

"I'm so sorry!" The young voice called into the cell. The deeper voice laughed at the youngsters worry and panic.

"I'm pretty sure his majesty is more appreciative over the rescue than a few splinters flying his way," the man stepped into the room. He was a shorter, round man, with a long orange beard that curled out around his jaw, a handlebar mustache that curled around the corner of his lips and shorter curly hair poking out around a bronze helm. The green button up shirt he wore was covered by a bronze breastplate with the Floria crest of a bear's head carved into the center. "Good evening, your majesty. We thought you might be needing some help." He reached his hand out for me to take, assisting me up from the floor. He took in my status, the tore up jeans, shredded shirt, and bare now bleeding feet. "This won't do. Boy! Bring me some clothes for his Majesty."

A small boy almost identical to Fennik, walked through the doors, arms full of clothes that looked like they might fit me on a good day. "I'm sorry your majesty, but this is all we have that might fit you and King Harold," he said, offering me the belongings. I take them, sifting through to find a pair of black jeans and a white t-shirt. It will do the trick for now. He brought in a pair of black boots with nice thick grey socks. He also handed me a roll of cotton wrap. "This stuff works wonders on healing wounds fast. It has an ointment built in to stave off any infection."

I took the roll from him and smiled, "Thank you. May I ask your names?" I looked between them. The burly man was keeping an eye out of the door and on the hallway beyond, while the boy was gathering up the clothes I didn't choose. They both had their backs to me so I could change without prying eyes. It was nice to have people that still believe in common courtesy. The guards weren't so kind.

"The names Alstrom your majesty. That there is young Elijah," The man, Alstrom, answered. A flicker of memory pushed its way to the forefront of my brain. Fuck, this is Fennik's half-brother. No wonder her looks like his fucking clone.

"It's a pleasure to meet you both. Thank you for the rescue," I truly appreciated their aide. I strapped up the boots and looked to them for a weapon. "Got a sword?" I asked. Alstrom smiled, grabbing a sword out of the guard's chest in the hallway. He wiped the sword clean on the guard's uniform before handing it to me.

"Sorry, hope you don't mind some iron on your steel," he laughed. I watched as Elijah just shook his head. "We have two more cells to break down doors on. You are in on the rescues right your Majesty?" Alstrom rose a long brow to me, testing if I was a King that watched others get their hands dirty, or if I was in fact a King who would fight with the people. Even if they weren't from my region.

"Lead the way," I grinned.

"That's the spirit!" Alstrom boomed aloud, taking off down the hall towards the other cells. Elijah just shook his head again before giving me an apologetic look. He followed Alstrom out of the cell, I kept hot on their heels. *Erina, I'm coming for you.*

CHAPTER 48
DAMIAN

I heard the door slam shut, my mates threat yelled into my skull, vibrating around in my head. I wouldn't put it past her to find a way to resurrect me just to kill me for leaving her if I died here. Allura hasn't moved from her spot in the doorway, her body angled in a way that I couldn't see past her. Something was wrong with her; a rotting smell filled the air around me, sweet and bitter all at the same time.

"Allura, where is Melody?" I called out, my cousin hasn't been seen by any of us since we arrived in Solaria. Allura acted as if she didn't hear a word I said, she leaned against the doorframe, one leg propped up on the wall, her arms crossed in front of her.

"Why did you really come her Damian?" She called back. It was as if I hadn't just asked her where her daughter was.

"I came back here to be close when my mate returned to us," my words echoed off the stone paths and walls around the courtyard. The moon blossoms were bright in the garden, shimmering white and silver. The flowers were a bad omen if they were blooming early in the day, it usually meant death or peril. I looked at my aunt, watching how she was just nonchalantly standing there as if she had any right to keep me out of my home. "Why are you inside my house anyway?"

"You're house? My dear boy, it belongs to the royal family. Since you, your mother, your brother and your aunt do not live here full time, this house is mine to take. I am the only one left of the Ashford name who lives here in Solaria full time. You should be thankful that I take care of things when you can't be bothered," she scoffed at me, arrogance radiating off of her like sludge.

"The house is my home. You have your own. I don't know what you think your claim is, but you would have to challenge me to run this land and seeing as you haven't, it still belongs to me. I never asked for your help with anything. I attend all council meetings that are required, and I deal with all inquiries and rulings as I am required. You haven't done anything for me, you haven't taken care of anything in my limited absence." I reply with utter disgust.

"I haven't?" She shrilled, pushing off of the wall. She began her descent down the stairs and into the courtyard. "I have been keeping the people calm and under control. Making sure they say their prayers to the gods, leaving offerings that are satisfactory for them. I remind them that the gods protect them, not their failed prince. I rule this land with an iron fist, unlike the likes of you! How dare you allow these people to forget to worship the gods who gave us life!"

Allura was in my face, shoving her bony finger into my peck as if that was going to cause me any sort of pain. I'm now even more grateful Luna isn't here. She would just fry my aunt for yelling at me and right now I wouldn't be opposed to that. I sigh, grabbing her wrist and holding it up high so she can't poke me any longer. "You do not rule the people here. You never have, and they don't respect you. They never have and never will. You believe in the old ways. Answer me this. Until my mate came into our lives, when was the last time you saw Vanalli, Undas, Ridalo, Undine, Vestial, Tirnag, Gilda, should I continue?" I watched as each name landed on her like a brand. The gods stayed in Valhime. She never entered Valhime, she was banished by Undas and Vanalli for coming in and starting a commotion during a sacred rite that was happening for a newly born god.

"You don't understand! They need me as their voice!" She screamed, trying to scratch at me with her free hand. I was so ready to throw my aunt across the courtyard, but my mother raised me right. I let her go so she could fall on her ass and stood over her. Footsteps approached from behind me, a deathly cold drifted across the ground.

"The Gods and Goddesses do not need some delusional fae speaking for us," Sirus's words were cold and cruel, but something tells me that's what she needed to hear. She knows who he is, but the Goddess behind him definitely needed no introduction.

"You have been stripped of your royal title after you were banished from Valhime. I only gave you grace by letting you stay in Solaria for your daughter's sake. Now, you mistreat one of my granddaughter's mates. Have you no shame Allura? Or are you angry with me for banishing you, so you went to the Isle of Souls to steal Otius's blade to get revenge?" Vanalli's words stabbed hard like daggers, but what she said had my head spinning.

"What do you mean she stole Otius's blade? The ruins are guarded by two powerful gods. How is that possible? She's never ventured off past Solaria, except to annoy you all in Valhime," I said, anger simmering my blood. If she stole the only fucking weapon that could kill my mate, family be damned, she will die by my hands.

"Go on Allura, tell your nephew who you refused to visit in Mistveil that you do actually leave Solaria. You just refuse to visit your family. Tell him how you brokered passage on a pirate vessel to sail to the Isle of Souls, acted innocent so Alric and Elucia would not think twice about you asking to make sure the blade was still be guarded safely, then leaving once you saw it was still there. Only you didn't sail home, no you went back after they went to town and stole the blade. Now Allura, you're going to tell me what you did with that blade." Vanalli was next to me in the blink of an eye. I didn't feel her or hear her movements.

Sirus grabbed my arm and moved me out of the way of his mother. I had never seen Vanalli cut anyone down before. I had also never seen her angry, but the fact that I was removed from her path by her son, I'm grateful to not be in the crossfire. I watch Allura as she stared up at Vanalli, and laughed. My aunt has fucking lost it. White flames licked up Vanalli's arm, a ghost of a flame compared to Undas and Luna. Shit!

"Vanalli wait!" I called out. "Luna had said we had to leave when she laid eyes on my aunt. I felt like something was off, but Luna was in a panic. My cousin Melody hasn't been seen at all. She," I pointed at my aunt, who was still cackling on the ground, "is the only person who would know where she is."

Vanalli took a long deep breath, the ghost like flames vanishing from around her arm. The air around us was charged with energy. I don't know if it was from one of us, or whatever was going on with Allura, but this wasn't like her. She respected the gods and normally would hold herself to a higher standard around them. This version of my aunt in front of me wasn't at all the woman that I grew up with. Regardless of how much of a pain in the ass she can be.

"You want to know where Otius's Blade is so badly? Go to Floria. His dark majesty has it," Allura sneered, a dark fury clouding her eyes. "He's coming back to this world, and none of you will have the strength to stop him this time."

Shit.

Footsteps echoed along the marble pathway behind us, but I didn't need to turn around to know who was approaching. Vanalli glanced over her shoulder to watch her eldest daughter and her mates join us.

"You really think Marcloff will return to Cerulia? You've got to be joking," Talissa said, her voice dripping with sarcasm as she placed her boot on my aunt's ankle. "You weren't around during his first failed reign... or maybe you were." She slammed her booted foot down hard on my aunt's ankle, cracking bone and tearing flesh.

"I guess you were right, Tal. She's not who she claims to be," a tall, muscular man with fiery red hair stepped forward. "Looks like Solaria has been infiltrated by Hilmers. Filthy scum."

Allura spat at the man, rage clouding her, "You better watch your tongue forgotten prince. You all were not strong enough to kill him before. Nothing has changed." I couldn't stand by any longer. Moving through the crowd back to the front I looked down at the Hilmer who held onto my aunt's body, her leg was broken from the looks of it, but that can heal.

"You may not think they are strong enough, but she's not alone this time. My wife is not one to mess with and you already pissed her off. I want my aunt back and to know my cousin is safe," I said, dropping to a knee before the thing. I've seen Luna kill a Hilmer when she was just freshly turned fae. I can only imagine what a freshly turned goddess can do to one.

"Your mate is just a fae, nothing more," she spat. News didn't travel quickly then, or the creature only knows what my aunt knew when it possessed her. Talissa put her hand on my shoulder, I glanced up at her before moving out of the way.

"My niece has more ethereal blood in her veins than even I do, and I am full blooded. My niece doesn't need her mates to surrender their power to her to succeed. But to take you out? I don't need to bother her with that," Talissa grinned as darkness crept around my aunt small frame.

"Talissa wait," Vanalli spoke up, halting Talissa from obliterating the Hilmer in front of her. "That is Damian's aunt. I may not like the woman for her antics, but I'm starting to believe that it wasn't her to begin with. I'm sure he would love his aunt in one piece, especially with his cousin missing." Talissa let out a sigh, stepping back from the creature possessing my aunt. I was grateful for Vanalli stepping up, but how were we going to get this thing out of my aunt?

"Then we need to get this thing to Luna. She will be able to exorcise the damn thing out of her," Talissa spat out, her voice thick with utter disgust. I caught a glimpse of River moving to her side, gently grazing her hand as she walked past him. This was an act for her, something that I can only imagine took a mental toll on her. I know it would take a toll on Luna if she was in the same position.

"Let's be quick about it then," Vanalli looked down her nose at my aunt, no, at the creature wearing her like a fancy suit. My skin crawled that the thought of something using her like that. The ghost flames licked up her arms once more, this time forming white shackles around my aunts' limbs. "Safety precautions. We just can't risk the vile creature escaping and running back to Marcloff. I assure you if there are any marks on her, we will get her fixed up at the Mor." Vanalli assured me. I nodded. This is just crazy.

"Luna and the others are heading to Floria. Drake and Erina can't be reached. Nor can my father. I told her I would meet them there. I still worry something happened to my cousin," I explained. Sirus clasped my shoulder.

"I'll stay here and look for her. I can join you all once I find her. Just make sure Holly is safe please," Sirus promised.

"Of course, I called it by the way," I grinned, pulling him into a hug so I could whisper into his ear, "welcome to the family." I let go of him, watching as his face turned a few shades of pink before he turned from me, stalking off to the castle.

I guess everyone is going to Floria.

CHAPTER 49
LUNA

I left my room shortly after midnight, the halls were quiet and warm. I could hear the crackling of the fireplace int he main room the closer I got. Low chatter could be heard through the crackling of the wood burning, my mates were all speaking low to each other while my brother snored on the couch. I had maps under both of my arms, stomach rumbling from not eating or drinking anything since I woke up, I wanted to just drop the maps on the table and grab food.

"Dinners on the table baby girl," Bastian said from behind me. I let out a small little yelp, dropping the scrolls to the floor. My scream woke up my brother who rolled off the couch into fighting position ready to sleepily fight off an invisible attack. "I didn't mean to scare you." Bastian dropped to the floor picking up the maps and scrolls I brought out with me.

"Nox, go back to sleep. I didn't mean to wake you up," I said, helping Bastian with the maps. Nox plopped back onto the couch, dropping one hand to the floor, the other across his face. I kind of felt bad for waking him up. Granted he didn't have too much time left to sleep. I know I told him three hours, but I know none of them have slept since I crossed to Celestia.

"What's all this princess?" Valyn asked, scooting to the side of the other couch, making room for me to take up residence on the warm vacated cushion. His turquoise eyes seemed so much brighter tonight; gold sparkles danced in his eyes. It had me thinking about an energy surge I felt when we all had sex when I woke up. He wrapped his arms around me, pulling me closer to his chest after I placed the maps on the table.

"It's maps and some texts from when I was studying the realms and their laws. Princess stuff my mother had me doing to make sure I as up to date with politics. Each realm is headed by one of my wonderful mates, all except Hellis. Each region in Hellis is under the rule of one of the seven kings. I was able to find some stuff on the King of Limbris, King Marcloff. Dude seems like a dictator, a real asshole if I'm being honest," I say, leaning back into Valyn's chest. I probably should've taken a nap. I could fall asleep in his arms like this. I looked at the table and noticed the pile of fruits and sandwiches, the smell of the bowl of fresh strawberries hit my nose as Bastian pushed it closer to me.

"Eat, I'm pretty sure that's one of the main reasons you're jumpy and on edge. Unless something happened that you're not telling us about," Bastian claimed as he watched me grab a strawberry and popping it in my mouth.

"Nothing happened, I mean, I was content on floating in the endless starry darkness. Aside from that, nothing happened," I said between bites of fruit. They all watched me, taking in the words that I just uttered. Maybe I shouldn't have said that out loud, but I wanted to be honest.

"You were okay not returning to us," hurt settled in Niklaus's eyes as he looked at me.

Shit.

"It wasn't like that; I just felt a peace I hadn't felt in a very long time," I stopped eating. "When was the last time we were able to just exist without being pulled in one direction or another? What about getting to enjoy our time being mated and married? We haven't even really talked about what we want out of our lives. I mean yeah, we've had some conversations, but have you all always wanted to take over the family mantels as Kings? I sure didn't want to be a part of a royal court. I wanted to explore the world and find rare artifacts and things like that. I didn't want my life to be scheduled for me. Not that I would change anything now, it just wasn't on my life's bingo card."

I watched as they each took a moment to ponder what I was saying. Their lives were planned out for them since their birth. Mine was a total lie. I forced myself to eat again, grabbing a sandwich that looked like ham and cheese. After I took a few bites Fennik let out a deep sigh, "You're not wrong. Honestly, if I could have a different life, I think I would be a librarian or historian. I love to read, and learning is my strong suite. I couldn't imagine a life without books in it."

"I never really thought about another type of life. I guess maybe when this war is over with, we can find something to do together,"

Valdis said as he turned one of the maps to look at what was on it. "Looks like you've been planning and plotting little one."

My cheeks heated at the nickname, his smoky voice caressing my soul. "Only some ideas, I was looking for a portal close enough to Floria but not in Floria. I don't want us getting ambushed. Looking at the distance, Fildery is too far north to fly or go by land. Leaving from here by air, land or sea would take way too long. Same if we left from Mirith. Looking at the portal layouts, the closest one is in the Temple of the Waters. It's about a five-minute hike to Port Ilsa, I was thinking we could get a ship and sail there. Nox and I could do aerial scouting when we got closer to the shore. At least if we can take a ship, that can give us some more time to rest up."

I laid out my plan just how I had thought it up. Not much of an attack plan, but it was something. Valyn looked over the map, I could see his mind working, his eyes taking in every little handwritten note I made in the corners of the map's edges. he slammed his fist down hard on the table, making the plates and cups shake. "The royal navy won't be much help with how far Floria is inland. There isn't a river close enough where we could get troops in. I can make some calls and get some troops off the shore. We have the fastest ships in all of Cerulia. I can have my personal ship waiting in Port Ilsa by morning, it can get us to Anchora within half a day's travel. You and Nox can do aerial scouting from the ship, it's big enough."

"Fildery has some mages that, as long as they're not corrupted, I can get them heading to Floria. My fear is they won't make it fast enough without the use of the portal," Fennik said, a grim expression crossing his face.

"They're mages, can't they just make a portal on the outskirts of town?" Bastian questioned. He took the seat opposite of Valdis, looking over the map trying to find something we didn't see already. "I can get the beast legions lined up within the hour, they can travel through the legions stone and set up camp around Anchora until we arrive. I'm sure Damian can do the same thing on his end."

"I think that's smart. The most I can do is send some soldiers and healers to the frontlines. Set up medical tents and things inside Anchora, use it as a base camp," Niklaus replied.

"I don't want to put the people of Anchora out with us bringing war to their home. It's not fair to them, can't we set them up elsewhere?" I objected to putting innocent people in danger because of someone else's fight.

"The people of Anchora are gracious people Luna. They would stand at our side if it meant keeping a dangerous power to overtake our land," Fennik assured me. I still wasn't sure how I felt about it. I knew what happened when soldiers came into towns during war.

"Promise me, that whatever men we send in will do no harm to any of the civilians," I looked each of them in the eyes, I wanted them to promise me that the people would be safe.

"Luna, I'm not trying to be dismissive of your feelings or any experiences you or others might've suffered at the hands of human soldiers, but fae aren't like that. Plus, most of our soldiers are female. Yes, we have a ton of males, but the females are far more vicious in battle," Bastian gave me the wickedest grin, exposing his fangs to me, sending a thrill down my spine at the thought of them biting into me again.

"As long as no innocent person gets hurt. That's all I care about. Fennik, if you say Anchora will welcome us with open arms, then fine I'm alright with us setting up camp there. At least for the purpose of food, shelter and medical needs, I want all camps set up midway between Anchora and Floria," they all just smiled at me. A glimmer shining in their eyes that I didn't notice before, a golden swirl of starlight lay in the irises.

Valyn kissed me on the cheek before excusing himself to set up the fleets. I just hope he's not waking anyone up or interrupting anyone from their own fun time. Bastian had sent off a quick text to Bertrum with the details we had discussed. At least he didn't call, Kira would've lost her shit on him if he woke her up.

I chuckled a little at the thought of one of my best friends living in the frigid cold of the winter realm all to be with the man she fell in love with. I'm happy for her. I knew it was too late to call Harper, but she needed to know I was okay. I fished my phone out of my pocket after the others stepped away to make their calls. I snapped a quick picture of myself and sent it to her with the caption, "I'm still alive."

My phone beeped a moment later with a red heart, it was too late to talk, but she made sure that I knew she got it. Who knows how long I would be gone this time around. I should message Lilly; I should tell Virgil that I'm alive. I glanced over a Nox, maybe he already told them.

Maybe me being out of their lives could help them move on without worrying about me.

"Send them the same picture you sent Harper. If you don't, I think they might cause chaos until we return," Bastian said, taking his seat with me again. Valyn was pacing back and forth arguing with someone on the other end. Niklaus was calmly ordering people on his end of the phone. Fennik wasn't pacing around like Valyn, but he was stalking up and down the hall as if stalking prey. I feel bad for whoever is on the other end of that call. I took Bastian's advice and sent a group text to Lilly and Virgil with the same message I sent Harper. I'm still alive.

I hoped I wasn't waking either of them up. I tossed my phone onto the table before grabbing a blanket off the back of the couch. Bastian decided that he didn't want me to struggle with the damn thing and helped me snuggle up inside of it. He wrapped his arms around me tightly, "What made you find a way for all of us to go together?"

"I didn't want to leave you or Fennik behind. I don't want to go into this without all of you with me. Did you call Damian?" the truth just rolled off my tongue. There was nothing to hide from him.

"Yeah, apparently some shit hit the fan with my aunt, but your family stepped in and helped. Talissa thinks that you might be able to exorcise my aunt and get the Hilmer residing in her out," he nonchalantly dropped the bomb of what my fear was. The darkness surrounding her was the presence of a Hilmer, but how was I able to sense that?

"I'll try whatever the need from me to save your aunt," I promised as the others rejoined us in the seating area. "What' the verdict?"

"Everyone is getting into place now. Valdis is currently on the phone with Gabrial and Kieran. We are going to have daemon forces on our side, hopefully that sends a message," Valyn said, pulling my legs onto his lap.

"I hope nothing that could cause the Noire family any issues," exhausted I rest my head back on Bastian's chest. I don't want issues for any of my family.

"Everything's in place. The Royal Guard of Infernia will be awaiting orders. My father is sending our shadow strike team to do an on-ground assessment in Floria now. They're going to report back with the layout of where troops are, and what the condition of the city is in. Fennik, we're going to need your knowledge to find the best way in once we are ready to go," Valdis announced, grabbing a bottle of bourbon from the liquor cabinet and a few glasses.

"The mages will be there, but according to them, Floria is under siege with dragons, daemons and what they believe to be autumn knights. If there are autumn knights there, I wonder whose orders they are following. We have to hurry," Fennik, grabbed a glass of bourbon from Valdis.

"Then let's go," I say, tossing the blanket off of me. Bastian reluctantly let go of me so I could wake up the sleeping beast. I padded over to where my brother lay, snoring like a chainsaw. "Nox wake up. We have to get going." I shake my brother's arm, resulting in him moving onto his side. I let out a low growl as I poke his shoulder with my nail.

Still nothing, just his hand brushing my nail away like a bug. Alright, we don't have time for this.

I close my eyes and think of the ocean and all of the waves, the rain pouring down in a heavy storm, the relaxing stillness of Lake Gilda. I feel a charge, a flow of energy burst forward. I opened my eyes as water formed above Nox's head and splashed down on his face. His eyes flashed open, his arms swinging. I dodged the hit, landing flat on my ass. A laugh burst out of me, Nox was drenched and clearly pissed, but I didn't care.

"Not. Funny." Nox growled, standing up. He glared at me before shaking his hair, flinging water all over me. I couldn't help but laugh harder.

CHAPTER 50
LUNA

Getting to the Temple of the Waters was the easy part, but getting into town in the middle of the night proved to be harder than we thought. A five-minute hike has turned into a thirty-minute hike through dense fields of flowers and grass. Sticks and hole littered the area. I almost snapped my ankle twice, causing Bastian to pick me up to carry me on his back. I grumbled in protest, but I knew I would be no good to anyone if I broke an ankle on my way to battle.

Nox and Valdis carried most of the weapons in bags and slung across their backs claiming that it was easier for them to get the weapons where they needed to go. Port Ilsa was finally within eyesight, the temple slightly far off behind us stood brightly against the contrast of the night sky.

It was oddly calm as we entered the small quiet port town. I looked around at the buildings that lined cobblestone streets. All were made of some type of stone, some looked like little brick homes, others looked like they were made of a type of sandstone. Lights flickered in certain windows as we walked through the streets.

Wooden signs hung outside of businesses, swaying in the breeze from off the sea. Valyn took in a deep breath as the salty wind played with my hair. It's been a while since he has been close to the sea. This must be highly relaxing for him.

"The Salty Sea Dog is just up ahead. They're open all night and they can get us a room, if need be," Valyn said, a smile gracing his lips.

"Think they'll mind the late-night intrusion?" Bastian whispered. He was probably the only one well aware of the time and the fact that people are sleeping.

"It's opened day and night, so I would assume it wouldn't be an intrusion. The owner Jasmine has always been accommodating when my fleet comes to town," Valyn replied, wrapping an arm around me as we walked. I quietly focused on Niklaus in my mind.

You're being too quiet. What's on your mind? I inquired, he didn't leave me waiting long for a response.

Just thinking about what we might be walking into. I can do some healing, but nowhere near the same level as my mother. I don't want her anywhere near this fight. I don't even want you near it, but I know better than to ask you to stay behind. I loved that he wanted me to stay and be safe. It's heartwarming, but I can't let them do this alone.

It's a part of our life. At least until we can end it, then we can create a new life. One without the worry of what might fall from the sky on us. I try my best to reassure him that we will have a life after this. One that will hopefully be bright and full of laughter and love.

I look forward to the days of calm. I'll help set up the medical tents when we reach Anchora. If you need me to do something else, just tell me. I could feel him gently reach out to my bond, caressing it.

I forced myself to focus back on the conversation around me. Valyn squeezed my shoulder twice. Great, so I didn't do that good of a job quietly talking to Niklaus. I really need to get that under control, just for fucking privacy's sake!

A large gray stone building stood before us by the sea, a wooden sign hanging from what looked like rusty hooks swayed in the breeze. The main floor was dimly lit by some sort of light, I couldn't make out if it was candles or sconces or even fae light at this distance. All I know was that it looked warm and inviting.

Valyn led us inside, a small bell dinged as we opened the door. It was a relaxing chime, not one of those loud obnoxious ones that rang out so loud when you walked in that you wanted to cover your ears. I looked above the door to inspect it, a small glass bell dangled above the door. How in the—

"Sea glass, reinforced by the fire of Undas himself. It won't break," a tall, tan woman called out. I turned to look at the woman, she was young, her skin looking kissed from the sun itself. As we got closer to where she was wiping down the bar, I was taken aback by her dark sapphire eyes. She tossed long dark braids behind her back as she took us in. "Prince Valyn, to what do I owe the pleasure of this early morning visit?"

"Good morning, Jasmine. Sorry for the early interruption, but would you be alright if we waited out a ship's arrival here?" Valyn was polite, moving me closer to his side. I don't know if that means that

I should be concerned that this woman and him had a relationship before and he's making a power play or what.

"You look so familiar to me," Niklaus speaks up from the back of the group. He moves his way to the front of the group, resting his hand on my lower back. "Have we met before?"

Jasmine smiled at Niklaus, her smile bright and filled with innocence. "No, we haven't met before, but I've been told that I take after my mother. There are plenty of pictures and portraits of her around the kingdoms."

Her words had me looking around the small room, wooden tables were scattered about with wooden chairs with two to four chairs sat around each. The sea glass lights hung from the ceiling above the tables, a soft light emanating from each. Then I saw it on the wall behind the bar, a huge portrait of a woman with the same features as the woman standing in front of us. I had seen her face before, heard the stories of the Goddess Undine. I know my grandparents were friends of hers, they told me stories before of how wonderful and blunt she could be.

"You're a goddess as well?" I uttered out. Jasmine smiled widely at me, giving me a strong nod. A shine sparkled in her eyes, a silver that swirled around her iris just like mine.

"You're Undas and Vanalli's granddaughter, correct?" she asked, looking me up and down. I hadn't met another goddess's child outside of my family and my aunts' mates. It was weird knowing that she knew who I was. I gave her a slow nod, confirming what she already knew.

"It's a pleasure to meet the goddess who threw herself into war to protect those she loves. I couldn't imagine what went through your mind as you were fighting."

"I honestly don't think I thought it through. I just went for it. People were being hurt. I couldn't let that continue," I replied. It was the truth, I couldn't remember what went through my head, just that I did what had to be done. What anyone of my mates would've done.

"Prince Valyn, is the whole fleet coming through?" She turned her attention to Valyn, I thought a jealousy would rage through me at the way she looked at him, eyeing him up from head to toe. But it didn't. I mean I had the desire to put my arms around his waist and pull him even closer to me, but not the murderous rage I felt with Rita.

"The Selestine will be the only one making port. The rest of the fleet will be heading straight to Anchora. Should I ask Victoria to come say hello?" Valyn said slyly.

I watched Jasmine's face turn fifty shades of red as Valyn had mention the name Victoria. I had heard that name before, Cassandra had asked Valyn to check on her the last time he was in Doria.

"Don't bother her. I highly doubt she wants to come visit. Feel free to have a seat, I'll bring out some food and drink while you wait," she turned from us, returning to her wiping up the already spotless counter before heading back to what I assumed was the kitchen.

I leaned into Valyn, "Who is Victoria?" I tried to keep my breath a low whisper while the others took up the largest booth in the room near the windows that had a gorgeous view of the sea.

"She's my cousin, but her and Jasmine have had this whirlwind romance for centuries. Victoria needs to stop running from her every time things start to get serious. She's afraid of commitment to anything but the sea. I'm sure Jasmine's love for Victoria is the only reason our fleet has the safe traveling's that we do," Valyn pulled me into a smaller booth that had just as equally of a gorgeous view of the sea. I watched as the stars twinkled over the almost black sea. Morning would soon be upon us; we need to be on our way to Anchora before then. I hope his ship is as fast as he proclaims.

"Rest up my love. We probably won't have much time for rest once we board and make landfall," he whispered into my hair. He placed his arms around me, cradling me to his chest. I let out a deep breath as I took in the room. The fireplace in the back of the room crackling from a well-kept fire, the paintings of the sea and ships that lined the room along with odd little trinkets of ship netting and anchors.

Jasmine reappeared with drinks and what smelled like bacon and eggs on a cart. My stomach grumbled as the smell of the food wafted through the room. She placed down a huge bowl of eggs and a plate of bacon and sausage on the table with the others. I heard grumbles of thanks and appreciations from the others. She walked back over to our table with a smaller bowl of eggs and a plate full of bacon and what smelled like maple bread.

"Our chef, Edith, was very happy to hear that we had some guests here for breakfast. She's been dying to try out her new stove," Jasmine said with a smile as she placed the bowls and plates in front of us. "Eat up, you're going to have a long journey ahead of you. Valyn, you said you're heading to Anchora?"

Valyn grabbed an empty plate and began filling it for me before responding, "Yes, we need a quieter way into Floria."

"I think it's a bad idea for you guys to head there. Noro has been spotted terrorizing ships that head anywhere near Anchora. Something has brought it out of hiding, I fear for the safety of the people on those ships," the look on Jasmine's face said enough. Too many of those sailors didn't return to town.

I watched Valyn's face drop, the chatter at the other table slowed to nothing. "What is Noro?" I asked.

"Noro is a sea wyvern. She is deadly and efficient. Legend says that she is a creature of immense strength that can cut a ship in two with her strong tail. Other tales say that she is only violent and aggressive when she is with child. The only problem with that one is that she is the only sea wyvern we know of," Valyn uttered.

"Why did you call Noro an it, Jasmine?" I asked her, watching her eyes flicker over to the picture of her mother. I wasn't sure if Undine was still walking this plane of existence or if she was in Celestia.

"Because my mother always called her that. She told me that Noro was very dangerous and that not even my powers could protect someone from her rage. It was clear that I must keep travelers far from her seas when she is active," Jasmine finally looked back at us. "Valyn, you're wrong about her being the only one. There are two others in the south Selpie Sea and another three in the north. Not including the handful of those in Hellis. Noro is just the only one seen by those on land."

Before I could ask another question, the door flung open exposing a tall, figure. I didn't have a fear of this person, but I still felt like shit was about to hit the fan.

CHAPTER 51
DRAKE

Alstrom and Elijah lead the way through the hallways, checking prison cells as we made our way to where they thought Harold was being kept. I can just imagine how he is faring in this dank dungeon. He was good on battlefields, but he suffers from claustrophobia. He didn't like being in small places that he couldn't easily escape. I remember one time we had to camp out overnight in a small ass cave and he about blew his top when I suggested we seal the entrance with a boulder.

"His Majesty's cell should be right around this corner," Alstrom called back to us. Elijah was helping a fae out of a cell when I heard metal on metal ahead of me. I saw two guards swinging their swords at Alstrom.

"Either get them a weapon or get them out of here!" I shouted at Elijah as I took off to help Alstrom. I swung the borrowed steel down on the arm of one of the guards. Blackish blue blood squirted out where the limb was severed from the rest of the body. Well fuck. "Alstrom! They're daemons! Be careful!"

The burly man swung his sword like it was a light stick and not a heavy weapon. He landed a nice blow against the creatures' legs, slicing through its' thighs. I watched as he hacked away at the guard parrying each attempted blow with his shield. I would be watching more if I didn't have to deflect the advancements of my own attacker. The daemon in front of me was clearly a grunt, very little armor covered its' body. Flesh and what looked like fur were completely exposed. I parried the final blow away from me before shoving my own sword through the daemons' chest. Blackish blue blood pooled on the floor around us, the swords and shields they had laid sprawled out where they dropped.

Elijah had come up with two other prisoners, each grabbing a sword. One of the smaller fae offered me one of the shields but I declined. I wasn't good with a shield, no, that was Harold's forte. "Save one of the shields for Harold. He's going to need something to protect himself with." The young man nodded as he checked the one guard for another weapon or keys.

"His cell should be over here," Elijah said, counting the number of cells that still had prisoners inside. I took a moment to take in the two young fae in front of me. Both were clearly from the autumn realm, but they looked like they were starving.

"How long were you both down here?" I inquired, they both had dark circles around their eyes, their skin a sickly ghost white. They looked at each other and shrugged.

"They were imprisoned by the Queen when they questioned her dealings with Hellis. They were advisors to the royal family," Alstrom said as he pulled some bread and water from a small pack. My head cocked to the side as I watched him dig out a map and another canteen before handing it to me.

"Marie has been dead for a little while now," I said bluntly. Alstrom shrugged his shoulders, I watched the other two men look over at Elijah. "Shit, I am so sorry. I forgot you are her son as well."

Elijah shrugged his shoulders, "In all fairness, your majesty, you probably knew her better than I ever did. One week a month isn't enough time to get to know someone." He took a canteen from his own bag. He took a deep drink from it before replacing it and pulling out a lock picking kit from his bag. "I'm more interested in my younger brother. Why did she have such anger towards him before she died? And if it's true that he killed her."

"I have the answer to that if you really want to know. I also can tell you why it went down like it did," I offered. He looked over at me and I couldn't tell if he actually wanted the answer, but it was Alstrom who answered for him.

"Tell us then. I don't see Prince Fennik as a murderer. I can't imagine he killed his mother the way Tanis described it," Alstrom said, his claim that Fennik was incapable of murder might actually break him when he finds out that he indeed did it.

"It wasn't in cold blood. He did kill Marie. Honestly, if he hadn't, I probably would've. Your mother killed my daughter. Well, we thought she killed her, and we weren't fully wrong. My daughter breathed her last breath as fae at the hands of your mother. Her hatred wasn't towards your brother, it was towards my daughter. Your brother is one of the final mates for my daughter. Your mother detested the notion that her son was mated to someone who had more than one mate. Words were exchanged when your mother slandered my daughter before their wedding. Fennik banned Marie from the wedding for her behavior. It was Luna who came here to convince Marie to come home to Mistveil when word got out that a daemon army was invading Floria. Fennik had anger towards his mother for her behavior, but my daughter wasn't about to let words come between them. Her drive to save your mother is what led to her demise. Your mothers' rage is what led to her own death. Fennik did it in a blind rage at the pain that ripped through him when Luna died that day," I told them. I watched the advisors faces drop, a tear streaming down their cheeks.

Alstrom and Elijah glanced at one another before speaking. "You said your daughter breathed her last breath as a fae. What did you mean by that?" Elijah asked.

"My wife is the Goddess Erina. My daughter is a goddess in her own right. I didn't know that the magical suppression her mother put on her also suppressed her goddess powers from developing. When she went through the changing last year, I assumed that was the only one she would undergo. I was wrong, she was in the middle of her finally changing when your mother stabbed her. Sending her essentially to Celestia, the healing realm where all the immortals go to rest and regain their strength before returning to our world. My daughter should be awakening soon," I reply, holding back tears. I wanted to be there when she woke up. I really hope everyone was right and that she has come back to us.

"I'm glad that my mother didn't kill your daughter forever," Elijah said, placing the pack back on his back before heading off.

"I'm sorry that your brother killed your mother," I repeated my condolences. Ones that I knew meant nothing more than pretty words at this point.

"There's no need to be sorry. My mother chose her path in life, and she chose wrong. If he didn't do, I would've. My father talked about the dissolving of a mating bond and how damaging it can be. You never truly recover from losing your mate. She didn't want Fennik to mate at all. Just like she never wanted a mate for me either," his confession had me glued to the floor. Was he right? Could he actually have killed his own mother?

A huge hand clasped my shoulder, "He had been preparing to take her life in the middle of the night. Hoping that if it looked like she passed in her sleep from an unknown illness that it would've spared the people a war. He came to the conclusion that no matter how she died, that war was inevitable. He's stronger than he looks." Alstrom assured me as he followed the young prince towards Harolds cell.

I followed them, the advisors close behind me. I looked at the one, he quickly wiped a tear from his eye. "My tears aren't for the Queen if that's what you think. Prince Fennik was always so innocent. My tears are for the loss of that innocence and the burden he now carries."

I nodded, fully understanding where he as coming from. The hall-way opened up to a large room, one cell door stood at the far end of the room. Harold was definitely behind it. I could hear him bitching and complaining as he rammed the door with what I can only guess was his shoulder. I called out, "Stop hitting the door or else we aren't saving you." Alstrom and Elijah both looked at me with shock.

"Drake you bastard! Get me out of here!" Harold bellowed from beyond the door. I laughed, looking at the young Prince next to me.

"What did you use to break down my door?" I asked, as I watched him try to regain his composure at my blatant disregard for royal conduct.

"It was an explosion spell. I'm not that well trained in magic, but I can at least make it work in a pinch. I couldn't get your door unlocked fast enough with the lock picking kit," he confessed. He seemed so unsure of his actions, clearly, he wasn't raised to fight. Tanis must've sheltered him and did a piss poor job of training him.

"Well, we don't have much time here either. I say use the same spell," I clasped Elijah's shoulders and gave him the best reassuring smile I could before yelling at Harold. "Stand to the far back of the cell unless you want to get blown up!"

I step away from the cell, giving Elijah enough room to concentrate. Alstrom tried to stand by his side, but I pulled him back. Elijah needed to do this on his own, Alstrom wanted to fight it, but it seemed like he finally figured out that I wasn't trying to pull him back for protection. Elijah took a deep breath before pressing his hands against the door, muttering a few simple words in Florian. The door splintered and shattered just like my door did. I was impressed with his abilities, maybe Fennik could help him learn his way around spells and natural magic.

Alstrom handed me some clothes as I stepped into the cell, Elijah was already working on the shackles. "The hell is this?" Harold questioned raising a brow at the strangers. The advisors were standing guard at the door, Alstrom standing behind them.

"This is Elijah, that's Alstrom, the other two were advisors who Marie threw in the dungeon for questioning her aligning with Hellis. Your wife was doing some very shady shit my friend," I said, offering Harold the clothes as he took in Elijah. To his credit, Elijah didn't back down or look away at the examining look that Harold gave him.

"You have my thanks. Any weapons to spare?" Harold asked as he got dressed. Quick and simple. He wasn't going to question me about the company I am keeping. They helped save his life and mine. I don't ask questions to those who help those in need. And right now, although we are royals, we were definitely in need of help.

"There are no spare weapons, only two guards were watching your cell. The advisors have their weapons, but don't fret. There are plenty more guards we have to get through," I said glancing at Elijah. "My wife is next on the rescue mission, right?"

"Yes, your majesty," Elijah said with a curt nod. He moved past me to head to the door where the others stood waiting.

"Call me Drake, enough of the formalities," I said, following him out of the cell.

"Same. The name is Harold. We're in the trenches together," Harold said, patting me on the back, "Let's go get your wife."

CHAPTER 52
TALISSA

Damian had informed us we weren't permitted to use the portals to get directly to Floria. It didn't set well with everyone, but I convinced them to head to the Temple of Rites. It laid on the outskirts of Floria closer to Anchora, someone with ethereal blood could only access it. Luckily for him, he just so had several people surrounding him that could make it open.

"So, who's bleeding for this excursion?" Claye asked, moving around to gently rest his palm against my lower back. We stood in front of the infinite portal that could lead us to anywhere we wanted to go. All we had to do was to have someone prick their finger and give a drop of blood to activate it. Then it's just a matter of thinking or saying where we want to go and with the snap of a finger, our entire party is there. Problem is, none of my mates would allow me to prick my damn finger.

"I already offered, but you all said no," I retorted. My father and mother were also on team don't let Talissa do shit. I'm not some damn fragile creature who can't handle a fucking little prick to the finger.

"I'll do it," River said, stepping up to the portal. He winked at me as he pricked his finger on his earring and forced a little blood into the portal door. "We'd like to head to the Temple of Rites." He announced it loud and clear, so there was no mistaking where we wanted to end up.

The portal lit up a brilliant white. Damian ushered his aunt through the portal, leaving us all the follow him and her. I wasn't keen on taking her with me, but for her safety, I guess we had to bring her with us so Luna could do some exorcist shit. I really hope I am right about her and her powers. The blinding white light slowly faded around us, exposing us to the dark night sky above us. The Temple of Rites had been long forgotten. Grass and vines snaked up and around the marble pillars. I couldn't help the feeling of sadness that flooded me. This place had once shined brightly. Humans that wanted to belong with their fae mates would proclaim their love here and go through the rite to be graced by the gods with fae immortality, their lives tethered to their mates' lives. Do the fae of this time not know that mates can span across not only gender but species?

I watch as the others take in the once brilliant temple and what it has now been reduced to. "Have the fae of now forgotten about this place?" I turn to Damian, who looks completely clueless as to what I am asking.

"Talissa, things have changed in the time since you were last here. Cerulia is much different now," my mother tries to explain. I know things are different, but who is to blame for that? Why aren't the gods making sure the people don't forget? We lived side by side with fae, humans, dwarves, and others for centuries.

"What happened to the dwarves of Mitos?" I asked my mother. A look of confusion flashed across Damian's face. He didn't know dwarves existed then. Maybe no one did, maybe they didn't exist anymore.

"We don't know. There has been no sign of dwarves since the first war," my father mumbled. The dwarves made the weapons we used, crafted them from the ores in the mountains from all over Cerulia. How could they have not been seen in so long? "We have tried looking, but no matter how close you get, you can never full climb the Mitos Mountains without getting lost, turned around or falling."

I nod, making a mental note to go check out the mountains once this all is over with. We need dwarven weapons if we plan on taking on Marcloff again. I walk over to the temple and place my hand on the marble pillar. I close my eyes and think about the last time I was here. The wonders of mates being united for their whole lives, the wedding ceremonies, the mating ceremonies, the parties that graced these hallowed halls. All dulled and faded.

I didn't hear the footsteps come up beside me, nor did I recognize the energy. "If it helps, my father still holds the sacred ceremonies to unite fae with their human mates. He calls it a challenge. If the mating bond is true, the human will survive the challenge and make it to their mate unharmed. However, if the claim is false, the human will perish in the challenge, leaving the fae to pick up the pieces alone." How is it possible that no one has seen them in such a long time? up the pieces. He tries not to hold it so often since there has been more people that would rather claim they are mated to the fae than to admit that they want to leave the human cities and live amongst us. My father has seen too many perish, so he only holds them for those that are worthy of knowing the truth." Damian's words helped heal my heart slightly. It hurts to know that humans must face such harshness when claiming to be mated to the fae, but I understand it. I can only imagine what one would do if they found out that they weren't truly mated, and the mating ceremony didn't take.

"I'm glad that your father still makes the offer, though. It's better than nothing," I said, taking a step back from the temple.

"Was it more common back then?" He asked me. The others chatted away by the side of the temple.

"Yes. They happened often, right here. Back then, the fae and humans mingled more with one another. They weren't afraid of each other. There were some mating ceremonies that didn't take, where people believed they belonged to one another, but they didn't. Instead of forcing them apart, the gods gave them the opportunity to explore their love. Even if they weren't mates, they were still allowed to love one another." I remembered the last time a mating didn't go as the couple planned. They were devastated with a child on the way. The gods allowed them to stay together for the child's sake. Hence us finding out that non-mated pairs could have children, debunking a theory the old gods had.

"What about the dwarves? I didn't even know they existed out-side of children's books." Damian's curiosity was a warm welcome. It's nice to know that someone out there is interested in the past.

"Dwarves are the reason we have weapons we do. They were key in helping us in the war. I plan on going into the Mitos after we're done here. I want to see if they have truly vanished or if they have just been forgotten like others," I paused to take a good look at him. He reminded me so much of Ignis. He just had a little less of a temper. "Any word from Luna?"

"I told her the minute we made it here where we are. She said she would contact me soon. I'm worried that she's not fully recovered and that she is doing too much," he looked to the town of Anchora and beyond it to the sea. His heart was pulling him to his mate.

"Something tells me this isn't the first time she's run headfirst into danger, is it?" I gave him a curious look. He rolled his eyes and recalled the story of how they met, the first battle in Mirith and everything that my brother had put them through during the winter. No wonder she was so strong. I watched as he talked about her, the love and pride he had for her was palpable. River and Voxis had joined us by the time he started recalling her and Nox flying straight at a foreign dragon and taking them down. Claye and Ignis joined as he gushed about her saving the people of Mirith as just a human, no magic to her name that she knew of. By the time he got to the fight that led her here before I met her, everyone was standing around listening to him.

My father clasped him on both shoulders, a warm smile graced his lips. "I am honored that my granddaughter has you and your brothers as her mates. Including Valdis. You all love her so much and it is rare that kind of love and admiration. Not all mates love as hard as you all do. Now only if my son can find his mate, then I'll be happy." He busted out with laughter.

"I think he already has," Damian said shyly. That caught my parents' attention, and mine. My brother has had many lovers, many partners in the past. Rimalu was one I thought was his true mate, but we were wrong.

"Well, speak up!" My father pushed, his eyes lit up with delight.

"My cousin Holly. He has been with her ever since the shit that went down in Taiga. Anywhere she goes, he goes, and vice versa. He told me to make sure she was safe. I already called my mother and everyone there is safe. Athena has had the castles on lockdown since my father left her in charge. No one is getting in or out with her on duty." Damian chuckled, and I watched as my parents smiled widely. She must be a good person then.

"I remember Holly. A little morbid that one, but that is perfect for him," my mother expressed. I looked past everyone at the woman sitting up against the stone with white flames surrounding her. How could a Hilmer infect a fae of the royal family? They had to have gotten close to her somehow. Unless she gave up her body to them for some reason.

"You said your cousin Melody was missing, right?" I asked Damian. He nodded in reply. "What if we can get her location out of the Hilmer? Not by torture or anything that can harm your aunt, but by deep diving into her brain?"

Lumina looked at me with a sheer look of disapproval. We had only done it a handful of times, but we were successful of getting the information we needed. My mother looked between us sensing Lumina's energy shift. The others knew better than to say anything or try to stop me with this one. "We need Sirus here, if he's back in Solaria searching for Melody, that puts us one strong power player down. Want to force Luna to attempt an exorcism that she has never done before? What if something goes wrong and she gets infected trying to save her?"

Everyone glanced at Allura, watching her gaze narrow on all of us. "If we do this, you are in and out. Find what you need and come back to me because I swear to Zephir that if something happens to you, I will personally torture you until you heal up." Lumina's threats were cute, but I also knew she meant it. She had a whole ass litany of spells that could cause me much discomfort.

"In and out. I promise." I held my pinky out to her. She rolled her eyes but entwined her pinky in mine. "Let's do this."

CHAPTER 53
LUNA

"Do you always have to be so over dramatic?" Valyn said from the table. The tall figure walked into the room, gently closing the door behind them. It was a woman, her long straight silver hair flowed just below her hips, a stunning shade of cherry red plumped and colored her lips. But it was the black liner that lined her turquoise eyes that told me exactly who this stunning beauty was.

"The damn wind took the door from my hand. I didn't mean to make such a grand entrance, but the wind made it, so why ruin a perfect entrance?" she grinned. Her eyes landed on Jasmine and her grin grew wide as she sauntered into the room, stopping a breath away from her. "You look as stunning as ever. Has anyone ever told you how beautiful you are when you blush?" Victoria pushed a stray braid behind Jasmine's shoulder. I watched Jasmine's face light up a bright pink before she shook her head and took a step back.

"Good to see you too, Victoria. Want some food before you head out?" she asked, leaving the naval captain speechless. I liked Jasmine. She seemed like someone I could be friends with. Victoria finally recovered from the subtle rejection.

"Uh yeah, can we talk?" She asked, as Jasmine turned around heading back to the kitchen.

"Not right now. I have to get you food and get them stuff for the journey. I'm not letting them go hungry. Trade ships haven't been able to anchor in Anchora in months. Luckily for them, they can grow crops to continue sustainable living. Most of the ships were bringing wines and other goods that the other realms make. I'll have supplies ready shortly. Have a seat." With that, Jasmine pushed open the door and walked through it.

Victoria took a seat across from Valyn and I, "You sure know how to leave an impression Vic." She rolled her eyes as she took in the food in front of us. I hadn't met her before, but she reminded me so much of Valyn. "Vic, this is my wife and mate Luna. Luna, my pain in the ass cousin and captain of the Selestine."

"It's a pleasure to meet you," I say by way of greeting. She gave me a quick smile before fixating her eyes back on the door. She was waiting desperately for Jasmine to walk back through those doors. "Why not just tell her you like her?"

Victoria's turquoise eyes locked on me, "because she already knows." Before I could respond, the back door swung open, revealing Jasmine and her cart of goodies. She trotted over to our table, placing a plate of eggs and bacon in front of Victoria before turning her attention to us.

"Here," she handed over a heavy sack to Valyn. "The food inside won't go bad as quickly as some of the other stuff. There's some bread and jams in there as well. Cheese would just mold before you reached Anchora. Remember what I said about Noro." She wasted no time leaving us to our meal. I could see the pained look on Victoria's face at the blatant dismissal.

"You know, if you actually would choose her over the seas, maybe she would be more receptive to you coming around. Or maybe if you called her or visited more often," Valyn leaned across the table to whisper.

"Valyn, you should probably stop trying to meddle in my affairs. Choosing the sea is choosing her. She just doesn't see it that way." Victoria scooped a forkful of eggs into her mouth. I decided I should mind my own business and turned my attention to my plate. Valyn opened his mouth to say something, but I gave him a slight nudge to his arm to stop him from getting in trouble with his cousin.

He wisely took my advice, focusing on his own plate of food so we could get on our way. The room fell into a quiet hush of forks scrapping on plates and the crackling of the fire in the fireplace. I couldn't shake the feeling that something bad was on the horizon and we were running straight for it. Maybe I was crazy, maybe even more insane than I originally thought I could be, but I need this. I need to save those I love. I look around the room at my mates and my brother, my heart wishing that Damian was with us. We will all be together soon. I just have to keep reminding myself that.

Luna, we made it to the Temple of Rites, it's on the outskirts of Anchora. Everyone is safe and here, minus Sirus. He stayed back in Solaria to look for my cousin Melody. We'll set up a base camp outside of the town about half a mile down the road from the temple. I miss you, please be safe.

Damian's words flowed into my mind as I finished up my way too early breakfast. I knew the others could hear the conversation; their heads all turned to look at me. "We should get going. The sooner the better." I began cleaning up the plates and glasses from our table; I didn't want to leave a mess for Jasmine to have to clean up. Nox was cleaning up the mess at their table as they all gathered their plates and glasses. I found a tray by the bar and began filling it up with the discarded dishes. Jasmine had returned to the kitchen when she was done with us at the table. I figured the least I could do was clean up our mess, it's not like she knew we were coming.

The others began talking amongst themselves, planning out a course of action. Victoria joined the group, sprawling a map out on the table and pointing at something on the map. I left them to it as I took the dishes back through the swinging doors that Jasmine wandered through. The smell of bacon filled the small room, the sound of sizzling bacon and eggshells cracking dancing in my ears. I watched as Jasmine cleaned up around the kitchen, moving shells off of the counter for the chef, cleaning up discarded potato skins from around the cutting board.

"Hey Jasmine, I thought I could clean these up before we leave." I said as I walked over to the trash can and begin to scrap plates before rinsing them I the sink. She watched me as I cleaned up the dishes and glasses.

"You're pretty handy around the kitchen," she said, admiring my work.

"Before coming to Mistviel and finding out who I really am, I used to take care of my sister and her father. They were ill, dying honestly. He passed away, but Maggie cured her at the Mor." I finish cleaning off the dishes before putting them in the drying rack.

"I'm sorry. I can't imagine how that much feel to take care of someone just to lose them in the end. Is your sister handling the loss well?" Jasmine asked as she finished up her cleaning. The chef must've taken some a break, so Jasmine was finishing up the cooking as well.

"She's good. She moved into Mirith from Celvenia to be with my mother. It's a long story and one that maybe when things aren't so hectic, I can tell you. I haven't really met a child of another goddess outside of my family," I replied, hoping to not sound so desperate.

"I have met none either. My mother kept me pretty sheltered as a child. It wasn't until the first war that I could finally break away and be free from her constant hovering. I love my mother, don't get me wrong, but she is afraid of losing me." Jasmine let out a deep sigh. She smiled at me, then looked at the door. "Is she mad at me?"

"Who? Victoria?" I asked, a little taken aback. "I think she's more upset with herself for not keeping in contact. Valyn was giving her some shit during breakfast. Should I assume something happened between you two?"

Her cheeks heated, turning a bright pink. "We were together for a long time. I thought things were good, but the moment the sea called to her or some other adventure came her way, she was off. I was used to it, but your heart can only take a certain amount of abandonment before you have to let go."

I could see the heartbreak in her eyes. I know what that feeling was like. Virgil would always pick his duties in the royal army over me, hell he would pick it over his own family. "Sometimes they won't realize what they imploded until it's out of their reach. My advice? Go tell her how you feel, if you want things to work out with her like she clearly wants them to. Tell her."

I grabbed a piece of paper from the table next to the door and jotted my number down on it. "Maybe when this is all over, we can get together and hang out. I would love another friend, especially someone as cool as you." I hand her the paper with my number and turn to walk away.

"Wait," she grabbed my hand and halted me from leaving. "I'll take your advice, but you have to bring her back safe to me. I can make sure you guys get there safely. As long as Noro doesn't get in the way. My gift is to make sure the seas and weather are good for safe travels. I'll do my best if you can promise me that."

I pulled her into a hug. "I can't make a promise that I can keep her safe because she seems super stubborn, but I'll do the best I can." She gave me a quick squeeze before composing herself.

"Then let's get you guys going before the sun fully rises, and the town wakes up," Jasmine said as she pushed her braids back over her shoulders, stood up straight and pushed her way through the door and back into the main room where everyone was talking amongst themselves.

"Let's get going," I smiled as I held my head high and headed out the door. The others followed me out, including Jasmine, as we headed for the Selestine. We would say our thanks and goodbyes, then set out to sea. My heart calling out to my mate, who's already out there waiting for me.

Today I will be strong. Today I will not fear the unknown. I take one last look at the port as we boarded the ship. I will keep to my word, Victoria will return to Jasmine. Even if I have to drag her back kicking and screaming.

CHAPTER 54
LUNA

The ship was a lot larger than I thought it would be, a mix of black steel and ebony wood made the entire ship. The dark black steel of the ship made it look like dark still water under a moonless night sky. It was a beautiful ship, everyone was already aboard making their ways around the ship, checking the harpoons thanks to Jasmine's warning about the sea wyvern Noro. She gave us her blessing of safe travels before we left port, a simple garnet teardrop pendant that Victoria fashioned into a black net necklace. The parting between them was loving and sad. My offer to Jasmine held strong in my heart. I will do my best to bring Victoria back to her in one piece, maybe then Victoria can tell her how she really feels.

Valyn ushered me below deck to the captains' quarters at the front of the ship. "I had Victoria make up the captain's quarters for you. There are plenty of blankets and pillows for you to curl up in and lose yourself inside of." Valyn said, pushing open the door to the most luxurious room I had seen on a ship. I had been on smaller boats back in Celvenia, and I had seen destroyers come to harbor in Galbranth, but I had never been on or seen a ship like this one. The ebony wood lined the walls and floor, the steel framing the door and the port windows looked more like accent pieces in the room. A lantern of fae light sat on the nightstand by a large fluffy bed, covered in red satin sheets and a huge black comforter that took up most of the bed. "You need your rest. As much as I'm sure we would love to devour you the entire ride to Anchora, that's not practical. So instead, we are going to stay in the officer quarters just down the steps."

He walked me over to the bed, helping me down onto the fluffiness. It was so soft and smooth; I knew I could fall asleep in this bed without hesitation. The rocking of the soft waves would be a big help with lulling me to sleep. Valyn had my shoes off and placed them next to the bed before laying me down. "Can't you just sleep in here with me?" I whined, throwing my arms around his neck.

He laughed and kissed me. "My love, if I stay here, you will not be getting any sleep until you're completely spent, and your body gives out. We both know you need your strength, as do I." I rolled my eyes and let go of his neck allowing myself to fall back onto the bed. I let out a huff, but I knew he was right. A tug on my heart had me looking toward the window. I know Damian is already there waiting on us, waiting for me.

I kicked back the covers like a defiant child being forced to go to bed when their siblings were allowed to stay up later. Valyn just laughed and covered me up with the comforter, stroking my hair from my face. His fingers traced the contours of my face lightly, trailing them gently down the bridge of my nose, across my cheekbone and down and around my jaw. The soft motions were a soothing familiar touch that I wanted to cling to, but sleep was weighing heavily on my eyes. The sound of the waves outside lapping against the hull of the ship was the last thing I remembered before drifting off to sleep.

A jarring screeching sound tore me from my sleep. The door to the captain's quarters flung open as Bastian entered the room, half dressed in nothing but jeans and a pair of socks, his boots in hand. His hair wild from sleep, his eyes trying to adjust to the darkness in the room. I'm surprised I can make him out as well as I can with such little light. "Princess, I'm going to need a little assistance if you don't mind."

I held up my hand, a soft iridescent light flared up from my fingertips illuminating the room. Bastian's eyes went wide, taking in the rumbled state of my shirt up high under my breasts. I watch him shake his head as if telling himself to behave. "What's going on?" I had to bring his attention back to the situation.

"Jasmine wasn't joking when she said Noro is a beast we wouldn't want to deal with. Crew noticed a blue glow under the ship following us the closer we got to shore. The rang the alarm a little too late. I think she hit the ship." Bastian grabbed my shoes and handed them to me. I grabbed them, shoving my feet inside without another needed moment. He was quick to do the same as we both headed out of the room and down the stairs leading back to the deck.

Another hit rocked the ship as our feet hit wood. Bastian grabbed me, pulling me close into his chest. I looked out at the busy deck, crew aiming harpoons at the water. I heard Valyn's voice ring loudly over the deck as he commanded everyone to hold tight and brace for another impact. Victoria was at his side, holding the helm with all her might, their matching silver hair dancing in the moonlight. If you didn't think they were cousins by their eyes, the hair would give it away in a heartbeat.

A sorrow filled me as I crossed the deck, a hollowness not of my own. I looked towards the sea, feeling a strong urge rage and sadness. I slipped out of Bastian's grip and ran for the railing. I watched as an eerie blue glow swam beneath us; purplish wings spread wide. I could make out the two arms that she had, both kept close to her body instead of slashing at the hull. She's not trying to hurt us; she's trying to move us away from something.

I listened as Valyn called out for a harpooner to take aim. Before he could utter the command to shoot, I screamed. "NO!" I ran up the stairs to the helm realization of what was happening. "We are invading her nest! We got too close! Don't you remember what Jasmine said. Noro only gets aggressive when she is pregnant or had just recently given birth. It could explain all of the vessels that never made it home. Her nest is close to the shore, look!" I point out where the glow from Noro is sitting by the rocks about fifty yards away from the port town.

She wasn't advancing any longer, she was definitely watching us. Her motherly instincts to protect her offspring is what made her attack us.

"She's right Valyn. Jasmine had always told me only a sea wyvern from Hellis would attack without cause. They are considered dangerous because they are big and can level a ship in one swipe from their claws. Our hull isn't dangerous." Victoria agreed with me, watching the creature circle itself around a tiny purple light. I admired the passion she had for her baby, the raw emotion to protect a part of her.

The sorrow and sadness I had felt moments ago had vanished. The rage and hollowness gone from me entirely. Instead, I felt joy and happiness. A sense of gratefulness and thanks filled me as Valyn called the crew to stand down. Something tells me Undine had told Jasmine to stay away from these creatures because while they are vicious and dangerous, there is something more from them. I can feel it.

As the crew and everyone calmed down, they all started to get ready to dock the ship in Anchora. Bastian joined us at the helm as Valyn and Victoria talked amongst themselves about the best way to proceed with docking. Bastian was listening intently to them, so I just stepped away to watch Noro and the little purple light. I closed my eyes and let the sound of the waves carry my thoughts, I don't know what I was doing or why, but I felt like it was something I had to do.

You're safe now.

I took a deep breath and exhaled, letting the scent of the salty sea overtake my senses, but there was another scent. A hint of sea and smoke danced across my tongue.

Thank you, your majesty.

The rumble of a sweet voice danced around my mind, a little echo following the other. Shocked, I opened my eyes and watched as Noro and her child peered above the surface to watch us pull into port. I looked back at Valyn and Bastian who had the same wide eyed shocked expression across their face. If they heard it, then I wasn't dreaming. I talked to Noro. I saved a sea wyvern. How in the hell did I talk to her?!

CHAPTER 55
DAMIAN

I felt a strong pull in my chest as Luna's voice sung out in my head. Who is safe? And who were those voices I heard? Talissa looked at me with a curious look on her face, but I didn't want to worry her as she was getting ready to dive into the brain of my aunt to force the Hilmer out and to find out where they have my cousin held. Ignis stepped closer to my side as the others gathered around Talissa.

"Are you okay?" He asked me, taking in the expression on my face. I guess I wasn't good at playing poker when it comes to Luna and my emotions when it comes to her. I let out a low sigh as to not distract Lumina from her duties.

"I heard Luna and two other voices just now." Ignis looked at me with a raised eyebrow like I should be used to this type of thing by now. I was used to voices that belonged to our group. "It sounded like a woman and a child. They said, Thank you, your majesty."

Ignis's brows furrowed as he took in what I said, "You don't have any other women in your group and no children either. So how in the hell did you hear someone outside of your bond?" I watched as he looked over at Undas, signaling to come stand with us.

"Something wrong boys?" His attempts at whispering were faltered by his deep voice. Vanalli watched us all with a curious eye, sometimes I think that woman can sense everything that goes through our heads without us having to say a word to her.

"Have you ever heard anyone else's voice in your head besides Vanalli's? Maybe you've heard of another mating group where they heard someone else in their heads?" Ignis asked in a hushed whisper. We watched as Talissa was preparing to mentally enter Allura's mind. Undas looked at us both with an odd expression.

"No, I haven't. Why do you ask?" Undas raised a brow at us. "There was a legend of an old god who could hear every voice of every creature and plant. Their name has long since been forgotten. Legend has it, they just vanished, leaving the world. I assumed everyone thought that the god died. Knowing now that gods don't truly die, we just rest. That brings in a whole different perspective to how I am going to view those older legends."

"I head another woman and a child in my head just now. Like a mother and child in unison. I heard Luna first say you're safe now, then I heard them say Thank you, your Majesty in return," I looked over my shoulder at the sea behind us. The town of Anchora was a dim gray in the rising sun. No lights had flickered since we arrived, nor has there been any commotion in these early hours of fishermen heading to their boats for the day. "Anyone else notice how quiet this fishing town is? For a port that is the only trades and fishing port close to Floria, you'd think it would be busy by now."

Undas and Ignis looked over at the still dark town and let out a collective hmm. I guess no one else noticed it but me. I know I should probably stay here and keep an eye on what is going on here, but something doesn't seem right. "Let's go check it out. You, me and River can head there while the others stay and keep an eye on things here." Ignis chimed in before I could make up my mind.

River was already walking our way before I could utter a simple yes. "Your brother is the prince of summer, correct?" River asked once he was close enough not to bother the others. I nodded my head and let him continue, "I would like to meet him when he arrives. I want to see if he has my sister's calmness or my brother's swagger." River laughed. Ignis just shook his head.

"This one reminds me of my sister, devoted, passionate and head-strong. Then again, I only have one sibling who could've fostered a bloodline. We're going to go check out the town. Damian pointed out that we haven't seen lights at all, and by now fishermen would be getting out to sea. Instead, there's nothing. No movement." Ignis pointed out. River turned from us and looked over at the town.

"If Luna and the others are planning to make port soon, maybe it is best that you guys go there anyways and meet them. This way Luna doesn't get lost." Undas recommended before heading back to the rest of the group.

"You heard the man. Let's go." Ignis said as he headed for the main road to the town. River just shook his head and followed behind him. I took one more look at my aunt, the expression of anger across her face left me sad. What if they can't get the Hilmer out of her? I turned away from the others, jogging to catch up to Ignis and River. I hope everyone comes out of this unscarred.

Anchora was silent, not even the sound of crickets or the scampering of felines could be heard. There was no snoring, no laughter, not even a drunkard in the streets yelling at anyone.

I peered into one of the row homes we came across when we entered the town. Not a light on, or any warmth coming from the window. I couldn't scent anyone either. I took a moment to change into my wolf to get a better scent for the families that should be here.

"Holy shit you're huge!" River gawked as I stepped around the building. Ignis's eyes widened when he took me in, but a smirk quickly replaced the shocked expression.

"Definitely my sister's bloodline," he murmured as we made our way to the next house. Each one smelled like the last soul that was living here left a long time ago. "Sensing anything?"

I let out a huff and shook my head. I ran off ahead of them when I heard noise coming from the town square. I thought maybe people were gathered there, but I was wrong. River and Ignis both ran behind me, following me on quiet feet.

The town square was battered down, the land reclaiming what originally belonged to it. Vines wrapped around the fountain in the center of the square. Grass and weeds popped up here and there through the stone pathways. A bulletin board with tattered papers caught my attention.

I padded over, taking in the multiple papers tacked up. Some were looking for missing children, some looking for missing family members. Most warning about the sighting of Noro, the deadly sea wyvern. Warning residents keep an eye on their children and livestock and to stay out of the water at all costs.

I had heard stories of the sea wyvern of the south. Deadly, merciless, child eater, but I always thought that was just legend. I shifted back, lucky for me I managed to have my clothes reappear on me instead of beside me like before.

"It looks like they civilians fled from here. There are so many missing persons posters hanging up on the boards that it almost covers the warnings up." I rip off a handful of missing posters to see beneath them. There were drawings of what Noro looked like. Or at least what they perceived the creature to look like.

"Noro? River do you know anything about this one?" Ignis asked as he ran his hands over the parchment that filled the board.

"Yeah. She is the mother sea wyvern. She's not a creature that would harm or kill children like they are making her out to be. She can be deadly but on when protecting her children or the spirits of children lost at sea. As long as she is not provoked, she won't harm you. These idiots probably didn't pay attention to their children, and they may have tragically passed. Instead of blaming themselves for piss poor parenting, they rather blame the big scary creature," Rivers hands were clench in fists, his knuckles bone white with rage. "They most likely tried to hunt her down and instead of them killing her, she took their lives as she protected the lives of those they didn't."

I watched as River ripped down every vile poster making Noro out to be a bloodthirsty beast. Ignis took the papers from his hands, lighting them ablaze before tossing them into the fountain. "The idiocy of people never ceases to astound me. The other missing persons flyers must be for the fools who went out there hoping to fight a majestic creature in a dingy."

I looked out at the sea. I saw the Selestine heading for the docks and pushed past the guys. "Luna and the others are about to dock. We should head there and greet them." We each took one look at the surrounding buildings. "If we find the citizens of Anchora, they will have to answer some hefty questions."

The sun began to rise higher in the sky, a shimmer raced from the horizon to the shore. My guiding light was coming home to me.

We prepare for war by midday, but for now, I prepare to see my wife.

CHAPTER 56
TALISSA

Lumina had already given me enough shit about doing this. The last time I mentally dived into someone's head, I was high as a kite off of dream silk root. I learned a lot about myself that night, and way too much about my brother. I almost didn't come out of it.

Luckily for me, Lumina recognized the benefits of smoking dream silk root and not just using it in teas and elixirs for sleep and anxiety. I just thought smoking it would give me a faster effect. I should've listened to my healer mate.

My grandparents were huddled around the fire, watching Allura as she snarled on the ground around the ghost flames that kept her in place. Lumina sat next to me as Claye and Voxis sat across from us. None of them were thrilled with the idea of me head diving into Allura's brain, but I don't want to add pressure to Luna. She's got enough on her plate, and the sooner I can get Sirus the location of Damian's cousin, the sooner he can save her and join us.

"Are you sure about this?" Lumina asked once more before handing me the joint.

"I's better than having Luna do something she didn't agree to. I wouldn't have liked anyone doing that to me. At least I can make this

412

decision. Also, I have an idea where to look." I grabbed the joint from Lumina's hand and leaned over the campfire. It lit almost instantly; the smell of licorice filled the air.

I watched as my mother gave me the biggest look of disapproval ever, but she can deal with it. I have to take dream silk root this way for it to work effectively. "Once in, I am going o search her memories for Melody and then try to force the Hilmer out."

"Be careful, you know how dangerous a Hilmer close to Marcloff can be. Even without a host." Voxis warned me. Like I needed the reminder of how disgusting and vicious they could be.

I moved closer to Allura, taking a long drag from the joint before blowing the smoke in her face. Both parties had to be pretty high for this to work properly. A few more hits and we'll both be soaring pretty good.

I didn't always care to have my cognitive functions disabled, but I've got enough people here to protect me if stuff goes south. The Hilmer inhabiting Allura's body slouched to the ground, her head lulled back onto the log we were sitting in front of.

I felt my head getting heavy as the world started to slowly slip away from me. Darkness lulled me into a nice, deep sleep.

I awoke in the middle of a cozy cabin, the fireplace being the only source of light. It was warm and inviting. The scent of cinnamon and apples filled the room. I looked down to notice that I was tucked into a nice warm bed, silver and white sheets wrapped around me.

"I know why you're here. I promise you'll be safe in here." A voice said to me from across the room. I recognized that voice immediately. I sat up throwing the covers off of me ready to get into a fight. "That's very unnecessary. I am not the creature you've had to endure. I promise."

She was right, the woman in front of me was not the same woman that I had given a broken ankle to. "Sorry about your ankle. Once I can get you free, I will make sure you're healed up and taken care of. My mate is an expert healer."

"There's no need for apologizes. You did what you thought was best to help get the answers you needed. I never question the gods. Everything is done for a reason." She turned to me, and I saw the same face as the woman I was unconscious next to in reality. Only this woman had much less of a fight in her.

"Not everything happens for a reason. Sometimes bad things happen to good people who don't deserve it. I hate to cut things short with you, but I need to find out where Melody is." Allura looked at me with wide eyes, horror-stricken. "What is it?"

"I don't know where she is. I hadn't seen her for at least two weeks prior to my run in with this creature." Allura fell back into the chair, her eyes fixed on the floor below. She would be no help to me.

"Do you mind if I take a look around? I need to get the Hilmer out of you. The sooner I do that, the sooner I can return and we can get to the bottom of where Melody might have gone." I made my way to the door, expecting her to stop me, but she didn't.

"There's an armory three buildings over. This place looks modeled after the Solaria of my youth. I don't go out there anymore. It's not safe for someone like me. The castle is down the road just a bit. The creature has been living there since taking control." She hadn't moved from the chair, only now turning her head to look at me.

"Allura, how did the Hilmer gain control of you?" I hesitantly asked. Knowing how she's gotten possessed might help us protect ourselves in the future.

She laughed a little. "I was in the temple, doing my normal cleaning and lighting of the candles. An old woman had come in, looking for a nice warm place to rest. I assumed she was a wayward fortune teller that was traveling with the circus that was in town, so I didn't think she was there to cause harm. Next thing I know, I'm being knocked over the head with a candlestick. I woke up, but instead of having control of my body, it was like I was watching a movie."

"How long ago was that?" It felt like a rock had just dropped into the pit of my stomach. I watched her as she counted out on her fingers. I didn't know if she was counting days, weeks, or months. I just hope she hasn't been counting for years.

"At least three years." Allura finally confirmed my worst fear. "I've been conscious enough in here to know that I have done irreparable damage to the once thriving relationship I had with your mother. If I cannot make it out of this hellscape, please let her know it wasn't me who did those things. My sisters probably think I hate them. My nephews probably think the worst of me. But what of my daughter?"

"Why hadn't you seen her before this unfortunate situation started?" I took a seat across from her, watching as she clasped her hands in her lap.

"She had a theory about a daemon uprising and she wanted to go talk to Harold. She said she had found evidence that daemons were walking amongst us in the flesh of others. I didn't believe her. I told her not to bother her uncle with such nonsense and to trust in the fate the gods gave us. She called me a coward and a blind fool." Allura sighed and my heart ached for her. "I guess she was right."

"Right or wrong, I will find her, and you can tell everyone yourself that you're sorry. I'm sure my mother has already figured it out and forgiven you. Damian was the one who said you were acting strange and stopped my mother from doing damage that would've removed you from this planet." I hated being so blunt, but I had no choice. "As for the armory, unless you're coming with me to help, I won't be needing anything from it. Normal steel won't kill a Hilmer, and my plan isn't to kill it in here." I stood up from the chair and looked down at her. "You can either help me help you, or you can stay here and let me take care of this by myself. Either way, I am heading out. I need to find out where Melody is, and I need to get this Hilmer out of you for your sake."

Allura sat there for a moment, her eyes shining with unspent tears. She took a moment before standing up, brushing her dress off of some invisible dust and walked to the door beside me. "I'll go with you. Just know, if I die in here. I die out there."

"No one's dying today. Let's get moving."

CHAPTER 57
TALISSA

Moving through the streets of this memory of Solaria was odd to see them looking like they did back in the day. Allura was much younger than me and probably was a child when the city last looked like this before the massive construction that changed it from the Solaria that I grew up with. I knew where the armory was, what I didn't know was what Allura was capable of.

"If you don't mind me asking, do you have any fae abilities that showed up after your changing?" I asked as we quietly made our way into the large stone building. The place looked just like it did when Ignis and I came here during the war to gather weapons for those on the front lines with us. Most of the fae back then didn't come into their powers until much later in life. Humans had no power, only their spirit which never faltered. Not even in the face of some of the most horrific creatures Hellis threw at us. I miss them, all the friends I had made from those days. I don't know how many of them were able to find their mates after the war and gain the blessing. Hopefully all who survived did.

"The most I can do is make a bright blinding light to distract and blind people. My father trained all of us girls to protect ourselves with a blade." She stepped up to a wall of daggers and grabbed a bandolier and quite a few daggers. "I was best with these."

A wicked smile flashed across her face but the crazy look in her eyes is no longer there. I let it go, knowing exactly the feeling of taking back your control feels like. "We should be able to get to the castle faster if we cut through the wards." I said as I made my way back outside.

"That's not a good idea. This may be my subconscious, but it's also theirs." Allura pointed toward the wards where shadows stalked between homes and fences. "They started showing up shortly after I got here. I don't know if they're my own inner daemons or the ones that thing brought in with it."

"Probably what they brought in with it. Okay, so we cut through the woods. It's not that far off of the path unless there's baskerhounds about. Then we might be screwed." I looked at the small patch of woods between us and the castle. I didn't hear the signature howling of the daemon dogs, but I didn't want to run into them just in case. They were bloody thirsty creatures with fur like an oil slick and teeth like razors. They blended into the shadows and the darkness around them, only glowing red eyes could be seen in the shadows.

"If there are any here, I haven't heard them. We should be safe." I shrugged my shoulders and headed across the path into the dark bit of woods. Allura followed me closely, keeping up with my quick pace. She was as silent as I was, narrowly missing sticks and branches that could give away our location. I was utterly shocked by how well she maneuvered through the darkness. Then again, she's been living in this darkness for years.

"The castle looks quiet. Are you sure the Hilmer is here?" I asked, as we stopped just inside the woods before the open lawn of the castle grounds sprawled before us. Allura said nothing, instead pointed to the shadows stalking the walls of the castle. They were much lighter against the grey stone walls. Either they were shadows or spirits of previous victims the Hilmer consumed.

I watched as the shadow guards moved around to the side wall and took that as a chance to move in. Allura didn't need my signal to follow me, if I moved my foot, she was mimicking my every movement. We made our way through the yard with no issues at all and posted up on either side of the doors. "Are you ready?" I asked her, she nodded, angling a dagger in each of her hands. I took a deep breath, focusing a dark cloud of smoke from my hand. Thick black smoke took the shape of a long scythe, silver and onyx took place of the smoke, startling Allura a little.

"Do you normally just materialize weapons?" She asked as she took in Oathbreaker. The bright silver steel was made from the dwarves back during the first battle of the first war. The scythe was made of black onyx and reenforced by dragons' fire to keep it sturdy for all these years. Erina decorated the onyx with a carved in dragon and the phases of the moon that spiraled around the scythe in a songlike dance.

"It's been with me for a millennium, it's my most trusted weapon that I have." I moved closer to the door and grabbed the handle. "Let's get this show on the road." Allura nodded as I pushed open the door exposing the bone white floor to the grey outdoors. The castle was eerily quiet, nothing like how it was back in the old days. I put my hand up, stopping her from entering the hall. I let a smoke like creature drop from my hand, "be my eyes, Ithika."

Ithika was a beautiful basilisk that I raised from birth. Her gaze could strike a man dead in his tracks, but she had other wonderful powers that most didn't know about. While you should never look one in the eye, she allows only those trusted by me to gaze upon her. She could take on the form of a larger dragon or the smallness of a black heart headed snake, all lethal in their own respects. Ithika grazed my hand before striking off down the halls, lending me her eyes and ears.

"What the hell is that?!" Allura yelped as Ithika rounded a corner at the end of the hall. I looked over at her, forgetting that my own eyes now resemble that of hers. "What's wrong with your eyes?!"

"Calm down and shut up. Ithika is a basilisk; she is one of the few that roamed Cerulia long ago. There is nothing wrong with my eyes. I am just seeing what she is seeing, so hush." I snap. Allura quickly shut her mouth, biting her lower lip hard. I rolled my eyes, refocusing on what Ithika was looking at. Upon the throne sat a dark, yet handsome figure. The Hilmer looked more human than daemon, but then again, they could take the form of whatever poor soul they devoured prior. I guess they preferred the look of the human over their natural flesh suit.

He was sprawled out on the throne made of alabaster and antlers, feet dangling over the arm of the chair. A shadow stood in front of it with a tray of what looked to be fruit. No, those were memory orbs. Ithika made her way closer to the throne, staying deep in the shadows as to not be noticed. I could hear the Hilmer laughing with the shadow. The closer Ithika got to them, the more details began to show in the shadows, hollow eyes, sunken in skin as ashen as that of wood after a fire. They were souls of the departed that the Hilmer dragged with him to keep him company. They were slaves.

"It's only a matter of time before that bitch gets here. Not like Allura will be brave enough to leave that damn cabin to help her. Weak little soul." His voice was a soft and velvety with a bone chilling echo to it. I halted Ithika so she wouldn't get any closer." Once she comes to her senses and realizes there is no getting rid of me and accepts her fate like you did, we can go." I looked past the vision of the throne room at Allura. I can't let her inside there, he's waiting for her to come to him.

I called Ithika back to me, her body shimmering into nothing but smoke. "Allura, you can't go in there with me." I told her, a stern look on my face. "Not if you ever want to see Melody or your family again."

She took a deep breath before speaking. "I've tried to come here and kill it before. I failed miserably and almost lost my life that night. I know what I— no what we are up against. I'm tired of being a prisoner in my own body. Let me fight him with you. His shadows can't do much besides blind us with their bodies and he will throw them at us to make sure we can't see. It's how I almost died that night."

"I can see through the shadows, and I can free them. Let them touch me, he won't like what happens when they do." I smirked at her. "If you are sure that you want to come with me, I can let you, but I can't protect you if you don't listen to what I tell you to do." She nodded that she understood and from that moment I knew there wasn't any turning back. We made our way through the halls, silently as to not alert the shadows or their capture to our presence.

The throne room wasn't that far into the castle, a quick right turn at the end of the hall opened to the large room. The bone white flooring stretched out into the large room covered only in the center by a large golden rug. One that I remember all too well from my youth. The throne that fool sat upon was my grandfathers, Otius, the matching one next to it for my grandmother, Illisandra. This idiot has no idea who he's pissed off this time.

I give Allura a look to stay in the shadows and she nods, slinking off into the darkness of the back wall. I walked into the main room, letting the hells of my boots click and scrape on the stupid floor. I would've caught so much shit for this if the person on the throne was someone different. The Hilmer looked up from the memory orbs in its hand, a serpent-like grin snaked across his face. A twinkle in his yes told me this was going to be a fun fight. I twirled Oathbreaker in my hand and smiled up at him.

"I was wondering who was stupid enough to sit upon that throne of blood." I said as I got closer to the throne. He wiped his hands on his pants and slowly began clapping his hands as he stood.

"Ah, royalty at its finest. Does King Zekon know you're still alive? If not, he would be very upset to know that you rather grace me with your presence than him." The Hilmer winked at me, there is no way a random Hilmer that belonged to Marcloff's ranks knew what Zekon meant to me.

"Why would I bother with such a pathetic daemon like Zekon?" I asked, rolling my eyes as he licked his lips. He was a soul eater, a different type of Hilmer than those who possessed those with the sickness. This could be a slight problem.

"Pathetic daemon? Oh, you haven't heard? He claimed that he killed you on the battlefield all those years ago. I'm sure King Marcloff would be very interested to know that you survived Zekon's assault." The Hilmer laughed, an eerie twisted echo reverberated off of the walls back at us.

"You think you're going to get out of here long enough to tell him I'm still alive?" I looked at Oathbreaker then back to the Hilmer. "That's not going to happen." I charged at it, swinging the scythe's long blade at it. A whistle sang through the air as it split the wind, missing the Hilmer by an inch. It jumped back hissing at the push of air that went its way.

"My shadows will protect me from your powers Goddess. I will not fall to you!" His soft velvety voice screeched loudly. I made another advance as he threw a shadow my way. I flashed a quick grin as I grabbed the shadow, a blinding white light exploded from my hand purging the creature from Allura's body. I could feel the shadows

424

gratitude soar through me as I granted it the release to finally pass on to the afterworld. "What did you do?!"

I swung again bringing Oathbreaker so close to tearing the Hilmer right in half. The grin that sliced across my face was wide. I caught a glimpse of Allura as she hid behind a column in the back of the room doing her best to stay from sight. "You must've forgotten what I am capable of in my long absence from Cerulia." He sent three more of his shadows at me in what he thought was a barrage of assaults. Little did he know they were running to me for freedom, not to harm me.

I let each and every one of his shadows grab me, a white light illuminating them once more before they vanished into the afterlife. The look at horror and rage creased his brows, he was out of options now. He reached behind the throne, pulling out a long black rapier made of iron and brass. It was an older weapon from the armory that I knew very well. I used to play with that exact one as a child. I could tell by the point of the rapier, dulled and half missing from me sparring with a block of wood. I knew it's weak spots.

"You'll pay for that!" He screamed, charging at me wildly. I moved a step the right avoiding the initial blow. I dodged his every move, sidestepping and deflecting the rapier with Oathbreaker. The more he missed the angrier he became, but my plan was working. His eyes were fading from black to grey, a sign of a Hilmer's power dying off. Without a teether back to Hellis the creature couldn't use too much power without it consuming its life force to stay alive.

The Hilmer stumbled over itself, now's my chance. I sliced through the air, severing the creatures' arm from its body, it let out an ear-piercing wail as its' arm thudded on the ground. Black and blue oily blood tainted the bone white floors of Otius's once great hall. A crashing sound reverberated through the hall, my eyes targeting Allura who knocked over a vase that shattered on the floor. The Hilmers scream must have startled her, but that alerted him to her presence. Allura was a lot smarter than I gave her credit for, she had her daggers out the moment the sound of the vase hit our ears. She wasn't going down without a fight.

"I see you!" The Hilmer hissed as it turned its attention from me to her, bolting off in her direction. She took off through the back of the throne room, heading for the door on the far side of the room. I followed her lead, taking off through the room. I could hear my grandmothers voice in my head telling me to stop running around, it was really annoying for my own memories of this place to play in my mind.

The Hilmer was slowing down as its blood leaked out in a trail behind it. Allura made it to the door right as I did. we spun on the Hilmer, forcing it to skid to a stop. I moved quick with Oathbreaker, slicing through the Hilmer's body. Its oily blood seeped out of its body in a pool around it. "Finish it off Allura. Put a dagger in its head." I offered her the truth final kill of the Hilmer that robbed her of three years with her family.

She gladly accepted my offer, raising the dagger high above the Hilmers head before plunging it into the right eye socket through into its skull. Blood spurted up at her, but she didn't flinch. She held herself together, but soon she will break. And when she does, I'll be here for her. "What happens now?" She asked, releasing the hold she had on the dagger.

"We wake up," I said with a smile as I touched the Hilmers body, turning the creature to ash. A blinding white light filled the room, I guess I'll see her on the other side.

CHAPTER 58
LUNA

Valyn and Bastian kept giving me looks as we made our way into port. We hadn't had a chance to talk about the voices that I know they heard judging by the looks they kept giving me. Victoria gave us a look as she kept talking to Valyn, forcing his attention back to her. I think I was annoying her by being on deck. Fennik and Niklaus joined us on deck shortly after Noro's thanks came through. Valdis didn't seem too bothered by the extra voices in my head. He just placed a kiss on the top of my head before speaking with the others about our next move. Nox was the only one not looking at me like something huge had just occurred.

We had finally docked at Anchora. The town was so quiet, despite it being early in the morning. There were no anglers at the docks, no boats in the water and no sounds of life at all as we made our way onto dry land. It had me worried about the people of the town. "It's too quiet here." Fennik said as he looked around the dock.

"That's because the people of this town have moved inland. They're a bunch of idiots, Fenn." Damian's smokey voice reached me before the bond in my chest had a moment to miss him. I spun around, taking in the sight of him, his red hair tossed up in a man bun. I looked past him to see River and Ignis heading our way.

"How's my favorite niece?" River teased as he pulled me into a big hug. I was grateful that everyone knew we were family and that I wouldn't have to deal with possessive fae dominance. I moved out of Rivers' arms and gave Ignis a quick hug before running into Damian's arms. His scent of bourbon wrapped itself around me, settling some deep nervousness that I had. He planted kisses all over my face as he held me tight to him.

"Why do you say the people of Anchora are idiots, Damian?" Valdis asked, looking out over the quiet town. It felt more like a ghost town, and I guess now I know why. Damian didn't answer, instead looked at Ignis and River.

"Because they blamed the sea wyvern for their inability to be attentive parents." River said with full disgust. "We found an announcement board littered with missing persons posters and warnings about the sea wyvern. They blame her for their children drowning at sea, falling from the high cliffs and dying. They blame her for the fools who died when they went into the seas to kill her. Noro is only violent when her child or those of the spirits she protects are threatened. Those children they failed to protect, she protects their souls. So much better than they protected their lives." A tear fell down River's cheek as he spoke.

"If this place wasn't important to the Autumn Realm, I would burn it to the ground. The people here needed a monster, and they created one, it's not right." Ignis stated before looking off into the horizon.

"Then I guess they won't have an issue with us setting up base camp here." I said coldly. Originally, I didn't want to displace anyone or push our way in, but a rage was now simmering in my soul towards these people. It's not right or fair to blame someone else for your problems.

"Baby girl, at you were against that. I thought we were going to set up a camp between Floria and Anchora." Bastian said as he came closer to us. The crew from the ship unloaded the ship, bring off weapons and food onto the pier. I looked at him, causing him to stop moving.

"I didn't, but since they clearly abandoned this place, why shouldn't we use it? It gives us access to the waterways. I'm hoping we do not need to bring in a full army, but we don't know what is waiting for us in Floria. It's best that we have a place set up for the healers. Did you guys see a hospital or at least a large enough building that if we need to set up a more permanent healing facility, we can?" I looked at River and Ignis. I could see a shine of pride in their eyes as I started deciding how things needed to go.

"There is a large town hall in the center of the town. There. Did is another larger building on the far side of the town. I'm not too sure what its original use was, but we could make it work." Ignis claimed as everyone moved out of the way of the crew.

"Princess, where would you like the crew to set up chow hall?" Victoria asked as she walked by with another crew member. It shocked me a bit because I honestly thought she disliked me. Maybe I was wrong.

"I'm not sure where exactly we should put it.. There I've never been here before," I said, looking at Fennik for help. He seemed to have gotten the hint that I needed help.

"They can set up in the local restaurant district, there's are three of them lined up, side by side with each other. It's just down the main road. I can take you," Fennik offered. Victoria nodded and ushered the crew who had supplies down the main road. Fennik gave me a kiss and headed off with the crew towards the restaurant district.

"I guess from here on out, we take over Anchora as a base camp. There is a portal at the Temple of Rites a few minutes up the road where we can bring in people. Only issue is we need a god's blood to use the portal." Ignis said as he looked over the weapons crate the naval unit was bringing off of the ship.

"You mean to tell me we could've used a portal to get here?" Niklaus uttered. The pale look on his face from being at sea was finally returning to its normal complexion. Valyn laughed, clapping him on the back.

"What? Didn't like the rocking of the waves? The sea breeze? Come on, the salty air did wonders for your hair," he teased. Everyone laughed a little at the way they acted, but we had to get moving.

"Damian, what happened to Allura?" Bastian asked. It felt like he doused us all with freezing cold water, reminding us of why we weren't together in the first place.

"A Hilmer possessed her. Talissa is current;y trying to force it out of her." Damian said, glancing down at mme,e remembering I faced one back in the fall of last year. I knew something felt wrong about her.

"Wait, Talissa can exorcise Hilmers?" Valdis asked, shocked by this revelation.

"Not exactly. She thinks that Luna actually possesses that power. She didn't want to put that on you though, with you being so fresh to your changing. Instead, she decided she would take a shot with dream silk root. She dream walked once into someone else's mind when she first tried it. They're currently doing that as we speak. Lumina, Voxis and Claye are there with your grandparents. They're all monitoring the situation, but we need to get back to her." River said.

I let go of Damian and looked at everyone. We all couldn't do this together. I need people to be here to set up the main camp. I took a deep breath before making my next decision. "Valyn, you and Niklaus stay here and set up the hospital centers. Damian, Bastian, and Valdis, you three will come with us and help set up the mobile camps outside of Floria. Your legions are going to need you to command them. Nox and I will do a fly over once we get to where Talissa and the others are. When Fennik gets back, send him to us, please."

Everyone stood there and looked at me. I watched their faces each fall. We promised we would never split up again, but we had no choice. "My mom can come run the hospitals here with Maggie and Bethany. I am not letting you go out into a war without me with you!" Niklaus pushed back.

"I second that. I'm not standing by and feeling useless while you put your life at risk." Valyn said, reaching for me, but I had to take a step back. The moment he touched me, I would cave.

"She's making the right call. Stop disobeying an order from your mate and wife. She's making the calls that you all can't make. Don't make it harder on her." Ignis stepped up, putting his hand on my shoulder. I looked at him, trying to hold back a rogue tear from falling. "I'll do as you and Talissa command. My fire and hammer are at your disposal."

River stepped up next, bowing at the waist. "My waters and spear are at your service. Just tell me where to go and I'll do so. Talissa won't fight with you on this."

Damian and Bastian moved from beside me to in front of me, side by side, then dropped to a knee reciting the same words. "We will listen to your orders, our swords at your service."

Valdis looked like he was about to be sick. "I love you Luna. I will obey your orders, but the moment you are in danger, all bets are off. Is that understood?"

Before I could answer, Ignis turned to Valdis. "You think River and I were okay leaving Talissa to take on an entire fucking army of daemons during the first war? You think we wouldn't have done things differently if we knew there was a better way? Listening to your mate and trusting them is one of the biggest things that is going to be hard for you to overcome. Trust me, I've been a part of this family for way longer than you all even knew of them. They are headstrong women who don't take no for an answer and walk into danger with a fucking smile on their faces. Deal with it."

They were speechless. By the time they regain their composure, Fennik and Victoria had returned to the docks. "Where do you need me?" Victoria asked me. She didn't bother with asking the guys where they needed her. No, she respected me enough to ask me for the plan.

"You, captain the fastest ship in the fleet. Preferably, I would like you to stay in Anchora to help get people to safety, and fast." I said. She looked over at Valyn, who just nodded in agreement.

"What about Noro? The safest way back passes her den, and I am not risking my crew." Victoria stood her round, and I respected the fuck out of her for that.

"She won't be a problem for you. You didn't fire upon her when she attacked the ship. I'll make sure you can get safe passage. Just make sure no idiots on board aim a harpoon at her or her kin." I replied, just as stern.

"Okay, you get people here who need safe passage, I'll take them to Port Ilsa. We can figure out where they go from there." I enjoyed her plan it made a lot of sense.

"Perfect. Jasmine can make sure people are at least looked after at her tavern until we can get the returned safely to Floria. Once we take out the army there, we need to make sure that we can rebuild the city from any damage. Fennik, any word on the mages?" I asked as he watched me.

He quickly shook his head, recovering from his gawking. "They'll be at the Endora Field's by midday. Should we head to the fields and set up a few tents?" I nodded and just like that, no questions asked, Fennik went off in search of tents and people to help get them to the site.

"Let's get heading out. Valyn, Niklaus," I paused taking in a deep breath. "If we can get your mothers here to Anchora, then you both can join me out at the fields. We're going to need you both out there once you both get things settled here."

I threw my arms around both of their necks, pulling them into me. "Promise me you'll be safe, and you won't do anything stupid until we get there." Valyn whispered in my ear.

"I'll do my best to not do something utterly stupid until the moment your feet hit the fields. Sound good?" I joked, but I meant it. I just couldn't make the promise. If things go sideways, I won't sit back and wait for them to join us before doing the right thing.

"It'll do. We'll see you soon." They both gave me a kiss on the cheek and pulled me into each of their arms.

It's time for action. "Where are we heading first?" I asked River.

"The Temple of Rites. Hopefully Talissa was able to save Allura and we go back to a dead Hilmer on the grass." River said.

"Alright then, to the Temple of Rites."

CHAPTER 59
DRAKE

Alstrom and the advisors made quick work of most of the daemons we came in contact with on our way through the cells.
Harold managed to get a sword a little while back. He was griping
about the quality of the weapon for a little while until he actually used
the damn thing. Of course it's not like his sword, it's not his fucking
sword. The damn things were rusted and looked like they sat around
since the first war, but they did the trick.

"Are you two alright back there?" Alstrom called out to us. He did
a really great job of making sure that we were still safe. In his words,
if he couldn't bring us back safely to our wives, he wouldn't be a great
solider.

"Yeah, we're good." I wasn't about to tell him that I was worried we
would never find Erina. "Do you know how much further we have
until we reach her cell?"

Elijah pulled out a map from his pocket and looked at it. The
others were searching open cells for weapons and food. Our group had
grown in size since rescuing Harold. I learned all about the Crimson
Rebellion that Elijah had put together after Marie and Tanis aligned
with Hellis. I give Elijah massive credit for having the balls to do what

most people wouldn't. Just goes to show you that you can't judge a book by its cover.

"Most of the rebellion was captured once you all were. We got locked away and promised a death fitting a traitor." A small teen smiled as he talked to Harold. "I'm grateful for Elijah for not wanting to see us die. I'll gladly follow him and Prince Fennik. Floria will rise again, we will make sure of it."

Shouts of joy and agreement echoed through the halls to the boy's statement. Elijah smiled as he looked over the map, "All the cells have been checked. The Queen isn't in any of them. That means one of two things." He paused as he checked the map once again. A pit was forming in the center of my stomach, I was immediately thinking the worst. "One, she is being held in the actual castle and not here or two, she was already rescued."

"Does your father know of your affiliation with the rebellion?" Hardold asked him. Elijah shook his head while packing his map back up.

"My father barely knows me at all. When my mother would make her visits to Floria, it was never to see me or Malicah, it was to see my father. We were just the burdens that had to be dealt with when they were able to be together. My father hasn't asked me about my life once in the last five years. So no, he has no idea who's running the rebellion." Elijah replied before heading off to talk to some of the soldiers we rescued from the dungeons.

Most of the Autumn army was locked away down here for rising up against Marie and her orders to allow the daemons safe harbor within the city walls. I feel for these people, and so does Harold. He's made more apologies since we rescued him since the deaths that happened in Mirith last year. The soldiers here didn't blame him, they all knew that his wives ruled their own realms and that he only stepped in when needed. Which clearly these poor people needed him to step in much sooner than we did.

"So, what now?" I asked Alstrom as he looked over the weapons that everyone was able to scrounge up from around the random cells. I looked at all the young faces surrounding us. These boys were mere teens, maybe young adults at best. They weren't around for the first war, nor the other battles that came after. There were some older men like Alstrom, but he said most of the older men left with the women and children in the middle of the night to head to Fildrey and Anchora. Hopefully everyone made it out safely.

"We go to the castle and march through the front doors. If your wife was rescued already, the castle would be in a panic. Just like they probably are now that they know you two are no longer in your cells." He replied.

Before he continued a loud roar ripped through the dungeon, shaking the entire place. Debris, stones and dust all fell from the ceiling. "We need to get out of here before whatever the hell that was gets to us!" I called out amongst the chatter and clattering of steel. Harold looked at me and nodded. We were always on the same page when it came to being on the front lines and it looked like we would continue that tradition.

"Valid point Drake. Let's make for the exit boys! Keep your eyes peeled for dragons and hellhounds. The daemons we'll see coming, the others we won't. Move out!" A chorus of ayes and cheers echoed through the hall. It was time to get moving and quick.

Howling and roaring echoed from behind us and our boots clanked and thudded against the stone floors as we ran through the halls towards the exit. Elijah was nimble and was the first one out of the dungeons making sure the way out wasn't covered in traps and guards. Considering he wasn't running back in here and I didn't hear metal clanking off of other metal, we must be safe to leave. Alstrom stalked out the dungeons before he would allow Harold and myself outside. Where he respected us as equals on the battlefield, we are still royalty to him, and he wouldn't be the one responsible if something happens to either of us. I could respect that.

He let out a low whistle letting us know it was safe to come out. Soldiers filed out on either side of us just in case there was an enemy they didn't notice. We walked through the tall grass that surrounded the place. The dungeon wasn't underground at all like I thought it was. It modeled the prison in the twilight realm.

That was probably the most terrifying thing that I could've saw when we came out of there. The Twilight realm was mainly known for being a prison that was inescapable. Hell, the guards there didn't venture in without a map and even then, they had to be careful or else the walls would change, and the way back would be lost to them.

At least whoever made this version didn't know about that little tidbit of information. "We all can't storm the castle. Is there anyone you could contact to see if they broke out Erina?" I asked.

"Already ahead of you. Beatrix has been in the castle undercover for the past year. She's managed to get the aid of the other maids and house staff on our side. I already sent her a message asking her to check the spare rooms. If my father has the Queen inside the house, he wouldn't be treating her like a prisoner. More like a child who was grounded to their room." Elijah huffed.

His phone buzzed, drawing his attention to the screen. "The Queen is in the high tower. Apparently, she made threats to level the castle so he had to put her some place where she couldn't see outside."

I laughed, that sounded so much like my Erina. "Glad to know that she wasn't stuck in the dungeon. But what does he think her not having access to seeing the outside world will do? If she wants to level the damn place, she will do it."

"I don't know, he made it seem to the staff that if she saw the outside world that she could destroy them all. Seems like no one believes it but himself, but they each are playing their part. She is safe. That's all that matters right now. We will get her out at nightfall. Beatrix will make sure of it," Elijah said as he looked at Alstrom who had a gleam of pride in his eyes.

"Where can we hide out for the rest of the day? It's not like we can walk into town and put people at risk." Harold inquired. He had a very valid point. I wouldn't feel right asking the people of Floria to hide us in their homes and put their families at risk.

"The townsfolk would gladly assist you, but we have a safe house on the outskirts of town. Well, more like a camp. Tanis knows something is happening out there, he just doesn't know if it's a daemon army or a refugee camp. Either way, he won't leave the castle to bother checking it out. He has no control out there and he knows it." Alstrom noted. A man in power with nothing but fear is a dangerous man indeed. This isn't going to end well for any of us.

"Where on the outskirts?" I asked as I followed Elijah and Alstrom behind the prison and towards a small dirt path that led into the woods.

"Endora field's," he replied. "Beatrix will meet us there. I promise you that the Queen will be returned to you safely."

I trusted the boy, but he shouldn't make promises that he can't guarantee. I guess I just have to trust this Beatrix and hope she doesn't fuck us over, even though every bone in my body is screaming to get to her now.

CHAPTER 60
LUNA

We made our way out to the Temple of Rites within a few minutes. I expected it to take a lot longer to get there. River and Ignis led the way while I caught up with Damian. He filled us in on what went down in Solaria after we left and how Sirus stayed behind to find his cousin Melody.

"Nice to see Victoria can actually take orders from someone besides Valyn," Damian commented as Bastian and Valdis walked ahead of us.

"Yeah, she isn't one to take orders from anyone. Sometimes she doesn't even listen to Valyn. You should be happy about that Luna." Bastian called back over his shoulder. Valdis had been really quiet since we left Anchora. I think he's mad about being told to just shut up and follow orders.

"I didn't think she liked me honestly. Her taking the orders like nothing was kind of shocking to me." I admitted. We turned around the side of the temple to see Lumina standing over Allura with her hand out, a white glow emanated from her.

We made our way over to the group, trying not to startle anyone. River and Ignis laid their hands on Talissa's shoulders as they each took up flank beside her. Damian and Bastian took their usual places at my back, with Valdis standing behind them. Protective mates at their finest.

"Luna!" Vanalli said my name, rushing to me. She pulled me into a deep embrace, practically sobbing into me.

"It's good to see you, too." I said, hugging her back. Undas was behind Vanalli, patiently waiting his own turn to get a hug.

"I'm so sorry we didn't see you as soon as you woke up. We had to take care of a situation." Let it to my grandmother to apologize for something that was out of her control.

"Getting to the bottom of who stole Otius' blade is a little more important than seeing me seconds after waking up," I reminded her. The information dump that I'd gotten since waking up has been intense.

"Yes, well, we think we have a lead on it." She looked back at Allura, who was wincing at whatever Lumina was doing to her.

"She didn't do it. Well physically she did, but mentally it wasn't her in the driver's seat mom. You have to let that go," Talissa said as she walked past everyone to give me a big hug. "Seems like you've been on an adventure yourself, my little niece."

"You could say that. It's been a long couple of days and will be even longer still. Fennik and Nox went ahead to the Endora Fields to setup a base camp. I think we should head out as soon as possible. We have to get the army out of Floria and rescue the people who might be trapped there." I said. The others looked at River and Ignis like this was a shocking thing for me to be discussing.

"She's been calling the shots since Anchora. I wouldn't bet against her if I were you. Her plan is sound, get the camps set up, then aerial scouting to see what we are in for when we need to infiltrate Floria." Ignis stated. His eyes locked on Talissa's, a grin on his face. She smiled back at him.

"Guess we're taking your lead. I'll help you if you need to make the hard calls and can't. Let's face it, this isn't my first rodeo." Talissa said. "She is right though. The sooner we get to Endora Fields and check out what's needed there, the better."

Everyone seemed to agree with the notion that we needed to hurry. Not knowing what is happening to Floria or what happened to my family has my anxiety at an all-time high. I just hope they are all safe and that I am just overthinking things.

"How long will it take us to get to the fields from here?" Bastian asked. Voxis looked up at the sky, looking at the birds that were flying overhead.

"It's about a two-hour hike from here. The sooner we leave, the better it will be for traveling. I feel a storm is on the horizon. Someone needs to get her somewhere safe first." She pointed over at Allura. Our attention now focused on Lumina doing her best to get her healed up.

"I healed most of her leg, but the Hilmer that possessed her was a soul reaper, according to Talissa. It had control of her body for three years, just taking from her the energy and life force. It did so much damage to her body that it starved her of food. She's lucky to be alive, honestly. She needs to get her strength back or else there is a very good possibility that she could die." Lumina said as she stood up, dusting off her pants with her hands.

"I can get her to Anchora so she can get to the hospital there." he paused, alive, looking at Allura. "That is, if you're okay with a daemon spawn touching you." Valdis made the offer from the kindness of his heart. I watched as shame glossed across Allura's face. Maybe parts of her were actually more aware than we believed. Either that or she was watching everything that was done with her body while being trapped inside it.

"I would appreciate it, Prince Valdis. I am so sorry for what I said before. It wasn't me," she whispered. None of the darkness I felt from her before lingered.

"Then I am at your service." Valdis bowed slightly to her. "Hope you're okay with flying." Valdis grinned.

"Before you go, where is Melody?" Damian asked Allura before she could leave. A shadow flickered across her gaze.

"The last time I saw her was three years ago, Damian. If she had been around during the last three years, I was kept in the dark." Tears slid down her cheeks. A mother's pain and love were both equally intense. My heart ached for her in that regard.

"I already called Sirus. He's on his was here. He said he checked the entire castle and the dungeons. Luckily, he found no evidence that she had been in either place recently." Talissa said as she placed her hand on Allura's shoulder. "We will find her, Allura. Hopefully, if she noticed something was off with you, she just went into hiding."

"Melody is anything but a coward. She's probably trying to figure out a way to save me if she has realized something was off." Allura stood gingerly on her feet, sway from side to side. "Save your sister first. Melody is a smart girl. I know she's safe. I can feel it."

"Okay, if you are positive that you think she is safe," Talissa hugged her. "Sorry again about your ankle."

"It's alright, consider it my atonement for the bad things the Hilmer used me for." Allura hugged her back before turning to Damian and Bastian. "I'm so sorry, boys. I owe you all so much more. After I am all healed up, I will head to Solaria and check the archives for any way I can find to help you in this war."

Vanalli stepped forward then, causing Allura to practically fall to her knees to bow. "Stand. Allura Ashford, I hereby lift your ban from Valhime and grant you access to the city of the gods once more. I will go with you to Solaria and from there, back to Valhime. I'm sure my mother and father have finally returned as well and I am going to need to play referee between the families. Undas, you better watch over our family and keep them safe, so help me."

Undas laughed and kissed his wife, negating her threat. "Of course, my love."

"I'm going to get Allura to Anchora. I'll check in with Niklaus and Valyn while I'm there. Please be careful. I know I can't stop you from putting yourself in danger, but can you just make sure you're still standing when I get there?" Valdis pulled me into a deep hug. The scent of his cologne, a gentle cherry scent, flooded my senses. I buried my face in his chest, inhaling deep while I still could.

"I promise I'll still be standing when you get back. No one will let anything happen to me." I said into his chest. Letting his scent wash over me to calm my nerves. I don't want anything happening to him either, but I can't voice that.

"Dude, she took on her half-brother and a dual headed dragon, not to mention the first Hilmer she ever encountered when she was still technically human. She was safe then, and she will be even safer now." Bastian declared from behind us.

I heard muttering between my grandmother and aunt. I guess they didn't know about what happened in Mirith. Or at least my part during the first attack. I wonder how much they knew about what happened over the last year.

"I think we should get heading to Endora Fields. Valdis, you better be quick. Don't leave me waiting." I gave him a kiss as he let me go. Allura tentatively took his hand, glancing at me.

"Thank you," Allura said to me as Valdis picked her up. He was going to carry her the entire way to Anchora. My surprise came when the jealous rage didn't occur. Maybe I am getting better at controlling my emotions. Vanalli gave me a hug.

"Stay safe, sweet child. I love you," she whispered in my ear before following them down the road toward Anchora.

I looked at everyone. "Let's get to Endora Fields. We need to get a good look at the vantage points we'll have or not have." Everyone nodded, breaking out into smaller groups as we made our way in the opposite direction from Anchora.

CHAPTER 61
LUNA

Getting to Endora Field's was a lot easier than I expected. Did it take some time? Yes, but it was time that I got to talk with Talissa and her mates. It was time that Damian and Bastian had with them as well. Learning history of what happened back when they were younger, explaining the most recent historical events that they had missed while in Celestia. It all helped the time go by so much faster.

"We can set up a makeshift portal from Endora Field's once we get there. We can link it to the Temple of Rites so people can be transferred quickly between here and the hospital in Anchora," Voxis said as we approached the area.

Tan and brown tents are already sprawled across the field. There were people already bustling around, some in armor, most in just casual clothing. It took me by surprise because I wasn't expecting there to be a camp here already. A sudden tug on my heart had my head spinning to see Fennik coming up between two tents from our right.

"Fennik!" I exclaimed, running over to him. I couldn't help but throw my arms around him. "What is going on?"

He nuzzled his nose into the crook of my neck, breathing in deeply to center himself. "These people are the citizens of Floria. They fled their homes thanks to Tanis and his iron grip ruling that he's been trying to force onto the people. There's someone you're going to want to see in the main tent. Come with me."

I took Fennik's hand as he led us through the small paths between the tents. The smells of stews and other assorted meats filled the air. I watched as children made their way into some of the larger tents as we passed. My heart broke at the little faces that looked back at me. Even if they had smiles on them, this was wrong.

"Can we get the families out of here? At least the children." Talissa asked as we made our way to a large reddish-brown tent.

"They refuse to leave. We have tried explaining that it is dangerous for the children, but the families don't want to lose their homes to looting when this is over." Fennik had a stern look on his face. A pang of anger simmered below the surface.

"Have they not seen the daemons? What of any dragons? They could be wiped out in no time and there go all the children in Floria. If the adults want to stay like idiots, that's one thing. I won't stand for children being neglected for petty materialistic things," Voxis raged. I wholeheartedly agreed with her sentiment.

"Houses and other materials can be replaced. The lives of the children cannot. If the families refuse to look at their children and save them, then I will force them to leave. It won't be pretty, but they will go." I said as we stopped short of the entrance.

"I couldn't agree with you more," a deep voice boomed from the tent entrance. I looked over to see my father standing there in what most would consider commoners' clothing. Fennik let go of my hand as I ran toward him.

"You're safe! Where's mom?" I asked, hugging him before pulling away to look around the tent. I saw Harold sitting around a table with another larger man and a male who looked way too much like Fennik for my liking.

"She's not here Luna. We haven't been able to find her yet. They weren't keeping her in the dungeons with us. According to Elijah, there is someone inside the castle that will rescue your mother tonight," he said as he looked over his shoulder at Fenniks' twin.

"Can we trust them to get her out safely?" I asked, my fear and anxiety creeping up. I don't want to think I can't trust Fennik's people, but I've seen how hearts can turn cold during wars.

"You can trust Beatrix. She wouldn't do you or the Queen wrong." Elijah stepped up to us and bowed at the waist. "It's a pleasure to meet you, Princess Luna." I gave a small nod of acknowledgement and looked at Fennik. I couldn't tell if I had missed something or not.

"Luna, this is my half-brother, Elijah. I just met him myself, so I have little to say about him, except he's the reason my father and your father are out of the dungeon. So, I am grateful for that." Fennik wasn't cold to him, but he wasn't very warm either. Why does it not surprise me that Marie kept something like another child from Fennik?

"Go easy on him, you hear me boy," the raspy round man called from the table. The man smiled at me when I looked over at him. "Nice to meet you, Princess. Sorry it isn't under better circumstances, the name's Alstrom."

"It's a pleasure to meet you both. Thank you for saving my father and father-in-law," I said, stepping up to the table and looking at the map sprawled out on top. Talissa moved up next to me as we took in the x's and o's on it. I placed my finger over the main castle, a big red circle surrounded it. "What's the red one for?"

"That is where Tanis is holding up with two commanders from Hellis. One a rider, the other a dragon. We're not sure why exactly they are here and why they chose here of all places to stage this battle, but we're ready for them." Elijah said as ice filled my veins. A rider and a dragon, there is no fucking way that it is Luther and Vikrum. I glanced over at the others, Damian and Bastian gave me a knowing look. They must suspect the same thing.

"What does the rider look like?" Bastian asked, stepping up beside me. He placed his hand on my lower back to keep me grounded, a small thing Valyn would normally do if he were here. I need him and Niklaus to hurry and get here.

"A tall blonde man. On the outside, he looked human, but something about him was off. He felt tainted or diseased. I tried to tell my mother that I didn't trust them, but she didn't listen to me at all. She never listened to anyone besides my father and we see how that turned out for her and our people." I watched as Fennik turned his gaze back out of the tent. I grabbed his hand, giving it a small squeeze.

"Well, you are right about one thing. The blonde man is tainted, or more so corrupted, if I am being honest." I watched as Alstrom and Elijah gave me a questioning look. "He's my brother. He used to be a commander in the Mistveil Royal army, the man with him used to be a General for the same army. Vikrum, the other man, corrupted my brother using the stupid lore that we grew up with."

"What lore is that? You're fae are you not? This man was human." Elijah retorted. Nox came up beside him placing a hand on his shoulder.

"She was living amongst the humans of Celvenia. She was raised by General Gunther Cromwell. I'm sure you've heard his name before. Her lineage was hidden from her by a magical suppression spell that our mother used. She is fae and goddess like myself. However, Luther was a byproduct of our mother thinking that the bond between her and our father was nothing more than her own infatuation. Sadly, she learned the truth after Luther and Luna were conceived." The way Nox spoke of my life like he knew it kind of bothered me.

"Look, my lineage doesn't matter. My brother thought he was fighting on the right side of the war. He is a good soldier, loyal to a fault. Vikrum knows I am a weak spot for my brother, and the last time I saw him before the attack on Mirith, we were already fighting. Vikrum used that doubt and planted a seed that I defected to the side of the enemy. As much anger and hatred that I have at him for being an idiot and the things he said to me before we parted ways in Celvenia, he is still my half brother. I don't want to kill him. I want to save him if I can." I watched as Nox looked at me, my father, as well. I have never spoken the truth that I don't want Luther dead. I want him back to how he used to be before Vikrum tainted his mind.

"Then let's get your mother and come up with a new plan. Just know that you might have to face him when we get in there," Elijah said, dropping any other questions he could've had. I'll keep that in mind for later.

"How long until Beatrix can extract my mother?" I asked, with little hesitation to jump right into business.

"Last meal is around eight, Beatrix has been personally seeing to your mother's needs. Tanis doesn't know she is a double agent working for the rebellion. He thinks she is one of the most loyal to him. He doesn't know that no one is loyal to him." Elijah pulled up a chair for me at the table.

"Have you seen a large silver sword lying around? I know that seems very odd since there are probably a ton of silver swords lying about, but this one is important." Talissa asked as she stood over my shoulder. Alstrom scratched his beard as he thought.

"Anything particular about his blade? Special markings or gems?" He asked as he looked at Elijah, who shrugged his shoulders in response.

"It is a blade made of silver and obsidian. If you have seen any depictions of the first war, you would recognize the blade immediately." Undas said as he entered the tent. I watched Alstrom and Elijah, along with several others, drop to a knee in front of him as if standing before him as a significant sign of disrespect. Alstrom tugged on Fennik's shirt, ushering him to bow to Undas. "That is over kill. Can you all please stand? It's very uncomfortable for me when people do this."

Everyone stood hesitantly, watching the god of fire and wealth. Undas rolled his eyes and moved next to the map, looking around at the surrounding areas. "The forests around the castle should provide enough coverage for archers to post up in the trees. I'd say we get a portal set up to get people to Anchora and evacuate the children. I don't care if I have to force parents to grow up. There will be no children's deaths on our hands."

"I wholeheartedly agree with you. I can be persuasive. They may not like it, but these children won't be tarnished and poisoned by war. River, Bastian," I paused as I looked over at all the mates standing in a line, waiting for orders. "You two take Lumina and get the portal up and running. Claye, Ignis and Damian gather up all able bodied men and women who have no children and bring them to here. If parents want to fight instead of protect their children, have the elderly and the teens take the children to Anchora. Fennik, you and Voxis can help get the children out of here fastest. Just be quick, we're going to need everyone here when night falls."

I bark out the orders and everyone obeys, leaving the tent to go get their respective tasks complete. A laugh barked out from the table. "For someone who has never been in battle, you are very good are coming up with strategies and plans. I'm proud to call you my daughter-in-law." Harold got up from the table and gave me a hug. "Where do you need me and your father? Both of us are fully capable of fighting on the front lines and are willing to do so."

"He's right Luna, you can't keep him and I in here out of fear of losing us. So, you're calling the shots. Where do we go?" My father stepped up next to Harold, both standing side by side, backs straight with a very stoic look gracing both of their faces. Talissa moved closer to me, her presence calming to my nerves.

"Nox and I are going to do air surveillance once night falls. I'd prefer to keep you all on the front lines here guarding the camp. Valdis should be here quickly once the portal is set up. He can stay in the shadows of the forest and help get mom back here safely." I paused and looked at Elijah. "Oh my goodness! I didn't mean to take over your operation! Please feel free to put my in my place. I am so sorry!" I panicked, not thinking that I could've been stepping on someone else's toes.

He let out a chuckle. "You aren't taking over my operation. You clearly came here with a plan to help take back Floria. I can't thank you enough for wanting to save our people. I am grateful for your assistance. The crimson rebellion is grateful for your assistance." He bowed once more towards me before looking at the others in the tent. "Princess Luna is in charge. All orders she gives are to be obeyed without question. If you have a problem with it, you can be on babysitting duty in Anchora."

Everyone looked at him before placing their feet together and crossing their right arms across their chests. In unison, they responded. "We are at your service!"

This would not be easy, but we will take Floria back and bring Tanis to justice.

CHAPTER 62
LUNA

All the citizens of Floria gathered in front of the main war tent. Women hugging onto their children and men holding their women. I watched the look in their eyes as they took us all in. Undas stood behind me, Talissa on my right, my father and Harold on my left. Fennik and the others stood on the opposite side of Talissa, each staring down at the citizens with mixed emotions. Valyn, Niklaus and Valdis joined us once the portal was up and running. Sirus took his place in the back of the group, saying how his presence could make those worry.

"Thank you all for coming. I am Princess Luna of Mirith. One of my mates is Prince Fennik of Floria. We came here not that long ago when we heard a rumor about an army from Hellis making its way to the Autumn Realm. Sadly, our last visit here didn't end the way any of us wanted or expected, and we were unable to stop the invasion. With that said, we are here to help take Floria back!" Cheers erupted through the crowd from the men and women standing around. This next part they won't be cheering about. "I will not tolerate children's lives being put in danger. I have faced a creature from Hellis face to face during the attack on my home, Mirith. We have a portal setup to take children, the elderly and those unable to fight to Anchora. We will not let the children be tainted and poisoned by this. I've seen firsthand what war does to children. I refuse to let that happen here. If you have a problem with that, feel free to come and speak with me."

Parents hesitantly looked at one another before hugging their kids closely. A young mother stepped forward, her head held high. "I am a single mother. Tanis and his minions captured my husband and took him away from his family forever. I cannot let my children lose me as well. May I please go with my children to Anchora? I am the only family they have left." Tears rolled down her cheeks, shattering my heart.

I moved away from my family and toward the young mother. I grabbed her hands, holding them in my own as I held back tears. "I am sorry for your loss. You and any other single parent here are free to leave with your children. What kind of monster would I be if I took their only parent left and forced them to fight in a war they didn't ask for?"

The mother fell into my arms sobbing. I gave her a hug, listening to the collective sighs of relief as children hugged their parents. I would never want to split a child from their parent. I know what it's like to lose a parent and not know what happened to them. I felt a soft gentle hand on my spine, a warmth came over me and flooded into the mother in my arms. "Thank you, your majesty." She whispered as her two young children bravely came forward, each blonde haired with bright green eyes. They looked no older than six and eight. I smiled at both of them as they ran into their mother's arms.

Talissa was behind me, helping me up from the ground. "You did the right thing, Luna. I'm proud of you. Most people in your position wouldn't care about the circumstances, they would see them as expendable bodies. If they were hesitant to follow you at the beginning of your speech, that hesitance is gone."

We walked back to our places in front of the tent as I turned back to the crowd. "Please gather your things quickly. It's best to get everyone to safety immediately. Prince Fennik and Lady Voxis will assist in the smooth transition from here to Anchora. You have an hour to get ready for the journey." I didn't dare look at my family or my mates. I would crumble the moment I did.

The crowd disbanded, leaving us alone to talk out the rest of our plan. Nox decided he was going to teach the crimson rebellion how to spot a dragon from afar. I knew he could camouflage his underbelly and scales to match the night sky, but I didn't think that others could do the same thing. We had still yet to talk about my acknowledging Luther as my brother, but in truth, he is our half brother, like it or not.

Everyone moved about quickly. Voxis and Fennik took off into the fray of people and tents to help in any way they could. I guess once the families found out that we would not split single parents from their children; it made them more receptive to getting the children to safety. Valdis and Bastian were talking things over with Claye and

Ignis, Damian was helping soldiers move crates of what looked to be weapons out to those outfitting themselves in armor to help. I watched as folks lined up to receive a weapon, some requesting swords, others bows. I hope they have a crossbow and a few daggers left for me.

As if he was listening in on my mind, Valyn brought up a bag full of weapons. "Your weapon stash, princess. My mom stopped by the house and gathered up a few things before coming to Anchora. I asked her to grab a few of your favorite daggers, along with the twin long swords and your crossbow." Valyn slipped the bag from his shoulder, dropping it to the ground with a satisfying thud. He unzipped the bag, displaying almost every weapon I grabbed during the first fight in Mirith. Talissa moved away from Valyn and me to give us some privacy while she took inventory of the remaining weapons for her and her mates.

"Do you think we will ever not have to deal with war?" I asked him in a low tone. I watched as his eyes closed, he paused for a moment before opening them and looking at me.

"I hope one day. I don't want to bring children into this world the way it is now. Sadly, I don't think this is going to be the last battle we have with Hellis. Regardless that you are now a princess of Hellis and Cerulia." His words felt like a weight pressuring down on me. I want children, but he's right. This isn't a world I would want to raise them in.

"Then we need to find a way to keep our people safe during this time. We can't afford to let harm come to our people." I said as I picked up my daggers and strapped them to my belt. I slung my cross bow over my back in its holster, and stocked bolts in my quiver attaching it to my back.

Night would be upon us soon, and I expect all hell to break loose.

The camp quieted down after the children and elderly had made their way to Anchora. Fires were lit around the edge of the camp, people eating what some might see as their final meal. I was sick to my stomach and refused the bowl of stew that had been offered to me. Talissa and my father gave me a stern talking to about needing the food for my strength. Luckily for me Nox had chimed in that he rather not have me puking all over him when we are in the air.

I gave him some space; we were about to be inside each other's heads for the next hour or more. Mom is our top priority at the moment. I know taking back the city is also at the top, but I need my mother to be out of this safe and sound. I've been ignoring my gut and the horrible feeling that something was wrong. I can't let my mind slip into dread and fear right now. She will be fine, and so will everyone else. I have to believe in them all.

My mates were all chatting with Talissa's group, getting to know one another, the ancestry between them all and the history lost from the first war. Valdis and Damian asking the most tactical questions and taking notes. I was so engrossed in watching everyone else that I didn't notice Talissa taking a seat beside me. She sat there in silence with me, watching our mates, her father and mine, and Harold.

"If Otius' blade isn't here, after we are done helping you take back Floria, we are going to head to Hellis and try to find the blade ourselves. I also want to see my other mate, my hearts been singing and pulling me towards every Hellis gate I pass. Zekon is waiting for me to come to him, and I need to get to him." Talissa said, staring out past the crowd of people in front of us.

"I know the feeling of being separated from your mates. I don't even want to talk about what happened during the winter. You do what you need to, we'll be here when you come back. Hopefully the blade is here, and we can take it back. Something tells me that we will need to find a new place to keep it though." I took a sip of water. Movement to my right caught my attention. "Looks like I have to get going." Nox sauntered up as he locked eyes with a few fae women who were obviously gawking at him.

"You two be safe tonight. I know this isn't your first time, but I don't want anything happening to either of you. Erina would kill us all if something happened." Talissa pulled us both into a hug before letting us make our way through the crowd. I gave each of my mates a kiss before heading into the woods. We all knew this wasn't going to be easy and any longer of a conversation with them would only make this tougher. They could all hear everything that was going on in my head anyways.

"You ready?" Nox asked as we made our way through the thick brush. I took a deep breath and nodded at him. "Are we going to talk about our unwanted brother?"

"You say unwanted, but he's not. Was he an ass? Hell yes. Did he annoy me and not treat me the best at times? Absolutely. But when mom wasn't around, he chased away the nightmares, he took care of me when I was sick after falling in the lake when I was twelve. He taught me how to be fearless in the face of danger. He also taught me how to forgive others when they don't do everything right. He was there for me when I had no one else. We aren't perfect. No human, no fae nor dragon or God. So, yeah I want to save him." I said as I made sure everything was secured tightly to me.

I watched Nox put his head down in guilt. I probably should've kept that last bit to myself. "If I could've been there for you sooner, I would've. I'm sorry I couldn't be the one to chase ay your nightmares or heal you when you were sick."

Nox took a moment to get himself situated. Once he has fully shifted, his fire and my weapons were all we would have to take down any daemons that could come our way. Florian archers were already high up in the trees, watching the city walls for any sign of life or chaos. Torches were lit outside the entrance of the gates. Guards patrolled the walls in pairs every hour. I guess Tanis was more paranoid than we thought.

"Let's get airborne. The sooner we have eyes in the sky the sooner we can make sure mom gets out safely." I said, expecting some type of push back from the lack of response. I know he would've been there for me if he could. I don't blame him for it, but he can't expect me to give up on the asshole who was there for me. No matter how much I want to punch him in the throat.

"Agreed, let's hope we can get up without being spotted. I don't feel like having arrows flying at me." Nox shrugged off his leather jacket and folded it, leaving it at the base of a tree. I raised a brow at him. "What? It's my favorite jacket. I don't want it getting ruined."

I rolled my eyes, taking a deep breath before reaching within myself search for the well of power that I had tapped into so many times by accident. I didn't have to look far; it was like a bubbling cauldron ready to boil over at any minute. It would be great if I could remember how I got that shield up before. Oh well, there wasn't time to practice a new trick or two.

We made our way to a large clearing, large enough for Nox to shift, secluded enough to not be seen by prying eyes. He rolled his shoulders back, his muscles coiling down his arms. Cracking his neck from side to side and cracking his fingers in front of him, I watched as his tan tattooed skin slowly was replaced by black and purple shining scales. His shortly cropped purple hair forming two horns on the side of his head accenting the long snout and teeth that he now bore. He was large, his wings were kept close here, the span as large as the entire camp when spread wide. Getting airborne here might be a little trickier than he anticipated.

Nox lowered himself to the ground for me to climb on. The one thing neither of us thought to grab was a saddle for me to stand in, but I can just focus my power to ground my feet in place. We've done it before, so I know I can do it again.

Hold on tight. Nox said through our familiar bond. He crouched down and sprung straight up into the air, wings beating hard and fast until we were high above the night clouds.

Sometimes I forget how sadistic you can be when there is no saddle for me to stand in. I huff back at him. His chuckle dances around my head.

I'm sorry, I had to take the opportunity while the clouds were above us. Look down, it looks like there is already chaos going on around the castle. Nox swayed gently so I could get a better look. Guards and daemons were in a panic running around the castle grounds and the streets of Floria. I knew Elijah said everything would go down after dinner clean up, but I didn't think they would have it down that close in timing.

A flash of blonde hair and red hair caught my attention as they were running through the streets. The red head was fighting off daemons with weapons while the blonde was creating walls of ice, blocking off the side streets as they made their way towards the side gate.

Mom has ice powers?! I yelled out. I had no idea she even had powers at all. I thought maybe she wasn't as gifted as her brother and sister or like Nox and me.

News to me! Luna! Daemon on their asses! Nox yelled back as I watched a nasty hellhound crash through the ice about a block away from them. I hooked a bolt into my cross bow and fired a shot straight threw its head.

Both of the women looked up to the skies, only catching a shimmering glimmer of Nox's underbelly. They were so close to freedom, hope swelled in my chest. The archers in the trees had fired arrows over the wall at the daemons that were climbing the houses to get to my mother and who I assumed to be Beatrix.

Things were going to well and I should've known this was too easy.

CHAPTER 63
LUNA

The ground began shaking as darkness emerged from the castle, ripping through the streets taking out ice barrier after barrier leaving shards of ice in its wake. Nox dove for the ground trying to get to our mother before the darkness. I tossed my crossbow back across my back.

"Grab on!" I yelled as I reached for the two women in front of me. Beatrix helped me lift my mother onto Nox's back. I reached back for her, but she just smiled up at me. Her emerald eyes sparkled up at me as she turned from us, bracing herself with her swords. I looked at my mom and saw the fear in her eyes. "I love you mom. Nox, take mom back to camp! I'll see you soon." *I'm sorry.*

Before anyone could register what I was about to do, I jumped off of Nox's back, landing on the ground next to Beatrix, bearing my own twin swords. She looked at me, eyes wide with shock. "Princess what are you doing?" Beatrix exclaimed as two daemon soldiers turned the corner, cocking their heads to the side smiling wide. Blood trickled from their mouths, dropping to the ground beneath their feet.

"You saved my mother. I am indebted to you. Consider this me repaying you while I can." I gave her a wicked grin before launching myself at the first solider, striking it at the knees severing it's calves from the rest of the body.

"Looks like I misjudged you princess. I thought you'd watch from afar while others fought in the war for you. My apologies." She smiled back as she severed off the arm of the other daemon soldier. These creatures were nothing like I had seen of the people of Infernia. These creatures looked half dead; pale grey skin drooped from their bodies hanging loosely as if they had been starved for centuries. The hair was matted against tehri skulls in patches. If they were fae at one point, I would never have guessed it.

"Where did these creatures come from?" I called out to Beatrix as we continued to dance around one another, slashing and stabbing at the creatures as they continued their onslaught.

"Where did all daemons come from? Hellis didn't exist until a millennia ago when your aunt took on Marcloff in the first war. At least not like we know it now. Some say they are fae who turned their back on the light. Others say they came from another world. Who knows." Beatrix called out over the screams of the creatures as they fell at our feet.

The darkness that tore ass towards them earlier kept its distance as if watching the battle, almost as if it was studying us. I pointed a blade down at the ground and let light strike down it creating one of the most beautiful snake creatures that I had ever seen. It's golden heart shaped head turned to look up at me, its shining opal eyes were so beautiful. I looked over at the shadows and smiled at my new little pet.

"I shall call you Lyria. See that shadow?" I glanced over at the darkness creeping around the battle. As if she knew what I wanted from her, she surrounded herself in light illuminating the street and casting away the shadow further down the street.

"Nice trick you got there," Beatrix marveled at the giant snake as she took her true form, she was larger than the townhouses beside her. I bet those at the camp could see her from here.

"I have a habit of making elemental snakes. Don't ask me why. Looks like we cleared out the mess here. You should get to camp, there are archers just outside the wall that can help you get there safely." I offered as I looked over at the gate behind us.

"No disrespect your majesty, but I am not leaving a member of the royal family behind as daemon bait." She wiped her blades on the tattered clothes on one of the creatures in front of her. I did the same, sheathing my blades back in their holsters reaching for one of my daggers instead.

"If you're staying, loss the princess and your majesty talk. My name is Luna, I assume you're Beatrix, right?" I asked her as I stepped over bodies. Lyria was coiled up in the following intersection waiting patiently for us to follow her.

"Assumption correct, Elijah tell you about me?" She asked as she followed my steps with less care for the dead. I looked over the street covered in bluish black blood and the bodies of the creatures. I couldn't leave it like this for the people of Floria.

"Yeah. Hold up really quick." She halted her steps once she passed me, turning to watch me. I closed my eyes, focusing on the white flames of purity that I read about during my night in Celestia. It took little effort to bring forth the white flames and cleanse the streets of the bloody battle that took place here.

I turned to see Beatrix go white as snow, her freckles looking like a stain on her face. "How did you do that?" she asked me, taking in the now clean purified streets. I shrugged my shoulders and moved past her. Lyria happily moved through the streets as I followed her. Beatrix was hesitantly on my heels, following me but not close enough to be able to touch me.

"Why do you seem afraid of me now?" I asked over my shoulder. Her demeanor changed once she saw the white flames and I didn't understand why.

"According to legend only the most powerful of gods can conjure that sort of magic. Only Otius and his daughter Vanalli were able to wield that purifying powers. It's how they were able to rebuild the world after the first war, despite the tragedy that Vanalli went through." Beatrix quoted a legend that I hadn't heard before.

"Makes sense that I can do it then," I said as we came to an intersection two blocks away from the castle. She cocked her head to the side in confusion. "My mother is the daughter of Vanalli. She happens to be my grandmother and Otius is my great grandfather. I guess it just skipped a generation." I shrugged my shoulders, but Beatrix dropped to her knees in front of me. Oh, dear gods did I just fuck up?

CHAPTER 64
NOX

I landed in the field right outside of the camp, my mother screaming at me the whole way to turn around and save my sister. I
didn't have the ability to tell her that Luna was very much capable of
handling herself. But it was the six large men stalking my way with
anger etched into their faces that had me more concerned.

Harold and my father were hot on their heels, followed by Undas
and Elijah. I debated staying my dragon form so they wouldn't dare
punch me, but that wouldn't go over well.

My mother jumped off of my back storming over to my father with
rage in her voice shrieking so the whole damn camp could hear that my
sister is psychotic and jumped into the battle with little self-preservation. I sighed and relaxed enough to shift back. "I swear if one of you
hits me, I will beat the ever living fuck out of you." I growled.

Valyn was pissed, but wisely moved back a few steps. Valdis and
Niklaus also seemed to value their lives. Fennik glared at me and moved
back to stand beside the others. However, my sister's two hotheaded
mates didn't back off. They didn't swing either, so that was a plus.

My father was ushering my mother through the tents and towards
base camp. I couldn't be more thankful to have her back, but fucking

skin me alive. "What the fuck happened out there Nox?" Bastian growled at me as Valdis stepped forward, putting his hand on Bastian's shoulder to keep him from advancing.

"Beatrix refused to get on and come back to camp. She was going to stay and fight. You all know my sister well enough by now to know she wasn't about to let the woman who risked her life to save our mother stay and be left to the daemons," I spat back at him.

"She is a good person, boys. She's also hardheaded and stubborn, like her grandmother and mother and aunt." Undas said as he joined us. "I think—" his words were cut off by a commotion at the edge of camp. Our eyes turned to see a bright light engulf the sky where Luna was just at. Panic clutched at my chest, but Valyn put his hand up stopping us from moving.

"She created it." He said, as if watching what was going on through her eyes. She did always say that Valyn had unlimited access to her, but he never overstepped. I guess that was why he was the first to step off. He may be angry with me, but he can keep track of her better than the others can. "It's a giant fucking snake! What the fuck is her creepy obsession with creating snakes?"

"Did you say she's creating snakes?" Talissa said, as she joined us. Valyn looked at her and nodded. "Well, serpents make the best helpers." She smiled as she waved her hand over the ground, letting smoke and shadows dance from her palm. An inky black basilisk stared us down as if it would strike us all with only a snap of her fingers. "Meet Ithika, she's been with me for a very long time. Be a good girl and go keep an eye on my niece and her new little pet. Something tells me she is going to need our help."

"Holy shit!" Valyn exclaimed suddenly; his eyes were wide. "She can conjure the white flames of purity?"

My world rocked, no one besides my grandmother and great grandfather could create those flames. I looked to Undas and Talissa who both went pale. We knew what it meant when someone could conjure the flames. Vanalli is believed to be the most powerful goddess to walk the earth aside from Talissa at full strength. But even Talissa can't conjure the flames.

"What? Why do you all look scared?" Niklaus said, panic lacing his words as they rushed from his lips.

Harold looked at his son, eyes wide with shock. "It means she's more powerful than we all had originally thought."

Undas opened his mouth next, his word freezing me in place. "She is the goddess of life and death, the goddess of all. She used the flames without training from Otius or Vanalli. She's conjured creatures from the elements without your help. When her power fully awakens, it will ripple across Cerulia, Hellis and Celestia like a beacon. It will signal a new era, an ending and a beginning all at once."

CHAPTER 65
LUNA

Lyria stopped short of the castle, watching the darkness slowly seep back into the stone walls. She shrunk down small enough to curl around my arm as I called her back to me. Beatrix was weary when it came to her, maybe she was just afraid of snakes. A small shadowy wisp coiled across the path in front of us, halting our advances before we could move.

Don't let your new pet hurt the little shadow, she belongs to Talissa. Her name is Ithika. Please don't do anything stupid. We will be there soon, the front gate beefed up on daemons after your display of power a little while ago. Valyn's voice was soothing as the little wisp took shape in front of me.

"You are so cute!" I chimed, resting my hand on the ground in front of me so she could climb my other arm.

"You're trusting a random shadow?" Beatrix asked skeptically. I nodded with a smile.

"Ithika belongs to my Aunt Talissa. She sent her here to be back up for us. Isn't she adorable!" I cooed as the little shadow serpent snuggled up to my neck. Lyria didn't seem to mind the company.

I love you guys. I am so sorry for jumping off Nox and running into danger. Don't be mad at him. He didn't know what I was planning. No giving him shit! I threw at them all. I could hear the huffs through the bond.

Fine, but we really need to talk about you running headfirst into danger princess. Niklaus's voice was like music to my ears. I missed him dearly.

Okay, I promise we will all talk when this is over with. I refocused my attention on Beatrix and the gloomy decaying statues in the courtyard in front of the castle. The apple trees that lined the pathway up to the main door we full of rotten fruit that were dangling and littering the ground.

"The earth here has been tainted by the rot. I don't know if it's fixable. We might lose Floria to Hellis." The sadness in her voice had me pausing, placing my hand on the tree closest to us. I let the tree speak to me, feeling it's pain and agony as if it was screaming. Most people forget that the plants and trees and the wind itself is all live.

I let the white flame dance its way up to the surface again, resting my head against the tree trunk searching mentally for the roots deep beneath the soil. Everything was covered in rot, black oil suffocating the ground beneath my feet. I wouldn't have it. *I promise this won't hurt.* I thought to the trees as I pushed the white flame through the tree that I rested against into the roots of all the others, decimating the black oil in the dirt and eliminating the rot at the core.

A feeling of joy and thanks flooded me after a few moments. An audible gasp pulled me back into my body. I took a few steps back to admire the trees. The orange, yellow and red hues all mixing together once more. Apples of green and red graced the branches of the trees once more. I reached up for one, holding my hand out waiting patiently for the tree to allow me it's fruit.

A candy red apple fell into my hand a moment later, Beatrix took a step toward me as if to stop me from taking a bit of the once rotting fruit. I took a bite, holding the apple up for her to examine. There was no rot, just sweet juicy nectar.

"Do you think you can use the flames to purge the creatures of Hellis?" She asked, looking over her shoulder at the decaying castle.

"I don't think it would work on them. Their blood is like the rot, blackish blue slime that is a part of them from the beginning. If they started off like us, maybe. But who knows what that would do to me in return." I had thought about seeing if I could purify a daemon, but I don't think they need purifying. Most of the ones I had seen in Infernia were different. They weren't depraved creatures; they lived like we did. I didn't want to put it out there into the world that a goddess was purifying those in Hellis. That would just be wrong.

"It would make our lives a lot easier, but I get it. not knowing exactly what it could do to you isn't a risk you should take." Beatrix seemed levelheaded at least. "So how do you want to go about this? We are running in there blind at this point."

Before I could open my mouth, Ithika nudged me on the cheek. I took her in my hands and looked into her eyes. A whole galaxy opened in them before they turned milky white. My vision blurred until I was looking back at myself. What the hell?

Ithika slipped from my hands and slithered into the castle through a small crack in the foundation. I watched each turn she made as if I was doing it myself. "This is trippy." I said aloud.

"What is wrong with your eyes?" Beatrix asked, startled by what I am only assuming is a milky white gaze staring at her.

"I think I am looking at what Ithika is seeing. Hold on," I said as a flash of light struck across my vision as she made her way into a main part of the castle. She seemed very good at keeping to the shadows.

She was inside the same room I had recently lost my life in. The fireplace was still crackling with a fire, only this time there was no familiar woman sitting on the couch. No, this time it was the familiar serpent smile of General Vikrum. His silver hair still cropped short, a light stubble gracing his jaw. His once bright silver armor had been replaced with a black suit of armor that no light reflected off of. Gone was the blue cape that he wore when he led the royal army of Mistveil, a crimson red cape replaced that too.

There were three other men in the room. The one sitting in the chair by the fire had short messy black hair with eyes as bright as twin emerald gemstones. He was tone and muscular by the looks of it but fading away. His skin was paling, turning from what I could only assume was tan to the slight greyish skin I was witnessing before me.

This man was dying. I could only assume from his looks that he was Tanis.

"This one know his sister is close and is fighting me like hell to get out to her," Luther's rough voice echoed in the room and time stood still as I took in my brother. His blonde hair was so much darker since I last saw him. His bright eyes had dark purple circles accompanying them now. He was paler than before. His muscles weren't as large as he once was. I as staring at a hollow version of my brother. My heart ached as I took him in. I can only imagine what my mother would say looking at her only other child in such disarray.

"Of course, did you expect anything less from the vessel? He is strong, but not as strong as his half siblings. He's a halfling, the only reason you can even be inside his body is because of the faint bit of gold blood running through his veins. He doesn't have enough to have any real powers, never completed their changing and if we are lucky, never will. He's expendable," a deep, velvety voice spoke from the couch.

Ithika moved around the corners of the room so I could get a better look at the man who is responsible for all this pain and bloodshed. King Marcloff, Ruler of Limbris. The man was by no means unattractive. Shoulder length black hair flowed over the front of his shoulders, his eyes a piercing violet stared down the Hilmer inside of my brother. He sat with his leg crossed resting on his knee, his arms sprawled out on the back of the couch swirling a glass of what I could only assume was bourbon in his right hand. His black button up shirt was unbuttoned down to the middle of his chest, exposing his pale chest and a dark black tattoo that slashed across it.

He wore a few different necklaces, a black moonstone moon pendant wrapped in silver caught my attention. I watched as he looked over at Tanis. "You look like the dead," a laugh rumble out from his throat. Tanis looked up at him, eyes void of expression and emotion. "I mean I guess you are dead. Now that Marie is gone, you are just a shell of a male. Don't worry, your suffering will soon be over."

"That princess is going to be a pain in our asses sir. She is not the sweet little innocent thing that she portrays. The boys father raised her, they both trained her on how to defend herself with just a bow and an arrow and some swords. She wont' go down easily." Vikrum said.

"You think I am worried about some princess with minor training. I am more concerned about her aunt who miraculously made her way back to the land of the living. That should have you all more than worried. She can take us down to nothing if she is at full power. That must not happen," Marcloff sipped from his glass. A simple knock came at the door, "Come in."

"Sir, the trees outside bloomed fresh apples again. I thought you should know," a small, framed woman clad in tight black fighting leathers kept her head bowed low. I could make out any features, but I could tell she recognized my work. Marcloff spat his liquor across the table into Vikrum's face.

"What did you just say to me?" Marcloff was pissed off. His eyes were wide as he looked at the woman in the doorway.

"The trees revived themselves. I don't know if it's because Prince Fennik is close by or not, but they have fresh fruit on them now," the woman bit back. She had no fear of this man in front of her. I wonder who she is.

Marcloff pushed up off the couch, stalking towards the woman. "Prove. It." He growled in her face as he gripped her by the chin, forcing her gaze up to his. On demand, she produced an apple from a satchel attached to her belt. His eyes narrowed on the bright red apple in her hand. "How in the fuck is that possible? The ground is rotting away beneath the surface. Soon Floria will belong to me. There is no way that bitch has regained enough strength to even remotely heal the land."

Ithika glanced back at the windows before focusing once more on the people in the room. *Come back, don't get yourself caught.* I thought to her hoping our connection would be strong enough that she could hear me. Hesitantly she pushed herself into the shadows more, creeping back around the room avoiding the pacing feet of a now enraged Marcloff.

"I think it's time we strike. I wonder how they would handle the grimlocks taking over their little camp?" Marcloff laughed before Ithika slipped out of the room and back through the halls. Her pace quickened once she made it through the crack in the wall. My vision cleared back to Beatrix in front of me as Ithika shot out of the wall and slunk to my side.

"Get to Talissa now and warn her," I said, commanding Ithika back to her owner. Without hesitation she slithered off into the streets toward the camp. *Valyn, get the archers out of the trees! They're grimlocks!*

Did you just say grimlocks? How the hell are there grimlocks in Cerulia? Valyn replied, his breath quick and heavy as his thoughts ran through my head.

Marcloff is in the castle, he is about to order the grimlocks to attack the camps. The only dragon here that I could see was Vikrum, Luther is here as well, but he is trying to fight the Hilmer that's inside him. We have to get everyone out of the camp who can't fight. I commanded back to him. *I am going after Marcloff, he's not getting away.*

Luna don't! Valyn said but I ignored him. I wasn't about to let this man kill those I love and care about.

"I hope you're ready for a fight." I looked at Beatrix as she fixed her hair into a high ponytail.

"Hell yeah. Let's do this." She replied with a wicked grin.

CHAPTER 66
VALYN

"**L**una's running into danger again!" I yelled over the roars of battle. Swords clanking off of armored daemons, shields and other swords. Luckily for us there were more daemon bodies littering the ground than there were fae. Bastian and Niklaus were the closest to me, both looked at me with an annoyed look on their faces.

"Why the fuck is she running into danger now?! She said she wouldn't!" Niklaus growled. She did promise us but unlike them, I knew better. Hell, I think Valdis even knew better when he made her promise.

"What are you all shouting about?" Talissa yelled as she slid her scythe through a daemon's chest. She was covered in the thick bluish black blood of the multiple daemons she slaughtered, her mates equally covered. We weren't expecting daemons to come to the camp, but they charged our way the moment Luna purified the street she was on.

"Grimlocks are coming!" I shouted over at her, "And your niece is deciding to take on Marcloff alone!" Everyone looked at me. Talissa went ghostly white. Her eyes wide with fear. Drake stopped moving, his eyes locking across the field at Erina who was pulling a sword of ice out of a daemon's chest. Fire rippled across the field, the mages from Fildrey had finally arrives on the backs of beasts and dragons.

"About gods damn time they show up." Damian growled, kicking a daemon off the end of his blade. He looked over at all the gods in our presence, "I meant no offense."

"We need to get to Luna before she gets hurt. Like really hurt." Lumina said as she joined us covered in blood herself. She had been healing everyone faster than I anticipated, with Niklaus on the front lines helping her, it made things easier for us to keep going. Bastian was probably the only one who needed the most healing, he'd been raging between wolf form and fae form this whole time.

"I agree, but we can't all abandon those here fighting for the home. She would never forgive us." Valdis chimed in.

"We'll go to her. It's not like we don't know our way through the city and the castle." Fennik said, looking over at Elijah who nodded his head.

"Alright, just be careful. We'll stay here and keep the daemons at bay. Once we clear them out, we will head your way." I replied. I didn't like the idea that I wasn't going to be the one rescuing her, but this is his home. Him and Elijah know this place best.

I just hope he can make it to her in time.

CHAPTER 67
LUNA

Beatrix was silent as a snake as she followed me through the shadows in the halls, unsure of what lurked around the next corner. The sconces barely lit up the halls, leaving an eerie sensation that we were being watched.

Two guards stood at the end of the hallway. These two looked nothing like the daemons from before. Their armor, the same matte black as Vikrums, was as dark as the midnight sky on a starless night.

"You take one, I take the other?" I whisper to Beatrix. She nods; her eyes already set on the guard closest to her. I size up the one nearest to me. It was much taller the closer we got, a smell of rancid sweetness tingled my nose. From the smell of the armor, I could only imagine the creature inside being most likely undead.

"Be careful," I warn Beatrix as she takes a step closer to the guard. Her dagger already angled, ready to strike. I knew if I wasn't ready as well, this wouldn't end well. Lyria peeked out from behind my hair to take in the scene. A low growl rumbled from her tiny little chest. I didn't think snakes could growl, but I could've been wrong.

I let the thought slip from my mind as I nuzzled her back into my hair. I needed to focus. Slipping a dagger from my waistband, angling the blade outwards.

I followed Beatrix's lead, slipping around the corner tightly against the wall, keeping to the shadows. The guards didn't move. It didn't even sound like they were breathing. Maybe they really are the undead. I doubt they would need to breathe like the rest of us.

Beatrix looked at me and began silently counting with her fingers. Alright count of three then.

One.

Two.

Three.

A squelching sound echoed off the hallway walls. Black blood poured from the identical slit wounds in the creature's throats. Beatrix pulled her blade from its throat. I followed her lead, cleaning my blade off on my pants.

The bodies thumped on the floor, their helms rolling off, exposing black bodies with rotting flesh beneath. The stench was so intense we had to cover our mouths with our sleeves.

"That is foul." She complained as she cleaned her blade off on her pants. I watched as she sheathed it. I wasn't about to limit myself by putting my blade away. Anything could be lurking around here.

"We need to find the sitting room. I forget how to get there," I grumbled. I really wasn't paying attention when we were here before.

"What are you doing here?" A soft voice trilled down the hallway. A petite woman walked towards us from the end of the hall. I readied my blade, but Beatrix put her hand down.

"Doing what you clearly wouldn't, Elenor." Beatrix said. "Why are you still serving these madmen?"

"How else do you get close to an enemy, dear sister?" Elenor said as she pulled back her hood revealing her short cut red hair. Her eyes were a stark blue against her pale skin.

"So, you're not drinking the tea?" Beatrix asked, he let hand now lay upon her dagger. Elenor just smirked.

"No, but I got closer to Marcloff. I know his plan. When I tell Prince Elijah, he will pick me to rule by his side." She boasted. Beatrix laughed.

"Prince Elijah isn't the one ruling Floria. Prince Fennik is. This is his wife and mate, Princess Luna. You're still obsessed with Elijah. He's told you he's not interested in you, Elenor." Beatrix's words looked as if they were physical stones being thrown at her sister.

"Prince Fennik isn't here to save his people—" I snorted out of disgust.

"My husband is at camp with the others fighting off the daemons and the grimlocks that Marcloff sent their way. Good thing for the camp that my family is there, though. Fire beats wood any day." I said as I flicked my wrist, sparking flames.

Her eyes went wide as she took me in. Lyria poked her head out once more to look between Beatrix and Elenor. She dropped to my side, growing to the size of a small dog. Rage settled in the face of Elenor as she gazed upon me. I didn't understand it.

"How did you know about the grimlocks? I hadn't had a chance to report it!" She screeched, her eyes turned wild and frenzied.

"The shadows speak to me," was the only reply I gave her.

Like a light switch had gone off in her head, she produced a dagger from her belt and charged at me. Beatrix stepped in her way, deflecting her sister with two daggers of her own.

"Move!" Elenor raged; a feral expression played across her face as she looked at her sister.

"No! You will not harm her! She can save us all!" Beatrix exclaimed, shoving her sister back onto her ass.

"You and I belong to the princes! Not some nobody!" She raged again, kicking her leg out at her sister's feet.

"We don't belong to anyone. That was your twisted dream for us, Elenor. Nothing more." Beatrix said as she jumped out of the way.

What is it with women wanting to claim my men? I stood back, watching the sisters fight. Both skilled and fast, almost too fast for me to notice the black smoke coming from Elenor.

"Wait! Beatrix, she's cursed!" I yelled. Elenor contorted her body in a way that made me believe I was in a nightmare. She was practically on all fours climbing the wall in the shadows to get around Beatrix. Lyria shot out from beside me to take away the shadows with her light.

Everywhere Elenor stepped where there were once shadows, she lost her grip. The bright light illuminating from Lyria kept her high on the walls. Beatrix was on her ass staring up at her sister.

"What's happened to her?" Beatrix stuttered. Her gaze locked onto Elenor.

"Something tells me she was made. Her desires are being used against her and turning her crazy." I said as I flicked my dagger in my hand.

A slow clapping rung out through the hallway, skittering Elenor across the ceiling to the man at the end of the hallway.

"Bravo, you figured it out. It's a shame you won't live to tell the others of your newfound discovery." King Marcloff was standing before me, a devilish grin across his face as he scratched under Elenor's chin.

I think I might've made a mistake.

CHAPTER 68
LUNA

Marcloff cocked his head to the side, looking past me at Beatrix. "Tsk tsk tsk. To think that we trusted you with such a valuable task. Caring for the Queen of Hildaria was a simple task, and yet, I find myself missing a very important queen. Why is that Beatrix?"

She just stared at him, like a child caught doing something they were told not to do. Instinctively, I put myself between her and Marcloff. "She doesn't need to answer to you anymore." I said, sounding much braver than I really was.

He laughed once more. A rumbling sound that echoed off the stone walls. Three men came up behind him, two of which I knew very well. I watched as the face of my brother looked at me with disgust. His eyes were not his own, they belonged to the Hilmer inside of his body.

"I told you she would be a problem, sire." Vikrum said with a smug look on his face. Marcloff grabbed him by the throat and squeezed.

"Did I ask for your input?" He growled, his grip going tighter around Vikrum's throat. I wanted to laugh and give that same smug look back to him, but I thought against it.

"No... sire..." he choked out. Marcloff let go of his throat, throwing him at the wall.

"Where was I?" He looked back over at Beatrix and I. "Ah yes. What to do with the two of you? Normally I would just let Vikrum and Ishtar handle you both, but—" he paused at the confused look on my face — "Ishtar is my most loyal Hilmer. He's the one inside your brother. Don't worry, we're taking good care of his body. But seeing as I need Vikrum and Ishtar elsewhere, Elenor and Tanis will have to do."

Marcloff made the biggest mistake next and turned his back on me. Within seconds, I had my crossbow out, already loaded, and pulled the trigger. A bolt shot him right in the center of his spine, dropping him. Elenor's scream ripped through the air as Vikrum and Ishtar caught Marcloff before he hit the ground. Tanis, however, didn't move an inch. His soulless body just stood there, eye void of any emotion.

"You bitch," he growled as he reached back to pull the bolt out of his back. "I was going to let Elenor and Tanis have their way with you but fuck that. You're mine!"

He stood up, blood oozing down his back, and turned to face me. Rage filled his eyes, his veins protruding in his neck. I just had to piss off the biggest Ritmer in Hellis, didn't I? He cracked his neck and let his claws come out. I knew I was fucked, but I would not die here.

I quickly put my crossbow back behind me and pulled Lyria back into me. Well, I tried too at least. She refused to return, instead giving me pleading eyes as if to ask for more. It dawned on me then. Every creature I've made of the elements so far has been serpents. Maybe I should give her sisters.

Lyria sensed my resolution and protectively got in front of me. Beatrix got to her feet and stood beside me. "Got a plan?" She asked as we stood there, swords now in hands.

"Actually, I do." I replied. I closed my eyes and focused on each individual element I could channel. Fire, water, earth, wind, smoke, darkness, and a celestial energy I wasn't sure where it came from. Each one formed a beautiful serpent, and with each thought, they came to life.

"What the fuck is she doing?" Vikrum yelled at Ishtar as if he had the answers to my abilities.

"The boy knows nothing of this from his time before." Ishtar replied bluntly.

"Parlor tricks won't help you here," Marcloff yelled as he charged at me. Lyria and my fire serpent blocked his path. One more serpent is all I need to call forth. The cosmic black serpent reminded me of Noro. She was larger than the rest, with wings on her back. Her black scales illuminated with stars as light touched her. She was gorgeous. Hell, they all were stunning.

"It's time." I said calmly as I walked down the hall where Lyria and my fire snake kept Marcloff at bay. The others stayed by my side, with the larger one at my back. Beatrix pushed herself against the wall, letting me and mine walk past her. Marcloff was still raging and swiping at my fire baby. His focus was nowhere near where it should be.

Elenor shrieked again, "Master, look out!" She pointed past the two serpents in front of him to us. I crooked a smile at them.

The water snake slithered up the wall chasing down Elenor, making the wall slippery enough that she fell to the floor. Vikrum and Ishtar went to join the fray, but Marcloff threw his hand out. "You two have somewhere else to be. Go! She's mine." He growled. Vikrum gave me a filthy glare before grabbing Ishtar and heading for the backdoor.

"Running scared?" I yelled, thinking that I should block them with my earth snake. She was a stunning brown, with ivy like scales twisting around her body. She followed them, my wind beauty in her tail. The white scales were shimmering baby blue. I watched the light sparkle along her scales as she slithered through the room. They would be my eyes and ears on where they were going.

"Beatrix, I hate to do this to you, but your sister is your problem. Got it?" I told her. She had a stern look on her face as she took in her sister. The woman before us was feral and practically foaming at the mouth.

"I got her. Be careful Luna." She replied before going after her sister. I turned my full attention to Marcloff, who was trying to get through my serpents, to no avail. I raised my blades and charged at him. Each serpent moving out of my way, reformed tightly to my side, acting as a shield.

Finally, Lyria moved out of my way as her larger sister was standing high above behind me. I drove my twin blades down hard into Marcloff's shoulders, thrusting down with all my might.

A loud roar echoed through the castle, causing rubble to sprinkle on top of us. I caught Beatrix in the corner of my eye as she took advantage of Elenor watching me. She took her sister to the ground, knocking her semi unconscious. My momentary distraction cost me. Marcloff plunged a dagger into my waist, tearing a scream from my throat.

The largest of my snakes struck, biting Marcloff around the throat. She looked at me waiting for my approval to destroy him, but I wasn't about to let her take the kill away from me. Why couldn't I create a snake that could heal me? That would've been helpful right about now. I followed the faint green light in my mind that I've seen tethered to Niklaus so many times before and pulled at it. His healing powers flowed through me, staunching the blood before I lost too much.

"You're going to have to try harder to kill me." I said, as I straightened up stalking over to him. He smiled at me as black blood dripped from his lips. "You're lucky that I don't just let her kill you." I looked at my beauty, an echo hummed through me, a name. Ophelia.

"I'll kill you just like I did Talissa all those years ago," he choked out. Ophelia bit tighter around his throat, his blood dripped down her face, tainting her midnight scales.

"Let him go, Ophelia. He's mine to kill," I said, pulling another dagger from my belt. Ophelia reluctantly let him go, dropping him to the floor with a huff. I stood above the Ritmer who has caused pain to my family and wondered how he did so much damage back then when he was no trouble now.

"Do let your guard down Princess." He hissed as he sprung up at me. He was only faking injured, fuck. I side stepped his swipe at me with his claws. Beatrix grabbed Elenor's limp body and ran for the exit.

"Get her out of here! Go!" I shouted at her. I watched the hesitation in her eyes, but she obeyed. Beatrix was out the door and on her way to safety. The guys would be able to help her if I didn't make it out of here. Marcloff was on my heels as I ran down the opposite end of the hallway. I had no idea where I was going here. I had never been here before.

Left. Fennik's voice echoed in my head. Go down the stairs and take the first right and run straight. I'll get you out of there.

I think I made a mistake. I whispered through our bond.

You didn't. You're just too stubborn to wait for help, and judging by how your aunt handled half the grimlocks without letting any of her mates step in, it must be a family trait. Focus on what's in front of you. I'll walk you through it until I get there. You'll come out in the dungeons, Elijah and I are heading there now. Fennik's reassurance pushed my feet faster. I forgot about my creatures following behind me. Lyria and Ophelia seemed to be working together to keep Marcloff at bay for now. But I need to call them back, I could feel myself draining the longer they were out of me. I called back each element one by one until Ophelia and Lyria were the only two left.

They both refused to return, I could feel them waging an internal battle between returning to keep me strong or staying out to protect me. I appreciated the desire to protect me, but without my strength I would be useless. I could tell the moment they agreed as they returned to me. I felt a surge of power gush through me the moment Ophelia returned.

I hauled ass through the stone tunnel, I didn't care that I didn't know the layout of the dungeon. All I cared about was that Fennik would be waiting there for me. "Run little mouse." Marcloff called out behind me. His voice a distant echo down the tunnel. I didn't chance looking back at him. I would fall flat on my face if I did. A door came into view as I got closer to the end of the tunnel. Almost there.

Suddenly, my feet were swaying beneath me as rocks and debris began falling from the ceiling. No! I picked up the pace, rushing to the door but I was too late. My only chance of escape was now blocked off by rubble. A deep laugh rumbled through the debris. "You thought you could outrun me? Run away to safety? Oh little mouse, you ran right into my trap." Marcloff stalked through fallen stones and dirt, a devilish grin on his face.

I looked around the tunnel for anything I could use to help me get out, but there was nothing. I searched deep inside of me to find the well of power lurking below the surface. Something tells me that the weapons I have on me won't do shit against him now.

"Nothing to say? Now that is refreshing. Your aunt would never shut up about how she was going to right the injustices that I'd caused to Cerulia. What about the injustices done to my kind huh? What about the mass number of deaths that happened by your great grandparents? Who would right those wrongs?" Marcloff growled.

"What are you talking about? You attacked the fae of Cerulia, the humans living above." I countered, fire engulfing my hand as I watched him stalk from side to side. He laughed, a horrible, hollow sound.

"Do you know nothing about the beginning of this world? The gods, fae, dwarves, and humans didn't exist here, we did! This was our home before they took it over, making us out to be the monsters to their creations. We lived in peace, our gods abandoned us, leaving us here on this planet to rot away once they found somewhere else to go. Those left behind took up arms to take our home back from invaders. Your kind are the villains, not us." Marcloff said, anger lacing each word. Could he be right? I didn't know anything about the history of Cerulia. Damn it.

My flame flickered, and he took his chance. Flinging himself over the rubble and throwing himself on top of me. He pinned my wrists to the ground, forcing one of his knees between my thighs. I struggled against him, panicking. His eyes roaming over my face as if something was stopping him from killing me right there. He leaned his head down and whispered in my ear. "This isn't over. You haven't learned the truth yet."

With that he dug his claws into my chest, shredding the clothes and flesh. Crimson blood flowed from the wound, soaking the clothes that remained. He got up and looked down at me, a smile crept upon his lips. "You and I are going to have so much fun." He held his blood-soaked hand up to his lips and licked it. My blood coating his tongue and lips as he licked them too. He turned from me ready to leave me where I was to die, but the joke was on him. That wouldn't kill me.

Smoke and flame surrounded my hand, forming a beautiful blade of steel and something more. Stars reflected in the dark steel, the hilt adorned with sapphires and onyx. I pulled myself up from the ground with the sword. "Don't count me out just yet. I'm just getting started." I gathered what little strength I had and charged at him, but he was ready. Our powers collided, crumbling the remaining parts of the tunnel around us. He caught my blade forcing it back at me, but I had more than my own strength with me. The power of every life on Cerulia was running through me. Pushing me back against him, stars and darkness began pouring out of me surrounding us.

His eyes went wide as I kept pushing harder and harder down. In a last-ditch effort to save himself, he threw a shroud of shadows around him, deflecting the blade away. He rolled back barely escaping the tip of my sword. His shadows struck at me, but my darkness consumed them, giving me more strength. The surge of power went through me, it was much more than I could contain.

A burst of power exploded out of me, full of everything and nothing all at once. An understanding of the world around me flooded through my mind. I could feel the world breathing, the plants, the animals, the waters and most of all the people. I closed my eyes letting it all soak in. What is this wonderful feeling? Warmth and love radiated through me, but something cold and distant lurked beneath.

I opened my eyes to an empty, destroyed tunnel. Marcloff must've made off during whatever that was. Sulking back off into the depths of Hellis. I clutched at my chest, the hole that should be there was gone. I could hear voices from beyond the rubble, some I recognized and others I didn't.

All I knew was that my mates were beyond the wreckage. And I needed to get to them.

CHAPTER 69
LUNA

A crew of autumn fae soldiers had dug me out of the remains of the tunnel. Rubble and debris were scattered across the courtyard, blocking out the beauty of the grass and earth below. I didn't like that one bit, nature needed to be set right. I thanked the crew and made my way over to the small little garden that was planted by a small stone wall. None of my mates or family came near me. They all watched from afar. The air seemed crisper, the wind caressed my skin as if it was the gentle hand of a mother caressing a sleeping child.

Talissa was the first to move closer to me. "Luna, how are you feeling?" Her underlying concern for me was evident. All of their concern for me was. I could feel the caress of my mates' bonds reaching out to me mentally.

Space. That's what they were giving me. Time. Another gift they were allowing me. They all had questions, they all wanted to know what happened. My clothes were torn to shreds, I can only imagine what images are going through their heads. What he could've possibly done to me.

"I'm... alive." I said. It was the truest response I could give her. She looked at me, hesitant to speak again. "Just ask what you need to."

"What happened down there? We all felt this wave of power flood the land then silence. Everything went completely silent until you came out of the rubble." She expressed.

"I know. The world was waiting to make sure I was alright. Clearly I'm fine. Well minus a horrible headache coming on. I feel so much better than I could ever imagine." I smiled and watched as bats began to fly in the dusk light. The sound of the earth settling below my feet was grounding. I felt so alive and so aware of every little thing. It was incredible.

"Let's get you checked out. Lumina and Niklaus are both itching to come check on you. Will you tell us what happened?" She asked once more. I just nodded. Only part of me was aware of what really happened down there. I felt the presence of Ophelia and Lyria wanting to come out and check on me. So I obliged. Each one took a much smaller snake form, twisting from my hands up my arms. Both rested gently atop each other on my neck.

Talissa stepped back, her eyes following Ophelia and Lyria. "Alright, alright. Fine!" She snapped. Smoke fell from her hand revealing Ithika. Ophelia was weary of her, but Lyria slithered down off of me to check on her little friend.

"You're fine Ophelia. She won't hurt you." I pulled her from around my neck and placed her on the ground. The moment she got close to Ithika the two locked eyes before speeding off playfully through the courtyard. Lyria slithered off behind them like an annoyed older sister.

502

"I'll tell you about what happened later. I want to enjoy myself for the night." I told her as I looked back at my mates. Each of them a hair trigger away from whisking me away from here and putting me in a keep with solid stone walls and iron bars on the windows so nothing can hurt me.

"My mates and I are leaving in the morning. I need to go see Zekon. I miss him and I can feel his bond pulling on mine." Talissa said as she took in her mates, all huddled together talking amongst themselves. I could only imagine what it feels like for her, I couldn't imagine that much time between seeing my mates. The brief time I was in Celestia was a lot on me.

"I'll fill you in on everything, let's walk."

***

I told Talissa everything as we followed Ithika, Lyria and Ophelia around the small orchard in front of the castle. I watched the wheels in her head turn as she processed everything that I told her. "I think he's lying, Luna. The only people we can really ask are all at each other's throats back in Solaria. I am not looking forward to that insanity that we will have to deal with." She was still covered in blood from her own battles today. I called Ophelia and Lyria back to me. Ithika returned to Talissa with a huff.

"I think our main priority now is to get everyone placed back in their homes. I also want to keep the crimson rebellion on a rotation patrol just in case. Something tells me this isn't the last time we will see Marcloff's forces in the autumn realm." I said as we made our way back over to our mates.

Seeing Elijah and Fennik talking and laughing was a warming feeling. "Good evening, Princess Luna." Elijah said as he bowed at the waist. "I know it's a lot to ask of you, but do you know what happened to my father?"

It took me a few moments to remember if Tanis even moved from the spot Marcloff left him in the hall. "Last I saw him, he was in the main hall, he wasn't moving Elijah. I think something might be seriously wrong with him."

"We will find him. I know he is your father, but he has to pay for his crimes against the people of Floria," Fennik declared. Elijah nodded at us both. "Luna, I know we agreed to never be apart, but I think I am needed here."

"I know. I was already thinking that myself. Each of you will be needed in your realms for the time being." I watched each of their faces fall. We had all just gotten back together, we hadn't even had time to process everything. "Look, I don't want to do this, but it's not what's best for us right now. It's what's best for our people. Look at what happened here. The royal family, no offense Elijah, wasn't here from the beginning. We're not spending enough time in our realms so we have been getting blindsided by daemons and creatures taking over towns and cities."

"She's right. I hadn't been to Solaria in a while. I've spent most of my time in Daglidell. If I had been to Solaria more than once in the last few years, maybe I would've noticed that Allura had been possessed. But," Damian paused, wrapping his arm around my waist and pulling me tighter against him. "That means we will have to set up a schedule for when you can be with each of us. Seems only fair if we have to be alone in our Realms."

He gave me a kiss on the neck, his beard tickling the sensitive skin there. "That sounds fair." I said breathlessly. "Tonight we shall celebrate as a family. Tomorrow we all go our separate ways and find a solution to keeping Marcloff at bay. Elijah, I would like the crimson rebellion to become the crimson army instead. I believe they are more than capable of keeping Floria safe. Don't you?"

"I couldn't agree more, your majesty." His bow this time was much more official than before. I noticed my brother, mother and father standing with Undas and Harold, pride on each of their faces, along with some daemon blood.

I excused myself, making my way over to them. "We are very proud of you. It's hard to make the decision for the people instead of for ourselves. I think you will make a great queen. Don't you, my love?" My father said, lovingly looking at my mother.

"I do. I think you are more than ready to take over. Each of you have proven yourselves worthy of the titles of Kings and Queen. I'm sure Harold and the others would all agree." My mother smiled at Harold and pulled me into a hug. "If you do anything as reckless and dangerous as you just did, we will have more than words." She whispered into my ear. I couldn't help but laugh as I hugged her tightly.

"Where is Sirus?" I asked, looking around, noticing my uncle's obvious absence.

"He went back to Mirith to be with Holly and check in on my wives while he's there. Luna, I need you to know that you are the guiding light for my boys. Continue to keep them in line. Just don't lose yourself in the darkness. My door is always open to you my dear." Harold confessed. I gave him a hug before turning to Undas.

"What's next for you?" I asked him as I watched him take in everyone.

"I'm going back to Solaria and Valhime. Your grandmother is dealing with stress right now with her parents and mine going at it like children. You should probably come say hi before they all threaten to hunt you down to meet you." Undas chuckled. I laughed, turning to look out over the city.

The city gleamed in the dimming sunlight, the people moving about the streets checking their homes and checking on their neighbors. The portal in the distance was lit up with a whitish blue glow. Children were returning to their families. The elderly return to their children. There were casualties on our side, thankfully not many. The battlefield around the camp was still flooded with the dead of the daemons and the few fae. I can't let the children see that.

I moved away from my family and stepped up to the small stone wall. All eyes were on me, and I didn't care. I closed my eyes and focused on the battlefield. I listened for the ground to guide me on my way, the wind to carry the scent of the dead to me. Cleanse all but our own, they must be buried. White fire erupted across the field, carrying away the rotting corpses of the daemons, the blackish blue blood that was staining the grass and the stench of death. All that was left was the bodies of our own, wrapped in sticks and grass, each with a sapphire bloom laid across their chests when the flames vanished.

I opened my eyes and turned around. Shock and awe filled the faces of those around me, but the praise and cheers from the streets let me know I wasn't being judged.

I was being accepted.

THANK YOU FOR READING!

Thank you so much for reading A Realm of Flowers and Light. Reviews are vital to authors and help others find our books. I would greatly appreciate it if you could take a moment to leave a review on Amazon and Goodreads, it would mean the world to me!

You can leave a review on Amazon here

You can leave a review on Goodreads here

The war continues in....

Cerulia Book 4

ACKNOWLEDGEMENTS

I hope you all aren't too mad at me for this one. I promise the journey will continue with our resilient Luna and her pack of mates in Book 4. I can't wait to continue their journey for you all to enjoy.

First off, I want to start by thanking you the reader. Without you, my dreams of becoming an author would have never come true. What are words in on a page if they are never read? Thank you for taking a chance on an indie author. It means the world to me to bring these characters to life and that you all enjoy them. I thank every one of you who have been following Luna's journey since A Realm of Wind and Rain. I hope you continue to love Luna as much as I do.

Next, I have to thank my boyfriend JD. He has gone through the trenches with me with this book from chapters being deleted thanks to software updates, late nights of me frustrated, me ranting to him almost every time we spoke about all my struggles. He helped me keep the house moving smoothly while I went into writing hyperfocus mode. I couldn't have finished this book if he didn't give me the time and space that I needed to finish it. I am forever grateful to him for being the biggest supporter in this journey of mine.

I want to thank my best friend, Jessica L, she has been dealing with me sending her every idea under the sun that I've had for this series along with several other ideas for other books. She has read every chapter of this book from the moment I started until the very last word. I am forever grateful that she has been a big supporter of me following this crazy dream of mine.

Lastly, I want to thank my ARC team and my street team for helping me promote these books for all to see. If it wasn't for you all and your love of these characters, I don't know where I would be at right now. Thank you all so much!

I'll be returning to Cerulia very soon to bring you the next installment of the series.

xoxo

Krystal Harding

ABOUT THE AUTHOR

Krystal Harding is a devoted mother, a full time barber with the ambitions of becoming a full time author. She loves to write fantasy, romance (fantasy and dark) and epic fantasy with epic world building and a vast wealth of enchantment and adventure throughout all of her books. When she isn't working or writing more, she can be found reading or making stuff for her books or her shop. She is a gamer, a writer, a mother and a creative mind fueled on caffeine and fantasy realms.

Her inspiration come from years of falling into different worlds through books and movies from Dragonlance to Dungeons and Dragons, from folklore and mythology to the magical worlds of old. Krystal grew up, like most elder millennials, on The Lord of The Rings trilogy, Harry Potter, Eragorn, The Vampire Diaries and Twilight. Krystal loved also finding books and movies that others didn't know about or didn't like.

Her love and passion for reading started at a young age and flourished over the years. She instills the importance of reading onto her children, teaching them that while some games can teach lessons, books teach many more.

Connect with Krystal

Website: www.authorkrystalharding.com

IG, TikTok and Threads @krystal.harding.author

Or on her Facebook Author Krystal Harding

Join the community at Krystal's Korner

Also by Krystal Harding

Cerulia

A Realm of Wind and Rain

A Realm of Fire and Earth

A Realm of Flowers and Light

Seven Deadly Sins

The Book of Wrath

Behind the Scenes

Join My Newsletter!

Join my newsletter for an exclusive behind-the-scenes look into upcoming events, releases, my writing process and sneak peeks of all the works that I have going. Also, get first pick at joining my ARC teams!

AuthorKrystalHarding.SubStack.com